Sycamore Souls
Steven E. Wedel

MoonHowler Press

MoonHowler Press

Contents

Copyrights   VI

1. Chapter One   1

2. Chapter Two   4

3. Chapter Three   9

4. Chapter Four   14

5. Chapter Five   19

6. Chapter Six   23

7. Chapter Seven   30

8. Chapter Eight   35

9. Chapter Nine   40

10. Chapter Ten   46

11. Chapter Eleven   52

12. Chapter Twelve   57

13. Chapter Thirteen   61

14. Chapter Fourteen   63

15. Chapter Fifteen   70

16. Chapter Sixteen   76

17. Chapter Seventeen   81

18. Chapter Eighteen   85

19. Chapter Nineteen   88

20. Chapter Twenty   94

21.	Chapter Twenty-One	100
22.	Chapter Twenty-Two	105
23.	Chapter Twenty-Three	111
24.	Chapter Twenty-Four	114
25.	Chapter Twenty-Five	120
26.	Chapter Twenty-Six	123
27.	Chapter Twenty-Seven	130
28.	Chapter Twenty-Eight	138
29.	Chapter Twenty-Nine	143
30.	Chapter Thirty	148
31.	Chapter Thirty-One	154
32.	Chapter Thirty-Two	160
33.	Chapter Thirty-Three	166
34.	Chapter Thirty-Four	172
35.	Chapter Thirty-Five	176
36.	Chapter Thirty-Six	182
37.	Chapter Thirty-Seven	187
38.	Chapter Thirty-Eight	190
39.	Chapter Thirty-Nine	196
40.	Chapter Forty	200
41.	Chapter Forty-One	204
42.	Chapter Forty-Two	208
43.	Chapter Forty-Three	211
44.	Chapter Forty-Four	214
45.	Chapter Forty-Five	220
46.	Chapter Forty-Six	225
47.	Chapter Forty-Seven	229
48.	Chapter Forty-Eight	235

49. Chapter Forty-Nine   240

50. Chapter Fifty   243

Epilogue   249

Also By Steven E. Wedel   253

Chapter One

K elsi stared upward and wished for an escape from what was coming.

The night sky was a jeweler's black velvet spread with all his inventory of diamonds. They twinkled and shone, coldly beautiful, distant but vital, something to reach for but never attain. There was no moon tonight and that made the gems seem even brighter in their infinite darkness so high above her.'p

Kelsi loved the stars and hated being in a city where light pollution dimmed them so that only the brightest and boldest could be seen. Maybe that's why she had ventured away from the shore in the little wooden boat she found pulled up on the sand. Going out on the ocean alone at night wasn't something she would usually do. Neither was stealing a boat. But that was the thing with dreams. They let you do things you wouldn't normally do.

She knew she was dreaming. And she knew how it would end. She was powerless to stop it.

The clouds came like they always did, and with the clouds came the waves. Small at first, almost pleasant sounding as they licked around the sides of the little boat, rocking Kelsi as she lay in the bottom, her head propped up on the rear seat. But soon enough, they were rocking the tiny craft. Kelsi didn't feel sick, but she was worried. The stars were gone. She sat up and the wind snagged her hair and pulled it around so that it blinded her and she had to fight to pull it away from her face while the boat lurched and rolled. Cold seawater splashed over the sides and wet her feet and legs, making them numb with the cold. Why did she wear shorts? She was always wearing shorts. What was she doing here? The seawater stank of decaying fish and salt.

The boat rose up on a bigger wave and raced down the slope of its back, the bow plunging into the black black depths, throwing icy water into Kelsi's face, making her cry out with the shock of it while already another wave was lifting her even higher and dumping the bow of her little stolen boat deeper into the next valley of icy ocean. She spat ocean from her mouth so that she could scream, but more salty, stinking water poured into her.

The only warmth was the track of tears running down her face.

Kelsi looked up, hoping to see the stars again, but they were long gone. She had only wanted to see their beauty, feel the peace of looking up at them, steady and reliable in the night sky. And now, she was sure she would die. Her body would be food for the millions of fish and sea mammals swimming beneath her. She would bloat and rot and become part of the stench of the sea.

The big wave loomed up in the distance, just as it always did. Her boat was sideways to the wave and she knew it would lift her up, tip the boat over, dumping her into the formless void of water where she didn't belong, couldn't find a foothold, had no sense of home or safety. There was no one to help her. There was never anyone to help her. She was pushed and pulled, lifted and dropped at the whim of something she couldn't control.

"I'm sorry," she cried. "I want to be back on the land. I want to sink my feet into the ground and never move again. I want to be safe!"

Up, up, up rose her boat and she tried to lean into the wave, to keep the boat level, but it was going over and she was about to ...

"Ahhhhh!" She sat up, fighting the heavy water off her body, only to realize it was not a cold, killing ocean wave but the sweat-soaked blankets of her bed. She sat there, wide-eyed, staring into the dark of her tiny apartment lit only by the LED lights of an alarm clock and the microwave at the other end of the room.

Beside her, Tucker snored, blissfully unaware of the drama that had played out beside him. He seemed to never dream. But then, he never seemed to have any deep, troubling thoughts when he was awake, either. Maybe it was all the marijuana he smoked. Kelsi watched him as she fought to get her own breathing under control. When it was normal, she carefully slipped out of the bed, though she knew she could have almost flipped the mattress getting out and Tucker wouldn't have noticed.

On bare feet, she padded to the refrigerator and took out a bottle of water, the brightness of the interior light like knives stabbing into her eyes. Blind for a moment, she felt her way to the little faux wooden table and into a chair. As her vision cleared, she opened the bottle and drank. The water was soft and cold, but not in the way of the seawater that had threatened to kill her in her dream. She wondered if she had screamed in her sleep. She knew she did sometimes.

As she always did afterward, she considered her dream. She had searched the internet many times for interpretations of the nightmare. There were variations. The boat was symbolic of a spiritual journey in most cases. The rough sea obviously meant turmoil, but what was causing that was too varied to have any real meaning to her. In every interpretation, being in a small boat on rough seas was not a positive dream.

And yet, Kelsi didn't feel unhappy. She felt she had come to terms with the loss of her parents. They weren't dead, but divorced and more interested in their new lives than their grown daughter. She had good grades in her college classes and her part-time job waitressing wasn't unbearable. Her boyfriend was ... Well, he was okay. He maybe could act a little more mature, hold her hand more than he held his Xbox controller, but she knew that was a common problem with men in her generation.

There was no reason for her to have a recurring dream about being in that stupid little stolen boat she couldn't control on an ocean that was trying to kill her. No reason at all.

A spiritual journey ...

That part intrigued her. She was on an educational journey. She supposed she was on a romantic journey. Or, at least a relationship journey. She had journeyed to the place she now lived. But a spiritual journey? She didn't feel that at all. Did the journey have to be spiritual? Maybe emotional? But she didn't feel that, either. She didn't really feel anything, except tired.

She drank the rest of her water and went back to bed. As soon as she was settled under the blanket, Tucker stopped snoring and rolled over. She felt his erection through his underwear and sighed as his sleepy but eager hands began groping her. She lay mostly still and made half-hearted appropriate noises as he did what he needed to do, then he kissed her sloppily on the forehead and slid off her and back into sleep without even tucking his limp penis back into his underwear.

Kelsi rearranged her own underwear and rolled over so her back was to Tucker. Despite what had happened with her parents, she somehow thought an established relationship would be more than passive acceptance of sex from a man-child who was still half asleep when he grunted and finished in her.

Is this love?

She pushed the question away, not wanting to deal with it. She'd come hundreds of miles to be with this guy.

It took a while, but eventually she slept again.

Chapter Two

"**Y**er not from around here, are ya?"

Kelsi looked up from the pad where she was writing the man's order for the kitchen. She gave a very brief half-smile and said, "No. Do you want the hash browns with that?"

"Sure I do," he said. "Where ya from?"

"I've lived all over, but I was in Wyoming for a while before I came here," Kelsi said.

"What brought you here?" he asked.

"A Buick," Kelsi told him. "Bacon or sausage patties?"

"Which do you recommend ... Kelsi?" he asked after checking out her name badge.

"They're both great," she told him. "Let's go with the bacon."

"Whatever the lady says."

Kelsi wrote down the rest of the order. This guy wasn't familiar, but his type was. They basically got two kinds of people for early breakfast at Sweet Pea's Diner, a small restaurant on the northern outskirts of Nokomis, Oklahoma. The diner was surrounded by industrial buildings and wheat fields. The early customers were either old farmers, usually with bulging guts, bald heads, and generally merry dispositions, and these younger men who were typically truck drivers or hired farm hands who often ate alone.

"I'll get this in and bring you some more coffee," Kelsi told the man. Under the grizzled beard, shaggy brown hair, and filthy Ford hat, she guessed him to be maybe five to seven years older than her.

"Can I get your number when you come back?" he asked. "My name's Kevin, by the way. Kevin McGee."

"Well, Kevin, my boyfriend has this thing about me giving out my number to other guys. It makes him a little crazy," she said. "And I miss him when he's in prison."

His eyes widened just a little, then he nodded. "I done a little time, myself. Just a county jail, though. Nothin' in the big house. Drunk and disorderly at a bar. Nothin' serious."

"I guess there's hope of moving up," Kelsi said, keeping her voice serious though she wanted to laugh. "I'll be back." She took the order to the window between the dining room and the kitchen and put it on the spinner. Jake, the young cook, gave it a glance and nodded acknowledgement to her. Kelsi scooped up the coffee pot and went first to the table of older farmers and refilled all their cups. They thanked her and called her things like "little lady" and "sweetheart" that for some reason, she didn't find offensive. Then she returned to Kevin.

"Why'd you really come to Oklahoma?" he asked. "Did you come for your boyfriend?"

The cocky light that had been in his blue eyes earlier was gone, and that softened Kelsi's mood toward him a little. "Yes, that was part of it. And to go to school."

"Yer in college?" he asked.

"Yes." She poured steaming black coffee into his white ceramic mug.

"I thought about that, but I ain't very smart," Kevin said. "I barely finished high school. What are you gonna be when yer done?"

"A social worker," she said.

"Oh," he said. "One a' them took my cousins away from my aunt when I was little. She drank and spanked 'em with a belt. Spanked me once, and I tell ya, it hurt like hell."

"I bet it did," Kelsi said. "I'll have your food out in just a few minutes." Kelsi was fully aware of Brenna, the other waitress on shift, covering her mouth to snicker at her from where she was wrapping silverware in napkins at an empty table. Kelsi returned the coffee pot and checked on Kevin's order. Brenna came over and hip-bumped her.

"I think he's gonna ask you out," she whispered.

"He already asked for my number," Kelsi whispered back. "I told him my boyfriend would end up back in prison if I gave it to him."

Brenna snorted with contained laughter. "Tucker Umber? In prison? They'd eat him alive. I know. I've dated a couple of cons."

Jake slid the plate with Kevin's food through the window and Kelsi put it on a tray. "I'm not surprised by that," she said to Brenna in a pretend haughty tone.

Kevin didn't bother her anymore, but was polite and left a decent tip. A few other customers came and went through the morning. As the day wore on, the wives of some of the farmers who had been in earlier came in for brunch, followed by some of the nearby factory workers who had an early lunchbreak. At eleven o'clock, Kelsi was relieved by Tammy and had four hours to herself before she had to return for the second half of her split shift. She had Jake drop some chicken strips and fries for her, then packaged them to go and slipped out the front door.

A little north of the restaurant, the old two-lane state highway curved, passed a few more businesses, then some farmland, and then came to one of the city's two cemeteries. Kelsi pulled off the highway and entered the cemetery, driving slow. She passed the office and the mausoleum, following the narrow, twisting gravel road to the back of the graveyard, where she parked by a shrub. Taking her food and the small throw blanket she kept in her car, she made her way to an old grave marker, where she spread the blanket and sat down.

"Good morning, Floyd," she said as she settled onto the blanket. She kicked her shoes off and put her feet in the grass over the grave. Her toes flexed as if grabbing the grass to hold on. Kelsi sighed contentedly, thinking of her body recharging now that her bare skin was connected to the electromagnetic body of the planet.

The tall stone in front of her marked the final resting place of Floyd Marion Duncan, who was born on July 25, 1899, and died on August 2, 1951. Under that bit of information were the words, "World War I." Kelsi munched on her chicken and fries, looking at the headstone as she had so many times before. It wasn't lost on her that Floyd Duncan had not yet turned twenty before the First World War ended. She wondered how old he was when he enlisted. Or was he drafted? She liked to think of him lying about his age and enlisting at sixteen or seventeen, then surviving the horrible war. But there was no way of knowing.

Despite having the same last name, Floyd Duncan was not related to Kelsi Duncan by any means she knew of. But somewhere in the dusty attic of her heart, she wished they were. The Floyd Duncan she had created was an honorable man. A good man. A man who could be counted on to take care of his family.

The cemetery was quiet and peaceful. The day was getting warm and Kelsi could hear sparrows singing from the tall cedar trees that ringed the cemetery. A gentle breeze played at her hair and made her hold on to the paper napkin she used to wipe the grease off her fingers and lips. To her surprise, a bright red cardinal fluttered to the top of Floyd's marker and stood looking at her with a cocked head and one beady eye.

"Hello, Floyd," Kelsi said. "I didn't know you, but you're not forgotten."

The bird twisted its head to fluff feathers under its wing, then looked at Kelsi again. She seemed to meet his approval and he flew away as quick as a dart from a gun.

Kelsi finished her meal and sat cross-legged with her eyes closed. The sun tinged the darkness behind her eyelids apple-red and warmed her face. The wind used her hair to tickle her neck. Kelsi tried to clear her mind, but she kept coming back to the man, Kevin, and his questions.

Yes, she had left Wyoming to come to Oklahoma and be with Tucker after they matched on Tinder. Yes, she was going to the local university. But she had also been running from her alcoholic mother and the parade of greasy, lowlife men she'd been dating since they left Sergeant Monty Duncan in San Diego. The sergeant had been a colonel at the time of Kelsi's first knowledge of military rank, but his indiscretions with female staff and then female enlisted members caused him to be shuffled around the country and demoted. Things would be okay for a while and he might even earn back a stripe, but then the cycle would repeat. Kelsi was born in Virginia. Every move was westward until they came to San Diego when she was sixteen.

That's how old she'd been the first time her father had "accidentally" walked in on her just as she was getting out of the shower. Then he started coming into her room unannounced, particularly at times he knew she was dressing for school. He took to spanking her on the butt when she passed by him in the house, and often, if she couldn't wriggle away, his hand lingered, cupping her buttock.

To her credit, when Jennifer Duncan saw him touch their daughter, she took immediate action. She and Kelsi and three suitcases were on a Greyhound bus as soon as Sgt. Duncan left for work. Casper, Wyoming, was as far as they could go on the money Jennifer had, and that's where they stayed. Her mother took a job waiting tables and entered what she proudly called her "whore phase," saying it was about time she finally got some good dick.

Man after man passed through the house and too many nights Kelsi lay in her locked bedroom listening to her mother and the stranger moaning to the accompaniment of squeaking bedsprings and the percussion of a headboard slamming rhythmically against the wall. Sometimes the man left right after. Sometimes he was still there at breakfast. Sometimes there were fights after and things were broken and her mother had red handprints on her face in the morning. And sometimes the men looked at Kelsi as if she might be a good second course.

At the age of nineteen, she met Tucker online and after a month of messaging and a couple of phone calls, she left her mother and came to Nokomis, a little city in northern Oklahoma.

Kelsi opened her eyes. There would be no meditating here today. She grabbed up her blanket, shoes, and lunch trash and went back to her car. The city wasn't big, and although her apartment was halfway across town, she was able to get there in less than ten minutes. She parked in her driveway and looked up at the one-room apartment built above a detached garage. It wasn't much, but she was able to pay for it herself with no help from Tucker, and that was important to her.

She knew the property was owned by some rich guy on the west side of town. He never came to check on his properties, of which she'd heard he had many, but instead used a property manager who always blamed his slowness to make repairs on the owner not authorizing the expenses.

Inside, she dropped her keys and purse on the tiny dining table in the kitchen area, then went to the small bathroom to relieve herself before crossing through the kitchen to the living/bedroom area, where she dropped onto the double bed. The bedding smelled like sweat, Tucker's Axe body spray, and stale sex. Kelsi remembered the dream that had awakened her again last night. She hated that dream.

There were about two and a half hours before she had to be back to work, so she set her phone's alarm for two hours, then dropped into a deep sleep that, fortunately, did not include dreams of boats and oceans.

Chapter Three

Her phone kept buzzing in her back pocket. It would stop for a while, then start up again. The floor was pretty crowded and she was busy with new orders and drink refills. It was almost forty-five minutes after the first silent ring before she was able to duck into the kitchen and pull the phone from her pocket.

Tucker. Six calls from Tucker. As she looked at the missed calls, her phone vibrated again. She answered it.

"Kels! I have big news. Huge news. Monumental!" he said, his voice almost exploding with enthusiasm.

"You won the lottery?" she asked without emotion.

"No. Can I see you after work?"

"So you do know I'm at work?" she asked.

"Hey," he said, offended. "I'm sorry. I just figured, you know, how busy could you be at the podunk little diner."

"I'm really busy," she said. "Please stop calling. Yes, you can come by. I should be home by about ten. I have to go." She hung up and slipped the phone back into her pocket.

Kelsi immediately felt bad for having been so rude, but on some level, Tucker was incredibly self-centered and that irritated her. He knew she wasn't supposed to be on her phone during her shift. Alan, the night manager, was one of those, "If you have time to lean, you have time to clean" managers that believed there was never time for personal messages during your shift.

Not that the rule applied to him, of course. He often leaned against the door frame of the office looking from his phone to the staff, barking an order at someone before returning his attention to Facebook or what sounded like stripper dance videos.

Kelsi went back to work, and she did wonder what it was that Tucker had to tell her that had made him so excited. Her shift ended and she helped clean the dining area, then counted and split the tips for the night. Even with the paltry morning shift, her take for the day wasn't very big, but it was better than nothing. She grabbed her purse and went to her car.

In the confines of her car, she could smell the fried food on herself. Some nights the smell of her chicken-fried clothes was so strong she felt like throwing up. She hit the switch to lower a window, started the car, and drove home. She really hoped she would arrive before Tucker showed up, but there was no such luck. His big Chevrolet pickup was parked in the driveway, which meant she had to park her own car in the street. He popped out of his truck as soon as Kelsi's car was still and met her at her back bumper.

"You took my parking space," she said as he leaned down to kiss her.

His lips pecked her unresponsive ones and he didn't notice. "My truck costs way more than your car," he said and tried to put an arm around her waist.

Kelsi slipped out of his grasp. "I pay for this driveway," she said.

"Maybe not for long," he said, and offered her a huge grin.

"What?"

"Let's go inside and I'll tell you all about it," Tucker urged.

Inside the little apartment, Kelsi flipped on a light and dropped her purse on a table by the door. The apartment had the peaceful, witchy smell of sage, but it was fading. Kelsi determined she would burn some more incense before going to bed. She just loved the smell, so clean and pure. Tucker dropped onto her loveseat. The space wasn't big enough for a full sofa. He patted the cushion next to him.

"Come to Daddy," he said.

"Gross," Kelsi said, but she sat next to him. "So, what is it?"

"They're going," he said triumphantly.

Kelsi stared at him dumbly. "Who? Where?"

"My parents," he said. "Dad accepted the acquisitions job, which means they're moving to Hutchinson, Kansas, for probably two years."

"Oh," Kelsi said. She remembered Tucker had said something about his dad considering a job with the sheet metal company he worked for, but it had sounded like a mean-spirited job. "Where he's going to shut down another company and fire all their employees?"

"Well, yeah, there'll be some downsizing. Not everyone's getting fired. We'll still run a shop up there," he said. "Dad has to clean up their books and oversee transitioning their production to making our stuff and some new products. The company is providing an apartment for him and Mom while they're there. We're talking, like, two years."

Kelsi didn't understand Tucker's enthusiasm. "Okay," she said. "So you'll have the house to yourself?" She hadn't wanted to say it. She didn't like acknowledging the fact that her boyfriend in his mid-twenties still lived with his parents.

"I was hoping I wouldn't be alone," he said slyly. He leaned over and kissed her on the forehead while Kelsi tried to process the implication.

"You want me to move in with you? In your parents' house?" she asked.

"Until they come back, it'll be our house," Tucker said.

"Are you making the payments?" Kelsi asked.

"Well, no. That's part of the beauty of it. Dad will still be paying for everything."

"And instead of you living there rent-free, we'll both be mooching off your parents?" she asked.

"Why do you have to be a bitch about it?" he asked, pulling away a little. "Don't you see how good this could be for us? For you? You won't have to pay rent to live above a garage. You can save that money or put it toward your college loans, or we can live the good life."

"I don't know," Kelsi said. "That's a big step." It was one thing for Tucker to spend a night, or even a few nights a week, but living with him? She wasn't ready for that.

"We've been together for a couple of years," he protested. "You came down here from Wyoming to be with me. Why not move in with me?"

What he said was only partially true, but even at that, it now seemed pretty pathetic hearing it said to her. Kelsi pulled a decorative pillow from the arm of the loveseat and held it across her stomach like a shield. "It's your parents' house," she said. "Their furniture, their pictures, their ... everything. I would never feel comfortable there. But I'll come over more."

"Is that really all it is?" he asked

"Yeah," she said. "What if I was vacuuming and broke something? I couldn't live with that."

"I guess," Tucker said. "But you'll really come over more?"

"Of course," she promised. "When are they leaving?"

"In a couple of weeks, but they'll be gone this weekend to look at apartments," Tucker said. "If you want to come over on Saturday we can have dinner."

Kelsi gave him a skeptical look. "You're going to cook?"

He gave her a sheepish grin. "I was thinking I'd get take-out, but light some candles. Make it a whole vibe."

And try to fuck me in your parents' bed. Kelsi smiled without saying her thoughts. Before she could respond at all, Tucker continued.

"There is one thing to this whole deal," he said. "On Saturday afternoons I have to take my grandpa to this old park so he can visit his tree."

"What?" Kelsi asked. "His tree?"

"It's really dumb," Tucker said. He twisted in his seat to face her better and crossed his right ankle over his left knee. He was wearing loose shorts and the movement clearly indicated he was not wearing underwear. Again. "Grandpa and Grandma planted a tree in the park when they were kids and now he has to go sit and look at it for a couple of hours every weekend."

"How is that dumb?" Kelsi asked.

Tucker shrugged. "It's just a tree. We have to set up two lawn chairs because he thinks Grandma's ghost comes and sits there with him sometimes."

Kelsi felt herself becoming more interested. "How long ago did she pass?"

"She died ... I guess it was about eight years ago now," he said.

"He's gone every weekend since then?" Kelsi asked.

"They used to go together, until Grandma couldn't. But yeah, pretty much every weekend. My mom takes him. But since they're leaving, she asked if I'd do it. She kind of made it sound like I owe it to her."

"You more than kind of do," Kelsi said. "Most guys your age have their own place and pay their own bills. Especially with the kind of money you make." This was dangerous territory, she knew, as they'd argued before about how much he spent on weed, video games, and truck accessories, with the discussion always ending in the fact it was his money and he'd damn well do what he wanted to with it.

"Hey, I take care of things around the house," he argued.

"You mow in the summer," Kelsi scoffed.

"And I take out the trash all year. Mostly," Tucker added. "Anyway, I'm taking Grandpa to the park at about one. You can come if you want."

"Okay," Kelsi agreed. She'd met Tucker's grandfather at a few family functions. He was a tall, bald man who didn't appear to be almost eighty-five. His eyes were sad and filled with loneliness even when his family was around. No wonder, Kelsi considered. They mostly ignored him or talked to him like he was a toddler. He usually slipped away from the table and went to watch television until somebody could drive him home. "I get off at noon Saturday. I can shower the smell of gravy out of my hair and meet you at your parents' house."

"I love it when you come home from work smelling like food," Tucker said, grinning again. "You're double the snack." He lunged forward and pinned her to the cushions as he began kissing and licking her face.

Kelsi let out a playful shriek of protest, but she didn't push him away. Eventually, his mouth covered hers, their tongues found each other, and she felt her body fully responding to the best thing about Tucker. She let him pull her off the loveseat and lead her to the bed.

Chapter Four

Saturday was always a busy day at the diner. Unlike most weekdays, there were kids in the restaurant, some crying, some running back and forth to the restrooms or the ancient jukebox that hadn't had a new record added to its collection since sometime in the 1980s. It was more about families today instead of the usual farmers and truck drivers. Tips weren't as good, but the work was harder.

Kelsi was glad to get off work. Her feet ached and her Sweet Pea's Diner uniform T-shirt had a big grease stain on the front from a plate of hash browns she'd nearly dropped when a kid popped out of his booth at the exact wrong moment. She'd hoped to get two days out of that shirt, but now it was going in the dirty clothes with the others. She would have to work a trip to the laundromat into the day's activities.

Showered, Kelsi spent a minute in her kitchen eating a banana and a couple of baby carrots, then took a bottle of water and went down the stairs to her car. She listened to a podcast about mindfulness as she drove across town to the nice brick two-story house where Tucker lived with his parents. It wasn't a gated community, but the housing addition was obviously for people with financial security. All the houses were brick or stone, with high, narrow porches and low-set but tall windows. Lawns were immaculate. There was no clutter of children's toys overturned in the grass, no oil stains on driveways or stray mixed breed dogs roaming around.

She parked her Buick in the Umbers' wide driveway. One of the two garage doors was open and she could see Tucker's red pickup, so she parked where he could back it out. Tucker opened the front door when she rang the bell and invited her inside.

"Hi, baby," he said, taking her in his arms. The house was cool and smelled of artificially scented wax melts that were never what they claimed. Tucker's hand strayed to Kelsi's butt and he pressed her groin to his.

"No," she said, pushing away from him. "We're going to be late."

"He won't care," Tucker said. "I bet he won't even realize it."

"That's awful, and I'm sure he will. He's not senile. I've met him," Kelsi argued. "Are you driving?"

"Yeah," he conceded, and got his keys.

They'd been driving for a while, going back through the downtown area, when Kelsi asked, "Where does your grandpa live?"

Tucker laughed. "Actually, not that far from you. He's an East Sider. He's lived in the same house since forever."

It turned out that Dennis Aiken lived less than a mile from Kelsi in a modest frame house with a big porch and white siding trimmed in light blue. The house was on a hill rising from the street, and the comfortably cracked and worn driveway, shaped like a camel's hump, led to a garage behind the house. There were pink and yellow roses planted in front of what was probably the master bedroom window and a flowerbed about three feet wide ran the length of the porch, though there were no flowers in it. The house was obviously old, but had been well taken care of. The houses around it, however, did not exhibit the same kind of care and upkeep. Tucker parked the truck and slid out the driver's door and headed for the front door of the house.

"So much for chivalry," Kelsi said, and pushed her own door open.

Dennis Aiken was just as Kelsi remembered him. He greeted them with a smile and invited them inside. The house smelled like lavender and old people and decades of home cooking. There was a calm, comforting feeling in the house, something Kelsi believed could only come from the love of the people who lived in the place. Dennis was dressed in jeans and a buttoned shirt of powder blue. His socks were bright white. He invited them to sit down while he got his shoes on, then he went down a hallway and into his bedroom with slow, shuffling steps.

"You'd think he'd be dressed and ready," Tucker whispered.

"Hush," Kelsi told him.

The room was decorated by a woman. That much was very obvious in the placement of family photos on the walls and on a nice set of oak shelves that included delicate figurines, mostly of birds. She picked out a school picture of Tucker and another of him as a young boy with his parents, probably taken at a Sears or JCPenney's store portrait studio. All the photos were dated, and Kelsi would have bet they hadn't been updated in the eight years since Tucker's grandmother died.

Dennis came back into the room wearing the obligatory white New Balance sneakers that it seemed every old man had to own. "Tucker, do you have the chairs?" he asked.

"Yeah, they're in the back of the truck," he said, popping up from the sofa and giving Kelsi a "hurry up" look.

Kelsi followed them out of the house, where Tucker bounded down the steps of the porch to his truck. Dennis stopped on the porch to lock the deadbolt of his front door.

"This is a beautiful porch," Kelsi said, looking at the two old-fashioned yellow steel chairs to the left of the door and the porch swing with faded white paint to the right.

Dennis pulled the key from the lock. He smiled at her. "A lot of memories on this porch. New houses, like the one Dennis lives in, just don't have porches like this. We used to have neighbors over and we'd sit out here and visit all evening. I guess people don't do that anymore."

"No, I don't think so," Kelsi agreed. "It's too bad."

He nodded. "It is."

"Are y'all coming?" Tucker called through the driver's window of his pickup.

"He was always impatient," Dennis confided.

Kelsi saw how the elderly man clung to the railing as he went carefully down the steps. Once off them, his steps were short shuffles that seemed even slower due to his height, which had to be at least six feet, and he was a large-boned man with hands that would swallow Tucker's in a handshake. Kelsi stayed beside him as they went around the pickup. She opened the door and pushed the front seat forward so she could crawl onto the smaller bench seat at the back of the cab.

"Oh, no, you sit in the front," Dennis protested.

"No way," Kelsi said. "You men take the front. I'm fine back here. Look, I can put my legs up here and take a nap while we drive."

Dennis gave a soft chuckle. "We're not going that far," he said. With effort he tried to hide, he climbed into the cab of the pickup and pulled his door closed.

"We ready?" Tucker asked.

"Ready," both Kelsi and Dennis answered.

The drive to the park took less than five minutes. Tucker parked the truck along the curb on 19th Street and got out. Dennis got out of the passenger side and tried to put the seat forward so Kelsi could get out, but she had to help him, which he apologized for several times. Dennis had the two folding lawn chairs out of the bed of his truck and he passed one of them to Kelsi. She scowled, but took it, and the three crossed the street to the park.

It was a long, narrow park with a drainage ditch running through it. There were the standard modern plastic playground pieces for kids to climb and slide on, plus a sidewalk that seemed to be part of a bigger walking trail. Dennis ignored the sidewalk and led them across the dry grass to a mature tree with white bark and spreading limbs, with the lowest about seven feet above the ground.

"What kind of tree is this?" Kelsi asked. She had seen them around, but her knowledge of botany was small.

"It's an American sycamore," Dennis said. "This tree is seventy-four years old. Well, older, I guess. It was a sapling when we planted it."

"You planted it?" Kelsi asked.

"I already told you that," Tucker said. He'd opened his chair and banged it down facing the tree. "Give me that one." He took the chair Kelsi had, opened it, and dropped it beside the first one. "There ya go, Pops. We'll be over here. C'mon, Kels."

Kelsi tried to hide her irritation and looked into Dennis's brown eyes in his lined face. "I want to hear that story someday soon. Promise you'll tell me?"

He smiled a real, warm, grateful smile and nodded. "I'll tell you," he said. "I've told it many times, but I like telling it."

Tucker had her hand and was pulling her away. Kelsi let him drag her away from the old man and the two chairs. They went to the empty playground equipment and sat on a bench meant for parents watching their children.

"You were rude," Kelsi accused.

"God, I don't want to hear that fucking story again," Tucker said. "I can repeat it to you, word for word. He's told it at every family gathering since I was a baby."

"I haven't heard it and I've been to some of your family gatherings," she argued.

"Do you want to hear it? I'll tell you and it'll be a lot faster than when he does it," Tucker said. "When he was eleven years—"

"Not from you," Kelsi said, cutting him off. "I want him to tell it." She looked over her shoulder and caught her breath. Dennis was sitting in the first chair Tucker had put down, a blue-and-gray one. At first glance, the chair next to him appeared empty, but then Kelsi saw movement. Except "saw" wasn't really the right word. She … detected movement. It was more a feeling, or a knowing. There was no physical person sitting in the red-and-gray chair beside Dennis Aiken, but the old man was not alone. Upon studying the scene closer, Kelsi saw that he had his hand on the armrest of the red chair and that his fingers were curled as if holding something. Something like another hand.

"What are you looking at? He's just sitting there looking at his tree," Tucker interrupted her thoughts.

Kelsi turned away. Her first instinct was to ask Tucker if he saw what she did, but she let that thought go. He wouldn't see anything. "How long does he usually stay here?" she asked instead.

"It depends. Hopefully not very long," Tucker said.

"Do you not like him?" Kelsi asked.

"What? Of course I like him. He's my grandpa," Tucker said, his face showing his shock at such a ridiculous question.

"You just don't respect him?"

"Look at him," Tucker said, turning so that he could see his grandfather. "He's sitting there staring at a stupid tree. He makes us set up two chairs, like Grandma's gonna come out of her grave and sit there and stare at the tree with him. He's living in the past. I can't believe Mom hasn't put him in a home."

"You're awful," Kelsi said, her voice low, her eyes still on Dennis's hand where it appeared to be holding a hand she couldn't quite see, but knew was there.

"I'm a realist," Tucker proclaimed. "And this has gone on long enough." He stood up and approached the two chairs. "Pops, are you ready to go?"

Kelsi, still on the bench, watched Dennis's hand open and fall back into his lap. His shoulders sagged and his head tilted back as his eyes tracked up and up the smooth white bark of the towering tree with its broad, green leaves.

"I am now," Dennis said, and there was a note of sadness in his voice. He struggled to get to his feet, so Kelsi went to him and held his left arm once he was standing.

"I'm going to walk him to the truck. You bring the chairs," she said to Tucker.

"Thank you, Kelsi. I'm not as steady as I used to be," Dennis said.

They left Tucker muttering behind them and Kelsi opened the pickup door and was about to climb into the back seat, but stopped herself. "Does she always come sit with you?" she asked.

Dennis's eyes widened, then a huge smile split his face. "You saw her?"

"Not really, but I knew," Kelsi said. She clambered into the truck's back seat as Tucker tossed the lawn chairs into the bed. Nothing more was said about the apparition, and Tucker dropped his grandfather off and didn't even help the old man get up the porch and into his house before he drove away, Kelsi fuming beside him.

Chapter Five

S he didn't spend the night with Tucker like he wanted, but she did sleep with him after eating pizza and watching the latest entry in the *Fast and Furious* franchise on Netflix. She insisted they use his bed. He tried to talk her into his parents' bed, but she refused, saying it was his bed, or she was going home. The springs in his mattress squeaked and his headboard pounded against the wall, the noise completely ruining any chance Kelsi had of enjoying the session.

She slipped out of the house around midnight to go home and sleep in her own bed without Tucker's snoring or the feeling of a strange house owned by real adults, not two twenty-somethings pretending to be grown-ups.

She dreamed of the boat on the turbulent ocean again, but it was different this time. There was a seagull and it was screaming at her as it flew past. She knew it was flying toward land and safety, but she had no way of turning or propelling the little stolen boat. She woke up sweaty and disoriented and gave up on getting any more rest that night. She made coffee and sat on her loveseat to read a Nina George novel while the Amazon Alexa device played soft 1990s pop at a low volume.

Eventually, the gray light of dawn spread around the edges of her curtain and she knew it was time to shower and go to work. She looked at her book and saw that she'd only read three pages, and she couldn't remember what had happened. Her mind had been on the invisible shape sitting in the chair next to Dennis Aiken yesterday.

It hadn't been invisible so much as just not visible to human eyes. The air had seemed to shimmer or have a transparent shadow in the shape of a person sitting in the chair. When looked at directly, Kelsi couldn't really see it, but if she turned her head away, it was there, but indistinct. The best evidence had been the way Dennis seemed to hold its hand, though no other hand was really visible.

Kelsi put the book away and went to shower, keeping the water cold in hopes it would help wake her up.

At work, she kept a cup of coffee out of sight of the customers and drank it strong and black every chance she got, fighting the urge to slump into one of the few empty booths and take a nap. Brittney noticed her swilling coffee.

"Somebody had a busy night last night, huh?" she teased when they met at the counter to pick up orders.

Kelsi shook her head. "It's a dream I keep having. I couldn't get back to sleep."

"Was that dream about eight inches long and attached to Tucker's pelvis?" Brittney whispered.

Kelsi gave a real laugh, then said, "I wish." She held up her left hand with her thumb and forefinger about three inches apart.

"You poor girl," Brittney said, shaking her head and picking up three plates of biscuits, gravy, bacon, and scrambled eggs.

When her shift ended at 11:30, Kelsi went to her car, sleepy but jittery from the coffee she'd drunk. She drove away, but didn't go straight home. Instead, she went to the park at the corner of 19th and Randolph, parked the car, and got out. There was a group of four black girls playing on the equipment and, on the other side of the drainage ditch, two Hispanic boys were using pieces of cardboard to slide down a big hill from where the park met the wooden fence of somebody's back yard. There was laughter and squeals and whoops and they made Kelsi smile a little. She hadn't made many friends when she was little because of the way her family kept moving around.

The tree stood there, impassive and completely normal, casting shade across a huge swath of the park. Kelsi walked around it, looking up at it's smooth white branches and wide, light green leaves. The leaves fluttered a little in the breeze, making a soft rustling sound and Kelsi suddenly wished she could sleep right here under the tree with that rustling as a lullaby.

She put her hand on the smooth, bone-like trunk of the tree and wished for a moment that the tree could give her a jolt that would reveal all of its history. But, of course, that didn't happen. The wood was cool, hard, and alive in the way a tree is different than a piece of lumber.

"Seventy-some years old, and most of that standing right here, watching the world change around you," she whispered, amazed at the very idea. "What have you seen and felt?"

The tree wouldn't answer her, but Kelsi knew where the answers were. She went back to her car, thinking she would just drive by Dennis's house now that she knew where it was. But when she saw the elderly man on his knees and hunched forward, she wheeled up his humped driveway and jumped out of the car to face his startled reaction.

"Kelsi?" he asked, squinting at her as if to make sure of what he was seeing.

"Mr. Aiken, are you okay?" she asked.

"I'm fine," he said. He was wearing an olive green button-down shirt and faded blue jeans and had a khaki cap on his bald head. "Are you okay? Is Tucker with you?"

Kelsi approached him slowly. "I just ... I saw you on the ground and thought you'd fallen. But you're planting flowers." She saw now that he had a small digging tool in one hand and a crate of small green plants in black plastic containers beside him. He laughed at her, but it wasn't a mocking laugh.

"You stopped to help the old man," he said. "I appreciate that. But you're right, I'm planting flowers. A little late this year, but April was kind of cold."

"Yeah, it was," she agreed.

"Did you come to hear about the tree?" he asked.

"Oh, no, you're busy. Maybe you can tell me this weekend. I think I'll be with Tucker when he takes you back to the park," she said. She realized that she hadn't heard from Tucker yet today and wondered if he was mad that she hadn't let him fuck her in his parents' bed and then she'd left without staying the night.

"Tucker made it pretty clear to you that he didn't want to hear the story," Dennis said. He saw the embarrassed look on her face and waved it away with his little spade. "I know he's heard it a million times. And yes, I could hear both of you talking behind me. My hearing's still pretty good for being eighty-four years old."

"I'm sorry he's like that," Kelsi said, not knowing what else to say.

Dennis shook his head. "It's his parents' fault, and I guess in a way that makes it my fault, too." He looked down at his dirt. "Have you ever planted peonies?" he asked.

"No. I've never done any gardening," Kelsi said.

"You're welcome to come and help me while I tell you about planting Woody," Dennis invited.

"Woody?"

Dennis smiled, but it was kind of a sad smile. "Gloria insisted we name the tree. She came up with a bunch of names from books, but I didn't want to name it after somebody else. I suggested Woody since I figured someday it would be fire wood. Turns out, old Woody is going to outlive both of us."

Kelsi knelt beside Dennis and felt her knees sink into the soft, turned earth of the flowerbed. She could smell the rich, dark soil and couldn't stop herself from putting her fingers in it. The dirt was cool from the shade of the porch and moist with the memory of the last rainfall.

"It feels good, doesn't it?" Dennis asked.

"It really does."

"Uh-huh. I knew when I first met you that you had an old soul," Dennis said. "Here, take this." He handed her the little spade. "Dig a hole just about as deep as the blade and a couple of inches across."

Kelsi buried the blade into the soft soil and turned it to further loosen the dirt, then lifted it all out. One more scoop and she had a hole that Dennis said was just fine. He handed her a little green plant in a container that seemed to be made of thin bits of cardboard that had been soaked in water and formed to hold a bit of dirt and a baby plant.

"These containers used to be plastic, but now they're whatever they are. Biodegradable, is what they call it," Dennis said. "Anyway, go ahead and put that in your hole, then fill around it with the loose dirt you took out."

Kelsi did as she was instructed, and couldn't help but feel a little motherly pride over the tender baby plant that now stood on its own in the great big earth between her knees.

"You done good," Dennis said. "Now move over a few inches and let's do another one. I'll tell you a story while we work."

Chapter Six

He had been attending Adams Elementary School in Nokomis, Oklahoma, since just before Halloween in 1946. Now it was the end of April and he didn't like it any more than he had that first day. The building was huge, hulking, made of dark red brick and filled with mean kids and meaner teachers. Dennis Aiken, age 11, in the sixth grade, wished he was still attending classes in the little country school and living on the farm near Drummond that his dad and his dad before him had owned.

But all of that had changed now.

He trudged up the sidewalk, into a flow of other kids, and into the gaping maw of the school, then upstairs to his classroom, where he put the books he'd had to take with him yesterday for homework, and his lunch, into the storage area of the desk. He took out a piece of paper, just as all the other students were doing, and wrote in cursive, "My name is Dennis Aiken. Today is Friday, April 26, 1946, and these are my assignments for the day." Mrs. Cousins, his teacher, made them do this every morning to practice writing in cursive and so they couldn't say they'd forgotten an assignment. She took roll while the students wrote.

Dennis knew his cursive writing wasn't very neat, but he didn't really care. Sometimes Mrs. Cousins would make kids rewrite assignments if she "Couldn't read that hen-scratching." Usually with the homework notes, she'd just say, "As long as you can read that mess" and let it go.

Today, the teacher seemed to be in an especially good mood. Compared to other teachers in the building, she was young. Her hair wasn't gray and she didn't curl it onto the top of her head. She wore brighter colors, like today's turquoise blue skirt and red top. She wore the clunky old lady shoes with the tall, thick heels like the other lady teachers did. Dennis figured those were required because even Miss Danbury, his teacher at the little country school, wore those kinds of shoes.

"We have a special job today, class," Mrs. Cousins said. She liked to stand in front of her desk and, when she was excited about a lesson, she would rock back and forth on her toes. She was rocking and smiling now with her hands clasped in front of her. "Today is Arbor Day. Arbor in Latin means tree. It's a celebration of trees. Every year, people plant millions of trees on this day. Why would we plant trees?" She paused, then pointed at a raised hand. "Doyle?"

"So we can have shade," the boy with oiled hair replied.

"Shade is good," Mrs. Cousins agreed. "But it's more than that. Melinda, what were you going to say?"

"So we can have wood to build houses," said a blonde girl in the front row.

"Yes, we need lumber," Mrs. Cousins said, smiling and nodding. "But what else do we need? What's something we're using right now?"

The girl in front of Dennis raised her hand and the teacher called on her. "Gloria?"

"Trees produce oxygen from carbon dioxide through a process called photosynthesis," the girl answered.

"Excellent!" Mrs. Cousin's head nearly exploded with pride. "How do you know that? You worded it so elegantly."

"My dad teaches science at the high school," Gloria said.

Dennis caught himself just about to mock the girl's smug know-it-all tone, but stopped himself just in time. Instead, he covered his mouth and fake coughed and stuck his tongue out at the back of her head. Nobody saw it, but the gesture gave him a small measure of satisfaction.

"Well, workers with the city of Nokomis have dug holes for us in a nearby park and they've left trees there for us to plant," Mrs. Cousins said. "So, we can take part in this Arbor Day, help beautify a city park, and contribute to everyone having plenty of clean, fresh air. Isn't that exciting?" There was a general murmur that sounded more like confusion than excitement. "Our class was chosen out of all the classes here at Adams Elementary. We have twenty-two students and there are eleven trees to plant, so I'm going to assign each of you a partner."

Dennis's heart sank down to his worn shoes. He hadn't made any real friends here. His only close friend was William Pierce, who lived across the street and over a couple of houses, but he was next door in Mrs. Rhinehart's class. Out of the options here, only Dwayne Maxwell had shown any friendliness to the new boy from the country. Dennis knew the chances of being paired with the one person likely to not make fun of him were pretty slim. Then, as Mrs. Cousins began naming off pairs, he realized she was choosing partners near each other on her seating chart. He barely stifled a groan when the inevitable happened.

"Gloria Light, you'll be with Dennis Aiken," she said. The teacher's voice skipped along, pairing up the rest of the class.

Gloria turned in her seat and glared at Dennis. "You better not mess this up," she whispered. Then she turned back around before the teacher could notice.

Mr. Grayson, the principal, came into the room and the low murmur of voices suddenly ceased. Mrs. Cousins smiled at the towering gray-haired older man with the serious face. "We're ready," she said.

Mr. Grayson cleared his throat and turned his body toward the students. "We are going to enjoy a walk to the park today," he intoned. "There will be no shenanigans. No horseplay. We will walk quietly in a single file line. Bring your lunches with you. Once at the park, a representative from the city parks department will be there to tell you what to do. You'll do as instructed, then eat your lunch. You will then be given a thirty-minute recess in the park, after which, we will walk back in the same orderly manner in we used going to the park. Are there any questions?"

"No, Mr. Grayson," the class said together.

"If anyone needs to go to the restroom, do it now," he added. "There are no restrooms at the park." Two girls and three boys immediately raised their hands and Mrs. Cousins dismissed them. When they came back, the principal told everyone to rise, and he led them out, with the teacher bringing up the rear of the line.

It wasn't a long walk to the park, but because they had to stay in line and not talk, it seemed to take a lot longer than it should have. Once there, they were greeted by a short, fat man in a tan shirt with the name Ben on one pocket and Nokomis City Works on the other.

"Gather round, kids," he called, and waited with a fixed smile on his egg-shaped face as the students clustered near him with their authority figures behind them. "Today you're going to help the city plant trees," the man named Ben announced like they hadn't already been told that. "We have oaks, elms, sycamores, and birch. Your teacher is going to give each pair of you a paper with a number and the name of the type of tree you'll be planting, then you'll go to the hole with a little white flag with your number on it, and plant your tree. It'll be just like the Land Run days you do at school." He smiled like the comparison was something special.

"Only sixth grade does the Land Run re-enactment," Gloria said. She had her hand up, but hadn't waited to be called on.

"Oh," Ben said. "Well, y'all get to watch it, right? So you know what I mean, right? You don't have to run to your tree,"

One of the girls raised her hand and Ben called on her. She pointed at the nearest hole and a tree on the ground beside it with its roots in a burlap bag. "Why do they have gunny sacks on their bottoms?" she asked.

The city worker explained that the bags kept the roots packed in the dirt they'd been growing in up until now and that they were often sprayed with water to keep them moist. "We'll be taking those bags off when you plant your trees," Ben said. "The burlap can keep the roots from growing the way they should." He paused as if there might be more questions, then looked over the kids' heads. "Mrs. Cousins, are you ready?"

The teacher and principal circulated through the students, giving each team a slip of white paper. Mrs. Cousins handed Dennis and Gloria's slip to Gloria, of course. She probably thought he couldn't even read it, Dennis guessed. He looked over Gloria's shoulder. The paper had a big 7 on it, and under that the words, "American Sycamore."

"Okay, friends, go find your trees!" Mrs. Cousins called like she was inviting them to the circus.

Dennis knew sycamores had white bark, so he immediately went for a tree that fit that description, but it was numbered 3 and said it was a birch. That left him confused, and his partner had not joined him in the rush to the birch tree. The two girls who had Number 3 glared at him. "This is *our* tree," the brown-haired one said. "Yeah, go away," her red-headed partner added. Dennis hurried away.

He found Gloria beside a sapling about seven feet tall. Of course it was the right one. "I thought you got lost," she said.

"I was just looking around," Dennis lied to cover up the truth.

"Well, this is our tree," she said. "It's a big one."

"It's not so big," Dennis said, looking at the tree. It was even taller than his dad.

"I'll untie this bag, then you can put the tree in the hole since you think it isn't so big," Gloria said. She squatted down beside the burlap-encased root ball and started pulling at the thick brown twine wrapped around the mouth of the bag and the very brown trunk of the sycamore. "It's really tight," she complained.

Dennis pulled his pocketknife from his jeans pocket and opened the blade. It was a good knife, one of his father's old ones, a Barlow with a wooden handle that was barely chipped at all and a single blade that Dennis sharpened often. "Let me do it," he said, and bent over the bag. He slid the blade of his knife under the top couple of wraps of twine and easily severed them. He noticed that Gloria smiled, but she didn't say anything, just quickly pulled away the rest of the string.

It took both of them working together to shimmy the damp burlap off the bulging ball of roots and soil. Finally, the bag was crumpled on the ground and covered in black dirt that had fallen off the roots. Both children's hands were dirty.

"Okay, you get to pick it up and put it in the hole," Gloria said and she only smirked a little.

Dennis put both hands around the trunk of the tree just above the roots and tried to lift. The tree moved a little, but the roots never left the ground. He wiped his damp, dirty hands on his jeans, something he knew he'd get in trouble for later, and tried again. The tree scooted a few inches, but that was all. "You could help," he almost growled at his partner.

Gloria put her hands on the trunk just above his and together they strained to move the sapling. It was then that Dennis noticed how nice her hair smelled. He had never noticed that kind of thing about any girl before. Not even his mom. But Gloria's hair smelled like sunshine trapped in a garden of bright flowers. His concentration was broken and he forgot what he was supposed to be doing.

"You're not even trying," Gloria accused, letting go of the tree and standing up. Dennis felt his face burning with blood as she glared at him, and then her expression changed to one of confusion. "What's wrong with you?" she asked. "Are you sick?"

"N-no," Dennis answered.

"Hey, partners." The man from the city came up and put a hand on the shoulder of both students. "You got the big sycamore. I bet you need some help getting it in the ground, don't you? Let's try it together."

With Ben's help, they moved the tree and lowered it into the hole. "Now, if you two will just push that pile of dirt back into the hole and pound it down tight with your hands, you'll be all done," he said, clapping them both on the backs before going off to check on another group.

"Have you ever planted anything before?" Gloria asked as they were on their knees pushing park dirt back into the hole. This dirt was more reddish brown than the black dirt trapped in the twisty roots of their tree.

"Sure," Dennis answered. "We lived on a farm before I had to come to this school. I helped plant wheat and oats and we had a vegetable garden I helped with."

"Did you like it?" she asked.

"I liked it a lot better than living in this big city," he answered.

"Nokomis isn't a big city," Gloria argued. "Last summer, my parents took me to Oklahoma City. That place is huge!"

"Then I never want to go there," Dennis said.

"I want to go to Paris and London and Rome someday," Gloria said. Dennis started to say something nasty about big cities and the kind of people who liked them, but something about how she said it stopped him. It was like she had admitted something private to him.

"Have you ever planted anything before?" he asked.

"Strawberries and cucumbers," Gloria said. "My mom grows them and makes pickles and jam from them. She lets me help her plant them and we pull weeds together."

"That's good," Dennis said because he didn't know what else to say. "I like strawberry jam."

They got the last of the dirt into place and patted it down firm with the palms of their hands. From their place on their knees, they both looked up at the tall baby tree with its thin, spindly limbs and tender young leaves. It stood straight and seemed to Dennis to be happy with its new home.

"I wonder how tall it'll get," Gloria said.

"I think these kind of trees get really big," Dennis said. "I hope it does." He looked back at the earth they had just patted down. "This ground is dry. The tree needs water."

"There's always water in the culvert," Gloria said. "Come on."

They raced to where the drainage ditch in the park dumped into a rough concrete culvert with a basin lower than the twin tunnels that would let the storm water run off to other parts of the city. Sure enough, there was a pool of stagnant water in the basin, along with bits of trash that included a couple of paper cups. The kids grabbed the cups and scooped up water. Dennis's cup had a hole in the bottom and he had to hold a finger over it as they hurried back to their tree. Other kids were already sitting around eating their lunch and watching them.

"Gloria! Dennis! What are you doing?" Mrs. Cousins called as she hurried to intercept them. She met them at their tree and demanded again to know what they were doing.

"Our tree needs water," Gloria explained. "So we got it some."

The teacher looked from the cups of smelly water to the base of the tree. "Fine," she said. "Dump that water on them, then throw away those nasty old cups and eat your lunch."

Dennis and Gloria shared a conspiratorial smile, then dumped their cups of water on either side of the tree's trunk.

Chapter Seven

"That's the sweetest story I've ever heard," Kelsi gushed. She felt herself grinning like a fool, but she couldn't help it and didn't really care. "You met the love of your life in the sixth grade when you planted a tree together. That is a meet-cute for the ages, and an enemies-to-lovers trope any romance author would envy."

Dennis's smile faded. "It's a what?" he asked.

They had finished planting the flowers and had retired to the big, shady front porch, where he had brought out glasses of ice and a plastic pitcher of lemonade made from powder, he'd said as if apologizing. He'd finished his story as they sipped their drinks.

"I took a creative writing course as an elective," Kelsi explained. "It was taught by a romance author. Meet-cute is when a couple has some cute way that they meet up or first get together. And enemies-to-lovers just means they don't like each other at first, but then fall in love later."

"Oh, well, then I guess you're right," he said, and smiled again.

"This is really good lemonade," Kelsi said, lifting the glass.

"Gloria always made it with fresh lemons and sugar," Dennis said. "But I've never been able to get it to taste right, so I just use Country Time powder. It's pretty good, but not the same."

"You miss her a lot," Kelsi said.

He sighed. "I do."

"Tucker said it's been eight years since she passed. Is that right?"

"Nine in July," he said.

"Does ... does she always come when you visit the tree? Woody?" Kelsi asked.

"No," Dennis said. He smiled and shook his head. "I like to think she's too busy on the other side to even know when it's the weekend over here. But sometimes she does. When I really need her, she's there."

"Can you see her?"

He nodded very slowly. "I see her more and more clearly now."

"What do you mean?" Kelsi asked.

Dennis took a long drink of lemonade, his sharp, old brown eyes watching her over the rim of his glass. He put it down and said, "Before I answer that, tell me what your faith is. I don't want to offend you."

Kelsi was a little taken aback. She'd never been asked this question and wasn't really sure what to say. "Well, my parents weren't very religious," she said. "Mom took me to Sunday school some when I was really little and I remember some of it, like the flood and the ark and the world ending in fire next time. And Jesus on the cross, of course."

"Uh-huh," Dennis said, his voice slow and maybe just a bit cynical. "Do you believe it? Do you practice it?"

"No," Kelsi admitted. "I'm more ... I don't know. Kind of earth-based? Like, the Universe is in control. Not some old guy with a white beard on a throne in the sky."

Dennis nodded. "I thought as much. I watched how you handled the dirt when we were planting. They would have burned you for a witch once upon a time. I grew up in church. United Methodist, and I was pretty involved when I was younger. But there are more things in the world, or the universe, as you'd say, than can be explained in the Bible."

"Like seeing your wife?" Kelsi asked.

"Like seeing Gloria," Dennis confirmed. "I couldn't at first, you know. I might catch a whiff of her perfume or her shampoo. She never changed her shampoo after I told her how I'd smelled it that day we planted Woody." He paused for a long time and Kelsi didn't interrupt his reverie. After a few moments, he used a knuckle to wipe away a tear. "She never changed it and I never got tired of smelling it."

A sudden lump rose in Kelsi's throat and she had to take a drink to push it back down, but it made a drop of water leak from her own eye. She turned her head and wiped it away quickly.

"It's the flesh that holds us back," Dennis said when she faced him again. "May I?" He pointed at her hand on the armrest of the metal chair. Kelsi nodded and he reached over and gently pinched the skin between her thumb and forefinger on the back of her hand. "See how thick and soft it is? How it springs back? Now do mine."

He held his hand out toward her and Kelsi couldn't think of a reason not to do as he asked. She lightly squeezed his skin where he'd done hers. She was surprised at the thin, papery feel of his flesh and how long it took for the pinched skin to settle back into its normal place.

"You look surprised," Dennis said. "Did you know your grandparents?"

"No," Kelsi said. "My dad's parents died in a flood and Mom never talked to hers. She never told me what happened. I never met any of them that I remember, but I have a picture sitting on my dad's mom's lap with Granddad beside us. I was just a baby. I don't remember it."

"That's tragic," Dennis said softly. "I'm very sorry. A child needs grandparents, and young parents need their parents for advice, even if they don't want it." He paused, then returned to his topic. "You felt how thin my skin is?"

"Yeah," she admitted.

He leaned closer to her. "It's getting thin so it'll be easier to release my soul when the time comes." He nodded his head once. "As my flesh gets thinner and my time to go gets closer, these old eyes that don't see so well in this world anymore start to see into the next one."

Kelsi swallowed, her eyes fixed on him. He was dead serious. That much was obvious. "That's ... is that what United Methodists believe?" she asked.

He snorted, then laughed. "No. Absolutely not. That's what I believe. It's what I know. I couldn't see Gloria at first, but then I saw just a shape in the air beside me. Then, sometime later, the shape had a tinge of color. Now, it's like she's a very faded old photograph that I can just make out if I look real hard." He paused and leaned back in his chair, lifting his face toward the ceiling of the porch. "What did you see?" he asked in a very neutral tone.

"The shape in the air," Kelsi answered quietly. "That's all I ever see."

"Your grandmother on your mother's side probably saw them, too," he said. "I've done a little reading on the topic. I guess you wouldn't know, unless your mom told you?"

"She won't say much," Kelsi answered. "She just says Grandma was crazy and talked to people who weren't there and told me never to mention that nonsense again. So I didn't talk to her about it anymore. After Dad ... after he left, Mom drank a lot and had other men over. We didn't talk much."

Dennis was facing her again. "You haven't had an easy life, have you?"

Kelsi shrugged. "I've gotten by. I'm doing okay."

"You are at that," he agreed. "I'm surprised we haven't heard from my grandson," he added, looking at the cell phone Kelsi had put facedown on the table with the lemonade pitcher.

"I think he's pouting," she said.

"What about this time?"

Kelsi couldn't stop a grin. "I doubt you want to know."

"Ah," he said and nodded. "I was young once. Is it still the job of the young man to be a billy goat and the young woman to set boundaries?"

"Not for everyone," Kelsi said. "But it is for me. And he's definitely a billy goat when it comes to ... well ... you know."

"It's called sex, Kelsi," Dennis said with a smile. "We called it that, among other things. He wants you to move into Natalie and Albert's house while they're away, doesn't he?"

Kelsi laughed. "I think you're still seeing everything just fine in this world," she teased.

"A blind man could tell you that boys and men think with that thing between their legs more than what's on their shoulders for most of the first half of their lives," Dennis said. "You just stand your ground. What did you say you're going to college for?"

"To be a social worker," Kelsi said.

"Is that what your passion has always been?"

Hesitantly, Kelsi admitted, "No."

"What did you want to do?" he asked.

"I wanted to be a photographer, but everyone said that was stupid because anyone can take a good picture with their cell phone these days," she said.

"Anyone can smear paint on a canvas, but are they Norman Rockwell?" Dennis asked. "Anyone can string words together, but that doesn't make them John Steinbeck."

"There isn't much money in photography," Kelsi said. "Especially if you don't have a studio."

"Do you have a camera? Besides your phone?"

"Yes. I bought one in Wyoming. It was used, but it's a good digital SLR."

"Take some pictures and show them to me next time you come," Dennis said. "Will you come again? I've enjoyed our talk."

"Of course," Kelsi promised, and she really meant it.

"And you'll take pictures? Of anything you like," he said.

"Yes. For you," she agreed.

"I'm going to go inside and eat since it's dinner time," he said. "You're welcome to stay, but I wasn't expecting company and only planned to eat tomato soup and a bacon sandwich. This old flesh doesn't require much food these days."

Kelsi laughed with him and thanked him, but said she should leave. They said their good-byes and she went back to her car. She saw that Dennis remained seated on the porch, waving to her as she drove away toward home.

Chapter Eight

K elsi slid the green button on her phone screen and put the phone to her ear. "What's up?" she asked Tucker. She'd found him waiting for her at her apartment after her visit with his grandfather three days ago. He'd had roses, a bottle of her favorite red wine, and take-out from Chili's restaurant. They'd eaten, drank, watched part of a movie, and ended up in bed together. He had never actually apologized for the way he'd behaved.

"Where are you?" Tucker asked.

Kelsi grinned, not that he could see it. "I'm lying on the ground looking up the thick white trunk of a certain sycamore tree, trying to find the most interesting angle for a photograph."

"You're what?" he asked, totally confused.

"I'm taking pictures of your grandfather's tree," she said.

"Why?"

"I like the story. I like the tree. I want to take a picture he'll like."

"Kels, this is kind of weird, you hanging out with my grandpa," Tucker said.

"Why is that weird? Hold on!" She dropped the phone and raised the camera that had been resting on her stomach. About twenty feet above her, a brown squirrel had appeared on a branch near the trunk. The little animal was perched there, looking down at her. Kelsi could hear Tucker's voice calling to her from the phone as she centered the squirrel in her viewfinder, snapped, then moved so that the squirrel was toward the edge of the frame with white limbs and shining green leaves filling most of the space. She took a couple more shots, then put the camera back on her belly and picked up her phone, keeping an eye on the squirrel. "I'm back," she said.

"What was that about?"

"A squirrel," she answered, then giggled about being distracted by a squirrel like a dog on a walk. "I got a few shots of him. He's cute and he's totally checking me out."

"Are you even the same person you were a week ago?" Tucker asked, and she wasn't sure how serious he was about the question. "Are you coming home soon?"

"No," she answered. "But you can come here. I want to go to Valleybrook Park, too, and take pictures of the ducks, and then downtown as the sun is setting."

"You're really into this photography thing," he said, his voice flat.

"I've always loved it. Your grandpa just reminded me of it," Kelsi said.

"He's never shown this much interest in me," Tucker complained.

"Have you shown interest in him? Really listened to his stories? Do you know about your grandma's shampoo?" she asked.

"Grandma's shampoo? What the hell? What about her shampoo?"

"Exactly," Kelsi said. She watched the squirrel run to the end of the limb and launch himself across about ten feet of space and into the leafy embrace of an oak tree on the other side of the walkway. "If you want to see me, you'll come here."

"Fine. I'm at your place. I'll be there in a few minutes," Tucker said, and he hung up on his end.

Kelsi pulled her feet out of her flip-flops. She'd had them on either side of the base of the tree. Now she stretched her legs up and flattened her feet against the trunk. She took a couple of pictures of her bare legs using an angle that made them seem very long. Tucker would appreciate that picture, she knew. She rolled away and into a sitting position, then crossed her legs and looked at the dirt where it met the trunk of the tree. She tried to picture young Dennis and Gloria right here where she was, putting this tree into the ground over seventy years ago and pushing dirt around it.

Kelsi reached out and put her hand on the hard, packed earth and closed her eyes. She didn't feel anything. No vision filled her mind and no vibrational memory tingled up her arm. But there was ... an aroma. Clean and floral, like flowers in summer. She opened her eyes, and for just a fraction of a heartbeat she was sure she saw the shimmery outline of a figure beside the tree, then the breeze blew her hair across her face and it was gone.

A shadow fell across her and she turned her head to find Tucker standing over her. He was wearing a black shirt with a picture of Johnny Cash flipping the bird and black basketball shorts with black-and-orange sneakers. "You look like some kind of guru sitting under the tree of Grandpa's knowledge," he joked.

"I'll take that as a compliment," she said, and held out a hand to him so he could help her up. He did, and she thanked him by allowing a quick kiss. "I took a couple for you." She showed him the shots of her legs.

"Now that's photography I like," he said. "Maybe later I can run my tongue up those legs."

"God, is that all you think about?" Kelsi asked as she slipped into her flip-flops.

"Like you don't appreciate what I do when I get to the middle," he said defensively.

She fixed him with a serious look. "We both know I do," she said. "But there is a mom with her kids right over there at the swings and she probably doesn't want her kids hearing you say that kind of stuff in a public park. It's crude." She saw his forehead wrinkling and knew he was about to go into a pout or say something loud and ruder. She stopped him by leaning close and whispering, "But yes, you can do that later." His brow smoothed out and he smiled happily. Kelsi shook her head and stepped away. "You drive," she said.

Tucker drove them across town to the city's biggest park. It had several playgrounds, a lake with pedal boats, and an amusement park with a carousel, a train that went around the park, and a few other rides for small kids. They walked along the edge of the lake until they spotted a group of ducks.

Kelsi began snapping pictures, but wasn't happy with the angle. She dropped to her knees, then lowered herself onto her belly and focused through some tall grass growing at the very edge of the water. Something cold and wet soaked through her T-shirt but she ignored it and took several more pictures of the ducks, all of which just happened to be facing and swimming right toward her. Kelsi pushed herself up and got to her feet.

"That's goose shit," Tucker said, pointing to three stains on Kelsi blue shirt and one of her blue shorts.

"Ewww!" she said, doubling over as if moving her skin further from contact with the soiled clothes.

"I guess you'll just have to take them off," he said. "You're not getting in my truck like that."

"This is so gross, you jerk," she said. "Don't you have a rag or something? Is there water around here?"

"There's a whole lake," Tucker said, motioning at the gray water.

"I saw a bathroom back there where we parked," Kelsi said, and began walking with long, determined strides back the way they'd come. Laughing, Tucker hurried to catch up with her.

"Those aren't usually open," he said. "And I bet they're really sketch, anyway. I wouldn't go in there."

"Then you don't have to," Kelsi told him.

They went past a little fenced in playground called The Tot Lot and Kelsi marched on to the pale blue cinderblock building with a darker blue sign with the outline of a woman in a dress on one side and a similar sign of a figure not in a dress on the other. She grabbed the steel handle of the door and for a moment feared it wasn't going to open, but it did.

A horrible smell of urine, body odor, and something she couldn't place wafted out, but Kelsi held her breath and rushed in. The water wasn't hot and there weren't many paper towels left, but she made do and scrubbed at her clothes until her whole front was wet, but the poop was gone. A small, accidental sound came from one of the battered stalls. Kelsi refused to look. No other sound followed. She tried very hard not to notice that there were empty, used syringes in the sink next to her. She left quickly and rushed into Tucker's surprised arms and pressed her face against his chest.

"Are you okay?" He held her tightly and petted her long hair, his voice full of real concern. "Babe? Are you okay?"

"It smelled awful and there'd been druggies in there. Maybe one was still in the stalls. I don't know. I got scared," Kelsi admitted. She breathed deeply of his clean human scent under the Axe body spray he used like he was still in high school. She wondered distractedly if someday in their future she would love the fact he had never changed that scent as long as she'd known him. "Can we go?"

"Of course." He kissed the top of her head, then kept an arm tightly around her as they went back to his truck. He let her go in front of the vehicle, still not thinking to open the door for her. Kelsi refused to be hurt by the thoughtlessness. She told herself he was trying.

"Do you still want to go downtown?" he asked.

"No. Not today," she said. "Take me back to my car, then we can go to my apartment." She wanted to be held. She knew he'd push that to include sex, which she really didn't want, but she was willing to pay that price.

To her surprise, Tucker was caring and gentle, holding her close on the loveseat as she showed him some of her pictures on the camera's little screen. "The legs are still my favorite," he said, "But I like the one with the squirrel on the edge, and the ones you took from the hill. You couldn't get the whole tree in it, though."

"I know," she said. "It's so tall and so wide. Just think how much it's grown since they planted it."

"Grown like their love," Tucker said, but he said it in a gently mocking voice. "I've heard the story so many times."

"It's a very sweet story," she argued.

"It is," he agreed, but his voice lacked conviction. He kissed her forehead, then put a finger under her chin and tilted her face up and kissed her on the tip of her nose, then on her lips. His own lips were warm, but dry. The kiss was gentle and comforting. He opened his mouth and she opened hers and felt her hand going instinctively to his neck. When he leaned her back against the arm of the loveseat and pulled her shorts off, she didn't mind nearly as much as she thought she would.

Chapter Nine

Another Saturday came and Kelsi found herself looking forward to the trip to the park with Dennis Aiken. She had to work another double shift, but had managed to make it a split so that she could have a few hours off in the afternoon. She ordered sandwiches as her shift ended, as she'd promised to bring a picnic lunch. She put the sandwiches, fries, and three cold bottles of root beer into a basket she'd bought especially for the occasion and she hurried away from the diner to the park, where Tucker was late arriving in his red Chevy pickup with Dennis, but eventually they made it. Kelsi left her car, with the basket in her hand and a folded blanket under her arm.

Tucker had parked and gotten the two lawn chairs from the back of his truck, but left his grandfather to fend for himself getting out of the tall vehicle. Dennis made it out, but Kelsi thought it was inconsiderate of Tucker to not have helped.

Together, the three of them approached the tree. Tucker asked, "Pops, do you want me to open these chairs, or do you just want to sit on the blanket with us?" Kelsi glared at him.

"I'd like to have the chairs, please," Dennis answered. "My old bones can't take sitting on the ground too much."

"Okay," Tucker said, his tone resigned.

"Be respectful," Kelsi said without moving her mouth any more than she had to as she walked past Tucker to a spot favorable for the blanket. She put the basket down, then spread the blanket so that one corner was nearly touching the chair where Dennis was settling in.

It wasn't a windy day, but there was a frequent gust of light breeze that caused the dappled shade on the ground to dance and shift in a way Kelsi found mesmerizing. She pulled the scrunchy out and let her hair fall around her shoulders where the breeze could maybe air out some of the restaurant smell before she had to put it back and return to work. She wore jeans and a Sweet Pea's Diner T-shirt and wished she could wear shorts to work, as the day was warm and her jeans felt confining.

"We'll eat together, then Tucker and I will leave you to your meditation with the tree," Kelsi said. "Is that okay, Mr. Aiken?"

He gave her a mischievous look and shook his head. "We've had our hands in the same soil and shared lemonade, young lady," he told her. "You call me Dennis."

Kelsi smiled and she felt a sense of joy all the way into her chest. "Okay, Dennis. Thank you."

"Putting your hands in the dirt is a bonding ritual now?" Tucker asked sarcastically.

"When's the last time you planted anything?" Kelsi asked.

"I don't really do that," Tucker answered.

"That's why you're not grounded," Dennis told him.

"What do you mean? Mom used to ground me from my phone," Tucker argued.

Dennis looked at Kelsi. "I was an electrician before I retired," he said. "We walk around on the biggest conductor of electricity and don't even think about it." He lifted his feet off the ground and pushed off his loafers, then put his bare feet in the grass. "You can look this up on your internet, but I know we've changed since the introduction of rubber-soled shoes. It keeps the earth's recharging electricity from passing through us. That's why it's important to take your shoes off and get your hands in the soil. It's healthy. And it connects you to where you are."

"That's crazy," Tucker said. "If the earth was so full of electricity, we'd be getting shocked all the time."

Ignoring her boyfriend, Kelsi gave Dennis a conspiratorial smile. "More United Methodist dogma?" she asked. They shared a laugh, then Kelsi untied her sneakers and pulled them and her ankle socks off. She stuffed the socks inside and put the shoes on the far edge of the blanket.

"You believe that?" Tucker asked her.

"He's the electrician," Kelsi said innocently. "But yes. It's called earthing. There's actually a whole movement based on the idea. I saw a documentary on Hulu or somewhere."

"Whatever," Tucker said. "I'll be keeping my shoes on. They were expensive, anyway. What kind of sandwiches did you bring?"

"I've got a pulled pork with barbecue sauce, a BLT with mayo, and a steak sandwich," she said. "And fries for everyone, plus root beer." They all looked at each other, nobody wanting to make a first claim. "Dennis, you pick first," Kelsi said.

"I think I'd like the bacon sandwich," he said. Kelsi handed it over with a side of fries.

"Tucker?" she asked.

"Nah, you pick and I'll take the other one," he said, and Kelsi was happy he said it. She knew he liked both sandwiches, but she just couldn't face the thought of eating the chicken fried steak, so she gave him that one and kept the pulled pork for herself. They munched in silence for a little bit.

"What have you been doing, Dennis?" Kelsi asked.

The older man swallowed. "I've been reading mostly."

"What do you like to read?" she asked.

"I like a lot of things," he said. "I reread some Louis L'Amour westerns I've had since I was a teenager, and a fantasy novel about gray orcs that cussed a lot, and one called *Hannah Fowler* that was one of Gloria's favorites."

"She was a reader, too?" Kelsi asked.

"Oh, yes. She always had a book with her. For as long as I knew her," he said, nodding. "She would read anything, but she really loved stories about pioneers."

"Did her parents come from farms or ranches?" Kelsi asked.

"No. At least, not that she knew of. Her father was a science teacher at the high school and his father was one of the first mail carriers in town. She came from a long line of city folk," he said and smiled. "She was always jealous that I got to live on a farm for a while."

"Why did you leave the farm?" Kelsi asked. She saw Tucker give her a what-have-you-done-now kind of look but ignored him.

"I was just a boy and didn't understand it all at the time," Dennis said. "Dad went to war after the Japs bombed Pearl Harbor. He was a paratrooper at D Day. He'd never talk about it much. Me and mom couldn't really keep the farm going much while he was gone. We did good to keep our personal vegetable garden planted, weeded, and harvested. Then, when Dad came home, he was different. Even I knew he wasn't working as hard as he used to. I remember one time, we couldn't find him at dinnertime. We looked all around the house and in the barn and he wasn't there, but the truck was in the driveway. I called for Duke, my favorite dog, and we went looking for him."

Dennis stopped, his head down as if he was examining the lettuce on his sandwich.

"Where was he? Was he okay?" Tucker asked. "I haven't heard this one."

"I found him sitting under a tree and he was crying," Dennis said. "It scared me pretty bad. He was a big, strong, hard man. I'd seen him throw bales of hay all day and face off against a bull that wanted out of the corral. He wasn't supposed to cry. No boy wants to see his father cry, but there he was, sitting on the ground crying like somebody had just died. I almost turned around and ran away."

He paused again and Kelsi prompted, "But you didn't."

"He heard me, I guess," Dennis said. "He looked up and called my name. I had to go to him, but I really didn't want to. When I got close, he lunged at me as fast as a mountain lion. It scared Duke. I remember him letting out a yelp and backing away. Dad pulled me close and I thought he was going to whip me again for bothering him, but he didn't. He ... He buried his face against my neck and squeezed me until I thought I might break and he just cried harder and kept saying he loved me. It was the scariest thing I'd ever experienced then, and only one thing has ever topped it."

"What was wrong with him?" Tucker asked.

"I guess they'd call it post traumatic stress disorder now," Dennis said sadly. "There wasn't a name for it then and nobody talked about it. I think Dad saw and did things in the war that changed who he was. He couldn't keep up with the farm and he sold it before he went into debt with it. I think that was Mom's idea. She was always better with numbers and managing money. We moved into town and I started school at Adams over there and met your grandmother." Dennis waved toward the east, where Kelsi guessed the school was.

"It doesn't sound like the farm was a very happy place," Tucker said.

Dennis smiled. "A boy on a farm is like being in paradise. Room to roam and a good dog. Good fishing. Hunting. Camping out in the pasture under the stars. Have you ever gotten out of town and looked at the sky at night? Even here in town we used to see a lot of stars a long time ago. Not so much any more."

"Yeah, but you didn't have computers or the internet or video games," Tucker said. Kelsi took a bite of sandwich and rolled her eyes where only Dennis could see it. "Were you even able to rent movies on those cassettes?"

"Tucker, almost nobody had a TV in their home in the Forties, especially out on a farm, and the VCR hadn't been invented yet," Dennis said. "We had a radio, a Bible, a collected works of Shakespeare, a few novels Mom had gotten somewhere, and the Farmer's Almanac. But I didn't read much then. I was always outside studying bugs or plants or looking for Indian arrowheads. That took a lot of my time. I found a few, too."

"What did your father do when you moved into town?" Kelsi asked.

"That was 1946. He went to work at Blue Dot Dairy," Dennis said. "It closed down back in the Seventies or early Eighties. Dad was drinking a lot by the time we moved to town. He died in an accident at work in 1950. Mom wouldn't talk about it much, but I found out from other people that he must have been drunk and sneaked off and fell asleep behind some crates. Somebody else was trying to move some big metal tanks and knocked over a rack of them. A couple of them crushed him. He never even knew he was in danger. I guess that was good."

"I'm so sorry," Kelsi said. "That's awful."

"I have some pretty vivid memories of my father," Dennis said. He shook his head. "But that one where I found him crying is the one that always comes to me first."

"Alcohol sure ruins a lot of lives," Kelsi said.

"It does," Dennis agreed.

"Mom and Dad drink, but I've only seen Mom drunk a few times," Tucker said. "Dad never. And Mom is really just kind of tipsy. Not black-out drunk."

Dennis nodded in acknowledgement.

"Let's finish up and give your grandpa some time with the tree," Kelsi said to Tucker. They ate quickly and she gathered the wrappers and empty bottles and put them back in the basket, then folded the blanket. "Tucker, will you walk me back to my car to put these away?" she asked.

"Anything for m'lady," he said.

As they were walking back, Kelsi asked, "Did you know the story about how your great-grandfather died?"

"Only that it was a work accident," Tucker said.

"That had to be hard on Dennis," Kelsi said.

"It's weird to hear you call him by his first name," Tucker said.

"I like it. It's awkward to keep calling him 'your grandfather'," she said. "And I can't call him that when I'm talking to him."

"I guess," he conceded.

They put the things in the trunk of her car and turned back to the park. Dennis's head was turned to the empty lawn chair and he was very clearly speaking to it. Kelsi tried to determine if the shape of Gloria was there in the chair, but the distance was too much.

"What the hell is he doing?" Tucker asked.

"He's talking to your grandmother," Kelsi said. She laughed at the incredulous look he gave her. "You don't believe in ghosts?"

"I don't believe Grandma is sitting in that empty chair," he answered. "I don't see her. Do you?"

"No," Kelsi admitted.

"I guess we're lucky he wants to come to a park instead of a cemetery," Tucker said.

"Where is she buried?" Kelsi asked.

"I don't know."

Kelsi looked at him. "You've never gone and put flowers on her grave?"

"Nope."

"That tree meant a lot to them," Kelsi said.

"Keep hanging around him and he'll tell you all about it," Tucker said as if it was a warning.

"I hope so," Kelsi said. She settled into a swing. "Push me until he's finished with his visit."

Chapter Ten

The classroom was warm despite the early hour. Sunlight poured through the windows facing the east, warming Kelsi's arm where she sat in the front seat of the aisle furthest from the classroom door and closest to the windows. There were about fifteen other students in the intersession class, all bleary-eyed with paper cups of to-go coffee or sealed tumblers from home. The room smelled of coffee and creamer on top of the aroma of old paper and old building.

Professor Gonzalez lectured from the front of the room and Kelsi tried hard to focus on what he was saying. Her small academic scholarship didn't offset much of her costs, but she needed every dollar of it and keeping it was dependent on maintaining at least a 3.0 GPA. She had already questioned herself numerous times on this decision to take an intersession version of Chemistry 3115 that started at 8 in the morning. She wondered if she really wanted to be a social worker. Maybe being a waitress wasn't such a bad career option. Her mind wandered down a pathway where she considered the possibilities of financial advancement waiting tables and compared it to expected future monetary needs. She was considering what size and condition of a house she could afford with a fifty cent raise when the professor dropped a book onto a table at the front of the room.

"Is everyone awake?" he asked, his tan face grinning. At least he seemed like a cool professor who understood how hard it was go get up early on a summer morning.

Kelsi sipped her coffee and vowed she would stay awake. When class ended at noon, she couldn't wait to leave. She couldn't decide if she was more tired or hungry. The desire for food won out and she made a stop at a Taco Bell, deciding at the last minute to go inside and eat instead of taking the food home to her empty apartment. The restaurant was busy with people from auto shops to nurses working in the area. Kelsi sat alone at a small table in a corner and watched them, wondering about their lives, trying to determine if they were happy based on the lines in their faces.

Lined faces made her think of Dennis Aiken, and she determined she would just drive by his house on her way home and see if she could see any flowers peeking over the brick border of his flowerbed. She was a little surprised to see the tall, elderly man on his hands and knees in the flowerbed, a straw cowboy hat on his head. She pulled into the driveway and got out of the car.

"Kelsi!" he called happily. "I was just thinking of you."

"I felt my ears burning," she said. "What are you doing?"

"Pulling weeds. It's an endless battle."

"You should wear shorts and wait for evening," Kelsi said. "It's pretty hot to be out here. Are you staying hydrated?"

"Oh, I'm fine. There's water on the porch and I've got my gardening hat on," he said.

"I see that. I thought it was Chris Stapleton out here in your garden."

"I don't know who that is," Dennis answered.

Kelsi laughed and considered explaining, but instead asked, "Do you want some help?"

"You'll get those bare knees dirty," Dennis said.

"They'll be easier to wash than your khakis," she answered. Kelsi kicked off her flip-flops, noticing for the first time that Dennis was also barefoot. She stepped from the hot pavement of the walkway in front of the porch to the cool, moist soil of the garden, then knelt down. "Where did all these weeds come from?" she asked.

"I think little devils come and plant them in the night," Dennis said.

The weeds — dandelions and sprigs and clusters of grass — weren't very tall, but there were a lot of them. Kelsi began pulling them out, making sure to get the roots just like Dennis was doing, and tossing them out of the garden. The soil felt good in her fingers. Even the weeds with their oily green life felt good as she ripped them out. She and Dennis didn't talk for a long while, just worked in silence, and Kelsi marveled at the feeling of peace she got from the work. After almost an hour, all the unwanted plants were removed and she and Dennis sat back on their heels and looked at each other.

"We're a good team," he said.

"The best!" Kelsi agreed. She held up a hand for a high five. He looked at it curiously for a moment, then understood the gesture and patted the palm of her hand with his own.

"If you'll help an old man up, I'll bring out some lemonade," Dennis offered.

Kelsi unwound and stood up easily, then offered her hands to him. She was surprised at the real difficulty Dennis had in getting his feet under him, and then he stood for several moments hunched over with his knees bent and his brow furrowed.

"Dennis, are you okay?" she asked.

He lifted his face to look at her, and she saw the pain and sadness there. "It gets harder all the time. I'm eighty-four years old and do okay for the most part, but there are parts that are wearing out faster than others."

"Let's get you up on the porch so you can sit down," she said.

"Would you mind if we go inside?" he asked. "I am kind of hot. Maybe you were right about the heat out here."

"Of course." With one hand on the wooden porch railing and the other around his waist, Kelsi helped Dennis up the steps of the porch, then she opened the door for him and followed him into the house.

Every house has a smell that is made up of the history and personality of the people who live in it. Dennis Aiken's house, though he had lived there alone for eight years, still smelled distinctly feminine. There was a good smell that couldn't be pinned down to one particular dish, but a tableau of homecooked meal after meal, seasonings and broths and basted meats all mingling together to become one comforting aroma, and mixed with that was the smells of powder and lotions and perfume. There was again a definite aroma of lavender. Kelsi knew without looking that there would be a crocheted cover over a spare roll of toilet paper in the bathroom and hand towels that were purely decorative and likely hadn't been washed in eight years.

There was clutter in the house, and dust, but overall it was pretty clean considering it was now inhabited by an elderly widower. There was a big floral sofa and a wide, dark blue rocking recliner, and another older rocker with worn wooden arms and wingbacks. They were all arranged mostly to look at the fireplace, but there was a medium-sized flatscreen television on the mantle. The floor was hardwood in need of mopping and buffing, with a rug under the coffee table in front of the sofa.

She could see through the living room to a dining area with a table on one side and an opening to a hall that led to bedrooms and the bathroom on the other. Beyond the dining area was the heart of the house, the kitchen.

"You go ahead and sit down and I'll bring the lemonade," Kelsi said.

"The glasses are in the cabinet to the right of the sink," Dennis said. He didn't protest, but moved stiffly toward the recliner and lowered himself into it.

Kelsi, of course, had never met Gloria Aiken, but the woman's presence was palpable in her kitchen. Dish towels with embroidered outlines of kittens and a hand soap dispenser shaped like an orange tabby stretching its neck to be scratched, cute kitty magnets on the refrigerator, and a thick oval rug in front of the sink gave hints about the woman. But more than that was just a feeling of her presence. Not like in the park where Kelsi thought she might catch a glimpse of the woman's ghostly shadow, but just the knowledge that she had been here. This had been her domain, the place where she worked hardest to make the house a home.

She had cooked in this room for decades, feeding her family, gossiping with friends at the small table in a corner, washing dishes, and Kelsi bet she'd been a fruit and vegetable canner.

Something deep inside Kelsi clenched and squeezed at her tear ducts. She couldn't understand it, but something about the kitchen made her feel a sense of incompleteness in her own life.

She washed her hands, then found two tall glasses in the cupboard. She filled them with ice, then poured from a plastic pitcher she took from the refrigerator, noticing that there were quite a few covered dishes of leftovers, some of which weren't looking too new. Taking the glasses into the living room, she put one in Dennis's trembling hand.

Kelsi sat in the corner of the sofa closest to her host, sipped while she watched him do the same, then asked, "Are you sure you're okay?"

"I'm okay," he promised. "I needed this. Thank you."

"Would you have stayed out there until all the weeds were pulled if I hadn't stopped by?" Kelsi asked.

She could tell he thought for a moment of telling her something less than the truth. He sighed. "I don't know," he admitted. "There is a real chance I would have ignored how I'm feeling and kept going." He shrugged. "But I might have decided it was too hot and the weeds could wait. I really just don't know. But I am glad you came along."

"I am, too," Kelsi said. "I'm worried about you being out there alone. Are you friends with your neighbors?"

An expression of sadness pulled the flesh of his face down as he took another drink. He shook his head. "Not anymore. There was a time, but those people have all either died or gone to retirement homes. Ruth Gadsden is still in her house four doors down, but she has a hospice nurse and probably won't last the summer. She hasn't been out of the house in weeks." He drank more lemonade. The shaking in his hand seemed to be less. "A lot of these houses are rentals now. It used to be an all-white neighborhood when we bought the house. Now we have a little of everything living here."

Kelsi tried to keep her voice completely neutral. "Does that bother you?"

"Skin color doesn't," Dennis said. "But I miss my old neighbors. The people I knew. The people my age. They kept their houses better than the people living here now. Maybe because they were a different generation. Maybe because they owned the houses. They're gone and the houses are still here." He paused and looked around his living room. "One day, not so far from now, there will be other people living right here in this house Gloria and I have owned for over fifty years. That's a strange thing to think about."

"It is," Kelsi agreed, but she was thinking about all the buildings she'd called home in her comparatively short twenty-four years of life. She wondered what it would be like to have one place to call home year after year. "Tell me more about your new neighbors."

He shrugged. "The Mitchells next door have been there for about ten years. They're a colored family. I guess they say black now. I used to talk to DeMarco some, but then he left the family. I don't know what happened. They'd fight sometimes and I could hear them, and then he was gone. Sanaya, the wife, she stayed with the kids, but she works a lot. Now the kids are grown and gone and I guess she's making up for getting married young. She comes home late most nights.

"People on the other side, I haven't met. Renters come and go fast in that house. You'd think it was haunted, but I guess it's probably too much rent and a shitty landlord," he said, then blushed. "Excuse me, I meant a bad landlord."

Kelsi laughed. "You can cuss around me," she said. "I've been known to drop a bad word here and there, myself."

"It's not proper," Dennis argued. "My mother would have taken a wooden spoon to my backside if she'd heard me say that, and in the presence of a young lady." He shook his head. "I just don't think much of the man who owns so many of the rental properties in this town." He took a bigger drink, then sighed. "Anyway, we've got two ... no, it's three Mexican families across the street in those houses. The Guzmans right across from me moved in first. He's a bricklayer. A hardworking man, from what I can tell. He's got three daughters. I think they're all teenagers now. He and his wife don't speak much English, so we pretty much just nod and wave. Same with his neighbors on either side.

"A lot of the rest of the neighborhood is made up of people from the Marshall Islands," Dennis said. "Again, not much English. You can tell their houses because of all the shoes on the front porch. When someone comes out to go somewhere, they just put on a pair of shoes. Usually not their own. You'll see them in stores wearing shoes that are too big or too small. It's the damnedest thing I've ever seen."

Kelsi had to raise a hand to cover a grin. She knew what he was talking about. She'd noticed the people he was describing in Wal-Mart and other stores, and she had seen that they were wearing shoes that didn't fit.

"I could walk up and down the blocks around here and tell you the names and histories of the people who used to live in every house," Dennis continued. "But I hardly know anybody around here now. And I'm sure I'm the weird old white man to them, but we get along despite it all."

"I guess that's what's important," Kelsi said. She finished her lemonade. "I'm dying to know more about you and Gloria. What happened after you planted Woody? But I'm afraid I have to go. I had class from eight to noon this morning and I have to be at work by four. Promise me you'll stay inside until evening?"

He smiled and nodded. "I promise," he said. "Thank you for caring."

Kelsi took the empty glasses back to the kitchen and put them in the almost empty dishwasher, then went back to the living room. Dennis seemed to be almost asleep, but he perked up when a floorboard creaked under her step. Kelsi had a sudden inspiration. "Where is your wife buried? Would you like to go put flowers on her grave someday?"

Dennis grinned at her. "You were sitting beside her for the past hour."

Kelsi followed his eyes as he looked from her to the end table beside the end of the sofa where she'd been sitting. In the center of the table, on a lacy doily, was a bronze urn that she had seen, but not registered as anything more than a decorative piece. "Oh," she said, realizing now what it was.

"That isn't where she wants to be, but your boyfriend's mother has forbidden me to carry out my wife's wishes," Dennis said, and for the first time since she'd met him, there was a bitterness to his voice.

"Woody?" Kelsi asked, knowing already.

"Of course," Dennis said, and he was himself again. He smiled at her. "Keep coming around here and you'll understand why."

"I'll do that," she promised. "Now you go ahead and take that nap you were almost into a few minutes ago."

"Practicing for the big sleep," Dennis said.

"Don't say that," Kelsi chided. "I'm just getting to know you. I'll lock the door as I leave."

She was filled with a sense of happiness as she drove home to change into her work clothes.

Chapter Eleven

"Can't you take a break from the schoolwork for a while?" Tucker whined. He lay on his back on the loveseat, his legs dangling off one end at the knee while he scrolled through the options on Netflix without choosing anything. Kelsi sat cross-legged on the floor in front of the little sofa, her laptop and textbook open on the battered second-hand coffee table in front of her. His fingers went back to Kelsi's raven hair and he made as if he was going to pull it in a dominant sexual way.

Kelsi twisted her body away from him, pulling her hair out of his hand. "This class meets every day at eight in the morning for two weeks. We talked about it. I'm giving up work hours for it. I will not skip the homework because you need attention. My dad isn't giving me a job."

She hadn't meant to let that last little bit out, but in her frustration at Tucker and with half her attention still on the textbook she was quoting from in her writing, it had popped out. The tension that suddenly filled the room was suffocating and she wished Tucker would yell at her instead of being hurt.

"You don't think I deserve my job?" he asked, his voice flat, emotionless.

Kelsi sighed. "You told me yourself that you've had that blue shirt since you started, that you never had to do the grunt work like people who aren't related to the superintendent," Kelsi explained. "I just need to focus on this homework."

"I listened to Dad all my life while he talked abut his job and how to do it," Tucker argued. "That's better than starting out picking up scrap metal and working my way up from the worst machines to the best."

"Can you operate every machine in the shop?" Kelsi asked, letting her annoyance get the better of her. "Shouldn't someone in your position be able to do that?"

"There's no reason for me to. Most of my job is in an office, running inspections," he argued.

"Whatever. Nobody's offering me any job, so I have to get this degree," Kelsi said, wanting to end the argument.

"I could probably get you a job," Tucker said.

"Couples shouldn't work together," Kelsi said. "What would we talk about after work if we saw each other all day? Plus, it isn't what I want to do."

"Working in a sheet metal shop isn't good enough for you?" he asked.

"It isn't what I want to do," Kelsi argued.

"That isn't what you want to do, either," he said, jabbing a finger toward her open book. "What happened to the artsy-fartsy photographer?"

"I have to pay the rent on this place," she said.

"You wouldn't for two years if you'd just move in with me," he shot back.

Kelsi was on her feet before she knew she was going to move, her bare feet running for the only closed off space in the studio apartment. "You're such a prick!" she shouted as she slammed the bathroom door. She sat on the toilet lid and tried to muffle her sobs so he wouldn't hear them and have the satisfaction of knowing he'd made her cry. It took several minutes to get over the crying, but still there was an ache in her belly.

Why? Why did I let him get to me? All he wants is sex. Is that all I am to him? And I do want to be a social worker. I want to help people.

A soft knock came at the door. "Kels, I'm sorry," Tucker said quietly. "I was being a prick. Just like you said. I'm sorry. Will you come out?"

Part of her had hoped he'd left the apartment. Part of her was glad he'd stayed and was apologizing. Did he mean it? He sounded sincere enough. Not sure what to say, she answered with, "Okay." Kelsi ran cold water in the sink and splashed it onto her face several times, then dried herself. She opened the door and Tucker was there.

"I'm sorry," he said again and reached for her.

Kelsi stepped into his embrace and nuzzled her cheek against his chest while his arms closed around her. He rocked side to side, his idea of dancing, and kissed the top of her head. She felt his right hand sliding down her back toward her butt.

"No," she said.

"No make-up sex?" he asked.

"Is that the only reason you apologized?"

"No," he said, defeated.

"I have to finish my homework," she said. "Then you have to take me out somewhere nice for dinner. No fast food. I want pasta. Show me you're really sorry." Tucker wasn't a fan of pasta and really hated paying restaurant prices for "twenty cents worth of noodles with a nickel of sauce on them." His idea of going out to eat was either steak or barbecue.

"I suppose I owe you that much," he conceded.

They went back to their places and she tried to get back into the swing of her homework, but it was harder to focus. Tucker had settled on a Marvel movie, so things were constantly blowing up on the TV screen. Kelsi's mind drifted to Dennis.

"Does anybody check on your grandfather during the week?" she asked.

"I mean, Mom has been. I'm sure she'll still call him," he said.

"He's alone over there. All of his friends have moved or died," Kelsi said.

"How do you know that?"

"I stopped by on my way home after class yesterday. I was just going to drive by, but he was weeding the garden, so I stopped and he let me help him," she said. "I think he got too hot. We went inside and drank lemonade and I think he took a nap after I left. He was telling me about all the neighbors he misses."

"It's really weird that you keep going over there," Tucker said.

"I like your grandfather," Kelsi said. "He's very nice and I want to hear the story about how he courted your grandmother." Tucker opened his mouth and Kelsi cut him off. "I want to hear him tell it to me." Tucker's mouth snapped closed. "Do you ever call him?"

"No," he admitted, and she heard the guilt in his voice.

"You should. Especially now that you're the caregiver," Kelsi told him.

"Caregiver? I just take him and his lawn chairs to the park every weekend. That's gonna be a real pain in the ass," Tucker said.

"Those trips mean everything to him. How can you say that?" she asked, turning to fully face him. He gave her a quick glance then kept his attention on Captain Marvel on the television.

"Why can't he just walk over there? It isn't that far," Tucker said.

"Have you watched him walk, Tucker? Really watched him? He doesn't do it so well," she said. "Why doesn't he drive?"

"He ran over some trashcans," Tucker said. "He said he never saw them. Smashed them up good from what Mom said. The city had to replace them. He made my Dad sell his car and said he was done driving. Something about thinking those trashcans could have been somebody's kids he didn't see."

Kelsi nodded. That sounded typical of Dennis. "You should just check on him more," she said.

"Sounds like you're doing enough for both of us," Tucker said.

"I'm hungry and you've watched that movie a million times," Kelsi said.

Tucker sighed. "Please pick somewhere with unlimited breadsticks so I can eat something with substance."

***

The next day, after class, Kelsi went to one of the big box hardware stores and bought a plastic window box, a bag of potting soil, and a package of geranium seeds after talking to a clerk in the garden section about what plants would grow best in a box she could keep on the small porch at the stop of the stairs to her apartment.

At home, she sat on the landing, her feet two steps below her, and filled the plastic rectangle with the dark earth. She plowed two furrows with her right index finger, then sprinkled in the seeds and covered them with dirt, patting it down gently over the seeds. She put the box at the edge of the porch, where the morning sun would hit it, then went inside for a pitcher of water. She gently poured water over the soil until it was leaking from the holes in the bottom of the box, then she sat down again and stared into the box as if expecting the flowers to burst from the dirt instantly.

The smell was different than Dennis's garden. It was like the window box and potting soil on her porch ten feet above the ground were a shallow imitation of the patch of actual earth where she and Dennis had planted peonies. She reached into the box and took out a pinch of the black soil, rubbed it into her palm, then sniffed it. No, it wasn't the same, but it was earthy. It would do for now.

Kelsi went inside her house and on a whim opened her computer and searched for Dennis Aiken's phone number in Nokomis, Oklahoma. It was an easy search and she copied the number into the contacts of her phone, then called it. Dennis answered on the fourth ring.

"Dennis? This is Kelsi Duncan," she said. "Tucker's girlfriend?"

"I know who you are without that tag, Kelsi. How are you?" Dennis asked, and she could hear his grin through the phone.

"I'm good. Just home between class and work for a little bit," she said. "Listen, tomorrow I'm off work. I was wondering if you'd want to make a mid-week visit to see Woody. You know, get out of the house. We could do other things, too. Go to the library or the grocery store or whatever you want or need to do."

"That is very thoughtful of you, Kelsi," he said. "Yes, I'd like that very much. I might have eaten all my cheese puffs last night and would like to have some more. I have plenty of books, but I appreciate you thinking of the library. I used to be on the county library board. Did you know that?"

"No, I didn't," Kelsi said. "That sounds like another story you'll have to tell me. But tomorrow I want to hear the next stage of your courtship of Gloria. After you two planted Woody."

He laughed. "You're a lot like her," he said. "She was a sucker for a romantic story with a happy ending, whether it was one of her novels or a movie or just gossip at the beauty parlor."

"Those are called salons now," Kelsi said, laughing with him. "I'll pick you up just a little after twelve. Right after class. I'll buy us lunch, we'll visit Woody and you can tell me your story, then we'll get your cheese puffs."

"I hope my grandson won't get jealous," Dennis joked.

"He'll just have to deal with it," Kelsi said. "I'll see you then."

Chapter Twelve

Kelsi rang the doorbell and waited until Dennis Aiken opened the door. He smiled at her as he pushed open the storm door and came out to the porch, then pulled the door closed behind him. He put a key in the deadbolt and turned it.

"Hello, Kelsi," he said. "How was class?"

"Long and boring," she answered. "I keep telling myself it's only two weeks and I'll have a full class finished instead of having to take it for a whole semester, but getting up so early and sitting in that warm classroom ... The professor doesn't have any inflection to his voice and I fight to stay awake."

"Some professors are like that," Dennis said as he pulled the key from the lock.

"Did you go to college?" Kelsi asked.

"No," Dennis said. "No, I didn't."

"You just went to work after high school?"

"Something like that," he said. Holding the handrail, he went down the two steps of the porch to the sidewalk. He paused and pointed at the garden. "Our flowers are getting some little buds."

Kelsi looked and, sure enough, the green stems they'd planted earlier now had tiny buds on their tops. "That is so cool," she said. "I planted gardenias in a box on the landing outside my door because you inspired me with all of this."

"Gardenias are very pretty," Dennis said.

"The guy at the store said they're almost idiot proof, so I thought I had a shot at growing them," Kelsi said.

"You'll be growing prize-winning roses pretty soon," Dennis said. He turned to look at her Buick. "That's a nice car. I guess you've figured out I don't drive anymore."

"Tucker told me about the trashcans," Kelsi said. "I'm sorry."

He waved it away. "It was time. The older we get, the more we have to give up. It's easier than you would think, too. We become more like children and then babies if we stay too long."

"Don't talk like that," Kelsi scolded. "Get in the car and let's go eat. I'm hungry."

They drove halfway across town to a little hamburger joint called Lotsa Burger. The place served huge hamburgers and the best fries Kelsi had ever had. "This is so good," she said as she swallowed a mouthful of cheeseburger. "I can't believe I've never been here."

"It was Gloria's favorite place for a hamburger," Dennis said. "We'd usually sit right here in this booth to eat and talk."

"What did you talk about mostly?"

Dennis smiled and shook his head. "Friends and neighbors. What Natalie was doing in school. City business and church stuff. Gloria was in the choir and worked as the secretary at the church for a long time. I was on the library board. I think I told you that. I was also a commissioner on the city council for a couple of terms. I didn't really enjoy that."

"You were so involved. Both of you," Kelsi said, looking at her elderly friend with new admiration. "I've never known anybody who really got involved like that."

"Well, it was all Gloria. She said it was our responsibility to give back and that if we didn't do it, someone else would. She was involved in all kinds of stuff over the years. Ladies couldn't do a lot of things back then, like being a city commissioner, but there was a ladies group for almost everything and they used us husbands to get things done." He laughed as he thought back on it and Kelsi wished he was like a movie projector and she could see the memories that were making him happy.

"All I have is school and work," she said. "I can't even imagine doing more."

"People your age don't usually get mixed up in city business. Especially these days," Dennis said. "Focus on what you're doing. Speaking of which, do you have pictures to show me?"

Kelsi felt her face coloring a little. "Yeah," she admitted. "I didn't think you'd want to scroll through my camera to see them, so I printed them out for you." She pulled a blue photo lab envelope from her purse and pushed it across the table to him. "I plan to document Woody as he goes through his seasons this year. I've got summer. There's other stuff, too."

She watched nervously as Dennis examined each picture. "I love this one," he said, showing her the one with the squirrel and the bright green foliage of the sycamore tree. He flipped through a few more, then turned the stack so that he was looking at them in portrait mode. "Back in the day we might have said that's a nice set of gams," he said, turning the pictures to show the one of Kelsi's legs stretching up the trunk of the tree.

"Oh God! I forgot that was in there," she said, reaching for the picture.

Dennis laughed at her and moved the stack out of reach, but flipped that picture to the back of the deck. "I suppose that one was for my grandson," he said. "He's a lucky boy. I hope he knows that." He winked at Kelsi. "Not just because of the legs, of course."

"I'm so embarrassed," Kelsi said, ducking her head and shielding it with a hand. "I did not mean for you to see that one. I just picked these up and forgot to pull that one out."

"I've seen legs before, and the picture showed a playfulness and was composed well," he said.

"You talk like you know about photography," Kelsi said.

"I had an interest for a while and took a class at the vo-tech back in the '70s," he said.

"You were an electrician, right?" Kelsi asked.

"I did a lot of things, but the thing I did the longest was electrician at the refinery," he said. "You can't tell it so much now, but out there on Willow and Thirtieth there was a big refinery owned by the a local family. Most of the jobs in Nokomis were either there, at the Air Force base, or the grain elevators. They said we were a target for the Soviets if it ever came to nuclear war." He shook his head, then shrugged. "The refinery closed, the wheat going through town became less, and we're always afraid we'll lose the base whenever the feds talk about closures."

"When did the refinery close?" Kelsi asked.

"During the Reagan years. The 1980s," he said. "Some of it was sold off and I was lucky enough to get to stay on with the new company. I kept the gages working and the air conditioning on in the offices for the bigwigs who stayed. I retired about twenty years ago, when they sold the whole rusty place to one of the mid-level oil companies."

"What did you do after you retired?" Kelsi asked.

"Mostly stayed home. There's a woodshop in a shed behind the house. I don't use it much anymore, but after retirement I was out there all the time making stuff. Ink pens and pencil sets, simple furniture. It kept me busy," he said. "But you're getting way ahead of the story. You wanted to know what happened after we planted the tree."

"Yes!" Kelsi said. "Are we done here?" All the food was gone. She and Dennis wadded up wrappers and dumped everything into a trashcan on their way out to her car. She drove them back to the east side, to the park where the white-barked sycamore stood sentinel near the playground equipment. "I don't have any lawn chairs," Kelsi said when she parked the car.

"If you'll help an old man up, I'd like to sit on the grass in the shade Woody makes," Dennis said.

"I can do that," Kelsi said.

They walked the short distance from the street to the tree. There was a noticeable drop in temperature as they entered the shade of the tree and Kelsi was grateful for that. The late May afternoon was getting pretty hot. Dennis walked up to the tree and put a hand reverently on the white bark. He stood there with his hand on the tree and his head down for a few moments and Kelsi remained quiet, watching, wondering if he was praying or thinking of Gloria. Dennis raised his head and patted the tree, then stepped back and awkwardly sank to a sitting position.

"Do you mind if I take off my shoes?" he asked.

"Not at all," Kelsi said, and gently kicked off her flip-flops.

"Gloria loved those kind of simple shoes," Dennis said. "We called them thongs back in the day. I guess that has a different meaning these days."

"Umm, yeah," Kelsi said. She sank down to sit cross-legged facing Dennis. "Tell me a story. You planted a tree together and realized you'd met the love of your life. Then what?"

He chuckled. "It wasn't quite like that," he said.

Chapter Thirteen

Dennis stood near the back wall of the gloomy elementary school, watching other boys from his class and the other sixth grade class play tag on the playground. He wanted to play, but hadn't been invited, so he stood away from them and watched the game as the touch of "You're it!" went from boy to boy.

From the corner of his eye he caught another motion and turned his head to see Gloria Light coming toward him, a piece of notebook paper in her hand. She was walking with determination, her face set as if she was going to chase a cat out of the henhouse and really didn't want to have to mess with such a task. She stopped in front of him and, without pre-amble, said, "I made a schedule for the tree." She handed the notebook paper over to Dennis.

He looked at it. In pencil, she had drawn a picture of a big leafy tree in the center of the page, coloring the leaves with two shades of green crayon and leaving the bark white although their tree still had brown bark. On one side of the trunk was her name and on the other was his. Above the leaves of the tree, written in brown crayon, were the words, "Tree Care". On the bottom, written in pencil, were the instructions.

We will take turns watering our tree. I will take the first week. We should water the tree on Mondays and Thursdays. We don't have to water the tree if it has rained a lot. You better not forget!

"You mean we're supposed to water that tree we planted?" Dennis asked. "People don't water trees. They find water with their roots and when it rains. Nobody takes care of a tree like it's corn or wheat."

"We are going to take care of our tree and it's going to grow up and be the tallest and best tree in that park and maybe the best in the city or the whole state," Gloria said, and her voice left no room for argument. "Are you going to help or do I have to do it all by myself?" She had gray eyes rimmed in hazel and they were flashing at him as she told him how it was going to be. Her eyebrows were drawn together over her nose, which had a light speckling of freckles. She wore a dark blue dress with shoulder straps over a white shirt. "Are you listening to me?" she demanded when Dennis hadn't answered her.

"Yes," he said. "Okay. Geez. I didn't think we had to take care of it. I'm glad we didn't adopt a raccoon or something."

"Raccoons are adorable and I would love to have one," Gloria said.

"I used to shoot them if they came around our barn," Dennis told her, and he knew what he'd said was mean even before her face crumpled into a horrified, sad frown. "We had to, though. They were eating the grain we were trying to sell."

"It's still mean," she said. "You'll take care of the tree?"

"Yeah, I guess so, if it means that much to you," Dennis agreed.

"Good. And he needs a name," Gloria said. "I've thought of some, but I want you to think of some and we'll see if we agree on any of them. My mom said that's the best way to start. That's how her and dad named me."

"I've never heard of anybody naming a tree," Dennis said.

"Well, we're naming our tree," she informed him. "Don't forget you have next Monday and Thursday." She turned to walk away, then stopped and turned back. She leaned toward him and said quietly, "If you want to play, just start running with them and let whoever's it tag you, then you tag someone else. Don't you know anything?"

With that, she turned and walked away with the same fast, determined steps she'd used to approach him. Dennis smiled. When Gloria had leaned closer, Dennis had smelled her hair again, and the memory lingered. He read the instructions about the tree again, then carefully folded the paper and put it in his pocket. He watched the boys playing their game and thought about Gloria's advice.

Hesitantly at first, with a quick lunge, a stop, a stutter-step, and then a full run as a pack of boys raced by him, Dennis joined the game. He deliberately ran slower than the other boys and the boy from the other class who was "it" slapped him on the back and yelled, "You're it, new kid!" Boys around him scattered like quail. Dennis picked out the slowest one, and gave chase.

Just as he reached out to tap the shoulder of the boy he was pursuing, Dennis saw Gloria Light standing with two friends near the fence. She was watching him. And she was smiling.

Chapter Fourteen

"Oh my God," Kelsi said, her hands on her cheeks. "That is just amazing. She was smiling at you? She already knew. Did you know?"

"Know she was, what did you call it, my one true love?" Dennis asked, laughing. "No. She was just an icky girl who liked to give orders and thought we should name a tree like it was a puppy."

"But she smelled good," Kelsi reminded.

"She did smell good," he admitted.

"What happened next?" Kelsi asked.

"We got married. Had kids. She died," Dennis answered.

Kelsi tilted her head and gave him a displeased look. He laughed at her.

"She used to give me the same look sometimes," he said. "I'll tell you more another time. It's your evening off and I suspect you have a date with my grandson. I feel a nap coming on."

"You're right," Kelsi admitted. "I'll take you home, but I have something for you when we get there."

"Why would you do that?" he asked.

"Because I wanted to." She got to her feet and extended her hands down to him when he got his shoes back on. Kelsi pulled Dennis to his feet and she slipped back into her "thongs" as he'd called them and they made their way back to her car and then to his house. "How far away from the park did you live when you were a boy?"

Dennis unbuckled his seat belt, then grinned at her. "We lived across the street from the park, but Gloria didn't know that for quite a while." His tone told her that was going to be a fun part of the story when he got to it.

They got out and Kelsi went to the hatchback of her car and took out a flat, wrapped rectangle. She followed Dennis up the stairs, him going slowly, a hand on the rail, then he opened the door and they went inside. The living room wasn't much different than it had been the other day, Kelsi saw, except that there was a book on the table beside Dennis's recliner. She inhaled deeply, but discreetly, of the homey, grandmotherly aroma of the house.

"What is that?" Dennis asked, nodding toward the gift wrapped in shiny green paper.

"It's not a picture of my legs," Kelsi said, handing it over.

Dennis tore the paper off and let it fall to the floor. Kelsi watched, eager for his reaction. He turned the eight-by-ten-inch framed picture so that it was right-side-up, then his face broke out into a big smile. "The squirrel," he said.

"It has so much of Woody's leafy greenness in it," Kelsi said. "I thought you might like it. I wanted to give you something for telling me to get back into photography. I'm really enjoying it again."

"I'm glad," he said. "I'll have to find a place to put this." He carefully put it down on the coffee table and admired it for another minute, then he straightened and said, "I have something I want to show you. If you don't mind coming into an old man's bedroom."

Kelsi laughed. "In most cases, I'd decline. But I think I can trust you."

Dennis led her down a hallway to the last bedroom. The door was open and he went in first. Kelsi stepped in and found a tall queen bed covered in what had to be a hand-made quilt of colorful patches. There were nightstands and lamps on both sides of the bed and the one she guessed to be Dennis's had another framed picture of Gloria as an older woman with gray hair and a loving smile. It appeared to be a studio picture.

"Look above the headboard," Dennis instructed.

Kelsi looked up from the simple wooden headboard to a document on a green matte in a black frame. "Oh!" She clapped a hand over her mouth and stepped forward as if pulled toward the framed piece of notebook paper. "That's it," she said. "The instructions for Woody." There, under glass, was the first written correspondence between Dennis and Gloria, with the colors in crayon and pencil, just as he'd so accurately described. "Who framed it?" Kelsi asked.

"That's what I gave her for our tenth wedding anniversary," Dennis said. "I'd kept the note in an old cigar box. You can see where it was folded. We had recently lost our daughter. Money was tight, but I wanted to give her something. She ..." He trailed off and Kelsi turned to see that he'd looked away and was wiping a finger under one eye. "She liked it."

"I bet she did," Kelsi said. "I didn't know you lost a daughter. I'm so sorry."

"It was a long time ago, but I can still picture her. Well, there she is." He pointed to a cluster of frames on the wall across from the foot of the bed. The biggest picture, in the center, showed a toddler standing on a small concrete porch, one chubby hand on a wrought-iron rail while she waved with the other. Pictures around it varied in size, showing the child as a baby in a bassinet, held by her mother and father (Kelsi was intrigued by how handsome Dennis was as a young man), and riding a tricycle, blowing out candles on a birthday cake, and other things children do.

"How old was she when you lost her?" Kelsi asked.

"She was three. It was an accident at Canton Lake. Nobody was paying attention and she went into the water," Dennis said.

"Oh my God. I'm so sorry," Kelsi said. She wanted very much to go to the elderly man and hug him, but felt like it would be an awkward gesture, especially standing in his bedroom. He pointed at the bed with a trembling finger.

"Gloria made that quilt out of Cynthia's clothes," he said, his voice shaking as much as his finger. "So we could feel her close when we slept. She had to repair it many times over the years."

Kelsi's hand went out and brushed over squares of crimson, sky blue, white, pin-striped denim, and prints with flowers, bunnies, and other animals. The fabric was cool to her touch, but comforting. She could imagine Gloria working on the quilt, crying so that she had to pause, then wiping her eyes and carrying on with the tribute to her lost daughter.

"Come on," Dennis said, waving her toward the door. "I want to give you something, too."

"You don't have to do that," Kelsi said as she followed him back up the hallway.

"I know," he said without looking back at her. In the dining room, he went to a wooden buffet and opened the wide top drawer. Kelsi watched him rummage through it, lifting out first one box that looked like something a bracelet would come in, then another. The fourth one, he turned, snapped it shut again, and handed it to her.

Kelsi didn't reach for it. "I really can't," she said, afraid he was offering her a bracelet or necklace that had been Gloria's. "Jewelry should be handed down in the family."

His face scrunched into confusion for a moment, then he laughed. "I agree," he said. "But this isn't jewelry. Take it." He shook the brown box at her.

Kelsi took it and opened it. Inside, held down by a little strap that matched the gray lining, was a pen and pencil set made from dark brown wood with shiny brass fittings. She took one out and twisted it so that the thick pencil lead peeked smoothly from the tip. Smiling happily, she retracted the lead and did the same with the pen. "These are beautiful," she breathed. "You made them?"

"I did," he said. "I still have a few laying around to give as gifts when I need to."

"These are almost too nice to use, but I'm going to," Kelsi said. "All of my notes at school and anything I have to sign, I'm going to use these."

Dennis chuckled and shook his head. "I'm glad you like them. Will you let an old man take his nap now?"

Here in the dining room, it didn't feel so awkward to step forward and put an arm around Dennis's shoulders. Kelsi did it, and planted a very quick kiss on his cheek. "You can't even sound grumpy because you're too sweet," she said. "Take your nap. I'll show myself out."

As she was about to step through the door, he called to her. "Kelsi?" She looked back and saw him standing with a steadying hand on the top of the buffet. He seemed to be a bit hunched forward. "Thank you," he said. "Thank you for a wonderful afternoon, for the picture, and the friendship. I hope Tucker appreciates what a treasure he has in you."

Kelsi stood in the doorway, very still, evaluating what he'd said. She looked around the house at all the obvious placements and influences of the woman this man had shared his life with. She looked back at Dennis. "I know what it means to be lonely. You're probably the best friend I've ever had. Lonely people need each other. I'll see you again soon."

She slipped through the doorway and pulled the door closed behind her before he could respond. In her car, she clutched the box with the handmade pen and pencil set to her chest, wondering if she'd said too much before leaving. She felt nervous, but no regret, so she started her car and drove home to shower before Tucker came to pick her up.

***

Kelsi wore a pale blue sundress with a pleated skirt and sandals and she curled her hair since she had time. When Tucker texted that he was on his way, she went downstairs and sat at the bottom of the staircase until he pulled up in the giant pickup. He didn't get out, but sat in the truck and waited for her. Sighing, Kelsi stood up and went to the passenger side and climbed into her seat.

"Whooowee!" Tucker said, lowering his sunglasses and looking her up and down. "Who is this passenger princess climbing into my truck?"

"Oh, hush," Kelsi said, but she felt her cheeks reddening. She buckled up, then realized he was still staring at her. "What?" she asked.

"You look amazing, baby. Really," he said. He leaned across the console and she met him for the kiss.

"Where are we going?" she asked. "You promised it would be good."

"It's your only evening off this week, so I wanted to make it special," Tucker said. "I have reserved us the best table at Sweet Pea's Diner. After that, I thought we'd go fishing. Noodling, to be specific."

"If you take me to the restaurant where I work, you won't like where I put my fork," Kelsi promised.

"Then how about we go to Venezia's instead," he offered.

"Italian? Again? Really?" she gushed.

"For you, yes," he said. "After that, perhaps some live music?"

"Who's playing?" she asked.

"I'm not sure. And I think it's mostly country," he said. "It's some kind of festival out by the airport. There aren't a lot of options for dates in a town without a movie theater, as we've discussed. Especially on a weeknight."

"It sounds wonderful," Kelsi said, and leaned over to kiss him again.

The restaurant was cozy, busy, and seemed authentically Italian, though Kelsi had never been to Italy. It looked like Italian restaurants she'd seen in movies, though, so she figured that was good enough. The service was always great and the food even better. She delicately lifted a forkful of noodles and creamy alfredo sauce. She chewed and listened to Tucker talk about his day in the shop, where he'd apparently had an argument with one of the machine operators over the specifications of some part.

"I mean, who did he think he was arguing with?" Tucker said. "Of course I was right and he had to fix it, but we had to scrap a lot of metal because he couldn't read a blueprint."

Kelsi wondered if Gloria had pretended interest in Dennis's daily work stories. Or had she actually been interested in what her husband did? Kelsi tried to imagine a life with Tucker in which she had to listen to his condescending attitude toward people who didn't have his background or dared to question the son of the superintendent.

"How was class? What did you do after school?" Tucker asked.

"I hung out with Dennis after class. We went to lunch, then went to the park," Kelsi said. "He gave me the coolest gift. It's a pen and pencil set that he made himself."

"You were with my grandpa again? Kels, that's really weird. Why do you do that? And yeah, I've got a dozen of those pen sets," he said.

"I like him," Kelsi answered. "He's lonely and needs company. And I still think he's not doing so good. Has he been tested for Parkinson's?"

"I wouldn't know," Tucker answered.

"He has the shakes a lot of the time."

"He's old. Isn't that just something old people do?"

"No, it isn't normal," Kelsi said, but honestly, she didn't know. It didn't seem like it should be normal, though.

"Well, you'd have to ask him about it," Tucker said.

Kelsi swallowed another bite. "That seems rude," she said.

Tucker shrugged. "Mom would know. I'll ask her if you want."

"She'll think it's weird, won't she?" Kelsi asked.

"Well, yeah," Tucker said. "Because it is," he whispered, but then softened it with an exaggerated wink.

"I guess there's nothing I could do for him if he does have it," Kelsi admitted.

"My grandpa isn't going to steal you away from me with his fancy pen sets, is he?" Tucker teased. "He's not rich enough to be a sugar daddy, you know?"

"You're ridiculous," Kelsi said, but she laughed. "I never knew my grandparents, and I don't think my parents ever loved each other the way Dennis and Gloria loved each other. And the whole story with the tree is very romantic."

Tucker looked at her as if he was thinking about saying something she wouldn't want to hear, then he changed his mind. "They had their problems, from what Mom's told me."

"Does she ever talk about the sister she had who drowned?" Kelsi asked.

"No. I mean, I know about it. She's told me it happened, but she never, like, talks about them playing together or anything like that," Tucker said. He moved some bits of ground beef around in his spaghetti. "She probably needs therapy over that, or something, but her generation doesn't go to therapy."

"Yeah," Kelsi agreed. "Gen X, bottling everything up until ... Well, forever."

"Right," Tucker said.

They ate and turned the conversation to other things. They agreed that when Kelsi's intersession class ended they would go to Oklahoma City for a weekend, eat at new restaurants, stay in a nice hotel, and see as many movies as they could. Then Tucker paid their bill and they drove to the far eastern edge of town, out in the country off the main highway, where they parked in one field, crossed a dirt road to another, and joined a throng of people standing, drinking, and dancing to country music played by long-haired men on a flatbed trailer.

They had been there for about an hour and had both had a few beers when Tucker's cell phone rang. He pulled it out of a pocket and put it to his ear, handing Kelsi his aluminum bottle so he could cover his other ear. "Hi, Mom," he shouted into the phone. Kelsi held a beer in each hand and continued to dance slowly in front of him, moving her hips as provocatively as she dared with so many other people around. "He fell? Is he okay?" Kelsi stopped dancing and stepped closer. "Which one?" Tucker asked. "Okay. Okay. I'm going now. I'll see you soon." He put the phone back in his pocket.

"Dennis?" Kelsi asked.

"He fell in the shower," Tucker said. "Mom is his Life Alert contact, so they called her. He's at St. Mary's Hospital and Mom's driving down here. I guess we need to go. I'm sorry."

"It's okay," Kelsi said. "But I'm going with you to the hospital."

Chapter Fifteen

Dennis was in surgery when Kelsi and Tucker arrived. A middle-aged nurse with graying black hair sat behind a big desk and told Tucker his grandfather had been in a lot of pain but had been coherent and had signed the consent form for the surgery. They obviously couldn't see him now, but if there were no complications he would be out of surgery in an hour to ninety minutes and one family member could be with him in the post-op room.

"How long is the recovery on an injury like this?" Kelsi asked.

"It varies, but typically nine months to a year to fully recover," she answered. "At his age, he may need a walking aid for the rest of his life. It's really hard to say with geriatric patients. The doctor will explain it all."

The nurse directed them to a waiting room, where they sat down on a sofa and stared absently at a television show about people buying houses. Kelsi waited for Tucker to say something, to express some emotion, but he just sat and stared blankly at the television.

"I feel so bad for him," Kelsi said at last. "How did anyone even know he was hurt?"

Tucker pulled his eyes off the television and glanced at her for a moment. "Mom had one of those Life Alert things installed in his house after Grandma died. You know, he yells something like, Help! I've fallen and I can't get up" and it signals for help.

"Thank God he had that," Kelsi said, then a new thought came to her. "Did they have to break in his door? Is his house all open to anybody right now?"

"I don't know," Tucker said, then he shrugged. "There isn't anything really valuable in there."

"Valuable to you," Kelsi said. "I can promise you there are things in there that he considers treasures. I wish I had my car. I'd go there. They won't let me in post-op, anyway."

"What would you do?" Tucker asked. "Stand in the door and shoot the blacks and foreigners that have been itching to get in his house and steal those treasures?"

"You're an asshole sometimes, Tucker," she said. Her blood was hot and she could feel it in her face. At that moment, she almost hated Tucker for his callus, selfish attitude. He must have recognized it in her face. He shoved a hand into his pants pocket and drew out his keys.

"Take the truck," he said, offering her the keyring. "Mom will be here soon. If you don't come back, she can bring me to his house to get the truck and take you home. You can text or call when you get there and let me know about the door. We can get somebody to fix it tomorrow."

Kelsi didn't say anything, but swiped the keys from his hand and left him sitting in the waiting room. She'd only driven the big truck a couple of times and she struggled a little backing it up, but she managed, and then hurried through the residential area back to Dennis's home. She was surprised and a little scared when she pulled into his driveway and saw two people sitting on the top step of his porch. The porch light wasn't on, but the living room light inside the house was. The people were a man and a woman, Hispanic, and they stopped talking to each other and watched as she parked. Kelsi considered calling the police, but felt she was being racist. However, she dialed in 911 and was ready to press the call button as she got out of the truck.

"Hello?" she asked. "Can I help you?"

The man said something in Spanish that didn't sound threatening. The woman got up and came toward Kelsi. "*Señor* Aiken? He is okay?" she asked.

"He's in surgery," Kelsi said. "Broken hip." The woman didn't seem to understand right away. Kelsi pointed at her own hip and said again, "Broken."

"Oh, *sí*," the woman said. "We watch his house. Nobody go in."

"Thank you," Kelsi said. "*Gracias. Gracias.*" She looked from the woman to the man as she thanked them. He nodded his head in acknowledgement. "You're neighbors?"

"*Sí*," the woman said. She pointed to the house next door. Kelsi remembered Dennis telling her about his Hispanic neighbors and their kids.

"Is the door broken?" Kelsi asked.

The woman, who was short and seemed to be in her early thirties, nodded. She turned to the man and spoke in fast, musical Spanish that left no doubt she was giving him orders. He nodded and stood up. He was wearing blue jeans with rhinestones on the back pockets, a maroon button-down shirt and, although it wasn't on his head at the moment, the ring impressed into his black hair told Kelsi he usually wore a hat, and she guessed it was a straw cowboy hat. He motioned at her to follow him and Kelsi followed his wife and him into Dennis's house.

The door and frame were splintered and broken where the rescue team had used a battering ram to make entry. Kelsi pushed the door as if to shut it and the chunk holding the deadbolt mechanism fell out and clattered on the floor. "I wish there was some way of sealing this door closed. We could still get out the back door."

The woman said more in Spanish, motioning at the door, and the man nodded and responded in Spanish, then he opened the door and left the house. The woman turned to Kelsi. "You are his granddaughter?" she asked.

"I'm dating his grandson," Kelsi said. "But Dennis and I have become pretty good friends recently."

"He's good man," the woman said, nodding. "My husband will put board across. No one can open door."

"Thank you so much," Kelsi said. She looked around the room, her eyes lingering a moment on Gloria's urn. "I should pack some things to take to him at the hospital."

"*Sí.* Yes," the neighbor agreed. "I will wait here."

Kelsi made her way back to Dennis's bedroom, where she found a very outdated set of brown leather luggage in a closet. She wondered how much traveling he and his family had done back in the day, then selected the medium-sized suitcase and began adding clothes from his dresser drawers and closet. She knew he'd probably be limited to the hospital gown for the duration of his stay, but he'd need clothes to come home in. And he might want his own soap and cologne and razor. She found all those things in the bedroom and nearby bathroom, then remembered his keys. She'd need to lock and reenter through whatever door she left by. The sound of power tools was coming from the living room and she was anxious to get back in there and see what was going on. At last, she noticed a ceramic dish like a kid would make in school on the dresser in front of the mirror. In it was a set of keys and a black tube of lip balm. Kelsi grabbed them both and put them in a pocket of her sundress, remembering how happy she'd been to see the dress had pockets when she bought it.

The neighbor man — Kelsi tried hard to remember the family's name, but couldn't — was using a cordless drill to put a two-by-four across the closed door, screwing the board into the door frame. Kelsi knew that would leave holes, but then she looked again at the damage done by the rescue team and knew that the whole door and frame was going to have to be replaced. As she came into the room with the suitcase, the man drove the last screw into the frame and turned away.

"Thank you so much," Kelsi said to him. "*Gracias. Muchas gracias.*" She wondered if her use of the few Spanish words she knew just made her sound racist.

"*De nada,*" the man said, and smiled at her.

Kelsi turned her attention to the woman. "Thank you both so much for watching over the house," she said. "I'll make sure Dennis knows."

"He would do same for us," the woman said, and Kelsi knew she was right.

Together, they all went through the house to the kitchen and out the back door. Kelsi hadn't been back here. She saw there was a thick cedar tree in one corner of the yard and a big workshop in the other. She locked up the door and they went through a gate in the fence back around to the front. Kelsi shook hands with both of them and got back into the truck. Her phone buzzed in her purse and she pulled it out to find a text message from Tucker.

R U OK?

She started the truck and called him after she backed out of the driveway. "Sorry," she said when he answered. "Some of his neighbors were at the house when I got there. They were watching over the place."

"Really? They hadn't gone in and stole the 1960s furniture?" Tucker asked, but he laughed and Kelsi knew he was teasing, or at least trying to be funny.

"They were very nice," she said. "The man sealed the door up so nobody can walk in. The rescue team must have used a battering ram to get in. He'll need a new door and frame."

"Well, that sucks, but okay," Tucker said.

"I packed a suitcase for him. I know he'll want his own stuff eventually. How is he? Any word yet?" she asked.

"He's in post-op. As soon as he wakes up, I can go in. Mom's about an hour away. Are you coming back?" Tucker asked.

"Yes, I'm on my way," Kelsi said.

"I'm sorry I was an ... asshole," he said, lowering his voice on the last word. "There are kids here now," he whispered.

"It's okay," Kelsi said. "But really, try to have some sympathy. Your grandfather is a nice man, and not everything valuable has dollar signs attached."

"I know. I'm sorry," he said.

"I'm in sight of the hospital," Kelsi said. "I'll see you in a few minutes."

Somehow, Tucker had arranged it with the nurses to allow Kelsi to go with him into Dennis's post-operation room and they sat on opposite sides of his bed as he slowly regained consciousness while a nurse with a clipboard stood at the foot of the bed. Dennis's head moved to one side, and then the other. His eyelids fluttered, relaxed, fluttered again, then opened. He was facing Kelsi.

"Gloria?" he asked.

Her eyes immediately watered, but Kelsi shook her head and reached for his hand. His skin was dry and papery. "It's Kelsi," she prompted.

Dennis smiled, then nodded. "Kelsi," he said. He turned his head and hesitated a moment on the nurse, then turned to find his grandson. "Tucker," he said. "Thank you both."

"How are you, Pops?" Tucker asked.

"It hurts," Dennis said.

"Mr. Aiken, I'm Danielle. I'll be your nurse until we get you into your own room," the nurse said. "Can you rate your pain for me on a scale of one to ten?"

He snorted, then tried to smile. "It's at least a five hundred," he said.

The nurse gave a practiced smile and said, "As soon as all the anesthesia has worn off we'll get you some Percocet for the pain. Have you ever taken that before?"

"A long time ago," Dennis said. His hand tightened on Kelsi's and his face twisted as a spasm of pain went through him. The nurse's pen scratched across her paper.

"I'll tell the doctor you're awake," she said, and left the room.

Dennis lay still, panting a little, his eyes cloudy and his mouth hanging open. He suddenly looked all of his eighty-four years, old, frail, and hurting. It made him seem smaller somehow. Kelsi squeezed his hand and he squeezed back automatically. He had called her Gloria. Did she look so much like his dead wife when she was younger?

"Did you put on fresh perfume?" Tucker asked from his side of the bed.

"What? No," Kelsi answered, but then she smelled it, too. Lilies and rainwater is what the aroma reminded her of. She looked around but didn't see anything like a Scentsy or can of air freshener. Then she saw Dennis smiling. "Gloria?" Kelsi asked.

He nodded. "I saw her while I was out," he confided.

Just then, the door of the room opened and Natalie Umber rushed in. "Dad?" she asked. Kelsi slipped out of her chair and Tucker's mom threw herself into it and took up the hand Kelsi had been holding. "What happened?"

"I got dizzy in the shower and fell down," he said. "I knocked myself out for a while. When I woke up, I couldn't move my leg. I kept yelling like in the commercial, but couldn't hear any answer until people were pulling me out of the bathtub wet and naked and cold. It wasn't flattering." He managed a mischievous smile.

Kelsi smiled and Dennis snickered, but Natalie wasn't having it. "Don't be vulgar, Dad," she said. "Are you in pain now? Have they given you anything?"

"I just woke up," he told her.

"The nurse said the doctor will be in soon," Kelsi offered.

Tucker's mother seemed to register for the first time that Kelsi was in the room. "They let you in here?" she asked. "I thought it was just for family."

"I want her here," Dennis said, his voice firm despite the pain. "Kelsi has become a good friend to me. But she has class tomorrow morning and probably should go home and get some sleep." His eyes locked onto hers and there was nothing she could do but agree.

"I'll come see you tomorrow," she promised as she closed the door.

As she turned to go, something caught her eye and she stopped, looking back in. There, beside Natalie, hovering over the bed, was the distortion in the air that Kelsi knew to be a spirit. In this case, undoubtedly, it was Gloria, come to comfort her husband in his time of need. The angle of his gaze told Kelsi that he knew the ghost was there and he was looking into her face. Kelsi wondered just how much his old eyes could see in the next world.

Smiling, somehow relieved to know Gloria was in the room, Kelsi summoned an Uber to take her home and was actually able to sleep.

Chapter Sixteen

During the break halfway through her four-hour class, Kelsi texted Tucker to ask how his grandfather was. After a few minutes, she got a reply.

> IDK I'm at work Mom is with him.

She texted back, asking why he hadn't checked with his mom, but then she deleted the message. She knew the answer. She finished her class, barely hearing anything the professor said, then raced to the hospital, where she learned that Dennis had been moved to a room on the third floor.

Kelsi knocked quickly at the door of Dennis's room, then pushed it open and went inside. She should have known Tucker's mother, Dennis's daughter, would be there, but the sight of Natalie Umber sitting in a chair pulled up beside the bed still surprised her. Natalie seemed just as surprised to see her.

"Kelsi," she said neutrally. "I didn't expect to see you here. Especially without Tucker."

Dennis, who sat propped up in the bed, looked from Kelsi to his daughter. "I told you we're good friends, Natalie. She's very welcome. I'm glad to see her."

"Well, come in," Natalie said. "In fact, if you wouldn't mind sitting with him, I'd like to go get some lunch. Did you eat?"

"No," Kelsi admitted. "I came here right after class."

"Oh, yes, Tucker mentioned you were taking a summer class. How is that going?" Natalie asked.

"The sessions are long and boring, but it's almost over. I think I'm doing okay in it," Kelsi said.

"I'm just going to go over to Braum's," Natalie said. "Do you want me to bring you back a hamburger or something?"

"If you wouldn't mind," Kelsi said. She reached for her purse, but Natalie waved it away, saying she would pay for it.

"I'll bring you one, too," she said, getting to her feet and quickly kissing Dennis on the temple. As she passed Kelsi she said, "They gave him pain medicine about fifteen minutes ago and he will probably be asleep soon."

"Come sit with me," Dennis said to Kelsi. "Tell me about class."

Kelsi took the seat Natalie had just vacated. "I couldn't tell you much about it today. All I could think about was how you're doing."

"I feel the pain, but it's like it's happening to someone else," Dennis said. "I don't like having to take such powerful drugs, but ..." He shrugged. "I remember how it felt waiting for the paramedics to arrive and I'd rather not have that, either."

"I'm so sorry this happened," Kelsi said.

"It was a matter of time, I guess," he said. Kelsi saw that his eyelids were drooping. "Natalie is talking about hiring someone to come over every day to clean, cook, and be there while I shower. I told you we become like babies again." He smiled, but it was a weak smile. One eyelid was completely closed.

"How do you feel about that?" Kelsi asked.

"I don't want a stranger in my house," he said, but it was more of a mumble.

"Go to sleep," Kelsi said. "Your daughter will be here with a big, juicy hamburger when you wake up."

He was already asleep. His face was completely relaxed, the lines in his forehead and cheeks deep. He was a little paler than usual, she thought, or maybe it was just the white hospital gown making him seem whiter. The thin bed sheet and blanket were pulled up to his lower chest.

She took a picture of Dennis's sleeping face and sent it to Tucker with a message.

> He's doing better. Drugged and asleep now.

OK

Natalie returned with food. She gave Kelsi hers and put Dennis's on the rolling tray that could go over his bed. Kelsi asked, "Should we wake him?"

"Not yet," Natalie said as she settled into another chair. She was a well-kept woman in her mid-fifties, brown hair, sharp chin, bright hazel eyes. Her throat was starting to crepe like many women her age and her hands also told viewers she was not young. She sat looking at Kelsi for a while as the younger woman ate. "Dad says you've been visiting," she said at last.

"Yes," Kelsi said. She kept eating, partly because she was hungry and partly because it gave her something else to do. Natalie wasn't exactly being frosty, but her tone wasn't benevolent, either. "He's a kind man and I'm just really fascinated with his story about how he met your mom and they planted the tree."

"The tree," Natalie said, and now she looked away for a moment. "I keep thinking a tornado will knock that stupid tree down."

"Why would you want that?" Kelsi asked, shocked.

"He thinks she visits him there," Natalie said. "Did you know that? I think that tree is playing into his dementia. The longer Mom is gone, the more he talks about the tree. He wanted to dump Mom's ashes around the base of the trunk." She said it like it was the most unthinkable thing she'd ever heard conceived. "Right there in a city park. Well, it's not even legal, I don't think. I forbade him to do that."

Kelsi ate without answering. There had been so much to process in that outburst. She wanted to say that Gloria did come to the tree, that she had seen her, and that if Dennis wanted to spread her ashes there, he should be allowed to do so. But she didn't say anything at all. Natalie picked up her own thread of conversation.

"We've all heard the story of how they planted the tree until we're sick of it," she said. "Sure, it was a cute way for them to meet and Mom took control of the relationship right from the start, but we've heard it already."

Kelsi looked at Dennis. He seemed to still be asleep. But was his breathing a little different than it had been before Natalie returned? A little shallower, maybe?

"I don't know how my parents met, and now they're divorced," Kelsi said. "My dad doesn't speak to either of us. He has a new wife who is about my age. Mom became an alcoholic. I never met any of my grandparents. Your dad has been kind of a grandfather to me. I enjoy his company and his stories."

Natalie seemed to soften just a little. "He's a fine man. Not perfect, of course. I could tell you stories from my childhood, but I suppose most parents, especially in his generation, were about the same. All work, no time to raise the kids, and that was the woman's job, anyway. He was a mess when Mom died. He didn't even know how to run his own clothes washer. Or dishwasher. He hadn't written a check in fifty years." She gave a sad smile. "He's come a long way."

"Do you love him?" Kelsi asked.

Natalie's face tightened in shock, then annoyance. "Of course I love my father," she said.

"I don't mean any offense," Kelsi said. "I was just wondering why you're moving away for at least two years when he needs people. Tucker isn't ... Well, he's busy."

"If the move was permanent, I'd put my foot down," Natalie said. "But it's up to two years and it could be a great chance for Albert to show he can be the general manager here when his boss retires in about four years. I know Tucker isn't the best at looking out for someone else, but he was the only option."

"What about me?" Kelsi asked. "Dennis told me you were thinking about someone to come in and take care of the house and check on him. I could do that."

Natalie sighed and studied Kelsi with her sharp eyes. "I know you and Tucker have been dating for a while, and I'm at fault for not getting to know you better. Honestly, I never expected it to last this long. When you agreed to come to Oklahoma from Montana to date my son, I assumed you were some kind of flake."

"No, I get that," Kelsi said, ignoring that Natalie had said Montana instead of Wyoming. "My mom called me a whore."

"I'm sorry," Natalie said. "I knew you were neither of those things fairly soon, but I honestly didn't think it would last. Tucker has never dated anyone else for very long. But here you are." She paused, smoothed the fabric of her wrinkleless jeans, then faced Kelsi again. "How do I know you're not a gold digger? Dad doesn't have much. Not much money and not much in the way of material possessions. How do I know you wouldn't take advantage of him?"

Kelsi put the rest of her hamburger down and looked hard at it, not daring to look at Mrs. Umber. There was a lump in her throat and tears threatened to spill from her eyes. Without looking up, she said, "I guess you'd just have to trust that I'm not like that."

Before Natalie could respond, Dennis spoke in a low but firm and rather groggy voice. "I trust her. That's really all that matters."

Kelsi looked up and saw that his eyes were open, though only slits, and he was looking at her, not at his daughter. She sniffled and used a brown napkin to wipe at her eyes and nose. "Thank you," she said.

"He's going to need at least ten weeks of rehab," Natalie said. "You have school and your job."

"It's just a summer intersession class," Kelsi said. "It'll be over soon. Then I can take online classes in the fall. My work is pretty flexible."

Natalie sighed, and it was a sigh of resignation. "Honestly, if this is what he wants, there's really nothing I can do about it. It's not like he is incompetent and needs someone else to make decisions for him. I'm not sure I like it, though. Please don't be offended. He's my elderly father and I just don't know you very well. I was going to go with someone who's had a background check and been vetted by an agency."

"Do you want to do a background check on me?" Kelsi asked, forcing her voice to be steady and making it as defiant as she could.

Natalie shook her head. "No. Are you sure you're up for this?"

"If I'm not, we'll go back to your way," Kelsi said.

Natalie actually smiled a little at that. She nodded. "Okay then. Dad, eat your food. It's getting cold."

Chapter Seventeen

Natalie Umber agreed to pay the early termination penalty on Kelsi's apartment lease and said any furniture she had could be stored in Dennis's garage since he no longer had a car. She promised that Tucker and a couple of friends would use their pickups to move her from the apartment to the house.

Tucker, however, was angry about the whole thing.

"You won't move in with me, but you'll move in with my grandfather?" he stormed when he visited Kelsi at her apartment for dinner that evening. "What kind of bullshit is that?"

"Don't be gross, Tucker," Kelsi said. "I'll be his caretaker and maid. Not his girlfriend." She had fried chicken breasts and served them with mashed potatoes and gravy and corn, with Hawaiian sweet rolls. It was one of Tucker's favorite meals that she could cook.

"Have you thought about us? How we won't have any privacy unless you come to my house now?" he demanded.

"Yes, I have. We've already done that. We can keep doing it. Not in your parents' bed, though," she said.

"How? If you have to be with Pops all the time? Have you really thought about all of this?" Tucker asked.

"He won't need me every moment of every day," Kelsi said. "Not after he finishes his rehab, anyway."

"Ten weeks?" Tucker said. "Ten weeks we can't be together? And that's if they have a place for him at the rehab center right off. It's bullshit."

Kelsi sighed and wanted to throw the salt shaker at her boyfriend. "He's in a lot of pain, Tucker. I'm taking the room furthest from his. He'll be on pain medication, especially at night. You can get a quicky right there in your grandparents' house. That should make you happy."

Tucker was quiet and focused on his meal for a while. Kelsi hated that she could guess the workings of his mind. He really did like the idea of having sex in his grandparents' house with his drugged grandfather sleeping nearby. She didn't like the idea at all and felt like it might even be a betrayal of Dennis's trust, but she knew it was a necessary compromise. She wondered again at his lack of empathy. His selfishness.

"Is your dinner okay?" Kelsi asked.

"Yes, it's good," Tucker answered. He looked up and gave her a weak smile. "I'm sorry. It's perfect, like always. If they find out how good you can cook, they'll make you stop waitressing and put you on the grill at the diner."

"That would be awful," Kelsi said. "All that grease all the time. My face would look like a pizza. I'm glad you like it, though."

"I'm sorry I was an asshole earlier. Again," he said.

"You'll help me move?"

"Of course." He looked around the one room. "It won't take long."

"No," Kelsi agreed. "None of the furniture is mine. I was too embarrassed to tell your mom. I don't really own anything but the clothes and linens and the pots and pans. I can have those all boxed up and ready to go. We won't need any help."

"Why would you be embarrassed to tell my mom that?" Tucker asked with a mouthful of mashed potatoes.

"Think about your house, Tucker. All you've got. You've never been poor. It's not fun. It's not ... something you want to tell your boyfriend's rich mother," she answered. "She was already worried I'm a gold-digger trying to steal from your grandfather."

"She said that?" he asked.

"She was polite about it," Kelsi said.

"That's my mom." Tucker cut off another bite of chicken. "At least there's a dishwasher at Pop's. You won't have to wash dishes in the sink anymore."

"Better and better," Kelsi said. "Be honest. Are you still mad I'm moving in with him?"

"I guess not," he said. "I know he needs somebody, at least until he can walk on his own again. Better you than a stranger. Is Mom paying you anything to be his nurse?"

Kelsi was shocked by the question. She hadn't even thought about that. "No," she said. "I mean, free room and board. That's plenty."

"You're giving up a lot of freedom. I'll talk to her about it," Tucker said.

"No, don't," Kelsi protested. "I don't want her to think that's why I'm willing to do it."

Tucker made a dismissive motion with his fork and continued to eat. When they were finished, he helped wash the dishes and they went to the loveseat, where they watched a romantic comedy movie. Kelsi mostly fought off Tucker's roving hands until the end of the movie, but when it was over she gave in and they retired to the bed. The lovemaking wasn't without pleasure.

***

Saturday came. Kelsi awoke with her alarm, her body sweaty and the remnants of the old dream about the little boat lost among the tremendous waves of a stormy ocean making her feel exhausted and off balance. She lay still for a few minutes, her hand over her closed eyes, getting her bearings and letting her heart settle into its normal rhythm. Then she got out of bed.

She'd taken the day off work over protest from Deena, the manager of Sweet Pea's Diner. Tucker arrived in the late morning and they carried the small collection of boxes down the stairs and put them in the back of his big Chevy pickup. While he waited in the cab, Kelsi ran up the stairs one last time for what she said was one last check to make sure she had everything.

Kelsi stood in the empty apartment, the first place she'd ever had by herself. She had moved hundreds of miles from Casper, Wyoming, to live here, above a garage, date a man she had never met in person, and attend a school she had never heard of a week before enrolling. She looked at the loveseat and the small table with its two chairs, one of which had a short leg that made the chair wobble. She'd been so proud of having her own place. She had hardly noticed the flaws for the first few months she lived here. Stepping over, she ran a hand over the bare mattress of the bed. She remembered the first time she and Tucker had made love here. Not a virgin by any means, but she had not been an experienced lover and had been very nervous that the man she'd left home for might find her beneath his standards. He'd seemed happy enough, though. He certainly came back for more often enough. She smiled at that.

The bathroom was tiny, but she had determined it was all she needed. Kelsi admitted to herself the idea of having a bathtub at Dennis's house was very appealing compared to the shower stall she'd made do with here.

She wandered to the front of the apartment and peeked out the window through the thin curtains. The view wasn't spectacular. The window overlooked the driveway and, beyond that, the houses across the street, but many of them had tall trees in the back yards and she had watched the seasons in the leaves of those trees. Turning, she looked back over the length of the apartment from the front window to the kitchen and determined she'd been happy here, but she didn't see giving up the apartment as giving up freedom. A new friend needed her and she was happy to go stay with Dennis and help him. She wanted to hear his story. She wanted ... She wanted to feel connected to somebody in a way that was not sexual like it was with Tucker.

"I'm giving up this for a chance to have a family," she whispered.

Her eyes were freshly dried when she put her box of growing geraniums into the truck bed and then climbed into the passenger seat of Tucker's pickup.

Chapter Eighteen

Dennis got his release from the hospital on Monday morning. His daughter drove him home and pushed him up the new wooden ramp she'd paid to have built over the steps to the front porch when the front door was repaired. Kelsi held the door open and prayed she had done a good enough job cleaning the house. She would die if Natalie Umber swiped a finger across a surface and it came away dusty. She had dusted. Swept. Mopped. Shined and polished until she thought she'd never get the smell of Pledge off her hands.

It was obvious from the grimace on his face that Dennis was in pain but trying not to show it. He sat stiffly in the wheelchair with his hands in his lap. Kelsi noticed his hands were trembling a little. She had a ream of paper filled with instructions for caring for a patient after a hip replacement.

Kelsi noticed that the first thing Dennis's eyes went to when he entered his home was the photograph of Gloria on the table beside her urn. Seeing the picture seemed to give him the smallest bit of relief. Then Natalie wheeled him past it and down the hall to his bedroom, where she and Kelsi struggled to transfer him into his bed.

"You won't be able to do that by yourself," Natalie said afterward.

Kelsi knew the older woman was right. "With the bedpan, he won't have to move much during the day and I can have Tucker help me in the evenings with his shower," she said. "It won't be long and he'll be able to put some weight on it. Right, Dennis? The doctor said you need to be walking on it soon."

"Sure," he said weakly.

"What's this?" Natalie asked, looking at the framed picture of the squirrel in Woody the sycamore tree.

"A gift," Dennis said. "From my photographer friend here." He waved a palsied hand toward Kelsi.

"You took this?" Natalie asked.

"Yes. It's the sycamore from the park. Woody. I got lucky and was under it when that squirrel was playing around," Kelsi said. She saw Natalie's face tighten at mention of the sycamore.

"It's very good composition and nice color," she said.

"Natalie taught photography classes once upon a time," Dennis added.

"That was a lifetime ago, Dad," she said. "Are you comfortable? Will you be okay?"

"I'll be fine," he said.

"Kelsi, you have my number," Natalie said. "Call me for anything. Anything at all. And I'll be calling for updates. Please don't think I'm being intrusive. He's the only father I have, and even though he can be irritating, I love him."

"Call anytime," Kelsi said. "I'll keep you updated on my schedule, too, so you'll know when I'm away."

Natalie chewed at her lower lip, looking from Kelsi to Dennis and back again. Finally she said, "Tucker says I should pay you and ask you to quit the diner job so you can be here all the time. How do you feel about that?"

"I told him not to mention that to you," Kelsi said.

"He told me that, which is why I hadn't done it yet," Natalie said. "But I'm worried about Dad being here alone for any amount of time."

"I'll be fine as long as somebody leaves me some books and maybe puts a television in here," Dennis said. "Judge Judy is ruling on cases without my advice and that can't go on."

Both women laughed, but Natalie's laughter died quickly. "How much do you make at the diner?" she asked.

"It varies," Kelsi said. She gave an average number.

"I can pay her that out of my retirement," Dennis said.

"Part of it," Natalie said. "I want to pay half. Will you do it?" she asked Kelsi.

"Umm ..." Kelsi began, taken aback. "I hadn't thought about that. I'd leave them short-handed. But ..." She looked at Dennis in the bed and thought about all the possibilities for injuries if the independent man decided he was going to get out of the bed unsupervised. "Yes, I'll do it," she said. "I have to go in tonight, though. I can't just ditch them and quit over the phone. I have to do that face-to-face."

"See why I like her?" Dennis said proudly.

"Yes," Natalie said. "Tucker is coming over this evening?"

"Yes," Kelsi said. "He promised me he would."

"His promises to you probably mean more than the ones to me," Natalie said softly. "Okay. Let's do that. I'll get the payments set up through my bank account to yours." She bent over and kissed her father good-bye and made him promise to do what Kelsi told him to, to take care of himself, and use the cell phone she was paying for him to have to call her more often. Then she asked Kelsi to walk her to the door, where she stopped and turned to face the younger woman.

"I've probably seemed like a cold bitch to you, and I'm sorry for that," Natalie said. "I'm a pretty good judge of character, and since we've seen so much of each other the past several days, I can tell you're a good person. And Dad loves you. You've probably figured out that you look quite a bit like my mom did when she was your age, and I'm sure he sees that."

"He's mentioned it," Kelsi said.

"You're a comfort to him, and he'll love telling you all his old stories," Natalie said. "I think my son is pretty fond of you, too, by the way."

Kelsi smiled and wondered what Tucker had told his mom about her to make her think that. "He's a nice guy," she said, and knew it sounded as lame as it was.

"He's still maturing," Natalie said, and reached over and squeezed Kelsi's arm. "They stay boys until they're at least thirty, sometimes longer. I look forward to getting to know you better. But now, I need to get back to the great state of Kansas and my husband. Please stay in touch."

"I will," Kelsi promised. "Drive safe."

The women parted and Kelsi watched Natalie drive away in her Landrover SUV. She closed the door of the house and stood there for a moment, trying to comprehend all the changes that were happening in her life. No more Sweet Pea's Diner. No more coming home smelling like chicken fried steaks. Her job — her income — was now tied to a man confined to a bed. A man who currently couldn't wipe his own ass. Maybe chicken fried steak wasn't so bad, she thought, then laughed.

She went to the kitchen and got Dennis a glass of iced tea and took it to him in his bed. "We've got to break that bedpan in, so we might as well get started," she said as she handed him the glass. His hand shook as he took it, making the ice rattle.

"You're not going to enjoy this job," he said lightly.

"We'll see. What else can I get for you?"

"A chair for yourself and the picture of Gloria from the end table for me," he said. "I want to tell you a story."

Chapter Nineteen

At the age of thirteen, Dennis Aiken had accepted some things about his life. He missed his father, but was glad he no longer had to worry about the angry man he became when he drank too much. His mother was on the hunt for a new husband and wanted one before the settlement money from the dairy ran out. His little brother, Ollie, was going to be a troublemaker all his life, and their little sister, Carol, would never get in trouble despite being a real brat. Having a newspaper route wasn't as much fun as he'd hoped. And he better do something soon or he was going to lose Gloria Light to the blockhead Devlin Shockley.

It had been two years since he and Gloria planted the sycamore tree in the park across the street from his house. Two years of watering the tree twice a week every other week. Two years of sitting at his living room window beside a framed portrait of his father in his Army uniform watching Gloria take her turn at watering the sycamore. At first, Dennis admitted, he had done it because he was a little intimidated by the bossy girl. Then he came to think of her as his only friend. But as time wore on and he did finally make friends — quite a few friends, actually — he continued to do it because he liked that connection with a girl who was growing up to be very pretty and stir strange feelings in him.

The tree, which they'd finally agreed to name Woody for the irony, was growing fast. Gloria had said the name was ironic. Dennis had suggested it because he figured the thing would die and end up in somebody's fireplace. Gloria had to explain what ironic meant. The tree was a respectable member of the little park's landscape now. Most of the other trees planted on that Arbor Day had died as saplings. Only an elm, a willow, and two white birches remained. Woody was taller than all of them and was shedding some of his brown bark to reveal the smooth bone-white trunk beneath.

Dennis liked watching Gloria when she came to water the tree. She came with a real watering can, the kind with a stem with a showerhead-type end that sprinkled water. She walked around and around the tree, holding the heavy can with both hands at first, but finishing with one hand holding the water and the other lightly touching the trunk of the tree as she circled it. From his vantage point peeking through the drapes, Dennis could see her mouth moving and he knew she was talking to the tree. As time went on, he wanted more than anything to know what she was saying. Was she talking about him? Did she even remember that he was connected to the tree with her?

She must. She never showed up to water the tree on his weeks to take care of that task.

And he knew she remembered him. He'd caught her looking at him in the halls of their new school, Longfellow Junior High. He was often looking at her, too, and she'd caught him at it more than once. But they almost never spoke.

Dennis had proven himself on the playground at Adams Elementary. He was skilled with a baseball bat and fast with a football, so he was often asked to be part of games at recess and after school. Once he had broken through that barrier, other kids seemed to find him acceptable and he made friends, even with kids who had tormented him in that first year off the farm. A few of them had even apologized for the way they treated him, saying things like, "You're okay, Denny-boy."

Dennis perked up as he knelt on the cushions of a worn sofa, facing the back and looking through the space between curtains on the front window. Gloria was crossing the street to the park, her watering can in her hands, her brown skirt swishing around her legs while her white blouse pressed forward where she was developing breasts that absolutely fascinated Dennis. He watched as she approached the tree. She said something to it, then tipped her can and began her circles around the trunk.

Dennis took a deep breath and let his right hand stray to his hip pocket, where it patted a thick bulge. He talked to girls all the time, he told himself. This girl was no different. But he still felt that feeling books described as butterflies in his stomach as he went through the front door of his house.

Gloria didn't seem to notice him at all until he was a few feet away from her. By then, her can was empty enough she was keeping one hand on Woody's trunk as she circled. She wasn't talking to the tree, though, and in later years Dennis would come to realize that was because she had known he was approaching as soon as he left his house.

"Fancy meeting you here," she said, looking up at him and smiling, but continuing her orbit around the tree.

"Just came down to check on the old boy," Dennis said, and wanted to kick himself in the butt for trying to sound cool like Clark Gable or Cary Grant when he was just talking about a tree.

"Woody's doing fine," Gloria said, coming around to face him again. "He's not going into anybody's fireplace for a good long time."

"I guess not," Dennis agreed.

"Just look at how tall he is and how handsome with his new spring leaves," Gloria said, pausing and looking up into the branches of the tree.

By this time, the sycamore was about twenty-five feet tall and loaded with big, bright green leaves and made wonderful shade on the grass around it. There was no doubt Woody was a strong, healthy tree.

"With all the rain we've gotten this spring, we hardly need to water him," Dennis said.

"I know, but I like doing it," Gloria said. Then she leaned close and said in a mock whisper. "But I think there's a guy living in that house who watches me through the curtain." She nodded toward his own house.

It seemed like every molecule of air in the entire world was suddenly sucked up and away and Dennis couldn't find enough of it to fill his lungs. He just knew he was going to explode because he couldn't breathe and that was going to be even worse than the fact he was blushing as bright red as a ripe tomato.

Then Gloria laughed and it was a musical sound that angels would dance to, he thought. He felt himself relax as suddenly as he'd tensed up and maybe it was in that moment that he realized he was already in love.

"Yeah, the guy who lives there is a real creep," he said, trying to sound like he was joking. "I kind of know him. He wanted me to give you something."

"He did?" Gloria asked. Her can was empty and she set it down in the grass beside her feet. "What is it?"

Dennis found himself struggling to get the cloth-covered black box out of his pocket. When he finally did, it popped open and a flash of gold arced through the air between them and slithered into the grass.

"Dammit!" Dennis cursed, then popped a hand over his mouth. He knew he wasn't supposed to curse in front of a lady. But Gloria laughed again and bent to pick up the thing he'd dropped.

"It's a little gold chain," she said, holding it up.

"There's a heart charm on it," Dennis said, then he saw that there was no charm hanging on the chain Gloria held up between them. "There was ..." He looked to the grass. "It must have fallen off."

He immediately dropped to his hands and knees and started pawing through the grass, looking for the charm. "It wasn't very big, but it's a gold heart," he said as Gloria lowered herself to her knees, careful to raise her skirt so it wouldn't be on the ground, which completely befuddled Dennis for a moment as he saw her knees and just a little bit of upper leg. Together, they combed through the grass all around where the chain had fallen, but the charm couldn't be found. At last, they sat on their heels and looked at each other. Dennis felt miserable. The bracelet was nothing without the heart. The heart told her what he wanted from her.

"It's a bracelet," he said at last, flopping a hand in the direction of her hand that still held the naked chain. "A charm bracelet without a charm now, I guess. I'm sorry. I ..." And this was it, the moment, the question, the thing he had to know. He took a deep breath and looked away from her, then told himself he had to look into her beautiful eyes to ask her. "I wanted to give you that and ask if you'd be my girlfriend," he said in a rush.

Gloria was a very pretty girl. He'd already decided that. But at that moment, as the blood rose to her face in a shy blush, he thought he might melt down and water Woody's roots with his own blood and goo. Then Gloria regained her composure.

"I don't know," she said slowly, looking at the chain. "Devlin Shockley has been calling me a couple of evenings every week for almost a month now. I think if old Mrs. Stewart wasn't listening on the party line he might have already asked me to be his girlfriend. He's pretty handsome, don't you think?"

Dennis wanted to jump up and run back to his bedroom as fast as he could. He wanted to close the door, crawl under the bed, and never come out. He'd been too late. For three months he'd worked his newspaper route, getting up before dawn to roll newspapers and deliver them on three neighboring streets, then coming home from school to do it all again with the evening paper. He had gone around and around to the houses on weekends with his collection book trying to get people to pay for the newspaper, tearing off tickets as receipts when he was lucky enough to find the person who controlled the money and happened to have it on them at the moment. He had begged and pleaded with his mother to take him downtown to the Woolworth's so he could buy something, embarrassed to tell her what it was until she refused to take him until he did. He'd endured her teasing and, worse, her encouragement as he shopped the jewelry counter and picked out the fourteen caret gold bracelet with a single heart charm attached to the middle. It had taken all but twelve cents of his savings, but he'd bought it.

And now the charm was lost and Devlin Shockley, a blond kid with shoulders wider that his IQ, had already beaten him to the girl he wanted.

"He hasn't asked me yet," Gloria continued. "And now you have. And with a beautiful gift that must have cost you a lot. Unless your mom paid for it."

"I paid for it myself," Dennis protested. "I have a paper route."

"I know that," Gloria said, her eyes glinting as she smiled.

"How did you know?"

"Girls know a lot of things boys don't think they know," she teased.

"Oh," Dennis said, confused. "Well, do you like me?"

"Of course I like you," Gloria said. "We have a tree together."

Dennis could only look at her, even more confused. "But, I mean, do you *like* like me?"

"For a boyfriend?" she asked for clarification in the same teasing tone.

"Yes, for a boyfriend," Dennis said.

"If I say no, do I have to give the bracelet back to the creepy boy who watches me from the window?" she asked.

Dennis hadn't considered that. "No," he said. "He wants you to have it."

"That means he has a good heart," Gloria said. "I like that."

"The bracelet had a heart on it because he ..." Dennis felt himself blushing again, but made himself finish it. "He wanted you to see it and know that you have his."

To his everlasting shock, at that moment Gloria Light leaned forward as fast as lightning and kissed him right on the cheek, not more than an inch from his mouth. If he'd flinched just a little bit, he'd tell himself later, their lips might have touched in a real kiss, just like in the movies. Then she was back on her heels and holding out her open palm. "You have to put it on me the first time," she said.

Dennis was ready for this. He had hoped he would get to do this and had sat for a long time practicing with the hasp of the bracelet. He now proudly showed his expertise by opening it, wrapping the thin gold chain around the wrist of his new girlfriend, and closing the hasp. Gloria wiggled her wrist and the gold flashed in the dappled sunlight falling through Woody's green leaves.

"I guess I'll have to tell Devlin to stop calling me now," she said with a sigh. "I hope he doesn't get too jealous."

That was something Dennis had thought of, but was willing to face if he had to. Devlin Shockley was bigger and stronger, but he wasn't very smart. Dennis felt confident he could win that fight if it came.

"I have to go home now, boyfriend," Gloria said, getting to her feet. "My mom is fixing dinner."

"Okay," Dennis said, getting up with her. "I'll keep looking for that heart. It has to be here somewhere."

"But you said I already have yours," Gloria said. She gave him a smile, blew a kiss at him as she picked up her watering can, then skipped away, calling, "Bye!" over her shoulder.

Had there been a breeze that evening, it would have knocked Dennis over right then.

When Gloria was out of sight, he got on his hands and knees again and continued looking through the grass for the missing heart until his mom came out on the front porch and called for him to come inside.

Chapter Twenty

Kelsi sat in the chair beside Dennis's bed and watched the man through wet eyes. He was exhausted, propped up on several pillows, but at that moment he looked incredibly peaceful as his eyes were looking toward the wall across from him but seeing back through the decades to another time.

"That's a beautiful story," Kelsi said.

Dennis turned his head toward her and smiled wistfully. With a shaking hand he pointed to the dresser, where a small cedar chest with a very faded forest scene glued to the lid rested on a lace doily. "Open that up," he said.

Kelsi went to the dresser and opened it the little chest. On top and pressed against the right-hand side of the box was a very worn black jewelry box. She looked from it to Dennis and he nodded. Kelsi lifted it out and opened it. Inside was a thin gold chain, a very dainty thing that showed a lot of wear. The fourteen caret gold, Dennis had learned later, was only a coating over copper and as the years wore on and Gloria continued to wear the bracelet, a lot of the gold chipped and broke away.

"She wore it right up to the end," he whispered. "I took it off her before they cremated her. It was the last time I worked the hasp on it."

"You never found the heart," Kelsi said.

"Never found it," he agreed. "It's still the damnedest thing I've ever seen. How did it just pop off and disappear?" He shook his head. "I'm tired, Kelsi. I think I'll sleep for a while, if you don't mind."

Kelsi replaced the bracelet and left Dennis alone in his room. He was already mostly asleep when she quietly closed the door most of the way. She went to the kitchen, where she had explored all the cabinets over the weekend and found a box of treasure. The box was small and rectangular with the word Recipes stenciled onto the wooden lid. Inside was a densely packed sheaf of index cards, bits of notebook paper faded beyond yellow to brown, and cutouts from antique food product boxes. It was the handwritten recipes that fascinated her more than anything.

The box held the penmanship of three different women. Two were in similar neat, flowing script, one with tight little loops and short tails and the other with rounder loops and a bit of a flourish on the tails, particularly at the end of words like *Spicy, Sugary, Baking, Celery*, etc. In her mind, Kelsi had decided the tight loops were Gloria's mother's, the looser ones Gloria's own. While these cards gave instructions for the making of many entrees and side dishes, there was almost an equal amount of desserts and even drink ideas with the appropriate season written in parenthesis in the upper right corner.

The third, though, was heavy, blocky printing where the pen or pencil had been pressed hard into patinaed index cards. These cards described simpler dishes with fewer ingredients and Kelsi believed they could only have belonged to Dennis's mother, the farmwife with little in the way of income even before her husband was killed at a city job. The only desserts here were for an interesting sounding chocolate cake and it's accompanying frosting that called for an insane amount of butter, and apple pie.

The thing Kelsi loved most about the collection of cards were the thumb and fingerprints on many of them. Though there had been attempts to wipe them away, she could see where the women had picked up or moved the cards, probably without realizing there was a smear of batter, gravy, grease, or sauce they hadn't completely licked off their fingers. It made her feel as if the spirits of the women were there with her, urging her to try this fresh tomato soup or that lemon meringue pie, or maybe some raspberry lemonade with a slice of cinnamon apple bread.

But what she'd pulled from the box now was a recipe for pinto beans and ham and another with instructions on how to fry fresh potatoes. She also had a box of Jiffy cornbread mix on the counter, unopened, with the instructions on the box, though she'd made this one before. The bean recipe was written in the heavy hand she'd attributed to Dennis's mother.

Kelsi whisked the dishtowel — called a T-towel on the card — off the top of the big green pot where she'd dumped the dry beans last night. She'd covered them with water and left them to soak. She was amazed at how they'd absorbed the water and puffed up. She took one bean up between her thumb and forefinger and found that it was much softer than when she'd put them in the pot.

Following the directions, she drained the water from the beans, then put them in a colander to wash them. Then back in the pot with water covering them by about an inch.

She put that on the flame of the gas stove, then opened a can of tomato paste and added it to the beans, along with salt and black pepper. The recipe didn't say how much salt or pepper, so Kelsi went a little heavier on the pepper and lighter on the salt because nobody needed too much sodium in their diet. Next, she crushed half a clove of garlic and cut up a small sweet onion and added that to the pot, stirring as she added each ingredient.

More than a little reluctantly, she put on a skillet and laid out six strips of bacon, spelled *baken* on the card, something that really confused her until she read on about how she was supposed to *"...dump the greeze and all right into the pot with the beans."* That sounded like an invitation to a heart attack, but she was determined to follow the instructions. While the bacon fried, she cut up a thick slice of ham she'd bought at the grocery store yesterday and added that to the pot. The bacon and grease went in last and she covered the pan with its lid.

By the time she had the skillet cleaned, the water in the pot had begun to softly boil. She let it boil for fifteen minutes, then turned the heat down and left it. The recipe said to let the beans cook for a few hours, until they were soft.

The instructions for fried potatoes was less complicated, but she feared all the popping oil that would be involved in that part. Fortunately, it would be a while before she had to worry about that.

When Dennis wakes up, she thought, *he'll smell the beans cooking and hopefully it'll be a comforting thing for him.* Maybe he would even sleep until it was time to start the potatoes and have the cornbread in the oven.

Kelsi went to the living room and settled onto the sofa with a copy of an old paperback novel she'd found in the middle bedroom, which was actually turned into a little library, with shelves mounted to every wall and lots of books on the shelves and in some dusty boxes. That room, she'd noticed, was dustier than all the others, as if it was seldom visited. Other than the books, the only thing in the room was a framed black-and-white photograph of a little girl in a pleated dress with an apron sitting on a photographer's box covered in a pale, wooly carpet. The girl had a big, open-mouthed smile that showed gums not yet completely lined with teeth.

How many people had Dennis lost to death already? His parents, a daughter, his wife, friends and neighbors. And hadn't he mentioned a brother and sister? Were they still alive? Kelsi told herself she'd remember to ask him.

The book she'd picked up was called *The Two Bishops* by Agnew Sligh Turnbull. There had been a whole shelf of novels by this author Kelsi had never heard of. This one promised a story about two bishops dealing with things like a man with two wives, a kid who kept trying to kill himself, and a convict. Kelsi knew they had been Gloria's books. Other shelves in the room held mysteries and she couldn't decide who was the reader of those, but the shelves of Westerns featuring men with horses and guns had to be Dennis's. She began to read, listening absently to the sound of a ticking clock and the water boiling the beans in the kitchen, the smell of the cooking food rising from the pot and joining the older scents of countless meals prepared and served in the old house.

Some two hours later, with the Pennsylvania bishops fully immersed in their problems, Kelsi made herself put the book down and go check on Dennis. He was still asleep, with his head turned to one side and just a bit of drool drying on the corner of his mouth. She considered stepping in and dabbing it away, but was afraid she'd wake him. His breathing was light but steady with just a hint of a snore. She smiled and closed the door, then went to the kitchen.

She picked up the wooden spoon she'd found in a drawer, something her own mother never would have tolerated because she hated the feel of wood against her teeth, and lifted the lid from the pot to stir the beans. Of course, she'd smelled them already, but lifting the lid sent a cloud of aromatic steam rising to her face, filling her nostrils with the earthiness of the beans, the sunshine of the tomato paste, the savory sweetness of the onion, and the irresistible smell of bacon. Her stomach rumbled and her heart swelled with pride. The food smelled incredibly good. She stirred the pot, lifted out a bean and pressed it between her fingers. Most of it smashed, but the center was still pretty solid. She covered the pot and put her clean skillet on another burner of the stove.

Kelsi let a quarter inch of vegetable oil heat in the skillet while she cut golden potatoes into halves, then quarters, and then eighths. The recipe had called for "lard", something she had to look up on her phone, her eyes widening in horror when she realized what it was. There was just no way she could cook anything in that much animal fat, even if she'd had it, and she was very thankful the house had been barren of that particular ingredient. Standing at arm's length, she dumped the potatoes into the oil and, as expected, the moisture on the potatoes caused napalm-like blobs of oil to pop and jump out of the pan. She plunked a lid onto the skillet and left it there until the popping and hissing mostly stopped, then uncovered the skillet and stirred the potatoes around, adding a couple of dashes of salt and pepper.

With the potatoes browning and the beans softening, she pre-heated the oven and mixed an egg and one-third cup of milk with the muffin mix and dumped the thick, pasty yellow blob of batter into a round cake pan she first coated with a light glaze of margarine, again, substituting anything for the lard the recipe called for.

"No wonder people didn't live long back then," she murmured as she spread the batter around to fill the pan. "Who cooks food in animal fat? It's disgusting and so unhealthy."

When she guessed the potatoes were nearly done and the beans were smooshy, she put the cornbread in for fifteen minutes at three hundred-fifty degrees and got out plates, bowls, and silverware. She put wedges of hot, buttered cornbread on the plates, along with a pile of fried potatoes on each, carefully drained and patted dry of oil, and then filled bowls with steaming spoonfuls of brown beans with chunks of ham and slippery-looking strips of bacon. Kelsi considered removing the bacon because of how it looked, but decided to leave it.

She found Dennis sitting up, his mouth and chin dry, a faraway look in his eyes. He turned to her when she came in carrying a tray Natalie had bought expressly for his meals while he was bedridden.

"Those smells take me back," he said softly, as if his throat was dry.

"I hope they're good memories," Kelsi said.

He smiled and nodded his head slowly, looking at the food as she put the tray over his lap. "Good memories. On the farm, mostly, before Dad died and Mom ran off."

Kelsi froze in the act of straightening up. "Ran off? Your mom? She ran off?"

"This looks as good as it smells," Dennis said. "Did you know how to make this?"

"I found a box of recipes," Kelsi said as if batting away a fly. "You can't drop a bomb like that on me and not tell the whole story."

Dennis put a loaded spoon of beans into his mouth, ignoring the steam, and chewed slowly with his eyes closed. Kelsi couldn't believe he wasn't yelping for cold water. He swallowed and smiled. "I haven't had these in almost ten years. Not since Gloria got sick. She learned to make them from Mom's recipe."

"Listen, mister," Kelsi said, pretending to be stern. "I want to hear the story." Then she realized it might be a painful memory that he simply didn't want to share. Her attitude changed. "I'm sorry, Dennis. You got me intrigued, but I guess maybe it's something you don't want to talk about."

"You're wrong there," he said with potatoes in his mouth. "God, these are delicious." He swallowed, then looked at her, his face very serious. "I want to tell you my stories. As many as I can. My family has heard most of them to the point they don't even hear them anymore. I want to tell you those, and the ones I haven't told anyone else." He paused and used his spoon to pluck at a bean in his bowl. "I know people in their eighties who break hips put themselves on the slide out of this world."

"Dennis —"

He waved her to silence with his spoon. "I've seen enough of it, and I used that silly phone Natalie gave me to look it up in the hospital. It isn't just anecdotal evidence. It's the truth. And I'm mostly okay with that, Kelsi. I am," he insisted. "I don't believe in death. Someday, not too far from now, I'll pass through the veil and I'll be with Gloria again. She's waiting. That's why we keep seeing her. She knows the time is close."

Kelsi stood beside the bed, stunned into silence. She heard what he was saying, but there was nothing she could offer in response.

"Go get your food and come back and I'll tell you about my mother," Dennis said. "But bring me a couple more pieces of this cornbread. I've never in my life had all I could eat of this."

Chapter Twenty-One

"Where's Mom?" Dennis asked.

"I don't know," Ollie answered.

Dennis closed the front door of the house and looked around. There was something different, but he couldn't put his finger on it. Outside, he could still hear the revving of the big yellow school bus as it moved on down the block, letting off other kids from the high school. Ollie, now at the junior high Dennis had left last year, got home about a half-hour earlier than his big brother. "What about Carol?" Dennis asked.

"Haven't seen her." Ollie was slumped on the couch with his feet on the table, looking through a comic book.

The house was very quiet. Still. Empty. Dennis dropped his books onto a worn-out chair cushion went upstairs to his sister's room. Six-year-old Carol wasn't in there. Her favorite doll, an orange dog in a sitting position, was not on the bed. Her dresser drawers hung open and they were mostly empty.

Dennis stood at the dresser, fingering a dress Carol had outgrown several months ago. It was the only thing left in the top drawer. He began to feel a sinking sensation in his stomach, but still told himself it wasn't possible. Quietly, almost as if in a daze, he left his sister's room and went down the hall to the master bedroom his mother and father had shared until Dad died. Even before he pushed open the door, he knew the truth.

Dresser drawers empty. Clothes gone from the closet. The ratty old suitcases that hadn't been used in years were gone, as was his mother's jewelry box. The bed was neatly made, just like it was every day. In the bathroom, both his mother's and Carol's toothbrushes were gone. Slowly, with all the implications of what was becoming obvious settling onto him, Dennis made his way to the kitchen.

The note was held on the refrigerator door with a round black magnet. Ollie had probably looked right at it and never even seen it, but Dennis knew it for what it was before he removed the magnet and sat down at the wobbly little table where his mother had served him breakfast before he went to school that day. He read the letter over and over and the meaning never changed.

My Boy's, I am real sorry to do this to you, but I've met a man named Amos Beggs and he's offered to marry me and take me to live with him in Arizona. He can't take care of 3 kid's, though. You are both big strong boy's and I know you will find a way to take care of yourself so I'm taking Carol and we're going with Amos to live in Arizona. Live good live's and make your mama proud. Please don't think I did this because I don't love you because I do but the money's all gone and I don't know what else to do. Love, Mom

Finally, Dennis couldn't read the letter any more because of the tears that filled his eyes. He blinked and the brine ran down his face. He put the letter down on the table and wiped at his cheeks. He looked around the kitchen and it was like a body without a heart now that he knew his mother was gone from the house. He and Ollie were maggots, living in a corpse. Dennis made himself get up and go into the living room and sit beside his little brother. Ollie barely looked over at him as he flipped through the pages of another comic book, mostly looking at the ads.

"They're gone," Dennis said in a shaky voice. "Mom left with some man named Amos and took Carol and they went to Arizona and left us here alone. She just ... left us."

Ollie's page-turning had stopped, but his eyes were fixed on the open pages of his book. "There's no one to tell us what to do?" he asked.

Dennis stared at his brother, wondering what wasn't registering. "She left us. She took Carol, but left us."

"Carol was annoying," Ollie said. He flipped a page. "Did she leave us any money? I want to buy these glasses. Think I could really see through girls' clothes with them?"

Dennis stood up and went to the front door. "There's no money. Not for glasses, not for food, and not for the mortgage on this house. I'm going across the street." He left Ollie on the sofa and crossed the street into the park.

It was autumn and the ground of the park was covered in crisp leaves of many colors. Dennis had never taken off his jacket when he arrived home from school, so he wasn't too cold as he walked slowly, aimlessly toward the familiar sycamore, kicking at or dragging his feet through the leaves, noting vaguely when more of them became the broad rusty leaves Woody dropped onto the earth beneath him.

"I wondered if you would come here." At first, the voice startled Dennis and he froze, but when he looked up, Gloria Light stepped around the sycamore's trunk and faced him. She was wearing the same white sweater and navy skirt she'd had on when they'd parted at his stop on the school bus. Her dark hair was pulled back in a high pony tail. At sixteen, she was tall and soft and everything Dennis needed at the moment.

"She left us," he said. "She just ..." He made helpless motions with his arms. "Left us." Gloria nodded.

"You know?"

"The neighborhood knows," she said. "Mrs. Bowers saw what was going on and confronted your mother. There was yelling. Mrs. Gray called the police, but by the time they got here, your mom and the man she was with and your sister were gone."

The story sapped the last of Dennis strength. He looked up toward the heavens, but all he saw was Woody's branches laden with dead leaves that had not yet fallen. Then he was enveloped in the warm smell of Gloria's perfume and shampoo and soft, perfect skin. Her arms were around him, holding tightly, and she was saying something he had to really listen to before he could absorb it. "I'm so sorry, Dennis. I'm so sorry."

He broke then, sagging against her, his face in her hair as he sobbed and clung to her with his arms as if she was the last thing holding him against the surface of the planet. He cried for a long time while Gloria rubbed his back and promised him over and over that everything would be okay. At long last, he got control of himself. He stepped away and wiped the sleeves of both arms across his face. In the glow of a nearby streetlamp, he could see that she had been crying, too.

"How is Ollie?" Gloria asked.

Dennis looked back up the hill, across the street to his home. He shrugged. "Ollie doesn't seem bothered by it. I don't think he understands it yet."

"He's young," Gloria said. "It'll be different for him."

"I guess."

"My mom sent me," Gloria said. "She told me what happened and then sent me to get you and Ollie so you could come have dinner with us."

Dennis had to swallow several times to push the lump back down his throat and keep from crying again. He nodded. "Your mom is a real mom. What a mom should be. She'd never pick one kid and leave the rest to starve or whatever."

"No," Gloria agreed hesitantly. "I'm getting cold, Dennis. Can we get Ollie and go?"

The three of them walked the few blocks to Gloria's house, which was bright and warm and almost thrummed with life after the corpse-like feeling Dennis now had about his own home. Mrs. Light, a taller, more angular version of Gloria, welcomed Dennis with a brief but intense hug and patted Ollie on the back. She smelled of pot roast and gravy and Dennis's stomach rumbled as she hugged him. He grinned awkwardly and she laughed. Gloria's father greeted both boys with firm handshakes and assured them that their situation was on his mind.

At the table, Mr. Light sat at the head and Mrs. Light at the other end. Dennis got to sit beside Gloria and Ollie sat across from them. On previous occasions when he'd been invited to dinner, Dennis had sat across from Gloria. Her parents seemed not to notice, or maybe ignored how every once in a while their hands were absent from sight as they clasped quickly below the surface of the table. The food was amazing. The pot roast was the most tender, most flavorful thing Dennis had eaten in a very long time. Even Ollie was impressed enough to offer his compliments to Mrs. Light. The meat was served with potatoes and carrots that had cooked in the same pot, and brown gravy made in the pot once everything else was removed, plus green beans and huge, fluffy rolls, with buttermilk to drink.

"I think that was the best meal I've ever had," Dennis said when his plate was empty.

"Sure better than Ma ever made," Ollie said, and that sentiment sucked all the joy out of the room, but only for a moment because Mrs. Light was a spark of joy that could not be extinguished.

"Well, thank you, boys. You'll need to come around more often. A woman needs to hear those compliments," she said.

"I'd like for you boys to come to dinner again tomorrow, too," Mr. Light said. "I'm going to talk to some men I know tomorrow and see what we can do to help you out. I want you to come over and I'll lay out what we know. Will you do that?"

"What are you having for dinner tomorrow?" Ollie asked.

Dennis shot him a murderous look, then addressed Gloria's father. "We thank you," he said. "If it's no bother, we'd love to come to dinner again. I really don't know what we're going to do now and want to hear your suggestions."

Mr. Light nodded gravely, his dark eyes penetrating Dennis's skin the way he felt they always were. "You're turning into a fine, responsible young man, Dennis," he said. "I'm pleased to see that."

"Thank you, sir," Dennis said. Gloria's hand in his squeezed happily and then slipped away to dab a napkin against her perfect lips.

Chapter Twenty-Two

"That was 1955," Dennis said, his voice and his eyes pulled back from six decades earlier.

"Did you ever see or hear from your mom again?" Kelsi asked. They'd finished their meal and the empty dishes were stacked on the tray that still straddled Dennis's lap. He turned a suddenly haggard face with haunted eyes toward her.

"Amos Beggs killed them both four months later," he said quietly. "Mom was the fourth woman he'd talked into running away with him. He killed them all. They say he did horrible things to the women. And to Carol. Their bodies were found in a ditch near Reno, Nevada. The police found him and he started shooting. They killed him in a little house in Needles, California."

"I'm so sorry," Kelsi said, struck again by how much death and loss this man had suffered.

"Ollie was already gone by that time," Dennis continued wearily. "It started with shoplifting candy from a corner store. He figured Mom wasn't there to yell at him, so why not? Well, the store owner caught him, of course. A judge lectured him and threatened him with the boys home. We were always terrified of being sent to a boys home, even though we didn't really know what it was. It was just a bad place for boys in trouble. Ollie wouldn't stop, though. He got in fights. Stole food and vandalized stop signs and bus benches and whatever. Three months after Mom left us, Ollie tried to steal a pair of boots from a store downtown. He got caught. The judge lectured him again, but had mercy on him because of our situation, and let him go."

Dennis paused and studied his hands where they rested on the edge of the tray. A tear rolled from one eye. Kelsi looked away for a moment, but was too interested and faced him again.

"He burned the store down that night," Dennis said in a whisper. "Burned it down and ran away. The police tore the house apart looking for him. They thought I was hiding him. I think he went to one of the grain elevators and hopped a boxcar out of town. I never heard. I got a letter from him after I found out Mom and Carol were dead. He was in jail in Nebraska. He'd stolen a car. The next time I heard from him he was in a prison in Oregon." Dennis shrugged with a gesture of his hands. "I don't know if he's alive or dead now."

"How did you stay in that house?" Kelsi asked. "What did Mr. Light do for you?"

"The sheriff dragged his feet evicting us. Evicting me," Dennis said. "Eventually he had to. By that time, Earl, that was Gloria's dad, had helped me sell everything valuable and put it in a savings account and he got me a job sweeping and stocking at a feedstore that used to be on the east side of downtown. I had to drop out of school to make enough to pay for a little apartment and my groceries."

"That's awful that you had to drop out," Kelsi said. Dennis didn't respond, so she asked, "How did Gloria respond to that?"

He smiled, but it was a tired, almost sad smile. "We had already been talking about being together forever, getting married, all of that," he said. "She told me I'd be the muscle and she'd be the brain in our partnership."

"Oh," Kelsi said. "How did you feel about that? Was there a career you wanted to do? College? Or something?"

"If I'm being honest, at the time, all I wanted was to be with Gloria," he said, his eyes moving from his hands to Kelsi's face. "Looking back, I do resent my mother for taking the choices away from me. From us, really. Gloria was sharp. She could have gone to college, but because I couldn't, she didn't. We might have had a completely different life." He moved a little and winced.

"Oh my God! I'm so sorry!" Kelsi said, jumping up. She lifted the tray off his lap. "It's past time for your pill and I need to clean up in the kitchen. I hope you liked the beans, because there are a lot of them. I'll be right back."

She deposited the dishes in the sink and poured a glass of cold water and took Dennis's medication to him. She found him trying to use the urine bottle by himself. He was using one hand to try to tent the blankets over his waist while holding the bottle with his other. There was sweat on his brow and he was trembling. Kelsi put the water and pill on the nightstand and took the urine bottle in her hand and looked him in the eyes.

"This won't work if you don't let me help," she said. "I know this is embarrassing for you, but you need help for a while. That's why I'm here. I'll hold the bottle, you work the hose."

His lips twitched, but it wasn't a smile, though she thought he wanted it to be. "You're bossy like she was, too," he said. "Can you ... not look at me?"

Kelsi turned her head. She heard the sound and felt the stream of urine entering the bottle. The level rose enough she could feel the warmth and was a little impressed he'd held that much for so long. When the whizzing sound stopped, she asked if he was finished and he said he was. She pulled the bottle away and asked, "Can you tuck back in there while I take care of this? If not, I'll be back and do it and you can just air dry for a minute."

"I can handle it," Dennis said. "There isn't much to it when you're wearing a nightgown."

Kelsi drained the bottle into the toilet, ran water from the bathtub into the bottle, swirled it around, and dumped that into the toilet, too, then flushed. When she went back to the master bedroom, Dennis was staring hard at the pill on his nightstand. Kelsi made him use a squirt of hand sanitizer before she let him have the pill and the water. When he was done, she took the glass and set it aside, then adjusted pillows until he was comfortable.

"Do you need anything?" Kelsi asked.

"No."

She tapped an old cowbell she'd put on the table beside his bed. She'd found it in the top of his bedroom closet. "You ring this if you need anything. Anything at all, okay?"

"That was Gloria's bell and I told her the same thing," he said. His voice faded as he said it and his eyes were already closed.

"Then you know how it's done," Kelsi said. There was no answer other than his soft, regular breathing.

In the kitchen, Kelsi put the leftovers into containers and loaded and ran the dishwasher. She checked on Dennis one more time, then went out to the bungalow's front porch and sat in the porch swing with her back against an armrest and her feet pressed against the other end. It was a pleasant, quiet evening, interrupted randomly by the laughter of children somewhere up the street or by the barking of a dog. She sat and thought about all she'd learned during the day and reflected on how she'd done in her first day as caretaker. Getting wrapped up in his story and forgetting it was time for his pill hadn't been so good, but otherwise she thought she'd done okay.

As dusk settled over the neighborhood, the peace was broken by the sound of an engine and the glare of headlights. Tucker's truck turned off the street and pulled into the driveway behind Kelsi's car. When he got out, he was wearing shorts and sandals, a gray T-shirt, and carrying a backpack that had definitely seen better days. He came onto the porch and Kelsi swung her feet off the swing so he could sit down beside her.

"What's up?" he asked, putting the backpack down by the porch rail.

"Just thinking," Kelsi said. She cuddled against him and he seemed surprised, but put an arm around her shoulders and held her.

"Thinking about what?" he asked.

"I don't know. Life, I guess," Kelsi said.

"You don't have your phone, do you?"

"No," she said. She hadn't even thought about it.

"My mom's getting agitated," Tucker said. He fished his phone from a pocket of his shorts and thumbed the screen a few times until the phone buzzed with a dialed call.

"Is everything okay?" Natalie's voice asked on speakerphone without any kind of greeting.

Tucker looked at Kelsi and mouthed, "Is it?" She smiled and nodded. "Yes, Mom, everything's fine. I found her on the porch. I'd bet anything she was sitting here thinking about one of Pop's old stories."

"Let me talk to her," Natalie demanded.

"I'm here," Kelsi said. "You're on speaker."

"Kelsi, I've been trying to call you," Natalie scolded. "Why didn't you answer?"

"I guess I left my phone in my room. Or maybe it's in the kitchen. I'm really sorry. I got wrapped up making dinner and then listening to your dad tell me about his mom and brother and sister," Kelsi explained. "He's fine, though. He's sleeping."

"Did he eat?" Natalie asked through the phone that Tucker held between himself and Kelsi.

"Yes. I made pinto beans with ham and fried potatoes and cornbread," Kelsi said. "He seemed to like it."

There was a long moment of quiet. "You made that?" Natalie asked.

"Yes. I found the recipe in a wooden box. There are a lot of them in there," Kelsi said.

"The recipes," Natalie said softly. "I know that box. You know, his grandmother used to make that, and then his mom, though he always said Great-Grandma's was better. Thank you for that. I should do things like that for him more. It's just ... life gets busy, you know?"

"I know," Kelsi said. "I enjoyed it, though. And ..." She stopped herself from saying the next, but Natalie insisted she continue. "It's dumb," Kelsi said. "I was just going to say that it felt good to see how happy the food made him."

Natalie laughed. "Tucker, you better hold on to this one," his mother said.

"I'm trying," Tucker promised, and he pressed Kelsi closer to him with the arm around her shoulder.

"Okay, well, if everything is okay, your father is taking me out to dinner since I'm back up here," Natalie said.

"We're fine," Kelsi promised.

"Bye, Mom," Tucker said, and ended the call before Natalie could answer. He stuffed the phone back into his shorts pocket.

"What's in the backpack?" Kelsi asked.

"I thought I might need a few things over here. A change of clothes, toothbrush, deodorant. You know," he said.

"Did your grandpa ever let your mom have a boy sleep over? Your dad?" Kelsi asked.

"I have no idea," Tucker said.

"I don't like the idea of sneaking you in and out of his house," Kelsi said. Tucker started to protest and Kelsi stopped him with a hand lightly over his mouth. "I said I don't like it, not that I won't do it. You are his grandson, not some random guy I picked up off the street. But when he catches on, and he will, he'll either say it's okay or not, and we're going with that. Agreed?" She took her hand away.

"In that case, I'll just have to be extra quiet so he doesn't catch on for a long time," Tucker said.

"You're never quiet," Kelsi teased.

"Do you want to go inside?" Tucker asked.

"Not yet. I'm in love with this porch," Kelsi said. "Just think of all the evenings Dennis and Gloria sat right here where we are and watched their neighborhood get dark." She pointed to houses across the streets with inviting yellow light seeping under blinds or illuminating whole windows. "Imagine the comfort of knowing your neighbors, seeing their homes occupied, feeling safe, feeling, I don't know, home."

Tucker used his long legs to push the swing gently while his hand rubbed her shoulder. "That's really a big thing to you, huh?" he asked. "The feeling of home?"

"I never had it," she said. "I went to nine schools in eight different states because my dad couldn't keep his dick in his uniform pants. Move somewhere, he'd go to work, screw some secretary or other officer's wife, usually get demoted and transferred, and we'd start over with less money. Until ... until me and Mom just left. The idea that your grandparents were together for almost seventy years and lived right here in this house for around fifty of those years is just ... it blows my mind, Tucker. You grew up here, too, with a stable home life. Went to just one high school. You got to put down roots."

"Roots in Nokomis, Oklahoma," he said, and there was an ironic tone to his voice. "Who wants that? I'd rather be one of those tumbleweeds."

Kelsi shook her head. "It sounds fun to move all the time, but it's not. I'd rather be like Woody."

"Woody?" he asked. "Oh, that tree. I thought you meant the cowboy in *Toy Story*."

Kelsi laughed softly and snuggled her head against his shoulder. "Maybe I just want to nest," she said. "Or I'm having some kind of break from my past. Do you know what I'm going to do in the morning after I get Dennis his breakfast?"

"I have no idea," Tucker said.

"I'm going to weed the flowerbed, and I cannot wait to get my hands back in the dirt," she said.

Tucker chuckled softly. "Who are you, and what have you done with the girlfriend who came here from Wyoming?"

Chapter Twenty-Three

Mornings proved to be the most difficult part of the day. The rising of the sun brought resentment, anger, frustration, and then depression for the elderly man who had never been bedridden before. He had a routine, one that had gotten him through his darkest days after the loss of his wife. He wanted to get out of his bed, go for a short walk, then have coffee with eggs and toast while he read the newspaper, then work in his garden until he felt the urge for a late-morning nap.

Most of that was simply off the table for him.

Kelsi did what she could. She exercised his good leg as much as his position in bed allowed. She prepared his breakfast and brought him his newspaper, and she did the work in the garden, showing him pictures on her phone of what she had done and how his flowers were growing. In the mornings, though, Dennis was crabby. While he was never downright mean to her, his tone was often harsh and ungrateful. Kelsi tried to not let it bother her. She knew that as the day went on, as his pain medication took away most of the discomfort and his inability to complete his morning routine faded, he would become the kindly man she had come to know.

Often, after he had his morning nap, Kelsi would help him out of bed and he would use his walker to shuffle into the living room and sit, exhausted, in his recliner. Kelsi would show him recipe cards and he would tell her stories about the food, sharing favorite memories of each meal and talking about the women who made them. Gloria, an avid reader, would often try to research and recreate meals she read about in her romance novels set in far away lands.

"Did you know they eat snails in France?" Dennis asked her during one of those sessions. "She read about some French people eating *escargot* and it sounded so good, she wanted to know what it was so she could make it for us." He shook his head, grinning. "She found it in the library. I remember her bringing that French cookbook to me and asking if it really said what she thought it did. Snails. They eat snails. I told her I wouldn't eat snails, slugs, or anything like them. Do you know what she did?" His eyes twinkled as he asked.

Kelsi, already laughing, could only shake her head.

"She threw away that romance novel where she'd read about *escargot*," he said, then he imitated a woman's higher voice. "I don't ever want to read about anyone kissing anyone after they've eaten snails."

They both had a good laugh.

Kelsi experimented with many of the recipes. Usually her creations were a success, particularly the entrees and sides, but she didn't fare so well with her desserts, not that Dennis ever complained. He just told a story about Gloria not doing so well in some endeavor.

"Cooking is witchcraft," he often said. "A little of this, a little of that. You sing while you stir it together, put it over a fire, and when you take it off, it's something new. Women's magic. Men can only put things over a fire and heat it until it's edible. It takes a woman to use herbs and spices and other ingredients."

"There are thousands of male chefs," Kelsi argued, though she liked the idea of cooking being a specifically female kind of magic.

Dennis waved that away. "Exceptions only strengthen the rule. Gather ten couples and I'll bet not more than one man in the group knows when or how to use any seasonings other than salt, pepper, onion, and maybe garlic. Maybe." He was quiet for a moment. "Gloria knew, though. When we were poor, just starting out, we'd have almost nothing in the cupboard, but she could always make a meal. Always."

"Like what?" Kelsi asked.

Dennis smiled as he remembered, letting his head fall back on the pillow Kelsi put on his recliner, his bright eyes looking up at the ceiling of the room he'd shared with the woman he was remembering. "Tomato soup and fried dough," he said softly. "She could always scrape together enough flour and lard to make fried dough. It's a poor man's bread and I knew it at the time, but she made it so fluffy that it was like having a dessert treat."

"Lard?" Kelsi asked. "You know what that is? I had to look it up. It's disgusting."

Dennis chuckled. "Times were different. And I say lard, but it was really Crisco shortening. It came in a can and everyone used it before vegetable oil become so popular." He turned his head to look at her. "Do you want to hear about the tomato soup?"

"Sure," she said. "Was it just Campbell's?"

He laughed. "Oh, no. We couldn't afford that. It was a little bit of ketchup in warm water."

"Really? That and bread was your meal? One meal, or for the day?"

"Sometimes it's all we had for the day," Dennis said. "We were too proud to ask her parents for help. They knew, though, and sometimes we'd wake up to find a paper sack of groceries on our doorstep. They pretended they hadn't left it and we pretended we didn't know they had."

"Why didn't they help you more?" Kelsi asked.

"We were a couple," Dennis said. "Married and on our own. We weren't their responsibility anymore."

"Still ..." Kelsi wanted to argue.

Dennis shook his head. "Parents didn't mollycoddle their kids the way they do now. Tucker, for instance. He's what, twenty-four years old now and still living in his parents' house. That didn't happen. Baby birds had to leave the nest."

"We really are a soft generation, aren't we?" Kelsi asked.

"It's not your fault, though. It's your parents' fault," he said, then winked. "There were other reasons Gloria's parents wouldn't openly help us," he said, his tone changing. "We disappointed them."

"How?" Kelsi asked.

"The world was a lot different back then, Kelsi," Dennis said. "There were things you were and weren't supposed to do."

Chapter Twenty-Four

It was a typical windy March day in 1957. A dust devil whirled to life on Randolph Avenue, making a new Chevy swerve out of the way. The boy on the sidewalk, just released from his shift of work, watched both the dust devil and the shiny green-and-white car until one died away and the other was out of sight, then he continued hurrying up the sidewalk toward downtown Nokomis.

The clerk was a thin man in a dark suit with a blue silk necktie and he visibly looked down his pointy nose at the boy with corn dust in his hair and on his shoulders as he entered the jewelry store, making the bell over the door jingle with his entrance. The boy looked up at the bell, as if he had never seen such a thing before, then looked around at the glass displays along the walls and in the middle of the store. The clerk looked at his two co-workers and they grinned at him because it was his turn to greet the next customer and they all felt sure there wouldn't be any commission earned from this boy.

"Can I help you?" the clerk asked before the boy could take another step into the spotless sanctum of the store. If he could send the kid out fast enough, maybe this wouldn't even count as a customer.

"I'm here to buy a ring," Dennis said. "A wedding ring. Or an engagement ring. I don't know what the difference is."

"Our jewelry is quite expensive," the clerk said. "Woolworth's might suit you better." His co-workers snickered quietly.

"No," Dennis said, stepping toward a counter filled with rings. "I bought her a bracelet there a long time ago and the charm flew off and we never found it. I have to do better this time."

Reluctantly, the clerk stepped up to meet the boy at the display counter. "What is your budget?" he asked.

"I can spend about thirty-seven dollars," Dennis answered. He glanced toward the back of the store when one of two men sitting there had a sudden fit of coughing. The thin man facing him seemed to deflate a little, too. "I know it's not a lot," Dennis said quietly. "But it's all I have and I want to get her the best ring I can. She deserves better, but I have to pay my rent and buy groceries, too."

"Yes, I understand," said the clerk, and his tone was different. Dennis looked into his face and the man's upper lip, which had been curled into a small sneer, was no longer so condescending. "My name is Frederick and I can help you, but I'm afraid your budget doesn't give you access to this particular cabinet. Come over here, please."

Dennis followed the man across the store to a glass case near the front door. The clerk went behind the case and opened a back panel. he took out a small cream-colored box with a gold band inside it and placed it on the counter. "This is a lovely wedding band. Simple but elegant, and in your price range."

Dennis looked at it, disappointed. "But there's no diamond," he said.

"Sir, I'm sorry, but we don't have any diamond rings in your price range," the clerk said.

"I really need a diamond ring," Dennis argued. "My girl deserves it."

"I'm sure she does," the clerk agreed.

"What about that one?" Dennis pointed to another ring in the case.

Sighing, the clerk took out that box and put it on the glass countertop. "It is fourteen caret gold with a cluster setting."

"What does that mean?" Dennis asked.

"If you look closely, you'll see that it is not a single diamond, but a cluster of very small stones that give the appearance of a bigger one," the clerk said.

Dennis picked the box up and looked at the ring very closely. He did see that it was a collection of tiny flecks of shiny diamond in a circle around one that was only marginally bigger than the others. "How much?" he asked.

"That ring is fifty-seven dollars," the clerk said.

"Can I give you the money I have now and pay you the rest later?" Dennis asked.

"A lay-away plan?" the clerk asked.

"What's that?"

"I would take your down payment and hold the ring for you until you pay the full amount," the clerk said, becoming haughty again.

"You wouldn't trust me to take the ring and still pay you?" Dennis asked. He stood still, fuming and red-faced as the dark-suited man with soft hands looked him up and down.

"Are you employed, sir?" he asked.

"Yes. I work at the feed store right down the street," Dennis said.

Although he walked out of the store with the small box gripped in his hand deep in his jeans pocket, Dennis felt like he'd lost something more than all his cash in the store. The clerk had grown even more smug as he read a credit agreement and emphasized over and over how important it was that Dennis pay the principal and the interest and how failure to do so would result in criminal charges and probably jail time. Had it been any other item he was purchasing, he would have left the store and gone somewhere else, but Dennis guessed it would be the same in any other jewelry store, and he was already deep into the process, so he saw it through.

Back in his apartment, he made a sandwich of bread and peanut butter and sat close to the far wall of his bedroom so he could hear radio station WKY on his neighbor's radio while he ate and read a couple of chapters of a Zane Gray novel from the library. As the room began to get dim, he put the book away and went downstairs to the commons area where there was a telephone residents could use for free to make local calls. There was an older lady already on the phone, so Dennis waited a respectful distance away and tried not to look impatient when he realized she was just gossiping to one friend about another friend and the "strange man from Chicago she's running around with." At last, the woman hung up the phone, gave him an exasperated huff as if he'd been bothering her, and clopped away in her heels.

Dennis called the Light house and Gloria picked up on the second ring. "I didn't think you were ever going to call," she said.

"I had to wait for the phone," Dennis explained. "How are you? How was school?"

"It was so boring," she said, and he could picture her standing in the doorway between the living room and kitchen, leaning with her back against the doorframe as she talked to him. "I'm so glad it'll all be over in just a couple more months."

"Can I see you after work tomorrow?" Dennis asked. "Mr. Zoladek said I can leave at four. Maybe you could make a picnic basket and we could eat in the park?"

"Sure, we can do that," Gloria said. "But it's Saturday and Mom will make fried chicken. Wouldn't you rather eat here?"

"I really want to see you alone," Dennis said. "I've missed you a lot."

"I've missed you, too," she said, her voice low, just above a whisper. "Okay, we'll do it. I'll meet you in the park at half past four."

***

Dennis was sitting on the ground, his back against the mottled trunk of the sycamore as he watched Gloria approach the park from her house with the familiar picnic basket in her hand. He had tried to ignore his old home up the hill and across the street, but he felt like the house was watching him. Did it miss him? Or was it content with the new family that lived there? Were they happy in the house where his own family had fallen apart? Would they do better? He hoped so, but it wasn't his main thought.

When she was under the shade of the sycamore's canopy, Dennis jumped to his feet and took her in his arms, hugging her tightly against him. She returned his hug with her free arm, but only allowed him a very modest kiss.

"Dennis, we're in a park. Anyone can see," she said, smiling and pushing him back. She took the folded blanket off the top of the basket and gave it to him. "Spread that out. Mom let me bring fried chicken, so you get to have it even though you wouldn't come to the house."

"That was very kind of her," Dennis said as he spread the blanket on the ground.

The chicken was delicious, but Dennis hardly tasted it. The bulge of the ring box in his pocket was like a burning ulcer. It was all he could think about while she talked about classes and teachers and lessons and homework. She talked and they ate and soon the food was gone and she was gathering up paper plates and napkins, still talking about a typing lesson where she'd erased a hole in the paper and didn't have time to retype it and was afraid she would get an F on that assignment.

"I'll take these to the trash and then we can sit and talk for a little while, but I have to go home and finish my homework," she said, holding the paper plates and other garbage from their meal. "I'll be right back."

Dennis watched her go, his heart beating like a jackhammer as her skirt swished to a green metal trashcan. Then she turned and was coming back, looking at him curiously as he studied her, his hands cupped in front of him. When she was a few paces away, he swung himself into a kneeling position and presented the open box.

"Gloria, will you marry me?" he blurted.

She stopped dead in her tracks and her hands flew up to cover her mouth while her eyes widened at the sight of the ring in its box. Dennis could see that her fingers were trembling. He didn't know if that was a good sign or a bad one.

"Please?" he added. "I love you. I think I've loved you from the day we planted this tree and I smelled your hair. I've never even thought about another girl. You're all I want out of life. Please."

Slowly, her hands slipped down to her chest and her eyes found his. She was crying, and Dennis just knew she was about to break his heart. "Yes," she whispered, then she nodded and said again, louder, "Yes. Yes, I will."

Dennis jumped to his feet and grabbed her in a tight hug, telling her over and over how much he loved her, then he stopped and held her at arm's length, the ring box still in his hand. "Do you love me?" he asked.

"Of course I do, dummy," she answered, laughing and crying at the same time. "Are you going to put that ring on me?"

Dennis plucked the ring from the box and held her left hand in his own and slid the golden circle down the length of her long, delicate finger. They admired it together in the fading light.

"I hope you didn't empty your savings for this," Gloria said.

"No. Like your dad said, that's for emergencies or a down payment on my own — our own — house," Dennis answered. "I was able to pay most of the ring off, but I have to make payments on the rest."

They settled onto the blanket, side by side, his arm around her and their hands clasped in her lap. "It's never a good idea to use credit. How much do you owe?" Gloria asked.

"I can't tell you that," he protested.

"We're a couple, and we'll be sharing finances," Gloria said decisively. "How much?"

"Well, I owe about twenty more dollars on the ring, and then some interest," he said. "I figure I can pay it all off next month."

"That's not too bad," Gloria said approvingly. She paused and snuggled her head against his shoulder, then said, "I'm not sure we should tell anybody yet."

"Why not?" Dennis asked.

"I'm still in school," she said. "Plus, you didn't ask my father if you could have my hand, did you?"

"No," he admitted.

"He might have something to say about it. I won't be eighteen until July," Gloria said.

"But he likes me," Dennis argued.

"That doesn't mean he'll approve of you marrying his little girl."

"But it should be your decision," Dennis said.

"And it will be," Gloria said. "But let's just wait a little while."

Reluctantly, Dennis agreed. He kissed the top of her head and breathed deeply of the smell of flowers and rainwater that lingered in her hair.

"You really remembered how my hair smelled all those years ago?" Gloria asked, raising her eyes to look at him.

"Yes," he whispered, and kissed her perfect mouth. She kissed him back and it was warm and soft. Their lips parted and their tongues found each other and the kiss went from warm to hot. Dennis found himself kissing her cheeks and neck while his hand cupped and squeezed and stroked her breast. They had done this before, but only rarely when they found themselves left alone for a few minutes in her house. Gloria shifted to move closer to him and her skirt rode up, showing a swath of milky thigh that Dennis couldn't ignore.

"Oh God," Gloria whispered. Her face was flushed and her eyes glassy. "I want you to touch me everywhere. I want ... I want you to make love to me, Dennis."

Like a distant memory from the deep past, Dennis recalled her stopping him from kissing her too much just over an hour ago. "Here?" he gasped, his hand creeping up her thigh and under her skirt. She panted faster in response.

"Bring the blanket," she said, and jumped to her feet, grabbing the picnic basket. She hurried across the center of the park, through the dry ditch to a big clump of bushes they both knew from childhood hide-and-seek games to have empty space in the middle.

They spread the blanket, asked each other if they were sure, promised to love one another forever as Gloria pulled her skirt above her waist and Dennis removed her underwear. He lowered his pants and they marveled at one another in the late evening, then he lay on top of her and they consummated the promises they had made.

Chapter Twenty-Five

Kelsi gaped at the bald man in the recliner. "You really did it right there in the park?"

"We did," he confirmed.

"You can't just stop the story there," she complained. "What happened next?"

"She got pregnant, of course," Dennis said.

"No way!" Kelsi almost shrieked.

"I assure you, there was a way, and of course it happened to us," Dennis said softly.

Kelsi's brow wrinkled. "But wait. You said that was 1957. Natalie isn't that old. She was born in the Sixties."

"I see your math skills are up to par," Dennis said. He was studying his hands in his lap. "I want you to help me out to the front porch tomorrow."

"What?"

"I want you to help me out to the front porch tomorrow," he repeated.

"You're not ready for that. Don't change the subject," Kelsi said. "What happened?"

"There are stories I tell Natalie and Tucker over and over because I want them to remember them when I'm gone," Dennis said, looking hard into Kelsi's eyes. "Those are the good stories. I want them to remember how much Gloria and I loved each other. I want them to believe that everything was perfect between us right from the beginning. Does that make sense to you?"

Take aback by his tone, Kelsi nodded and said, "Yeah, it does."

"But for some reason, I want you to know the truth. All of it," he said. "Maybe so you can tell them when I'm gone. Maybe because it'll do you some good. I don't know why, but I want you to know it all. Making love in the park that night almost ruined us."

There was a long, awkward moment of silence and Kelsi didn't know if he was going to continue or not. She reached over and put a hand on one of his. "I'm sorry," she said. "If you don't want to —"

"I *do* want to," he said. "But that doesn't make it easy. She got pregnant. She called the commons at my apartment a couple of weeks later, on a Tuesday, and left a message that I needed to meet her at Woody's as soon as possible after work. Well, I paid a neighbor with a souped up Ford to race me over there and I found her under the tree. She told me she was late and I said, 'But you got here before I did'." Dennis paused and shook his head. "I was as dumb as a cob. I didn't know what she meant. She had to spell it out that her period was late. I still didn't get it. She had to say she thought she was pregnant."

Kelsi watched, fascinated, as the man looked at his hands, opening and closing them as he told his story, his eyes looking back to a scene that played out a lifetime ago.

"We had to tell her folks what we'd done," he continued. "We talked about whether it would be better if I was there or if she did it alone. I insisted I be there to take whatever punishment her dad wanted to give. I thought her mom would be hysterical, but she only nodded and said she already knew. She wouldn't explain how, other than saying mothers knew those kinds of things. Her dad sat very quiet for a really long time. His face was set and hard. He had dark brown eyes, almost black. Gloria said he had some Indian blood in him. I remember his eyes were like holes in his head and I was afraid of what was happening at the bottom of those holes."

Dennis took a drink of water from a glass beside Gloria's urn and photo. His hands trembled as he put it back. "He asked to see the ring and Gloria went to her room and got it. He looked at it and just nodded. After a few more minutes, he said we were going to have a wedding soon after Gloria graduated. That's what we did. We got married on June 1, 1957, but the marriage license said we got married on April 2nd." He stopped and looked up at Kelsi. "There was a huge stigma on pre-marital sex and conceiving babies out of wedlock back then. Things have changed quickly, all things considered. Back then, though, the baby would have been a bastard and we — especially Gloria — would have been shamed. A lot of birth certificates had dates older than their ink."

"She was really pregnant?" Kelsi asked. "She wasn't just late?"

"She was really pregnant," Dennis said. He sighed and looked up toward the ceiling. "She miscarried on June 22, 1957. We decided it would have been a boy and we would have named him Anthony Wayne. But ... no."

"Dennis, I'm so sorry," Kelsi said. There were tears running down her cheeks. "You lost so many people. It just isn't fair."

He turned his lined face toward her and there were tears cascading down his weathered cheeks. "She miscarried again in October of 1959. I blamed her. Do you understand? I blamed her. I accused her of not loving me and not wanting to have a baby with me. I was crazy and stupid and ignorant and I blamed her when she was at her weakest." His voice was tight and clipped with emotion, his fists balled in his lap and his eyes hard and sharp under the fountain of tears. "I hurt her so much."

Crying herself, Kelsi could only shake her head. "But she forgave you," she argued.

Dennis shook his head violently. "She left me," he said savagely, then repeated softly in a defeated voice. "She left me."

Kelsi gasped, her hands going to her face. "But ... She left you?"

"She left me."

They both sat quietly for a long while, wiping at their eyes. Dennis seemed to wither and shrink right in front of Kelsi. He collapsed into the recliner and it was like the chair was swallowing him. He was limp until a spasm of pain caused him to wince. "I didn't want any more pain pills," he said in a dry whisper. "But I've clenched up and it's hurting. Would you help me back to bed and then get them? Please?"

"Of course!" Kelsi got up and pulled his walker close, then kept an arm around his waist as they shuffled back to his room. She helped him back onto the mattress and covered him up, then hurried to the kitchen, coming back with a fresh glass of ice water and a Percocet. She handed them to Dennis and returned to the living room to take the old glass of water back to the kitchen. When she returned, he was lying still, the glass held in both hands in his lap. She took it and put it on his night table. "That's enough story for tonight," she said.

Dennis rolled his head toward her and looked at her with wet, rheumy eyes. "You're a good listener," he said. "It hurt to tell you that, but I already feel lighter. I guess you get to wipe my butt and be my confessor."

Kelsi laughed softly and adjusted his blankets. "I'll be whatever you need me to be, Dennis," she promised. "You're a good man. Whatever mistakes you made in the past. We've all made them. I already know the end of your story and she forgave you eventually."

"Mmm," he said. "I'll tell you about the dark times later. But it isn't fair that I'm the one doing all the talking. You're young, but you've lived some life already, and I want to hear about it."

"It isn't interesting," Kelsi said and turned off the overhead light. "Get some rest."

"Porch tomorrow," he insisted.

"We'll see," she said, and closed his door.

Chapter Twenty-Six

T he first visitor arrived the next morning as Kelsi was washing up after a breakfast of eggs, bacon, and pancakes. She hurried to the door, drying her hands on a dish towel, and opened it to find a man a few years older than herself with neatly combed hair and blond beard. He was wearing black slacks and a maroon button-down shirt. He smiled at her when Kelsi opened the storm door.

"Hi," he said. "I'm Pastor Zook. I've come by to see Dennis, if he's up to it."

"Oh. Come in," Kelsi said, opening the door wider. "You're from the United Methodist church?"

"That's right," the minister said. "He's talked about the church?"

"Only a little," Kelsi said. She thought that might sound like it wasn't important to him, and she really hadn't determined if it was. "He sleeps a lot because of the medication."

"I understand," the man said, nodding. "Are you his nurse?"

"I'm not a nurse," Kelsi said. "I'm not sure what you'd call me, but I'm watching over him. Making sure he eats and doesn't do anything to hurt himself more. I cook and clean."

"That's very nice," the pastor said. "What is your name?"

"Oh, I'm sorry. I'm Kelsi. Kelsi Duncan. I'm dating Tucker, Dennis's grandson."

"Oh, I know Tucker," Pastor Zook said, smiling and nodding. "Your accent tells me you're not from around here."

"I moved here from Wyoming," Kelsi said. "Let me just go in and see if Dennis is up to seeing you. Is there anything specific you came for?"

"Just to check on him. He's part of my flock, you know," he said.

Kelsi went to Dennis's room and found him reading one of his Western novels. "Did somebody knock on the door?" he asked.

"Pastor Zook is here to see you," Kelsi said. "Are you okay with that?"

Dennis's face split into a big grin. "Peter's here? Tell the bastard to come in here."

Kelsi was more than a little shocked. "He's a preacher," she said. "You can't call him that."

"I'll call him what I want in my house," Dennis said, but he was still smiling. "Bring him back here. You'll like him."

Kelsi went back to the living room, where she found the pastor studying the photograph and the urn containing Gloria's ashes. He turned as she came in. "Did you know Gloria?" Kelsi asked.

"Of course," he said. "Magnificent woman. As involved as anyone could be in the church and the community. I was in her Sunday school class once upon a time."

"What's your best memory of her?" Kelsi asked.

Pastor Zook laughed. "Shortly after I took over the church here, she came to me and asked about organizing a ladies' book club to meet in one of the church rooms on Tuesday evenings," he said. "Of course I approved that. The first book they read was one she recommended, and I had elderly ladies absolutely up in arms because she had them reading smut. I'll never forget Virginia Lacroix and how she called it, 'Porrrrrrnagraphy'." He laughed. "I can't remember the name of the novel now, but it simply said something like the new wife enjoyed her wedding night. I called Gloria in and suggested she choose books that didn't include any carnal activity. It was my first year as minister, and I was really young for the job and was pretty intimidated to be asking that of my former Sunday school teacher."

Kelsi, remembering Dennis's story about the first time he and Gloria made love, smiled at the story. She asked, "What did she say?"

"Well..." The pastor cleared his throat. "She told me she picked that book for that very scene and that it was important women know it's okay to enjoy making love. I pretty much stayed out of the book club after that. I did notice that none of the women quit the club despite the complaints."

"She does sound like a fun woman," Kelsi said.

"Peter?" Dennis's voice called from the back of the house. "Leave that young girl alone and get back here."

Kelsi and the pastor both laughed, then she led him through the house to the master bedroom. The men shook hands and Peter Zook took the chair Kelsi usually sat on. She hovered near the foot of the bed as the two men spoke.

"It took you long enough to come around," Dennis said.

"And I'm terribly sorry about that," Peter answered. "I only just learned of your accident after services on Sunday. It's been a busy week. I've performed two weddings this week and have another one coming on Saturday."

"Women always want to get married in the spring," Dennis said. "New beginnings and all of that."

"You can't deny the symbolism. Didn't you say you got married in the spring?" Peter asked.

"Something like that," Dennis answered, glancing at Kelsi. He changed the subject smoothly. "What do you think of my helper? I stole her away from my grandson."

"Kelsi seems like a fine young lady," the pastor said.

"Yeah, until Tucker shows up here after they think I'm asleep," Dennis said with a wink at Kelsi.

Kelsi stiffened and felt her face flaming with shame at having been called out, and in front of a preacher, no less. It hurt, too, that Dennis could do that to her. If he was bothered by it, he should have told her privately. It was so unlike him to blurt out something like that in front of somebody who was a stranger to Kelsi.

"Relax, Kelsi," Dennis said. "You're both grown adults and I don't care what you're doing. I just thought you should know it's not a secret. That should make it easier on you."

"You didn't have to say it in front of a preacher," she said.

"You might as well forgive him, Kelsi," Peter said. "Dennis has an ornery streak. He wasn't trying to shock you. He was trying to shock me. He thinks I'll be scandalized by any mention of sex." He looked from Kelsi back to Dennis, then added, "Something to do with a scandal about a novel."

"Gloria loved telling the story about how embarrassed you were" Dennis said.

Peter sighed, but he was laughing softly. "I was young and inexperienced and did not expect the woman who taught me about the plagues of Israel to argue in favor of a book with sex in it."

"You would have made a great priest," Dennis said. "You're so uptight."

"No, I wouldn't have," Peter assured him. "How's your recovery going?"

"I'm supposed to be moving around some, but Kelsi keeps me in bed unless I'm going to the bathroom," Dennis said. "But she promised me we'd go out on the front porch today."

"I said we'd see about it," Kelsi said. "And you weren't supposed to be up and moving around while you were taking your pain medication regularly. You've been stoned most of the time you've been home."

"I'm cutting back on those," Dennis said. "Peter, you're a strapping young man. Getting out of the bed is the hard part for me, so why don't you help me get up? Get that walker thing over there first." He pointed to the red walker with faded and worn tennis balls on the back legs. It had been in the garage since Gloria's death, but Dennis had sent Kelsi to find it and bring it inside.

"Is it okay for him to do this?" Peter asked Kelsi.

"Yes. He's supposed to put some weight on it as much as he can. I've just been really worried about him getting hurt again," she admitted.

Together, Kelsi and Peter got Dennis out of the bed. He was still wearing a hospital gown that opened down the back because it was easier and more comfortable with his incision. He got his hands on the grips of the walker and began a series of shuffles, clomps, and slides out of the room. Kelsi grabbed a throw blanket from the linen closet in the hall and they made their way to the front porch, where Dennis lowered himself into one of the metal chairs, panting and sweating even with the pastor's help. Kelsi put the blanket over his lap and let it drape down to cover his shins and most of his bare feet.

"That took a lot out of you," Peter said.

Dennis made shooing gestures with his right hand. "I'm fine," he said.

Peter sat in the other chair — Gloria's chair — and Kelsi retired to the porch swing. "Can I mention your name in prayer at church this Sunday?" Peter asked.

"Of course you can," Dennis said. "I'll appreciate the congregation weaving a spell for my recovery. That is what you'll pray for, right?"

"Yes, but a prayer is not a spell," the pastor said, an edge of exasperation in his voice.

"It's all ritualized intent," Dennis answered. His breathing was almost back to normal now. He was looking out at the neighborhood and Kelsi knew he was basking in the feeling of sunlight and fresh air. "Line up the energy of the Universe to make me walk again."

"God is not the universe," Peter insisted.

"Toe-may-to, toe-maw-toe," Dennis said, and offered his minister a grin. "You know where I stand."

The pastor looked to Kelsi, who only shrugged. "He's a step away from being an unredeemed New Age heathen, but the man knows his Bible stories," Peter said.

Despite his earlier embarrassment of her, Kelsi felt the need to defend Dennis. "We've talked about some of what he believes, like the electric charge we get from being barefoot on the earth, and I agree with him. I doubt God cares what we call him as long as we lead good lives."

Dennis laughed heartily at that and slapped Peter's shoulder with the back of his hand. "I'm making converts faster than you," he teased.

"Well, you two are quite a matched pair," the minister said, but he was smiling. "At least we can all agree on the leading good lives part." He paused to compose himself. "Dennis, if you're doing okay and there's nothing I can do for you, I'm going to have to move on. I have a couple of other members to visit this morning."

"I'm doing fine, Peter, and I really do appreciate you coming by and putting up with me," Dennis said, all hint of playfulness gone from his voice now.

The men shook hands again, then the minister shook hands with Kelsi and said it was nice to meet her. They watched him off the porch and into a brown Toyota that he backed out of the driveway and drove away up the street.

"You were awful," Kelsi said. "I can't believe you embarrassed me like that and were so disrespectful to your own preacher."

"I'm sorry I embarrassed you," Dennis said. "I really am. I didn't think you young folk got embarrassed by stuff like that. I should have known better. You're an old soul in a young body. As to Peter, he knew what he was getting into when he came here. We're actually good friends and do respect each other a great deal. He's a good man. I've known him since he was just a boy. A real good man, and he is a blessing to this city. But I have to stir him up every once in a while."

"Just when I think I'm getting to know you," Kelsi teased.

"Now, you watch," Dennis said. "Mark my words. Peter was here first, but over the next few days there will be a parade of people, mostly older women, show up here with casseroles and pies and cakes and cookies. Some will bring Jell-O, and I'm not a big fan of that stuff. Some will bring macaroni salad, and I really don't like that. We may get a brisket, fried chicken, or who knows what."

"People really do that?" Kelsi asked.

Dennis gave her a surprised look. "Sure, they do. That's part of what makes a town a community. Looking out for each other."

"I got the impression you didn't have many friends anymore," Kelsi said.

"I don't. Not really. These people who'll come aren't people I'd go to a bar with or socialize with. Most will be younger than me. I think dirt is younger than me at this point. But they're good people. And bored. Helping other people gives them something to do and they'll feel good for doing it and we'll feel good that they did it, though I think you're beginning to really like cooking."

"I really am," Kelsi admitted.

"Well, we'll be eating gifted entrees for a while, but we'll need side dishes." He paused and studied the street. "I have to admit, I'm not so good with names, so you're going to be the buffer. You introduce yourself to them when they come and they'll tell you their name and I'll either remember it or learn it. Sound good?"

"Sounds like something George Castanza would have come up with on *Seinfeld*," Kelsi said.

"I knew you'd watch old TV reruns," Dennis said and grinned. "You promised me stories about your life. I'd like to hear one."

Before Kelsi could even think about what to tell him, they were interrupted by the Mexican lady from across the street who had greeted Kelsi the night of Dennis's fall. She came into the yard carrying a heavy plastic bag from Wal-Mart that she carried onto the front porch.

"Good morning, Marrah," Dennis said.

"*Buen día*," the woman replied. "You are doing well?"

"*Si señorita*," Dennis said.

"No *señorita*," Marrah said with a smile, pointing at the wedding ring on her finger. "I bring you tamales." She held up the bag.

"Real Mexican tamales?" Dennis asked.

"Of course," she answered.

"Did you hear that, Kelsi?" Dennis said, turning to her.

"I did," Kelsi confirmed, smiling at both the gift and his excitement.

"I shouldn't get up, Marrah," Dennis said. "First, it would hurt. But more importantly, you'd have to see my scrawny, wrinkled-up white butt in this gown. Will you give those to Kelsi? She'll take them inside."

Marrah gave the bag to Kelsi. It was heavy and Kelsi had to wonder just how many tamales were in there. She took it inside and put it in the refrigerator. When she got back to the porch, Marrah was already back in her own yard and disappeared into the house as Kelsi settled back onto the swing.

"She seems very nice," Kelsi said.

"Yes, she does."

"Again, I got the impression you didn't know or talk to your newer neighbors," she said.

"Tragedy brings people together," Dennis said. "And curiosity. Back there in Wyoming, would you have gone and checked on a neighbor after an ambulance hauled him away?"

Kelsi thought about it. "Probably not," she admitted. "I sure wouldn't have cooked for him."

Dennis just nodded his acceptance of her answer. "There's our first food delivery. Now, about your story. I know about your folks splitting up and why you had to keep moving. I want to hear about three good memories you have. Anything from birth until the day we met."

Chapter Twenty-Seven

"I was four years old," Kelsi said. "We were living in the Midwest. One of the states that begins with an I. Iowa, Illinois, Indiana ... I can't remember. It was spring. I didn't really know what spring was, but I knew it had been winter for a long time and the snow was finally gone and the trees had turned green. The sun was warm. I was barefoot and playing in the back yard. I had a playhouse. I think the people who lived there before left it behind. I remember it was faded from the sun. Plastic. Yellow with a green roof and pink door."

Kelsi paused and smiled. "It's funny the details you can remember. I didn't know I remembered those things. I just started talking and there they were."

"The mind is a funny thing," Dennis agreed. "Is that the memory? Playing in your little house after a long winter?"

"No," Kelsi said. "I was playing with my doll. I called her Bessy. We were baking pies for a tea party. You've eaten chicken pot pies?" She waited until Dennis nodded. "We ate a lot of those when I was growing up. They're cheap and easy to cook. Anyway, I had a couple of the little pot pie pans and had filled them with mud and sprinkled seeds from a mimosa tree seed pod on top of them for seasoning. They were in the oven of the little house. I had my little white plastic tea pitcher full of water from the faucet in the back yard and I had poured cups for me and Bessy and was talking to her when I heard my dad's voice."

Kelsi interrupted her story again. "I bet you were a great dad who played with your kids all the time," she said.

Dennis's face seemed to fall, to lose its smile and animation. His eyes clouded and he looked away from her for a long moment, then shook his head once and faced her. "I think it is a common failing of fathers that they get too focused on their jobs and earning enough money to keep the family's bills paid. They're tired, and they don't make the time to play with their kids like they should. Then they try desperately to make up for it with their grandchildren."

Kelsi listened and nodded. "Maybe," she agreed. "Maybe that's how it is for most dads. Did you play with your kids?"

Dennis sighed. "I can remember times we played together. Board games. Hop scotch. Trips to the zoo. I bet you didn't know Nokomis used to have a zoo, huh?" He paused and shook his head sadly. "But I remember most of the time coming home to a hot dinner and then falling into my recliner to read the newspaper and telling my girls I was too tired to play with them. I remember it well, and I regret each and every time."

He sounded sad, and that was not what Kelsi had intended. "I'm sorry," she said. "I didn't mean to make you feel bad. I was just drawing a contrast to my own dad. He never played with me. Never. But there he was, bent over and looking through the open window of the playhouse at me. I remember him smiling and how his eyes twinkled when he did.

"'What're you doin', Scamp?' he asked me. I told him about the tea party and mud pies. He asked if he could join us. 'You're too big,' I told him and I remember I laughed at the idea of him trying to come into the little playhouse. He said he could sit outside and I could serve him through the window, like it was a restaurant, except I was eating with him. 'The pies aren't done cooking,' I told him. 'Well, how long do I hafta wait?' he asked. I told him about five minutes. He agreed and sat down in the grass outside the house, looking in at me through the window. He asked for some tea. I only had two teacups left out of my set. I told him, 'Bessy isn't drinking hers. You can have it.' And I handed the cup through the window. It was so tiny in his big man-hand. He drank that tepid water and pretended it was the best tea he ever tasted. I took a sip of mine and laughed at how he was smacking his lips and saying how good it was."

Kelsi paused again, thinking, and Dennis took the opportunity to ask, "Didn't you say your father was ... well ... harsh and cheated on your mom often?"

"Yes," Kelsi said. "That's why this day stands out so much. I served him his mud pie and gave him a pink plastic plate. He pulled out his pocket knife and made a big show of cutting out a slice of pie from the first pie pan. He put one on his plate and one on mine and we pretended to eat and talked about how good it was. He asked me for my recipe and I told him it was dirt and water and magic beans on top. He stayed out there with me for quite a while, then said he had to go back inside and asked if I minded cleaning up and putting away the leftovers myself. Then he went in. I don't remember him ever playing with me like that again."

"That's a good story," Dennis said. "It obviously means a lot to you. Your recall of details is incredible. Thank you for sharing it. You still owe me two more."

"Are you going to tell me three stories next time?" Kelsi asked.

"You have to do three because you're so far behind," Dennis argued playfully. "Come on. Tell me another happy story."

"Fine," Kelsi gave in. "I was nine years old when this one happened. We didn't go on vacation very often. Maybe we weren't really on vacation then. It might have been while we were moving from one base to another. I don't know. But we were staying in a little cabin in the woods. I think it might have been Arkansas, but I'm not sure. It was hot and there were mountains covered in green trees. The cabins were made of logs and flat rocks and I thought they were really cool, like the *Little House* books a teacher had read to the class a year or so earlier. I had to leave the class before she read the whole series, but the cabin reminded me of what I thought the Ingalls' house would have looked like in the big woods in the first book."

"I bet it was a state park with cabins built by the WPA in the 1930s," Dennis said since Kelsi had paused again.

"Maybe," she said. "I don't know. I sure didn't care. Mom and Dad took me swimming in a creek. It was the first time I'd ever swum in a natural body of water. I remember it was warm and so clear I could see the bottom. It was covered in little rocks of all different colors and I thought it would hurt to walk on them, but mom said the rocks were worn smooth from the water and they didn't hurt my feet at all. But while we were there I met two other kids, Charlene and Greg. They were on vacation and lived in Tennessee. Greg was the same age as me and Charlene was a year younger. I started playing with them and Mom and Dad went away and sat on some rocks or something."

Kelsi looked at Dennis, who was watching her. His lips seemed dry. "We need some lemonade," she said.

"No, ma'am. Not right now," he said. "Go on."

"This story is so dumb," Kelsi said, but his look gave her no reprieve. "I didn't make a lot of friends," she said. "Remember your story about fourth grade and how you were the new kid from the farm? Well, imagine that happening almost every year you were in school. That was my life. I didn't make friends because I was always the new kid and nobody was going to like me, and even if they did, it was just a matter of time before I had to move again." She paused, thinking back. "But with Greg and Charlene, we were all just kids on vacation. We were all new kids. None of us lived there or would stay there, and that felt so good when I realized it and I was able to really play and bond with them even though we were only together for two days.

"This is the part where you're going to think I'm cheesing it," Kelsi said. "That last night we were there, the three of us were playing in the street that ran past all the cabins. I think we were catching fireflies. At one point, though, it was like time stopped. I could still see them and I could see the fireflies and hear the cicadas and I knew my dad was sitting on the porch drinking beer, but it was like everything had just frozen and in my mind I knew this was a memory I would keep forever and I had to imprint it there in all its detail."

She looked at Dennis to see if he was about to laugh at her, but his face was as serious as a stone. "I remember the trees. One of them behind Greg had a broken limb with dead leaves on it like it was winter for that one poor branch. Charlene was running and her hair — light brown and wavy — was flying out behind her and she had a huge smile on her face. Greg had a stick in his hand that he'd been using like Harry Potter's wand. There was the chittering of the cicadas and somewhere further away a crow cawed. I remember the softness of the twilight. It's all there like a frozen picture in my mind, but the weird part is just knowing at the time that it was a memory I would always look back on as a happy time. Does that make sense?"

"It does," he said. "I can't say anything like that has ever happened to me, but I've read books where it happens, so it isn't unbelievable. And you were right. You do still recall that as a happy memory."

"Yeah," she said, still turning over the details of the experience in her mind. "It's just always felt weird to me how it all seemed to stop."

"I'm getting tired," Dennis said. "Why don't you get us some lemonade, then tell me your third story before you help me get back to bed for a nap? I wish I could just nap right out there."

"I could tell you the other story later," Kelsi offered. "I don't want to keep you from your nap."

"The suspense is too much," Dennis said. "I'd never be able to close my eyes for wondering about the third story."

Kelsi stuck her tongue out at him quickly, then said, "You're a horrible old man." But she laughed and Dennis laughed with her. She went inside and poured two glasses of lemonade and brought them back outside. There was a woman on the porch and she was holding a Tupperware cake dish.

"This is Kelsi, my caretaker and my grandson's girlfriend," Dennis said as Kelsi came through the door. "Kelsi, this is Beverly Rhine, an old friend. She was the secretary back when I was a city commissioner. She brought us cake. Chocolate, I think."

Beverly Rhine appeared to be in her sixties, with gray-and-white hair and bright blue, lively eyes. She was wearing khaki shorts to just above her knees, sandals, and a lemon yellow blouse. She shifted the cake and offered a hand to Kelsi, who shook it. "Do you want me to put this inside?" she asked.

"I'll take it," Kelsi said. "You can sit down and visit if you want."

"I can't stay," Beverly said. "I watch my grandson during the days in summer and I just dropped him off at his piano lesson. I have to be back when it's over. The lesson is only an hour long. It was so nice to meet you, Kelsi. Dennis, you be more careful."

"If I'd known what it takes to get one of your cakes I would have broken a hip a long time ago," Dennis teased.

"Oh, you," Beverly said and laughed. She waved at them and left the porch. She'd driven up in a white Cadillac, which she now drove away in.

"Do you want some cake with your lemonade?" Kelsi asked.

"Oh, hell yeah," Dennis said, rubbing his hands together. "That woman knows how to bake. Make it a big piece."

Kelsi went inside and cut two slices from the round three-layer cake. It smelled incredibly fresh and the devil's food cake was fluffy and moist, with chocolate frosting that was like a cloud. Kelsi sneaked a lick off the butter knife she used to cut the cake and knew immediately that the frosting was not out of a can. She was in awe, and told Dennis that when she handed him his plate of cake.

"I told you," he said.

They ate and drank and Dennis didn't ask for her last story until he'd scraped the last stain of frosting from his plate and set it aside and licked his lips. He took a sip of lemonade and put his glass down. "Okay, Shahrazad," he said. "Continue with your tale."

"I know that name," Kelsi said.

"She was the smart one in *Arabian Nights*," Dennis said. "But you're going off on a tangent."

"You opened the tangent by calling me names," Kelsi argued.

He turned his head sideways and cocked an eyebrow at her. "I'm an old man in need of a nap and you're keeping me from it by not telling me your story."

"I don't know how Gloria put up with you," Kelsi said. "Fine. Last story. It maybe isn't such a happy one, but it's an important one in my life, which so far is much, much shorter than other people's on this porch, so don't blame me if it's boring."

"Nothing you've said has been boring yet," Dennis promised her.

"Okay, well, I was older," Kelsi said. "I was sixteen and Dad had been moved to Long Beach, California. It was the best place in the world as far as I was concerned. I absolutely fell in love with the beach. I was there all the time. I loved the warmth, the feel of the sand, the sound of the ocean, the smell of people's suntan lotion, the scream of the gulls, and how I was just one person in a crowd of strangers. Oh, I figured out that there were groups of regulars, but mostly it was tourists. I didn't bond with any of them. It wasn't like with Greg and Charlene. I lay on my big towel and was just one more nameless person on the beach."

Kelsi fought it, but she knew her face changed as the story changed. "One day, it was late evening, and Mom and Dad had been fighting again. I ran out of the apartment and went to the beach. It was deserted. It felt so strange to be there and be the only person on the beach. Like visiting a body in a funeral home. The sand was cool instead of warm. I could see people's footprints, like they had just been there, but now they were gone. The water didn't sound the same. It was loud. Booming, almost. The gulls were quiet. The only smell was the fishy smell of the water. The sun was gone, like it had drowned, and the sky at the horizon was the color of blood. It was eerie. How could this be the same place that during the day was so crowded with life that you couldn't walk a straight line more than a few steps without having to go around someone? Where did they all go? Why was nobody here in the evening?"

Kelsi stopped and shook her head. "Not a good memory, but another one that has stuck with me forever."

Dennis was looking at her and his eyes told her he knew. She looked away, but she was caught and she knew it even before he said it. "There's another reason you remember that evening, Kelsi. Tell me."

She shook her head. "I don't want to."

"I think it would do you some good," he argued.

She couldn't face him. She felt the first tear and she slashed at her cheek with an open palm to wipe it away. "None of them are happy stories," she said.

His hand, dry and papery, with skin so thin she could almost feel the blood coursing through the fingers, closed on her forearm as he reached across the small table between them. "Tell me," he urged softly. "You know about so many people I've lost. Life is hard and it isn't fair and sometimes too many bad things happen to people who don't deserve it. All we have is each other, the comfort one human can offer to another."

A sob broke from Kelsi's chest, but she still couldn't face him. "The mud pies," she said, and the tears came freely now. "When I went in the house after the tea party, Mom had a black eye. He'd hit her and then went outside and found me playing and joined in like he hadn't just hit my mom. His wife. I saw it and I got so mad and I threw myself at him, hitting him as hard and as fast as I could. He spanked me and sent me to my room. We had to move again after that. I guess he'd been caught with another woman."

Dennis's hand squeezed her. "And the kids at the cabins?"

Kelsi looked up at the ceiling of the porch. Her nose was stopped up and the tears were still coming. "When I went inside that night, Mom told me I couldn't play with those kids anymore. I asked her why and she said my father didn't want me to. She tried to stop me then, but I screamed at him and demanded to know why I couldn't play with my friends." She sniffled and lowered her face, but still couldn't look at Dennis. "He told me no kid of his was going to get mixed up with a couple of 'damn Jew brats.' That's what he called them. The best friends I had in all my childhood. I didn't even know what a Jew was. They left the next day, anyway, so I never had to tell them I couldn't play with them."

"And the beach?" Dennis prompted.

Kelsi was very still, remembering the sound of the surf smashing into the sand, the sucking as the water retreated. The blood in the sky and the eerie quiet between the waves rolling in. "Dad never loved me. Mom was already starting to drink and wasn't defending me like she used to. She didn't say she loved me anymore." She stopped.

Dennis's hand tightened on her wrist again. "Go on. You have to say it," he urged.

"I decided to walk out into the water and just keep walking until it sucked me under and pulled me out to sea and drowned me," Kelsi said. "I was so tired of moving, of starting over, of Dad yelling and hitting Mom and Mom drinking and never standing up for herself. Dad had ... he had started walking in on me when I was showering and I was scared of where that was going to go. So I was just going to let the ocean take me. I'd heard drowning wasn't a bad way to die, but what I liked was being pulled away from them, out to the open sea where nobody would ever find me." She finished in a whisper and then sat quietly.

When Dennis didn't say anything for a long while, she looked at him and found him watching her with tears running from his eyes. "So young," he said finally. "So young to have lived all of that pain. What kept you from doing it?"

"A ghost," Kelsi answered. "Most times, like with Gloria, all I see is kind of a ripple in the air. Maybe it has a human shape. Maybe not. That time, it was a full human woman with features I could see. She had a thin face with gray eyes and brown hair. She appeared between me and the water when I was close enough to feel the wet sand under my toes. She mouthed the word 'No' at me and pointed back the way I had come. I was surprised and confused. I couldn't walk through her. I mean, I could have, physically, but mentally I couldn't make myself do it. And I never even thought about going around her."

"So you went back?"

"Yeah," Kelsi said. "I went back and I told Mom about Dad coming into the bathroom. He'd left to go to a bar he liked. Mom told me to pack my clothes and anything else I wanted and could fit into one suitcase. She had a little bit of money hidden in an old salt shaker in the kitchen. She called a taxi and we went to the bus station and she bought tickets to the furthest place she could get to, which was Casper, Wyoming. She kept drinking and dating one man after another when we got there. I worked as a waitress and saved money until I met Tucker on a dating app and moved here."

Dennis patted her arm and withdrew his hand. "Do you feel better?" he asked.

Kelsi smiled. "I do," she said.

Dennis nodded. "The Catholics got it right with confession," he said. "It helps to tell somebody else."

"Was I confessing my sins?" Kelsi asked.

"No, Kelsi. You didn't sin. Unless it was holding all of that in and nursing it like a cancer, letting it eat at you," he said. "You feel better now, and I'll bet you the rest of that cake that you'll keep feeling better because now we're sharing the burden of what happened to you."

Kelsi laughed a little. "For a high school drop-out, you're pretty damn smart."

"I'm glad we can agree on that," he said. "Now help me get out of this chair and back to my bed, and I would prefer if you do it without marveling at my bare ass in this stupid gown. Tomorrow I'm at least putting on pajamas. For your next story, I want to hear more about the ghosts. When you started seeing them and what you've learned from them."

Chapter Twenty-Eight

O ver the course of the next three days, eleven women appeared on the front porch with covered dishes. They were all late middle-aged to elderly and knew Dennis either from his work on some committee or they were friends of Gloria who said they felt a sense of responsibility to look after the man she'd left behind.

"When she died, poor dear, Dennis didn't even know how to start his clothes washer," said Ida Showalter, a lifelong homemaker and wife of a retired banker as she sat with Dennis and Kelsi in the living room, all of them drinking lemonade.

"I've come a long way since then," Dennis said, taking the ribbing with good humor. "Thanks to your teaching, I know how to pick the best rocks to clean my laundry."

"He's just awful," Ida said. "I don't know how Gloria put up with him all those years."

"She probably went out and got the cancer just to get away from me," Dennis said. Kelsi was a little shocked by the joke, but their visitor took it in stride and laughed him off.

Lenora Allred proclaimed later on the same day, "Would you believe, the man had never made a grocery list?"

"Really? Never?" Kelsi asked, feigning shock as she looked at Dennis, who only shrugged guiltily.

So it went with every female visitor talking about some mundane task they'd had to help Dennis with after his wife's death. He never contradicted or corrected any of them, but would join in with self-deprecatory jokes, then thank them for coming, for the food item they had brought, and implore them not to be strangers.

Some men came, too, and they talked about changes in the city, politics at every level, and caught Dennis up on their family lives. He told them about his daughter and son-in-law working in Kansas for a while and bragged about Tucker's position at the sheet metal company. He also introduced Kelsi to all of them and boasted about her skills with both a bedpan and a saucepan.

"I've only mixed them up once and he never noticed," Kelsi said, joining in with the jokes.

On the fourth day, Dennis insisted Kelsi take him to the park to sit under the shade of Woody before the day became too hot to be outside. She helped him into a charcoal gray pair of linen pants and a dark yellow button-down shirt with some loafers, and, with him using his walker, they made their way out to her car and she drove to the park.

"You're a fantastic caretaker," Dennis said, "But I'm damn glad to be out of that house for a while."

"I can't blame you there. It's early summer and you should be outside more. Sitting in a lawn chair watching me pull weeds out of the flowerbed shouldn't be the highlight of your morning," Kelsi said.

"It gets my feet in the grass and the sun on my skin," Dennis said. "And you're getting really good in the garden. You look right at home in there with your new sunhat. Gloria would have approved of that floppy thing."

Kelsi laughed. "I'm glad. When I saw it at Wal-Mart I thought it looked like something she would have worn."

Dennis sighed, then chuckled softly. "It's almost like you knew her," he said.

Kelsi parked the car and helped Dennis get out. The park, not being one of the major ones in the city's system, didn't have a dedicated parking lot. Visitors parked along the street, which meant Dennis had to navigate getting over a curb. He did it, though not without a groan, and pushed his walker along through grass that needed to be mowed while Kelsi hovered beside him, carrying the folding lawn chairs. Dennis moved slower as they progressed and by the time they were under the shade of the tree he was clinging to the handles of his walker to hold himself up and sweat was beaded on his bald head.

"Oh my gosh. Just a second," Kelsi said. She quickly tossed open one of the folding chairs and helped Dennis sink into it She unslung her backpack and pulled out a chilled water bottle and opened it for him. Dennis took a big drink, sighed, took another drink and nodded.

"Thank you," he said. "That was harder than I thought it would be."

"You have to work back up to it," Kelsi said. "You've got a brand new hip and that's a big thing. This is the furthest you've walked since you got those new parts."

"Yeah, yeah," he said, still catching his breath. He pulled a white handkerchief from a pocket of his pants and dabbed at the perspiration on his head and neck.

Kelsi opened the second lawn chair and put it beside Dennis. She laid a hand on his shoulder and said, "I'm going to take a short walk and leave you alone for a few minutes." She moved away, trailing her fingers over the mottled trunk of Woody, then went to the sidewalk and walked slowly along, looking at the other trees and trying to remember which ones Dennis had said were planted at the same time as Woody. Across from the drainage ditch that ran through the north part of the park she saw a large clump of shrubbery and paused.

Dennis and Gloria had made love for the first time inside a ring of shrubs in this park. She glanced back and saw that Dennis was sitting still, his head tilted back and it looked like his eyes were closed. Kelsi left the sidewalk, scurried through the ditch and was behind the shrubs and out of sight of Dennis. On the north side, facing the hill that went up to meet the back fences of the neighborhood, there was a place where limbs had been consistently broken or pushed aside to allow entry into the ring. Kelsi pushed through and came to an open space about five feet in diameter.

The ground was littered with beer and soda cans, a couple of empty pint-size whiskey bottles, and a lot of burned down cigarette butts. Kelsi nudged some butts out of the way with her foot and sat down on the soft green grass.

"Right here," she whispered. She put her hands palm down on the tops of the grass and moved them back and forth, letting the blades tickle her skin. "What was it like to be with someone you love for the first time?"

Her own first had been shortly after her seventeenth birthday. His name was Dakota Shepherd, also seventeen. They had dated a couple of times and he was already pushing hard to do more than just kiss. They'd gone to a well-known make-out point on their third date. She got into the backseat of his crossover SUV willingly enough and they started kissing. She didn't protest when he popped her bra open and put a hand up her shirt. She tried to stop him when he moved the hand and pushed it into her shorts and underwear. When he touched her, she was wet and it did feel good, but she didn't want to go further.

"Your body is saying yes," Dakota argued, then he pushed a finger into her. "You're seventeen. Probably the oldest virgin in school. It's time."

And so it went, cramped in the backseat of a Ford Escape. It took maybe two minutes, but at least he'd had a condom. He'd known what he was going to do when he picked her up. She hadn't had any particular feelings for him before, but afterward, she broke up with him. He told his friends she was an easy lay and several other guys asked her for sexual favors. Not even dates. Just blowjobs in parking lots or quickies in school bathrooms. A few asked her out, and she went with some, but when they made their intentions known in the first twenty minutes, she ended the date. She hadn't had sex again until she was eighteen and even then she hadn't wanted it so much as just wanted to know if it could be any better than it had been that first time. It had been better, but she still wanted to experience it with an emotional connection.

Tucker?

There had been times she thought there was a real connection. Her head told her it was fine. He was a good person with a good job and good parents, but her heart knew the truth.

The truth.

She had never fully admitted it to herself before. She liked Tucker, but she didn't love him. She let it sink in. Then asked herself, "What do I do now?" She couldn't face that at the moment. She pushed herself to her feet and slipped out of the ring of bushes. She went around it and checked on Dennis. He was sitting in his chair, his hand on the armrest of the empty chair. Kelsi paused and studied the chair, trying to determine if the spirit of Gloria was there with her husband. She didn't see any shimmering in the air to indicate a ghostly presence. Slipping through the ditch, she returned to the sidewalk and made her way back to her patient.

"How are you doing?" Kelsi asked.

"I'm fine," Dennis said. He grinned at her. "There's no trace of what we did left in there. But I guess you know that now."

"You'd be surprised what I found in there," Kelsi said.

Dennis gave her a quizzical look but didn't ask anything more.

"Did she visit?" Kelsi asked.

"No, not today," he said. "I imagine she's busy on the other side. She can't come here every time I come to visit."

"You know she was with you in the hospital, right?" Kelsi asked.

He nodded slowly. "I thought so," he said.

"Do you think she'd mind if I sat in her chair?" Kelsi asked.

"I think she'd be okay with that." Dennis nodded toward the chair and withdrew his hand to his own armrest.

Kelsi settled into the chair and asked, "Was Woody's bark always falling off like that?"

"No, it was all brown when we planted him," Dennis said. "The brown flakes off as the sycamore grows. Eventually he'll be all bone white."

"That'll be pretty," Kelsi said.

"In winter he'll look even more like a skeleton," Dennis teased.

"That's morbid," Kelsi told him.

"I want to ask you for a favor," Dennis said. He fixed her with his eyes, waiting for her reaction.

"Of course. Anything," Kelsi said, meeting his gaze.

He smiled. "Careful with that," he said. He took a deep breath, held it for a second, then exhaled. "The next time we're getting a good, soaking rain, I want you to bring me here and help me spread Gloria's ashes around the roots of this tree. It's what she wanted. Natalie is against it. She thinks the ashes are some kind of holy relic that are supposed to be saved. That isn't what Gloria wanted. She wanted her ashes to nourish the earth for our tree. It's what I want for my own, too."

Kelsi held his gaze, but she wanted to look away and think about what he was asking. "Why in the rain?"

"So the ashes will start soaking in immediately," Dennis said.

Kelsi nodded. "I see. Natalie will be mad, won't she?"

"Yes. She'll fight you on my ashes, but I'm going to put it in my will that I want it done, and I want you to do it," Dennis said. "It'll be vague. Just saying I'm leaving my mortal remains to you and you know how to dispose of them. Will you do it?"

Natalie would be a formidable enemy. Kelsi knew it. But it was only fair that Dennis and Gloria get what they wanted. "Yes," she said. "I'll do it. But you have to tell me the rest of your story. I want to know about her leaving you. I want to know about her coming back. About the children, them growing up. And I want to know about Gloria when she was sick and how you dealt with her passing."

Dennis reached out and gripped her wrist in his big, dry hand and squeezed. "Thank you," he said. "I should have spread her ashes a long time ago. I was torn between what she wanted and making my daughter happy. As to your conditions ... yes, I'll tell you. I want to tell you."

He stopped talking and looked up into the leafy branches of the sycamore tree. Kelsi thought he was simply promising to tell her at some future date, that he wasn't going to pick up the thread of his autobiography right then. She was wrong.

"I became a drunk," Dennis said.

Chapter Twenty-Nine

The smell of cigarettes, stale beer, sweaty men, and desperate failure filled the empty spaces in the little bar on a spring evening in 1959. It was a place where men came to get away from wives, jobs, girlfriends, bill collectors, and anything else that made life harder for them. They sat at the bar, at the small tables, or gathered around the two pool tables, all with a glass or mug or bottle in hand and talked about what was holding them back.

Dennis sat alone in a corner under a dim, greasy lightbulb in a dirty fixture hanging from the ceiling. In front of him was half of a bottle of cheap whiskey and an empty glass. He stared at nothing, his eyes glazed with sorrow, fear, and alcohol. Bits and snatches of conversation flowed past him as if he was a stone sunk in the bed of a river.

"She's been busting my balls harder than usual ..."

"That motherfucker thought I stole his calipers ..."

"Cindy's on the rag and Marge's husband is home for the weekend ..."

"I can't pay it. I just don't have the money. We got the final notice ..."

"Six ball, corner pocket."

"... promoted that sonofabitchin' Wainscot over me, a white man ..."

"Nobody 'round here's gonna vote for a fuckin' Catholic, I can tell ya that ..."

Dennis filled his glass and drank it in two quick gulps. The voices bubbled down like a potion in a witch's cauldron for a few minutes and he heard no individual words or phrases. He sat with his eyes closed, but that brought back visions of Gloria, her face covered in sweat and tears, her hair matted and plastered to her head as she lay in the hospital bed. He'd turned away from her even as she reached for him. He walked out of the hospital, through the rain, to this bar near an elevated railroad bridge on Maine Street.

Here he sat, waiting and drinking. Eventually, his wait was rewarded. Jeff Washburn came in and pushed between two other men at the bar and ordered a beer. Dennis watched him, and when Jeff's roving eye passed over him, Dennis waved him over. Jeff waved back and came to the table carrying his bottle of beer. He had a smile on his face, but it fell away when he saw Dennis's expression.

"They said you called in sick today," Jeff said as he sat down. "You're not looking good."

"I'm not sick," Dennis said. "Remember what you told me a couple of years ago when my wife miscarried?"

Jeff only looked at him, not comprehending. He finally shook his head.

"You said your brother is a doctor and he told you women can control that," Dennis said. "That if they don't want a baby, they can make their bodies kill it."

"Oh. Yeah," Jeff said, nodding, then taking a pull from his beer. "But that's my cousin's husband's brother. Teddy." He nodded again. "Yeah, he's a doctor."

"And he said that?" Dennis asked.

"Well, yeah, I don't remember his exact words, but he said something like that," Jeff confirmed. "Why?"

"Gloria did it to me again," Dennis said. "She miscarried today."

"Oh, Jesus, Dennis, I'm sorry," Jeff said. "Listen, I'm not sure I heard Teddy right. I wouldn't put a lot of stock in that. Ask your wife's doctor."

"No. I believe it. That bastard Devlin Shockley is behind it," Dennis said. "I think she's in love with him. She regrets marrying me and wishes she was with him. That's why she keeps losing our babies. She doesn't want to have a baby with me. But oh boy, if I was Devlin Shockley, the football star, it'd be different."

"Dennis, man, have you drunk all of that bottle?" Jeff asked.

"I'm not finished with it," Dennis said and poured another glass and slurped it down.

"That's a lot of whiskey," Jeff said.

"Not enough," Dennis said.

"Shockley's not a football star anymore," Jeff argued. "He's just a guy selling record players and televisions downtown."

"Gloria bought a new record player two weeks ago," Dennis said. "She said it was so the baby could hear classical music and grow up smarter." He paused, his hand on the bottle, his eyes on his co-worker. "We have a fuckin' radio, Jeff. We didn't need a record player. I'm not made outta money. But she had to go buy a record player from Devlin Shockley." Dennis poured and drank. "I should go beat his ass."

"He's still a big guy," Jeff said. "Where is Gloria?"

"I left her at the hospital. Saint Mary's," Dennis said.

"She miscarried and you left her at the hospital?" Jeff asked. "Dennis, that ain't like you. You love that woman."

"Not if she's gonna kill our babies," he slurred. The bar seemed hot and crowded. He was having trouble focusing on the man across the table from him. "I should go back to my car and go home."

"You're not driving, Dennis," Jeff said. "Come home with me tonight. I've got a good couch. Sleep it off. This will all seem different tomorrow."

Dennis poured another glass of whiskey. The bottle was almost empty. He tipped it up over his mouth and let the last quarter inch run out, but it missed his mouth and ran down his cheek and chin. He swallowed and put the bottle down. "She doesn't love me," he said, then threw back the glass, swallowed, grimaced, and missed the table when he tried to put the glass down. It hit the wooden floor and rolled away. Dennis didn't realize he was sobbing, or that his friend had pulled him to his feet and was guiding him through the crowded bar to the door while everyone stopped what they were doing to watch. He just kept wailing, "She doesn't love me. She won't give me babies."

When he awoke the next morning, his head throbbed, his body ached, and his tongue felt as thick as a bull buffalo's. He stared up at an unfamiliar ceiling and breathed in the unknown scent of an alien home. He didn't know where he was or how he'd gotten here. He was on a sofa, though, and he tried to sit up, but the swirling in his head threatened to reach down into his guts like the funnel of a tornado and wreak just as much havoc. He fell back onto the pillow and closed his eyes, focusing very hard on not vomiting. He slept again.

The next time he woke up it was to the smell of fresh, hot coffee, the feel of someone poking his bicep, and a man's voice asking if he was ready to wake up. Dennis forced his eyes open and looked into the face of Jeff Washburn, the operator of the drill press next to him at the factory. "Jeff?" he tried to ask, his voice as thick as molasses in his dry throat.

"You really put it away last night," Jeff said. "Sit up. I brought coffee. I called McEwan and said you wouldn't be at work. I told him about the miscarriage. I hope that's okay. You know how they are about missing days."

The miscarriage. It all came flooding back on him. Dennis swallowed coffee and it was like choking down all the grief again. Gloria didn't love him. She killed their baby because she wanted to be with Devlin Shockley. She thought he was a better man than her husband.

"Why would she do it?" Dennis asked. Tears ran down his face as he sat on the sofa with a cup of coffee in his hands. "I've always loved her. I've given her everything. I'd die for her. Why would she kill our babies?"

Jeff shook his head. "I don't know, Dennis. Nobody really understands women."

"The first time, I thought maybe it was an accident," Dennis said. "We were younger. We didn't know anything. But now she knows."

A woman in a thick blue bathrobe stepped into the living room from the kitchen. Despite the robe and curlers, Dennis recognized her as Lily, Jeff's wife. She had a spatula in one hand and both hands were on her hips. She pointed the spatula like a gun at her husband. "Are you repeating the lies that idiot Teddy Hoops told you about women being able to end their pregnancies?" she demanded.

Jeff visibly shrank back, but his voice was strong. "He's a doctor. He knows more than we do about it," he said.

"The man is a veterinarian and a religious nut," Lily snapped back, slapping the spatula hard against her thigh. She didn't flinch. "Maybe a horse can end its pregnancy, but a human woman can't simply decide to kill a baby growing in her belly. Think about how few bastards there'd be in the world if we could do that."

Both men were silent.

"I'm going to make breakfast," Lily said. "Then you're taking Dennis back to his car." She pointed her kitchen weapon at Dennis. "And you better get back to that hospital and apologize to Gloria and tell her you're an idiot and lucky to have her." She spun around and disappeared into the kitchen, leaving the men in shocked silence.

"I'm sorry," Jeff whispered. "She doesn't always remember her place."

Dennis stared into the black depths of his coffee. "Her place," he repeated. What was Gloria's place? How would he react if she had an outburst like the one Lily had just performed? Dennis considered. Gloria would never do something like that unless she was sure she was right. Was it her duty to remain silent, like Jeff clearly expected of his wife? Dennis asked himself if that's what he wanted. It wasn't. He wasn't totally convinced that Lily was right and Jeff — or his veterinarian friend — was wrong, but suddenly Dennis wanted to be with his wife.

"I have to go," he said. He looked up and faced Jeff. "I have to go. Will you take me now?"

"Without breakfast? No," Jeff said. "We both need it. Then I'll see if I can find you a toothbrush. Your breath would kill a skunk."

Dennis allowed himself to be led to the table in the kitchen and he fought his stomach's revulsion and managed to eat a little bit of scrambled eggs, a crispy piece of bacon, and a piece of toast. There was no extra toothbrush, but he used some mouthwash and was waiting in Jeff's pickup when his friend finally came out of the house with his lunchbox for work.

Back at the bar, Dennis jumped into his old Ford and flew back to St. Mary's Hospital. Gloria was gone. A nurse said her father had picked her up earlier that morning.

Dennis drove home as fast as he could. As soon as he entered the house, he felt her absence. In their bedroom, he found all of her clothes gone, the quilt her grandmother had made them was gone from the bed. Her jewelry, makeup, perfumes, even the big green cooking pot that had been handed down from several generations back in her family were all gone.

Dennis dropped to his knees in their living room, wailing and pounding his fists into his torso.

Chapter Thirty

K elsi sat very still. The morning had worn away into afternoon and they had moved their chairs to follow the shade of the sycamore as Dennis told his story. She thought he would go on, but he seemed to be stuck at that point where he collapsed in the living room, crying over the loss of his wife.

"She came back," Kelsi prompted.

Dennis seemed to pull himself back from a faraway place and Kelsi saw his eyes refocus on her and the present moment. "Mmm. She came back," he said. "It was about six months later. Her mom and dad wouldn't let me talk to her when I called or showed up at their house. Her dad stood in the doorway with a hunting rifle and told me not to come back. He said that if Gloria ever wanted to talk to me again, she would let me know."

"Oh, wow," Kelsi said. "A rifle?"

Dennis nodded. "I don't blame him. I became a drunk," he said. "I lost my job. This was after the feed store but before I went to vo-tech to learn to be an electrician. I was unskilled labor in a machine shop, drilling holes in parts. I just quit going to work. I stayed home, with the lights off, and drank. At first it was because I wanted the dark, and then it was because the power company cut me off. I burned through all of our savings just to hold on to the house and buy my alcohol. I was guzzling the cheapest, nastiest stuff you can imagine just to get numb and not feel anything."

"But she came back," Kelsi insisted.

Dennis smiled at her. "You're in such a hurry for the happy ending, Pollyanna" he said. "You know, it's more common that there isn't a happy ending."

"Yeah, yeah. I know," Kelsi said. "But in your case there was. Tell me!"

"I ran out of money in February of 1960," Dennis said. "I was going to bars and begging for drinks. Hanging around outside of liquor stores begging for change. I started getting letters from the bank about foreclosure and eviction. Gloria still wouldn't talk to me. I didn't go to her house anymore and the phone had been turned off a long time before."

"You're slow-playing me, Dennis," Kelsi teased.

"No," he protested. "I'm making sure you understand just how far I fell. I was one of those people you see begging on the streets. Unwashed. Unemployed. Dirty clothes. Most people considered me hopeless. My friends had all abandoned me. I was alone all the time, even when I was successful in getting someone to buy me a drink at a bar. They didn't sit with me. They gave me the drink to make me go away."

Kelsi studied the man sitting next to her. It dawned on her that there was no alcohol in his house. She hadn't thought much of it before. No wine. Not even a six-pack of beer to drink while watching a game on the television. There hadn't been any when she moved in and he had never asked her to put it on a grocery list.

"You don't drink anymore," she said.

Dennis smiled and nodded. "That's true."

"You're just creating more suspense," Kelsi said.

"On the one hand, I feel so much shame over the fact I got so desperate I found myself standing in the parking lot of the First Methodist Church asking people for money as they were leaving morning service," Dennis said. "And yet, there I was, and that's where things turned around for me. Or started to." He paused again and Kelsi was about to prod him on when he pulled himself out of another reverie and winked at her. "I know. Keep going. Someone reported me to the minister. Not the one you met. This was ... at least four ministers back. Reverend Charles Freely. He was an older man. Not as old as I am now, but he was probably close to seventy. He was tall and straight and bald as an egg." He grinned and reached up to rub his own bald head. "His head was shiny and I thought that was funny at the time."

"No way you found religion and it saved you," Kelsi said. "That isn't you."

Dennis shrugged. "Yes and no. What I found was kindness. And wisdom. I found them in a church and I hadn't found them anywhere else," he said. "Keep in mind, Gloria and I had been regulars at the Baptist church she'd grown up in. None of those people tried to help me. I wasn't hard to find. I begged on every corner until the police moved me or took me to the drunk tank. But Chuck Freely came out to the parking lot of his church and shook my hand and asked me to come inside with him. I told him I didn't want to hear any sermon. He just smiled and said he'd already delivered his sermon and was about to eat some lunch and wondered if I'd like to break bread with him. That's what he called it, breaking bread." He smiled at the memory.

"What'd you have to eat?" Kelsi asked.

"Sandwiches," Dennis answered. "Roast beef. I remember him telling me someone in his congregation had given him the roast. And he was glad to share it. I was hungry, but mostly I just wanted to get drunk. I remember eating and wondering if Methodists did communion and if there was any wine in the place. Would he give me any money I could spent on whiskey? I was in a bad way. I think he knew it, too. Knew what I was thinking. He kept me talking. He asked if I'd always lived in Nokomis and I told him about the farm. He asked about my family and I told him about my dad, my mom, and my brother and sister. He asked if I was married, and I remember I was quiet for a long time before I nodded my head. Then he got the whole story out of me. I thought it would make him feel bad for me and he'd give me money or wine, so I told him the whole thing."

"He didn't, though, did he?" Kelsi asked.

"Of course not," Dennis said and laughed. "Later, he might have wished he had, but no, he didn't. He excused himself and went to another room. When he came back he said he'd asked a friend to come talk to me. I thought this is where they're going to start pushing me to join their church. 'Hold on,' I said. 'I'm already a Baptist.' He just laughed at me and said that was fine. Well, I recognized the man as soon as he came in."

Dennis paused and Kelsi knew he did it for dramatic effect. She tried very hard not to get frustrated, but finally she couldn't hold it in. "My God, you're awful," she said. "Tell me!"

"He was the doctor who'd been at the hospital when I took Gloria in that day," Dennis said. "He was kind of a young guy. Not much older than I was at the time, and he listened while Reverend Freely told him my story, including what Jeff had told me about women choosing to end their pregnancies. The doctor — I can't remember his name — he looked at me like I had just walked out of the Middle Ages and he went on a rant about how ignorant most people are about birth and delivery. He had to apologize to the minister several times while telling me what a fool I was. Then he explained to me in terms I couldn't comprehend even if I hadn't been consumed by the need for a drink, about fertilization, gestation, and birth.

"I looked at him and asked, 'So, Gloria didn't decide she didn't want to have a baby with me?' I thought the man's head was going to explode. 'She may well have decided she didn't want to have a fool's baby, but she didn't concentrate all her mental powers and kill the baby in her womb like you seem to think,' he said."

Kelsi laughed. "What did you say to that?"

Dennis chuckled. "I asked him if he was sure."

"No!"

"I did," Dennis confirmed. "I'd held on to that belief for a long time."

"Did his head explode?" Kelsi asked.

"I really thought he might hit me then," Dennis said. "But Reverend Freely spoke up and assured me the doctor never lied, especially about medical stuff."

"And you believed him?" Kelsi prompted.

Dennis nodded very slowly. "I'd wanted to believe something like that for a long time, I guess. But there was nowhere to go to learn that kind of information. I couldn't just google it in 1960, and I didn't know any real doctors to ask." He paused, then said, "I broke down. I cried and cried and called myself a lot of names that probably shouldn't be said in church. I remember the minister thanking the doctor and the doctor leaving. I couldn't stop crying. I fell on the floor and just kept crying because I'd run her off by being so stupid."

"So he called her?" Kelsi asked, trying to guess the ending.

"Fortunately, no," Dennis said. "I wasn't ready. I promised Chuck Freely that I would never touch a drop of alcohol if he would help me. I told him I'd convert and become a Methodist. I'd do anything he wanted if he would help me get her back." Dennis stopped and pointed up into the tree. "Your squirrel is up there, probably wanting you to take his photograph again."

Kelsi looked up and saw the little brown animal about thirty feet above them, poised on a limb, looking down at them, flicking his tail from side to side. "I think he's waiting for the rest of the story," Kelsi said.

Dennis laughed a deep belly laugh. "Nokomis was — and in many ways still is — a town where knowing the right people can get you anything. Chuck Freely was well connected. He got the bank to back off. He got me a job as a janitor in one of the office buildings downtown. He gave and gave of his time. I stopped drinking. Went from Wild Turkey to cold turkey is how I always told the story. But I still had dark moments where I knew I'd never get my wife or my life back. But Reverend Freely was always there for me. And then, yes, Miss Impatient, he called Gloria."

"Finally!" Kelsi said.

"I found out later he'd been in contact with her from the day I showed up in his parking lot," Dennis said.

"So, he arranged a meeting?" Kelsi asked.

"Oh no," Dennis said with a laugh. "She wasn't going to be caught that easy. She told him that if I really loved her, I would know where and when to meet her."

"Obviously, that was right here," Kelsi said.

"Obviously," Dennis agreed. "But when? That's what had me stumped. Finally, Chuck pulled out an almanac and the answer became clear. Can you guess it?"

"Your wedding anniversary?" Kelsi asked.

"No. Thank God, no. I didn't have to wait that long. It was April 29, 1960. Arbor Day," he said.

"The anniversary of you planting Woody," Kelsi almost squealed.

"Yes," Dennis said quietly, his eyes drifting to the base of the tree. "I was sitting right there from just after sunup until I saw her cross the street." He pointed back to where Kelsi's car was parked. "She was something else. I don't know if she had it down to the minute, but it was damned close to the very time of morning we planted this tree. Well, I started crying as soon as I saw her. I hadn't seen her in over six months, and then, there she was." He traced the path she'd walked with his pointing finger until it came back to the tree. "I stood up when I saw her, but I didn't go to her. Maybe I was afraid I'd scare her away. Maybe I didn't trust my legs to walk. I just stood here and she came to me and stood right in front of me."

Kelsi felt the emotion closing her throat as she imagined the young Dennis and Gloria of the pictures in the house coming together after such a long absence. "Tell me you grabbed her and kissed her," she said.

Dennis shook his head. "No. I didn't dare. I didn't dare touch her after how I'd hurt her. I raised my hands like I was going to put them on her arms, but then I dropped them. I told her I was sorry. I told her how stupid I was. I told her about Reverend Freely and his doctor friend and was trying to repeat stuff about gestation when she reached up and put a finger over my lips."

"She kissed you?" Kelsi asked, picturing them standing feet away from where she sat.

"She asked if I trusted her," Dennis said. "I told her I did. She told me that if I ever had any question about anything, that I better come to her first and that if I ever hurt her like that again, I would never see her after that."

"I love that woman," Kelsi said, wiping at her eyes. "I love how sassy and independent she was. I wish I could have met her."

"I do, too," Dennis said. He gave Kelsi a mischievous look. "And then she let me kiss her."

"Fuckin' finally!" Kelsi said, then popped a hand over her mouth. "Sorry," she said.

Dennis laughed for a long time, even wiping at his own eyes before he got himself under control. "I wish I could say believing she could pinch off a pregnancy as easy as taking a crap was the last dumb thing I ever did, but of course it wasn't. But I never doubted her and we always talked about anything we needed to. Maybe not immediately, but we did."

"Did she move back in right away?" Kelsi asked.

"She did. And she got right to work sorting out the financial mess I had made. Since I had promised to become a Methodist, she left her parents' Baptist church and we became Methodists. Chuck Freely soon got tired of me questioning all of his sermons and told me I should go to seminary if I wanted deeper answers than he could provide. But I just read a lot instead."

"Thank you for telling me all of this," Kelsi said.

"It's just the story of two people's lives," Dennis said. "Not two significant people. We didn't change history in any way. We were just regular people." He paused, then asked, "Will you help me get my shoes on? I'm feeling kind of stiff and it's hot. I think I'll take a nap. All this talking has made me tired."

Kelsi knelt before him and slipped on his right shoe. She was putting the left one on when she felt a feathery touch on the side of her face. She flinched away and looked up at Dennis, thinking he had touched her and that it was really inappropriate, but he was looking over her head and his hands were on the armrests of his chair.

"Yes, she is," he said.

Kelsi twisted around and there, beside her, was the shimmery outline of a human figure. She couldn't make out any details, but it was obvious to her that Gloria had come to visit at last. It was the closest Kelsi had ever been to one of the apparitions she sometimes saw. She didn't know what to do, but she slowly reached out a hand toward the vague distortion in the air. There was a moment of cold, and then the shape was gone. Still kneeling, with her hand in the space the ghost had occupied, Kelsi asked, "What did she say?"

Dennis had tears cascading down his cheeks and his eyes stayed where his wife had just been. "She said you're just like she used to be." He blinked and more tears fell. "Let's go home."

Chapter Thirty-One

Days went by. At least once every day Natalie called to check on her father, as she had since she'd left to return to Kansas. Sometimes she called Dennis's phone, other times she called Kelsi's. The conversations were never long. Both Kelsi and Dennis reported that his progress was going well, he was up, he was walking, he was doing more and more on his own. Yes, he was eating and drinking plenty of water. He read a lot and sat on the porch or in the yard with his bare feet in the grass while Kelsi worked in the garden. In one call, Natalie seemed eager to talk to Kelsi.

"I'm not on speaker, am I?" Natalie asked. "He's still asleep?"

"I think so. I'm in my room. Do you want me to go check on him?" Kelsi asked.

"No, I just want to be sure he won't hear. I'm not on speaker? You know how sound travels through the air vents in that house," Natalie said.

"Umm, yeah," Kelsi said, remembering Dennis commenting on her lovemaking with Tucker.

"Well, I just want to thank you," Natalie said. "Dad sounds amazing. I don't mean just mending after the accident. I don't want to say he was depressed before, but he was ... listless sometimes. Does that make sense? Just like he didn't have much purpose. But with you there, he sounds happy. Even though he can't garden or work in his shop or go see that silly tree, he —"

"We go to the tree," Kelsi interrupted.

"You're kidding?" Natalie said.

"No," Kelsi said. "He struggles walking through the grass, so we go slow. I think he's getting better. Then we get there and sit for quite a while, until he's ready to push through back to the car. We go early or late, when it isn't too hot."

Natalie sighed, then gave a soft laugh. "I should have known he wouldn't give that up," she said. "He claims he talks to her there. Did you know that? Does he talk?"

"I know," Kelsi admitted hesitantly. "I haven't noticed him talking to anyone." It was a small lie, and she didn't like it, but she felt she was protecting Dennis's privacy. "The walk from the car to the tree is the longest walk he makes, and the walker doesn't move through the grass all that well, so it's a workout for him, but I think it's good for him."

"Probably so," Natalie agreed. "I tell you, as a girl, Mom and Dad took me to that park all the time in the evenings after Dad got home from work. They'd sit on a blanket under the tree, or one would sit and the other would lay there with their head in the other's lap. I thought it was so embarrassing."

"Do you still think that?" Kelsi asked curiously.

There was a long moment before Natalie answered. "No, I don't. In fact, I'm a little jealous."

"Me, too," Kelsi said, then remembered she was talking to her boyfriend's mother.

Natalie only laughed softly, then said, "Thank you, Kelsi. You've really been a blessing. I'll suggest to Tucker that you might like to have a picnic in the park."

"No, don't do that. Please," Kelsi said. "If he doesn't think of it himself, I don't ... Well, I want it to be his idea."

"I understand," Natalie said after another pause. "In that case, don't hold your breath. He's a good boy. Well, a good man now. But they don't mature very quickly, and it seems each generation takes longer to mature and develop empathy."

The conversation ended, and Kelsi lay on her bed — Natalie's old bed — and thought about Tucker. At first, when she'd moved in with Dennis, Tucker came over every evening and they sat on the porch swing or on the sofa and watched movies on DVD, or they played board games with Dennis. Then he skipped a night, calling on the phone to say he was tired from work. A couple of nights later he was having a video game night with friends. She hadn't seen him in three days now. So far today, all she'd had were a few text messages. The last one had been hours ago.

For the first time, Kelsi wondered if he was seeing someone else. The thought surprised her, but she was equally surprised to realize she hadn't considered that option earlier, and that the idea didn't bother her all that much. Before Dennis's accident, she would have been devastated. She would have questioned whether she should stay in this city, or this state, or finish her degree.

She punched in a quick text message to Tucker.

Whatcha doin'?

Kelsi searched her heart, wondering if she missed Tucker. She had fun with Dennis. They played games. He was teaching her poker and they played the classic board games that looked like he'd owned them since at least the 1970s. They often read together. Gloria had a collection of very steamy romances mixed in with her books about the American frontier. Plus the cooking, cleaning, gardening, and helping Dennis with the tasks he still struggled with. She was always occupied with something.

Watching the Royals game and eating tacos
You?

Nothing. Just lying here.

Coming over?

Kelsi thought about it. She did want to go. She wanted to get out and do something. But Dennis ...

Let me check on Dennis.

k

She went down the hall and peeked into Dennis's room. He was lying on his back, eyes closed, snoring softly. Smiling, Kelsi closed the door and went back to her bedroom.

I can't tonight. He's asleep. I don't want to just be gone when he wakes up. Tomorrow?

K sounds good

What will we do?

Can we go out?

Sure

See you then.

Yep

Kelsi went to the bathroom and ran a tub of steaming hot water, lit a vanilla candle she'd bought, and slipped into the bath, putting her head back and closing her eyes. Tucker could have said he missed her. Could have said he loved her. He hadn't. She hadn't, either, though. She was still. The water was motionless. The candle flame was small and steady. Only the steam moved, rising from the water and disappearing before it reached the ceiling.

***

"When we're finished eating here, will you get out all the dishes from the ladies who brought us food?" Dennis asked.

"Of course," Kelsi answered as she turned bacon in a cast iron skillet. "Is someone coming to get them?"

"In a sense," Dennis answered. Kelsi looked over and saw him grinning.

"What?" she asked.

"I've made arrangements for you to get out of the house today," he said.

"What?" Kelsi asked, thinking of her pending date with Tucker. "I was going to talk to you about going to see Tucker this evening. What do you have planned?"

"Yes, yes, go see my grandson. I've pretty much taken you away from him," Dennis said.

"Okay, well, we'll talk about that," Kelsi said. "What did *you* plan for me today?"

"Peter's coming to pick you up in about an hour. The two of you are going to deliver those dishes to their owners," Dennis said.

"What? This morning? To all those ladies?" Kelsi almost forgot about the bacon and had to quickly lift it out of the popping grease. She laid the strips out on a paper towel. "I'll have to dress nice for that."

"Nonsense. Just don't flash too much skin at them and you'll be fine," Dennis said.

Kelsi drained most of the bacon grease, then replaced the skillet on the burner and poured in a slurry of milk and flour, adding salt and pepper, then stirring constantly with a wooden spatula until it became gravy. The oven dinged to say the biscuits were done. She turned off the burner and put on an oven mitt to take out the pan of biscuits. She carried it, then the pan of gravy, to the table, added the bacon, and poured orange juice for both of them.

"If I wasn't here, would you return those dishes yourself?" Kelsi asked.

Dennis snorted. "Of course not. A man doesn't call on married women like that."

"How would the dishes be returned?" she asked.

"Oh, they'd come around eventually to pick them up. After they felt sure the food would be gone," he said.

"But we're not doing that?" Kelsi asked.

"Nah. Peter probably needs to visit them, anyway. Check on their souls and all that," Dennis said. He had a spot of white gravy beside his mouth. "But somebody from here needs to go to thank the ladies one more time. That's a lot of porch steps and walking for someone with a brand new metal hip and Frankenstein stitches. So you have to do it."

"Won't you need me here?"

"I'll be fine. Probably won't leave the recliner the whole time you're gone. I'm rereading *Lonesome Dove*. You don't mind going and seeing those ladies, do you?"

"No," Kelsi said. "I don't mind."

"Good. Tell me about your date tonight," Dennis said.

"I made him promise to take me out to eat," Kelsi said. "But that was before this. If I'm going to be gone most of the day, I should be here tonight." She ate more biscuits and gravy. They were really good. Just canned biscuits, but the gravy really made for a delicious breakfast, if maybe not the healthiest thing in the world.

"No, you're going," Dennis said. "You've been cooped up in here for too long. You're a young woman and need to get out. Keep that grandson of mine in line. I'm doing fine. Think of it as resting up for another trip to the park tomorrow."

"Are you sure? You'll call immediately if you're not feeling right? You're not completely out of the woods, you know? There's still a chance of blood clots."

"I'm fine," Dennis said. He pointed at his plate with his fork. "This is amazing. I haven't had gravy like this since Gloria passed." He took another bite and chewed and swallowed. "I wish I could help you move those casserole dishes."

"I can do it. I'm glad you made me write down who brought which one," Kelsi said. Then she looked at him with new revelation. "Were you planning this when they were bringing that food?"

"Well, you know, it's just customary," Dennis said, grinning around a piece of bacon.

They finished eating and Kelsi cleaned away the dishes, then brought in all the dishes and bowls that had contained donated food and she laid them out on the table. From a drawer in the kitchen she took the spiral notebook where she'd written what each lady had brought and which dish it was in. She left that on the table, too, then went to her bedroom to put on her best khaki shorts and a modest black top with white piping around the collar and ends of the sleeves.

Chapter Thirty-Two

The Reverend Peter Zook arrived a few minutes before ten o'clock. Kelsi invited him in and the three of them sat at the dining table and drank coffee while he talked to Dennis about his condition and what he'd been up to. He asked the same of Kelsi, and she asked about him.

"I've been well. Thank you for asking," he said. He motioned at the dishes on the table. "This is what we're returning today?"

"I guess so," Kelsi agreed.

Peter began taking the dishes out to his car while Kelsi fussed over Dennis, making sure he was settled in his recliner, had an insulated bottle of ice water beside him and his walker within easy reach. He was only about one-eighth of the way into the thick Western novel, so he had plenty of reading to do. He finally shooed her away and Kelsi helped load the rest of the dishes into the trunk of the minister's sedan with folds of old newspapers between the breakables. She got into the passenger seat and they backed out of the driveway.

"You know where all those women live?" Kelsi asked.

"Oh yeah," Peter answered. "Most are in my congregation, but I'm on good terms with all of them."

Nokomis had a population of over fifty-thousand. It wasn't like a small town where people couldn't help knowing everyone in town. Kelsi said as much to the minister.

"That's true," he said. "I certainly don't know everyone in Nokomis. Like I said, most of these ladies are in my congregation. They're friends with or on committees with or were in clubs with the others, so we've come in contact that way. Also, I'm blessed with a really good memory. I seldom forget a name or face. That's convenient in my line of work."

"And they're all ..." Kelsi gestured with her hands as if they were wounded birds. "I don't know. Connected?"

"We're all connected, Kelsi," Peter said.

"Connected in Christ?" Kelsi asked, and she couldn't keep the cynicism out of her voice.

"Of course," Peter said, flashing a smile at her. "We can think of it that way. But if you look at other religions, most of them will tell you that we're connected. That we're all a piece of God trying to get back to form the one being, or there's only one spirit and we all just have a little spark of it. And then there's the more practical things like, if you do a good deed for another person, it may give them the motivation and ability to do something good for someone else, and on and on."

"Ripples in a pond," Kelsi said, unsure where she'd heard that philosophy.

"Exactly. Every drop of water is an individual, but also an important part of the pond," Peter said.

"Is that United Methodist belief?" Kelsi asked, and she remembered asking Dennis the same thing once.

Peter chuckled. "Not exactly."

Kelsi smiled. "No wonder you and Dennis get along so well," she said.

Peter pulled the car into the driveway of a modest white house with black trim and a second story built over the garage. "This is Jordan Arnold's house," he said.

Kelsi remembered Mrs. Arnold as soon as she opened the door. She was a very old lady, hunched, with thin red-dyed hair that was a translucent poof on top of her jowly head. She wore huge square glasses with pale pink frames. She smiled a lot and liked to reach out and touch the person she talked to. Mrs. Arnold invited them inside, pulling Peter Zook in, then reaching a bird-like hand to take Kelsi's arm and pull her inside, too.

"I brought your dish back," Kelsi said, raising the glass cake pan with the red plastic lid.

"Thank you, dear," Mrs. Arnold said in a voice that rattled in her throat. "How is Denny?"

Kelsi smiled at the nickname. "He's doing really well," Kelsi said. "He's not ready for a lot of driving and walking, though. He's home reading a book."

"That's fine, just fine," the woman said, moving ahead of Peter to lead them through a hallway to the kitchen. "I have cookies I baked yesterday. Will you have some?"

"We'd love to," Peter said. "But only one for me."

"Same for me," Kelsi said

Peter pulled out a chair at the dining table and sat down, so Kelsi did the same and put the cake pan on the table. Mrs. Arnold brought over a cookie jar shaped like a golden apple. She put it on the table and took off the top, setting it beside the jar. She told them to help themselves and asked if they wanted a drink. Both declined, so the elderly woman gently lowered herself into a chair.

"It's going to be another hot day," Peter said.

"Yes," Mrs. Arnold agreed, smiling happily and nodding.

"Thank you again for the cake," Kelsi said. "It was so good. I've never tasted one like it."

"Mrs. Arnold is one of the best confection chefs Nokomis has ever seen," Peter said. "At least, that's what I've heard, and I haven't tasted anything better."

"Oh, you," Mrs. Arnold said, leaning back and blushing as she brushed at the minister's arm with a small, wrinkled, bird-like hand.

They stayed with Jordan Arnold for about half an hour before Peter announced they had other stops to make. It was obvious the elderly lady was reluctant for them to leave as she followed them back to the front porch.

"I'll see you Sunday," the minister said.

"Yes," she agreed, then turned her attention to Kelsi. "You come back soon. Bring those recipes and we'll see about sharing some of them."

"I'd like that," Kelsi said.

The next stop was Wilma Baker, a small, hunched black woman with thinning hair and half-moon glasses hung on a chain around her neck. She was sitting on the front porch of her old bungalow house, an extension cord run under the front door to power a small oscillating fan. At her feet were three wicker baskets. She paused what she was doing and looked up at them with a slender green thing held in one gnarled hand.

"Reverend," she said in a shaky voice. Her eyes moved to Kelsi and she thought for a moment. "You're the sweet young girl looking after Denny. I'm sorry, love, but I can't remember your name."

"Kelsi," Kelsi answered. "It's nice to see you again. We brought your casserole dish back. It was amazing. Thank you so much for it."

"Oh," Wilma made a shooing gesture. "Reverend, will you take that to the kitchen and wake Arthur up and tell him all about the sin of sloth? You'll find him in that recliner. It's like a monster that swallows him up every afternoon and most evenings."

Laughing, Peter took the glass dish and went inside. There were three empty chairs on the porch and Wilma waved in their general direction and told Kelsi to get comfortable.

"How is Denny getting along?" the elderly lady asked. There was a snapping sound in her hands, then she dropped raw peas into one of her wicker baskets and the empty and broken pod into another. She took a fresh pod from the first basket and repeated the process, then noticed Kelsi hadn't answered. She glanced up.

"I'm sorry," Kelsi said. "He's doing really good. We finally got his physical therapy approved and he starts that tomorrow."

"He'll be tired and cranky after that. He's got a temper," Wilma said. "Gloria used to put him in his place." She grinned and snapped another pod.

"Can I try that?" Kelsi asked, motioning to the baskets.

"Have you never snapped peas, child?" Wilma asked, amazed. "No, of course not. You've always gotten yours at the supermarket, haven't you?"

"Yes, ma'am," Kelsi said.

"Ayuck," the woman said, shaking her head like she had a bad taste in her mouth. "Don't 'ma'am' me. I know I'm old. You call me Wilma. Now, reach in there and get you a pod."

Kelsi did as she was told and watched as the other woman held up her pod and snapped the top off it, then pulled a string-like piece down the seam, almost like unzipping the pod. She rolled the peas out and into the basket assigned to them. Kelsi tried it and broke off the stringy part and ended up tearing the pod to pieces to get the little round peas out of it.. Wilma cackled as Kelsi separated the peas from the mangled pod. They both picked up another and Wilma showed her again how to snap the top off the pod and pull the zipper down. Hers came open easier and she rolled the peas into her basket. Kelsi tried again, and this time it worked, though not as gracefully as Wilma's.

"I did it!" Kelsi said proudly.

"You sure did," Wilma said. "When I was a girl, this is the only way we got our peas. For a while, anyway."

"You have a lot here," Kelsi said, looking at the baskets. "Do you have a big garden in your backyard?"

"Most of the yard is given over to a garden now," Wilma said, her hands moving automatically from basket to basket as she talked. Kelsi tried to keep up, but averaged about one pod to Wilma's three. "We couldn't do that when we had Duke. He was an Irish setter Arthur had to have. Duke was a good dog and I guess I can admit to you that I miss him. He was a digger, though."

"Is most of your garden peas?" Kelsi asked.

"No. We have potatoes and okra and tomatoes, of course. Why have a garden if you're not planting tomatoes?" Wilma said. "Cucumbers and carrots and a couple of watermelon and pumpkin vines. Not a lot, but it keeps us busy. Keeps our hands in the soil." She looked up at Kelsi as she said this. "That's life, you know? There's nothing like the feeling of good, damp soil in your fingers, knowing you can make things come to life in it."

Kelsi nodded slowly. "Dennis feels that way about his flowers," she said. "He really hates he can't get down on his knees and get his hands in the dirt. He loves it and I guess it's always been important to him."

"It has. It has," Wilma said, nodding and slowing her shelling. "He was one of the farm kids who moved to town when his parents lost their place. Him and Gloria used to carry water to a tree they planted in a park by our school."

"You know about that?" Kelsi asked. She'd assumed that had been kind of a private thing between Dennis and Gloria.

Wilma cackled again. "Everybody knew, even though they never really talked about it. We all knew way back there in grade school that they were destined to be together."

Kelsi smiled and snapped her peas. "I think that's pretty amazing," she said. "Not just about them as a couple, but ... I don't know. How connected you all are." She grinned, remembering the conversation with Peter Zook less than an hour ago.

Wilma sighed and leaned back in her chair, an empty pod seemingly forgotten in her hand. "The minister would tell us otherwise, but in the end, all you've got are the people whose lives you've touched. Hopefully you've made the journey better for another person, or many. Younger generations don't seem to think like that anymore."

"No," Kelsi agreed softly, and she was ashamed that her thoughts went to Tucker.

Then Peter came through the front door and announced they still had several stops to make. Kelsi hugged Wilma and told her good-bye and thanked her for the lesson.

"I'll send some of these peas around to you," Wilma promised. "You'll never buy another can of peas, I can promise you that."

The rest of the afternoon went pretty much the same. Everywhere the minister and Kelsi went they were welcomed, treated with snacks and drinks and stories until he finally said they had to be moving on. As they drove back toward Dennis's house on the east side of town, Kelsi tried to sort and process all of the visits.

"I never would have believed what we did today could be fun, but I loved it," she said. "These people, they're ... they're like Dennis and Gloria's tree. They've got deep roots in this town and it's like all their branches reach out and touch each other."

Peter laughed softly. "That's a good way to put it," he agreed. "Of course, it isn't all like that. Nokomis has it's problems. Like any city, we have drugs and violence and homelessness. Times change. The people making and spending the money and making decisions aren't raising gardens or listening to people calling in to a radio show to sell things while they iron their clothes. The people you met today are a dying generation. I think we'll be a lot poorer when they're gone."

"Me, too," Kelsi said, thinking of Dennis and his walker and the grimace on his face when he put too much weight on his repaired hip. "Definitely me, too."

Chapter Thirty-Three

Soft violin music was piped in through speakers mounted high on the walls and plants with trailing vines were placed on shelves just a little lower, trying hard to give the impression of an Italian villa with the reproduction paintings in ornate frames. The waitstaff all wore matching uniforms and smiled and spoke kindly. The smell from the kitchen is what sold the little restaurant, located in the city's downtown area, as an authentic Italian eatery.

"It smells so good," Kelsi whispered after their young brunette waitress left them. She inhaled deeply and smiling excitedly. "Do you smell those fresh tomatoes? I bet they make their own sauce."

"Buying a can of it would be easier," Tucker said with a grin.

"Mrs. Lucas gave me a bag of tomatoes from her garden today and I can't wait to go through the recipes and decide how to use them," Kelsi said.

"I'd just slice them up for sandwiches," Tucker said over the top of his menu. "I wish they had a steak."

Kelsi couldn't help but give him an irritated look. "You picked this place. If you wanted steak, we should have gone somewhere else."

"You love Italian," Tucker said without lifting his eyes.

Kelsi clamped her mouth closed instead of telling him to stop complaining. She opened her menu and decided on the bruschetta for her appetizer and cheese raviolis for her main course. She lowered the menu and found that Tucker had already done the same. The waitress came back with their first glasses of wine and pulled out her order pad. Kelsi gave the girl her order.

"I'll have regular old spaghetti and meatballs," Tucker said when it was his turn.

"Did you want an appetizer?" the waitress asked.

"Just some bread sticks," he told her. "I'm not as fancy as my date."

Kelsi knew he probably didn't mean it to be an insult, but she felt her face burn at the words and the waitress flicked a knowing glance her way before hurrying away from the table. "Am I too bougie for you?" Kelsi asked.

"No, baby, that's not what I meant," Tucker said, leaning forward. "I'm just ... a caveman. You know, bread, potatoes, a piece of meat. Nothing fancy."

"Fancy? Or pretentious?" she asked.

"Baby, don't be like that. I didn't mean anything bad," Tucker said. He reached for her hand and Kelsi let him take it. "I'm sorry."

"Okay." Kelsi shook her head as if to clear it all away.

Tucker smiled and squeezed her hand. "Did you really spend all day visiting old women with a preacher?"

"I did. It was fun," she said. "I even learned to shell peas."

"Shellpease? What's that?" he asked.

Kelsi giggled. "It's two words. Shell. Peas. You know, the vegetable? They grow in pods and you have to break the pod open to get the peas out. Hey, that's why people say something is like two peas in a pod." She laughed. "I never thought of what that really means."

"I think you really did like that," Tucker said, his voice full of wonder. "You light up when you talk about it. Maybe you should change your major to old people studies. Who'd grow their own peas when you can buy them in the store?"

"You've never grown anything, have you?" Kelsi asked. "I haven't grown vegetables, but I helped plant some of Dennis's flowers before he got hurt and I've done most of the caring for them since then. You get connected and you feel like you're just part of the earth, part of the life cycle."

Tucker shook his head. "There'll be time enough for that when I'm dead."

Kelsi clamped a lid on her irritation. "Okay, tell me about your day at work."

"I'm loving this with Dad being gone," Tucker said. "I wish they'd make his transfer permanent. Me and a few guys have been taking dabs at lunch and it makes everything better."

"You're what?" Kelsi asked, stunned.

"We go out to Brian's car and hit our pens," he said. "No biggie."

Kelsi stared at him as if he'd lost his mind. "First of all, you're at work. Second, you're supposed to be a supervisor. Third, I don't like you doing drugs."

"It's just weed, Kels. C'mon. Nobody thinks of weed as a drug anymore. I've got my med-card," he argued.

"But you don't have a medical need. Those cards are a joke. I hate it when you do drugs," she said.

"I don't do drugs," he continued to argue. "It's just weed. You know, a plant, like your peas and tomatoes."

"Don't even," she said.

The waitress returned with their appetizers. She seemed to sense there was still tension between the couple, so after asking if there was anything else she could get them, she hurried away.

Tucker took a long breadstick from the basket and pretended to smoke it, then laughed.

Kelsi carefully placed her fork on her plate and looked Tucker in the eyes. "Take me home," she said.

"What? No. I'm sorry, Kels. I'll stop. I promise," he said, dropping the breadstick onto the table.

"You'll stop what?" she asked.

"I'll stop teasing you," he said.

"But not getting high?" she asked.

"It's just weed. It's better than getting drunk," he said.

Kelsi shook her head. "Let's pretend it's not a character issue. You work around machines that could kill you. You're a supervisor. What are you going to do when one of your pothead buddies gets mad because you make him do something he doesn't want to do and he tells your boss you need to be drug tested?"

"My dad is my boss. He won't do anything," Tucker said.

"Your dad isn't there," Kelsi reminded.

Tucker shrugged. "Nobody's going to take the word of a floor hand over a supervisor," he said.

"You're an idiot," Kelsi told him. She took another bite of her bruschetta, then asked, "What have you been doing in the evenings you don't come over?"

He shrugged again. "Some of the guys come over. We watch movies and play games."

"And get high?" she asked.

"Yeah, maybe," he admitted.

"Are there girls there?"

His hesitation was all the answer she needed. She put her fork down again and stood up, slinging her purse strap over her shoulder. He jumped to his feet and was beside her before she could turn away. "Kelsi, don't do this," he said, his voice a whispered hiss.

"Leave me alone," she said in a stiff, staccato tone that made him drop the hands that were reaching for her. "I'm leaving. You stay here. Don't call me anymore."

"You live with my grandfather," he whispered again. "Don't you think I can put an end to that?"

"Your grandfather is five times the man you are and he'll make his own decisions about who lives in his house," Kelsi said, then she strode away from him, aware that all other conversation in the restaurant had ceased and every eye was on her and Tucker.

Kelsi left the restaurant and didn't pay any attention to where she was going. She just walked, her pumps clicking on the sidewalk beneath her. She passed people and some looked at her with concern. Everyone moved out of her way. It was mid-evening in July and most of the businesses downtown were closed for the night, while those that were open were turning on their lights and creating islands of illumination that she passed through as she moved.

"Kelsi?"

At first, she ignored the call, then she realized it was a woman's voice, not Tucker's. Kelsi stopped and turned back. A woman her age with brown hair and freckles on a pale face stood in the doorway of a little shop watching her.

"Are you okay?"

A tumbler turned over in Kelsi's mind and she found a name. "Kinley," she said. They had been in English Composition II and Biology together. They had spoken a few times, but not often. "I'm fine," Kelsi said, but then wiped her eyes, which made her give a short bark of laughter.

Kinley walked over, her long, bare legs moving smoothly while her ankle boots clicked on the sidewalk. She wore sky blue shorts and a breezy white blouse tied in the front to show her belly button jewelry. She hooked an arm through Kelsi's as if they were life-long friends. "Guy problems, huh? Alcohol or tea?"

Stunned by it all, but thinking she didn't want to go home to Dennis drunk, she said, "Tea, I guess."

Kinley spun them around and pulled Kelsi back into the little shop she had just left. Inside, they sat at a bar and looked up at a menu of flavored teas. A middle-aged brunette came over and greeted them.

"I thought you left," she said to Kinley.

"I found my friend crying and walking like she was going to hurt someone," Kinley said. "This is Kelsi. I can't remember your last name."

"Duncan," Kelsi said. "I can't remember yours, either."

"Baker," Kinley said.

Kelsi perked up and looked at the other woman. "Is your grandmother Wilma? Wilma Baker?"

"Yeah. That's weird you'd know that," Kinley said, her nose wrinkling a little and rearranging her freckles.

Kelsi laughed. "I shelled peas with her today."

"You can tell me that story after we order some tea," Kinley said. She turned back to the proprietor. "What do you have to heal a heartbreak?"

"I have just the thing," the woman promised.

"I'll have another one of those raspberry ones like earlier," Kinley said. The older woman moved off to complete the order. "Why were you hanging with my grandma today?"

Kelsi gave a run down of what had been going on with her since the spring semester had ended, not giving away everything, but how she'd left her waitressing job to become the caretaker of her boyfriend's — no *ex*-boyfriend's — grandfather and all the food he'd received after his injury. As she talked, the shop owner returned with mugs of tea and left them.

"That's a lot going on," Kinley said. "And now you've broken up with that guy but you still live with his grandfather. Is that gonna be weird?"

"I don't know. I doubt it," Kelsi said. "It'll be his mom, Dennis's daughter, who'll decide to make it an issue or not, I think."

"Try your tea. This place is ah-MAZ-ing," Kinley said, nodding at the brown ceramic mug.

Kelsi lifted the drink and held it under her nose. The steam brought soft, comforting aromas of spearmint and vanilla. She blew to cool the surface, then sipped. She had never tasted anything like it. She took several more swallows. There was an ending flavor of some kind of berry. Mulberry? Kelci pictured the flavor as coming from something small, clustery, and deep, dark red with sticky juice. The shop owner came back over and asked if she liked it.

"It's delicious," Kelsi told her. "What's in it?"

"A little witchy recipe that isn't on the menu," the woman told her with a smile.

"Not on the menu?" Kinley asked. "Can I taste it?"

Kelsi handed over the mug and her new friend took a sip, then another. Nodding, she handed it back.

"That's good," Kinley said. "Did you say a spell over it? Tina's a real witch," she added to Kelsi in a lowered voice.

"I did," the owner, Tina, responded. "A spell that she'd find her own power and you'd leave a bigger tip this time." Then she gave an exaggerated cackle and moved away to tend to other customers.

The women finished their tea and talked about school and the coming semester, then exchanged phone numbers. Kelsi got up the nerve to ask, "Do you think you could give me a ride home?"

"Of course!" Kinley said. "Good thing we didn't decide on alcohol, right?"

Chapter Thirty-Four

The expected call from Natalie came early the next morning. She called Dennis instead of Kelsi. They were both seated at the breakfast table, eating pancakes and sausage patties Kelsi had made for them. Dennis told Kelsi who was calling, then growled at Natalie that, "She's sitting right here with me and I'm putting you on speaker."

"... do that. This is between you and me," Natalie's voice said as Dennis put the phone on the table between he and Kelsi.

"Too late," Dennis said.

"Good morning, Natalie," Kelsi said, trying to force her voice to be cheery.

"I'm sorry you have to hear this, Kelsi," Natalie said curtly. "Dad, since she broke up with your grandson, I just don't think it's appropriate that she continues to live in your house and get paid to take care of you. We can get a regular nurse to come by and check on you."

"Natalie, this is my home and I will decide who lives here," Dennis argued. "Kelsi is welcome to stay here as long as she wants. She's all the nurse I need. I enjoy her company and she's doing just fine."

"Dad, you're not ... You and her ... "

Kelsi's mouth dropped open at the unspoken question. She saw Dennis's face redden, but it didn't seem to be embarrassment.

"Absolutely not," he said in a voice that could have cut stone.

"From what Tucker said, she's ... flighty," Natalie argued. "Unreliable."

Kelsi and Dennis both laughed at that. She had confided in Dennis the whole truth of what had transpired the evening before, but she didn't want to tell Tucker's mother everything.

"Natalie, Tucker admitted he's been having parties at your house with other girls while I've been watching over your dad," Kelsi said. "Do you think that's appropriate?"

There was a little hesitation before Natalie answered. "Maybe not, but it's something that could be worked out. It doesn't justify you throwing your wine on him and making a big scene in a restaurant before walking out."

Kelsi couldn't stop the laugh that erupted out of her. "That is so Tucker," she said when she had control of herself. "There was no wine thrown on anyone. He always has to make things so dramatic and make himself a victim."

"Tell her the rest, Kelsi," Dennis prodded. "Tell her what started the argument."

"No," Kelsi protested. "No, that's too much. It's too ... I don't want to tell his mom that."

"I don't want to violate your confidence, but this is important," Dennis urged.

"What?" Natalie demanded from the phone. "Tell me what?"

"You can tell," Kelsi said softly.

"Tucker is smoking pot at work with some of the men under him," Dennis said. "That's an accident waiting to happen. A lawsuit waiting to happen, Natalie. He's also doing it in your house at these parties, but that's purely between you and him."

"He told you this, Kelsi?" Natalie demanded to know.

"Yes," Kelsi admitted. "I told him he could get fired or someone could get hurt and he said it was no big deal. I told him one of the other guys could get mad at him and report him and, as a supervisor, he'd be in trouble. He got mad at me."

"Marijuana isn't that big of a deal anymore," Natalie said. "He has that card. The doctor said he has ADHD and it's supposed to help."

Kelsi rolled her eyes, but Dennis asked, "I'd be willing to bet smoking grass on the clock is not allowed by the company policy, legal or not. They wouldn't put up with him drinking whiskey on his breaks, would they?"

"This is easy enough to confirm. I'll just have him drug tested," Natalie said.

"No! He'll know I told," Kelsi argued.

"You broke up with him. What difference will it make?" Natalie asked.

"I don't want him slashing my tires or something if he gets fired," Kelsi said.

"Tucker would never do something like that," Natalie argued, her voice an octave higher than usual.

"He does a lot of things you don't know about," Kelsi said quietly. "I used to be okay with that, but ... I guess I've grown up a little."

"Things like what?" Natalie demanded.

"Just stuff," Kelsi said. "I really don't want to talk about it. Not any of this. And I don't want to be a problem in your family." She said the last part looking at Dennis.

Dennis swallowed the bite of pancakes he was chewing, then shook his head. "You are not a problem. Instead of being my friend and my grandson's girlfriend, now you're just my friend. It's no big deal."

"Dad, I'm just not sure—" Natalie began.

"If it's the money, I'll pay her myself," Dennis snapped.

"This is what you want?" Natalie asked, her own voice tight.

"It is," Dennis answered.

"Fine. We'll re-evaluate the situation later," she said.

"Sure thing," Dennis said, then ended the call.

"I'm so sorry," Kelsi said. "I really don't want to be a problem between you and your daughter. I should go."

"You better not," Dennis said in a warning voice. "I can't drive myself to this stupid physical therapy. And I can't get down on my knees in the garden. Are you going to leave and let this July heat murder all of our flowers?

Kelsi hung her head, but it was more to hide her grin. "I suppose not," she said.

"Good. Now, if you'll clean up in here, I'll go get dressed for this therapy thing. I can't wear my pajamas," he said.

"Sweatpants," Kelsi reminded. "Or shorts. You've got to be able to move easily. Do not come back out here in jeans or khakis."

Dennis shuffled away with his walker, muttering something about having so many bossy damn women in his life, while Kelsi scraped plates and put them, the silverware and orange juice cups into the dishwasher. She rinsed out the heavy cast iron skillet she'd used for pancakes and the newer, non-stick one for the sausage. She finished to find Dennis in a pair of gray sweatpants, white New Balance sneakers, and a T-shirt that said, "I read banned books" with artwork of book spines.

"Gray sweatpants, huh?" Kelsi teased, then had to awkwardly explain why women liked it when men wore gray sweatpants.

"I should change," he said, starting to turn his walker. "I don't want the ladies staring at my package."

"No time. Let's go," Kelsi said. "One of your bossy females commands it."

Dennis laughed and clomped after her with his walker. "I need you to do something for me while they're torturing me," Dennis said. He paused in the living room and picked up a thick book from an end table. He waved it at Kelsi. "This needs to go back to the library."

"We can drop it in the return slot," Kelsi said.

"No, you need to put it in the hands of a young librarian named Evangeline Bradford. She'll be on the second floor," Dennis said as Kelsi took the book. "There's a note for her inside the front cover."

Kelsi looked and saw an orange sticky-note that simply said, "This made all the difference. Thank you!" with Dennis's scrawled signature under it. She looked back at the title on the cover. There was no dust jacket and it was an older book with a gold cloth binding. "*The Teachings of Krishna* made all the difference?" she asked him.

"Yep. Let's go," Dennis urged, nudging at Kelsi's flip-flop with the tennis ball of a walker leg.

Traffic was light and the drive was short. As they pulled into the parking lot, Dennis looked over at Kelsi and asked, "You're really against him smoking grass, aren't you?"

"Nobody calls it grass anymore, Dennis," she said. "But, yes."

"Even though everyone does it? So I've heard," he asked.

"Even though," she said. "It's ... an escape for most people. They don't need a medicine. They just don't want to feel reality, so they smoke or use edibles or whatever to escape reality. It's like ... like my mom's drinking."

Dennis nodded. "You don't drink?"

"I don't get drunk," Kelsi said. "I'll have some wine with dinner, but not to numb myself."

Dennis turned back to look through the windshield. He nodded, his whole torse rocking forward. "I respect that. I know what you're talking about. I numbed myself enough once upon a time." He paused, then turned and smiled at her. "We better go inside."

Chapter Thirty-Five

Kelsi sat with Dennis in the reception area of the rehabilitation center while he filled out the necessary paperwork, grumbling about it most of the time as he did it. Kelsi looked around at the other patients filling out forms or waiting for treatment. There was another elderly man with a stabilizing boot on his left leg, a middle-aged woman with no visible hint to her malady, and a teenage girl who had to be a cheerleader wearing a back brace. The girl was called back as Dennis worked on his paperwork.

About twenty minutes after Kelsi turned in Dennis's paperwork, he was called to come to the rehab room by an attractive blonde technician Kelsi guessed to be about her own age. As he used his walker to make his way to the door, Dennis paused and looked over his shoulder to Kelsi and said, "Don't forget about the library."

"As soon as that door closes behind you," Kelsi promised.

The door closed and Kelsi grinned and shook her head. She asked the receptionist how long the session would be and was told a little over an hour. She checked the time on her phone as she left the center and returned to her car. The drive to the library, like every drive in Nokomis, didn't take long. Kelsi took the old book from the back seat, climbed the steps, and pushed into the air conditioned, bookish air of the library. The stairs were next to the front door, so she went up them and found a desk, where she waited for a couple of minutes before a woman who couldn't have been more than three years older than herself hurried over.

"Hi," she said in just above a whisper. "What can I help you with?"

"I'm looking for—" Kelsi noticed the girl's badge on a lanyard around her neck. "I'm looking for you," she amended.

"You must be Kelsi," Evangeline Bradford said, smiling at her.

"Yes. I have a book for you," she said, handing over the old volume. "There's a note inside."

Evangeline opened the cover and removed the note, glancing at it quickly and shaking her head. "That Dennis is something else," she said. "We all miss him being on the board and coming in to check on us."

"He's a nice guy," Kelsi agreed. "Did he leave the board recently. I thought he left ... well, before you or I were born."

Evangeline laughed quietly. "No, it was just a couple of years ago. When his term ended after Gloria died." Evangeline checked her watch, then smiled at Kelsi. "Are you ready?"

Kelsi blinked several times, wondering what she'd missed. "Ready for what?" she asked.

"Tea and cookies," Evangeline said. Her smile faltered for a moment, then came back with a twinkle in her eye. "He didn't tell you, did he?"

Kelsi sighed, then grinned. "Nope. What has he done now?"

"He asked me to take you across the street to the tea shop during my break. He said you need to meet people your own age," Evangeline said.

"Lord," Kelsi said, trying not to laugh. "Yesterday he had me visiting elderly women who'd brought him food after his accident."

"With the hot preacher," Evangeline added. "I heard about that."

"You think Peter's hot?" Kelsi asked.

"Don't you?" Evangeline countered.

"I guess," Kelsi said with a shrug. "I didn't really think about it. I have ... I *had* a boyfriend. Until last night."

Evangeline nodded. "You were dating Tucker. Dennis told me that. You broke up?"

"Yeah. We didn't agree on some things. He was doing drugs and other girls in his parents' house."

Evangeline leaned forward and whispered, "He was an asshole in high school, too. Let's go. My break is only supposed to be fifteen minutes."

Evangeline was a fast walker and Kelsi had to adjust her pace to keep up. They left the library through the front door and turned and crossed a busy street. As Evangeline pushed open the door of a little shop Kelsi realized it was the same tea shop she'd been in with Kinley the night before.

"It's breaktime, huh?" the dark-haired proprietor said as greeting to Evangeline.

"Yep," the younger woman said. She turned to Kelsi and added, "I come here almost every morning."

"I recognize you, too," the woman said to Kelsi. "But I didn't get your name."

"I'm Kelsi Duncan," Kelsi said, offering her hand across the counter.

"Jessie Hayes," the woman said. Her handshake was firm and quick, her eyes gray, and her smile genuine. "Are you new in town?"

"I've actually been here a couple of years, going to school. I just haven't gotten out much," Kelsi said.

Jessie nodded. "Are you doing better today than you were last night?"

"I am. Thank you," Kelsi said. "Honestly, now that it's happened, I don't feel much. I think I knew it was over."

"It happens that way sometimes," Jessie agreed. "Now, what can I get you two?"

Suddenly the aromas were overwhelming. Spices and herbs and warm cookies and bread filled the air with their scents, making the little shop a wonder to the senses. "It smells so good in here," Kelsi said. She ordered a cup of tangerine tea that Jessie said would give her positive energy, and a big, thick chocolate chip cookie.

"I'll have my mint tea and peanut butter cookie," Evangeline said.

Taking their drinks and treats, the two younger women made their way to a small round table near the shop's front window and sat down. "Tell me the Cliff's Notes version of your life," Evangeline urged.

"I moved around a lot as a kid. My parents separated and I lived in Wyoming with my mom, but she was drinking all the time," Kelsi said. "I met Tucker online, saw there was a university here, and moved to Nokomis. I had my own apartment, but gave it up to move in and take care of Dennis."

"Oooo, so much to unpack there," Evangeline said. "I grew up mostly in foster homes, but did well in high school and have enough Native blood that I qualified for and won the Gates Millennium Scholarship. I could have gone all the way to a Ph.D., but a master's in library science was all I needed, so I got that and found a job here."

"Do you like it here?" Kelsi asked.

"I do. It's an hour and a half to Oklahoma City if I have to shop for something I can't find here," she said, then added, "But Amazon does deliver here, so I don't have to go very often. There's not a lot of night life here, but I'm more of a homebody. I'm too clumsy to dance in public and getting drunk once was enough for me. Tipsy on wine at home is another matter, but ..." She trailed off and smiled over her steaming teacup.

Kelsi grinned and swallowed her bite of cookie. "No wonder Dennis introduced us," she said.

"I figured," Evangeline said. "You like to read and play board games, don't you?"

"Yeah," Kelsi admitted. "I never had video game consoles. Board games seemed like something families would do, so I was always interested. I usually had to play alone, though."

"That's sad, but you don't anymore. We have a game night at my house on Fridays and you have to come," Evangeline said. "When we go back to the library I'll give you my number and get yours and give you my address."

"It sounds fun," Kelsi said. "What game do you play?"

"Pfft. I have a ton of them and the other girls bring some and we just pick something," Evangeline said.

"How many come?"

"It depends," Evangeline said. "There were nine of us one night, but it's usually four or five."

"No guys?"

"Absolutely not! This is a girls' night. We play games, we drink wine, we usually have food, and we gripe about guys," Evangeline said.

Kelsi laughed. "Sounds amazing," she said.

"It is." Evangeline popped the last of her cookie into her mouth and chewed quickly. "I have to get back to work." She drained her tea. Kelsi did the same and they returned the mugs and plates to Jessie and walked back to the library.

"I've hardly ever been downtown," Kelsi said as she worked to keep up with her new friend. "Between school and my old job I didn't have a lot of time, and Tucker told me that downtown was just a bunch of lawyers' offices."

"There are a lot of those," Evangeline said. "Old people tell stories about all these businesses that used to be downtown before the mall opened in the 1980s. It killed downtown, and now it's pretty much dead, too."

Back upstairs, the women exchanged numbers and said their farewells. To Kelsi's surprise, Evangeline gave her a hug before they parted.

Kelsi drove back to the rehab center and scrolled through social media in the waiting room until the blonde tech opened the door and Dennis came out. He was almost hanging in his walker, his face drawn and pale and she could see his legs shaking. Kelsi jumped from her seat and went to him.

"Dennis, are you okay? What happened?" She directed the second question to the tech.

"This is common with the first few visits," the woman said. "He'll probably be really tired and have some aches. Try to avoid pain meds he might have gotten after his surgery. Advil or Tylenol, or even Aleeve is okay. We'll see you back in two days."

"It's like the Spanish Inquisition in there," Dennis complained in a weak voice, but he did offer a half-smile.

"Hopefully you didn't confess," Kelsi said. "Let's get you home."

She opened doors for him, stopped at a Sonic drive-in for lunch, then got him home and settled into his recliner, where he took two Advil and ate half his chili cheese-dog before falling asleep. Kelsi finished her burger and put his leftovers in the refrigerator. She thought about taking a nap, too, but instead she took out a deck of cards and played solitaire on the kitchen table for a while as her mind turned over everything that had happened during the past day and a half.

"I'm single," she whispered to the cards. The words didn't have any real impact. After two years with Tucker, she just felt nothing at the end of the relationship. She wondered why. Maybe her heart had known it was over before her head figured it out.

Suddenly bored with the game, Kelsi gathered the cards and put them aside. She added ice to Dennis's drink without waking him, then slipped out the back door of the house. The back yard wasn't large. It had a good size storage shed that Dennis had built in his younger years, and a storm cellar with its top covered in concrete. In a far corner of the yard, though, there was an old mimosa tree. Barefoot, Kelsi walked across the springy, perfectly-cut grass lawn. The afternoon sun was brutal and she felt drops of perspiration form along her brow, but she didn't turn back. Once in the shade of the tree with its beautiful pink, white, and green flowers, she sank into a cross-legged position and looked back at the house.

It was such a neat, trim home. Nothing was out of place. Nothing was sagging or in need of paint. The yard wasn't weeds and dirt. She had never lived in such a place. Usually, her family had settled in apartments or houses that had been rentals for years and years and were not at all well maintained. She thought of the lives Dennis and Gloria had lived here. So many years. Two people who had chosen to come together, live together, work out their differences, and after all those years, it seems that they were still happy to be with each other when Gloria had to leave.

Obviously they'd been happy, Kelsi corrected. Gloria's ghost visiting Dennis was proof of that.

Kelsi leaned back until she was lying on her back, looking up into the branches of the mimosa, watching the long, thin leaves sway softly in a very faint breeze. She decided when she went inside she would take some of the flowers from the tree and put them in a bowl of water in the living room. Did they have a fragrance? She honestly didn't know. She'd check before she plucked any.

A gray female cardinal fluttered onto a branch of the tree, hopped onto a thinner branch, then turned its head and cocked a black eye to look down at Kelsi.

"Hello, Gloria," Kelsi said quietly.

As if in response, Kelsi's phone buzzed in the pocket of her shorts. She pulled it out and saw it was a text message from Kinley.

> Hi Kelsi. Enrollment party at my place tonight. Pizza and wine while we pick classes for the fall. Wanna come?

Kelsi considered, then wrote back.

> Dennis had his 1st rehab today. If he's okay to be alone, absolutely! He's asleep. I'll let you know soon.

> That's a yes until you say otherwise.

Kelsi laughed and lay the phone in the grass beside her. Meeting Dennis had changed her life, she mused. She got rid of her boyfriend and was making friends in her generation and Dennis's. Not in Natalie's, though. Kelsi wondered about that. Did Dennis have a coven of middle-aged women he was going to send her to meet next? It wouldn't surprise her at all.

The cardinal was gone, which made Kelsi think it was time to go back inside and check on her friend and benefactor.

Chapter Thirty-Six

The following Tuesday morning, as she was having tea and a cupcake with Evangeline during her break while Dennis did his rehab, Kelsi's phone buzzed. She glanced down at it and saw that it was a text message from Tucker, the first he had sent since the breakup. She bit off some cupcake, licked pink frosting from her lips as Evangeline told a story about a library patron getting upset that he couldn't take books into the library restroom, and opened the message.

> You fukkin cunt!!! I hope ur happy Tez and Mike were fired and im being send to fukkin kansas bitch!!!

"What is it?" Evangeline asked. "Kelsi? Hey! Are you okay?"

Kelsi looked up, blinking and confused and hurt. She tried to speak and couldn't, so just pushed her phone toward her new friend. She watched Evangeline read it, then look back at her.

"I guess this is your ex?" she asked. Kelsi nodded. "Nice spelling. Did you get him in trouble at work?"

"No," Kelsi said. Her voice broke and the first tear leaked from her eye. She wiped at it angrily. "I didn't tell anyone what he was doing. Except ..."

"Who?" Evangeline prompted.

"Well, Tucker's mom. And Dennis. But he wouldn't. Would he?"

Evangeline dipped her biscotti into her tea and stirred slowly before taking a bite, chewing, swallowing, and answering. "It's hard to guess what Dennis might do."

"It's his grandson. He wouldn't get his own grandson in trouble," Kelsi argued.

Evangeline shrugged. "I know he holds family up to a higher standard than he does other people. I could rob a bank and he'd shrug and say I probably had a good reason. What was he doing? Tucker?" she asked, nodding at the phone.

"Getting high at work with those other guys," Kelsi said. "Getting high at home and cheating on me, too, but that wasn't work."

"Why Kansas? Why wasn't he fired?" Evangeline asked.

"His dad is a big supervisor in the company," Kelsi said. "His mom and dad are in Hutchison, Kansas, right now overseeing the takeover of another shop the company bought."

"Ah, nepotism. Gotta love it," Evangeline said. She finished her biscotti and gulped the last of her tea. "I"m sorry, Kels, but I have to run. You stay and finish your cupcake. Don't let that asshole spoil that for you. And whatever you do, *do not* respond to that message. Ask Dennis about it when you pick him up."

That's what Kelsi did. As soon as she was on the road toward home, she ignored Dennis's groans and his closed eyes and made him read Tucker's message.

"That boy needs a trip to the woodshed," Dennis said, putting the phone in the car's center console. "Talking to a lady with that language."

"Dennis, did you tell somebody what I told you?" Kelsi demanded.

He leaned his head back and closed his eyes, but didn't hesitate in saying, "Yes. Jim Hayes owns that company. I worked for him for a couple of years when he was just getting started. I let him know what was going on. He called me back last night and said he'd reviewed weeks of video of the parking lot, watching those guys smoking in a car. He took security with him and busted them on Friday. Just happened to have a mobile drug lab visiting that day to randomly test a bunch of employees. Tucker's lucky he didn't get fired. His dad's a hard worker and important to the company and that's what saved him. He's always been lazy and spoiled."

"He thinks I did it," Kelsi said. "Natalie is going to be so mad at me."

"I'll take care of that. She'll know by now. Get me home and drugged and in my recliner and I'll call her," Dennis said. "You might want to go to the grocery store during that conversation."

"Yeah," Kelsi agreed. "I don't want to overhear the names she'll call me."

***

Sitting on the porch after a dinner of fried chicken breasts, mashed potatoes and home-made gravy, and fresh green beans, Kelsi read while Dennis fussed with the potted flowers Kelsi had originally bought for her old apartment. Kelsi knew from his stories of what they did at the rehab center that he could get onto his knees in his flowerbed, but he refused to have the neighbors see him struggling to get back to his feet, so he contented himself to feeling the soil in the pots to determine if it was too dry. He trimmed leaves and turned the pots so that the geraniums got sunlight on all sides. When he finally sat back, as satisfied as he could be with the pots that were separated from the earth he loved, Kelsi put her book down.

"How bad was it?" she asked.

"Oh, it was bad," Dennis said.

"She hates me."

"Natalie is a good person," Dennis said, his eyes and his voice far away. "A good woman. She's lost something. Humility, I guess. Maybe empathy. The more money her husband makes, the more distant she becomes. I don't know. I hope she'll change." He pulled his eyes back and looked at Kelsi. He smiled. "They're moving. She says the family has been humiliated here, so they're going to take the permanent transfer to Hutchison and sell their house here."

"She *really* hates me," Kelsi said softly.

"She had some pretty strong words for me, too," Dennis said. "But they are only words."

"They can hurt, though," Kelsi said.

After a long moment, Dennis agreed in a whisper. "They can hurt."

"We need to go to your tree," Kelsi said, putting her book on the little table beside her.

"I'd like that," Dennis said, his voice far away again.

Kelsi drove them to the park and pretended not to notice how long it took Dennis, still tired from his rehabilitation exercises, to shuffle from the car to the tree with his walker. She opened the two lawn chairs in the shade on the east side of the tree. The canopy of green leaves rustled above them as if welcoming them back. Kelsi looked around as she stood beside Dennis. She thought she might see the shimmer of Gloria's presence, but there was nothing like that.

"I'll leave you alone for a little bit," Kelsi said, then impulsively she bent over him and hugged Dennis, kissing him on the temple. "Thank you," she whispered, then turned and nearly ran down the sidewalk toward the far end of the park. She slowed about halfway across the park, but kept walking until she reached the other north/south street. She stopped, leaned back and filled her lungs with air, then turned to look back. Dennis seemed very small and alone sitting under the shady tree with the empty chair next to him. She could see that he was talking, though. His mouth moved and his hands made small, hopeless-looking gestures as he faced the tree.

"He stood up for me against his own daughter and grandson," Kelsi whispered to no one. She wondered why. What did he want in return? She couldn't think of anything. He had never said an inappropriate word to her, so she felt sure he was not a pervert-in-waiting. Slowly making her way back, Kelsi took out her phone and texted Evangeline, giving her a brief summary of the latest development and asking her if she could explain why Dennis was doing all of this for her. The response came almost immediately.

> Dennis is genuinely the nicest man you will ever meet. There isn't a selfish bone in him. God doesn't make them like him anymore. I've talked to a lot of people. Everyone knows Dennis and I've never heard a bad word against him.

> Thank you. I knew that. I've just never had anyone be so nice to me and I don't know how to act.

> When he passes, we'll lose a real treasure to the human race.

> Yeah. Thanks. Don't wanna think about that.

Kelsi put her phone away as she approached her friend in his chair. He was no longer talking, but his eyes were brighter and more focused than when she'd left him. He smiled at her and motioned toward Gloria's empty chair.

"Take a load off," Dennis said. "Gloria said it's okay."

"She was here?" Kelsi asked, sinking into the lawn chair. It was surprisingly cool and for the briefest moment Kelsi was sure a soft, cool wind swirled around her and disappeared.

Dennis laughed. "She was," he said.

"She helped your mood," Kelsi said.

His laughter faded and his face relaxed and looked very old for a moment, but then he sighed and smiled. "She always did," he said. "I miss her. I'd give whatever days I have left to hear her hollering at me from the kitchen, telling me to get out of the garden and come to dinner or open this jar for her."

Kelsi reached over and took his large, dry hand with its papery skin and wrinkled fingers. "I know," she said. "But don't talk about things like that. You're the best friend I've ever had. The best parent figure. You can't leave me."

He squeezed her hand softly. "Can you take me downtown tomorrow morning? I have some business to take care of."

"Are you going to send me off on another errand to meet another network of friends?" Kelsi teased.

"No," Dennis said, grinning. "Not this time."

"Of course I'll take you," Kelsi promised.

Chapter Thirty-Seven

The summer dragged on, hot, dry, and mostly still. The humidity was high, causing one to sweat immediately after stepping out of air conditioned buildings or cars. In the parks and yards that weren't tended to, the grass grew, turned brown, and the soil cracked open in long, crooked lines that might have reached all the way to the planet's molten core. Afternoons were lifeless. Dogs didn't bark. Squirrels didn't run along fence tops or highline wires. Children stayed indoors.

In the evenings, Kelsi pulled weeds in the flowerbed, then Dennis, now using a cane instead of the walker, held the water hose and sprayed the flowers that were beautiful bursts of color no matter the heat and humidity of the day. After, they usually took a thermos of lemonade or sweet tea and cups to the park and sat in the shade of the sycamore tree while the long days faded to purple evening.

Many afternoons on the days when Dennis wasn't too exhausted from his rehabilitation exercises, they would go visiting. Kelsi's favorite was when they went to see Wilma Baker, who was always on her porch with the previous evening's peas or green beans or carrots. Kelsi finally got to see her garden, which took up almost all of her back yard, with everything planted in neat rows with wooden stakes announcing what was planted in that area. Wilma always patiently showed Kelsi what needed to be done with that days vegetables, and then she and Dennis told stories about the city and the country life in the days before they moved to the city.

Sometimes they went to the old shopping mall that was nearly empty of stores but offered a nice, air conditioned indoor space that seniors used for walking. Dennis was slow with his cane, but they met other elderly people there and walked together. Dennis took many breaks on the benches placed in front of the faceless cages of the closed shops.

Kelsi spent some evenings with her new friends her own age. They would gather and take turns making elaborate dinners and spend the evenings eating, drinking wine, watching movies or playing games while talking about those things that are important to women in their twenties. With Kinley's group, the college friends became more and more aware of the passing of summer and the coming classes at the university. Bits of information about professors and classes and the best restrooms were shared and promises were made to continue their meetings despite the busier schedules.

Sometimes they met in Dennis's house and the young women loved Gloria's big kitchen and handwritten recipes. Phones always came out and pictures were taken of the yellowed cards with the neat or blocky handwriting as the women worked to recreate the dishes, filling the house with laughter and sounds of delight while the aroma of food wafted through all the rooms. Dennis appeared sometimes and the young women treated him something like a mascot or a sorority house supervisor who never quoted rules. He took food and complimented them, then faded back to his own room, giving them the run of the rest of his house.

There had been one weekend when Dennis sent Kelsi away. He gave her a hundred dollars and told her to go to Oklahoma City and bring him a new Western novel from a Barnes and Noble store.

"We can order it from Amazon. You don't have to give me all this money," Kelsi argued.

"I just need you to leave for a day," Dennis said solemnly.

"You're not having a woman over for …" Kelsi tried to think of a nice way to ask if he was going to get laid.

"Of course not," he said with a snort. "If you must know, Natalie is coming over to collect a few things she wants from the house. I thought it would be best if you weren't here. Call one of your girlfriends and go to the city. Shop, go to a new restaurant, ride that Ferris wheel they put downtown. Make a day of it."

Evangeline was off work and not busy. Kelsi had come to really value the other woman's company, even more than the group of other students. Maybe because she was a couple of years older, already had her college degree and was working in her chosen profession. She seemed older, more mature, while still able to identify with and appreciate the things Kelsi liked. She was glad to go to Oklahoma City with Kelsi and they had a good time. Kelsi only used the money Dennis gave her to fill her car's gas tank, discretely leaving the rest of it on his dresser the next day.

The things Natalie took were mostly from the room where Kelsi slept. They were things from her childhood and teenage years. A jewelry box that held costume or cheap jewelry. A shadowbox or Nokomis High School pom squad memorabilia. Yearbooks.

A handmade quilt that had been in the top of the closet and Kelsi had secretly looked forward to using when the weather cooled off.

She didn't hear anything more from Tucker, though for weeks she expected to go outside and find the tires of her car slashed. She guessed he was gone, off to Kansas with his parents. Dennis would have told her, but Kelsi didn't want to ask. She felt guilty for coming between Dennis and his family and knew asking him about it would make him sad and increase her own feelings of guilt.

The approaching school year reminded her of her old life, her old job, and she was surprised at a sense of nostalgia. She looked at the package of round steaks thawing in the sink and impulsively put them in the refrigerator. Dennis was watching a TV judge in the living room. "We're going to Sweet Pea's Diner for dinner tonight," she announced.

Dennis looked up at her and grinned. "Yes, ma'am," he said. "Tell me when and I'll put on some shoes."

"When your show is over," Kelsi said. "Bring your appetite, and eat some Tums if you need to."

Thirty minutes later, they were in the car and driving through the steamy late afternoon.

Chapter Thirty-Eight

Kelsi knew she shouldn't be, but she was surprised to enter the restaurant where she used to work and the staff — and many customers — greeted Dennis before her. Rhonda, the crusty old cashier who always reeked of cigarette smoke, left her station to hug Dennis, then held on to his biceps as she told how she'd heard about his accident and was wondering how he was doing. The woman who had seldom had a kind word for the wait staff was absolutely bubbly with Dennis.

The pair made their way to a table with Zoey, the green-haired waitress, grinning right behind them. She waited impatiently while Dennis settled into the booth and put his cane behind him, then asked, "What'll you have to drink?"

"Sweet tea, Zoey. Thank you," Dennis answered.

"Same," said Kelsi.

"How ya doin'?" Zoey asked her with a quick look as she wrote on her order pad.

"I'm good," Kelsi said. "Just trying to keep Dennis from breaking anything else."

Zoey left to get the drinks and Kelsi and Dennis studied the menus. "You really do know everybody," Kelsi said, smiling but not looking up. "Did you ever come in here when I was working here?"

"Probably not," Dennis said. "Once I gave up driving, I stopped coming in. I used to be a Saturday morning regular." He nodded toward the restaurant's largest booth, which was almost a complete circle in the corner farthest from the door.

"The farm club?" Kelsi asked.

"Oh yeah. I've known those guys since I was a kid, before my folks moved us into the city," he answered.

Zoey returned with their drinks and took their food orders. Dennis ordered a pulled pork sandwich and fries, so Kelsi got the same. Once she had the orders scribbled onto her pad, Zoey put a hand on Dennis's shoulder and said, "You better make Kelsi here bring you back more often. We miss you around here."

"Are the boys still coming in on Saturday mornings?" he asked.

"Oh, shoot, you know they are," Zoey said, slapping playfully at his shoulder. "We can't hardly keep enough coffee brewed when they're here."

"Well, I'll see about it," Dennis said. "I don't think my chauffer would be entertained by the conversation."

"Oh, we'll put her right back to work," Zoey said and laughed. Kelsi and Dennis laughed, too, and for just a moment Kelsi missed the hustle of the busy restaurant. Zoey moved away to put in their order.

"I think she's flirting with you," Kelsi whispered loudly.

Dennis nearly choked on his drink of tea. He put his glass down and wiped at his mouth, his eyes twinkling. "Do you think so? She's probably a third of my age."

"I think she'd have to fight Rhonda for you," Kelsi said. "I've never seen her treat anyone like that. Not even her husband the one time he dared come in and bother her at work."

"Her dad was a friend of mine," Dennis said. "I've known her since she was a baby."

"Does anyone in town not like you?" Kelsi asked.

Dennis chuckled. "I'm sure there are people who don't like me. I've had some arguments with city commissioners and library board members, but I always tried to keep it professional, not personal." He shrugged. "I can't say how they feel, though." He traced a small circle on the table, his smile fading. "Losing your spouse softens people's opinions of you, too."

"Oh. I guess I can see how it would," Kelsi said.

During dinner, they talked about Dennis's rehabilitation, about Kelsi's activities with new friends, and the health of Emelia Dunn, one of the ladies who'd brought a casserole and had just been diagnosed with the covid-19 virus.

"Emelia's husband, David, loves meatloaf," Dennis said.

Kelsi grinned at the hint. "How about if we make him one?"

"Ummm ... I think it would taste better if I stayed away from that process," Dennis said.

"Surely you cooked before I came along," Kelsi teased.

"Simple stuff that didn't require mixing ingredients. Or frozen dinners," Dennis said. "I can cook frozen chicken strips with the best of them."

"It's a miracle you've survived," Kelsi said.

Despite Kelsi's protests, Dennis insisted on paying while Rhonda gushed about how good it was to finally see Dennis again. The wait staff and half the customers waved as Dennis and Kelsi left the restaurant. In the car, Kelsi hesitated starting the engine, her eyes running across the road and to the north where the tall cedar trees marked the border of the cemetery.

"Kelsi?" Dennis asked. "What's wrong?

She shook her head once. "Nothing," she said.

"Tell me. You look so sad right now." His voice was gentle and coaxing, almost like a spell, drawing the information out of her.

"On my breaks when I worked here, a lot of time I'd go over there to the cemetery," she confessed. "I didn't have any friends or family. I was either at work, at school, or with Tucker for two years. That was my whole life."

"Why the cemetery?" Dennis asked.

"At first, because it's peaceful. It's so quiet there, and nobody expects anything from you in a graveyard," she said.

"At first? Then what?"

"I found Floyd Duncan."

Dennis asked, "Who's that?"

Kelsi gave a tiny laugh. "What? Somebody you don't know?"

"Yeah, he missed out, I guess," Dennis said, but his tone told her he was waiting.

"Floyd lived and died a long time ago," she said. "He was born on July 25, 1899, and died on August 2, 1951."

"Oh yeah, *that* Floyd," Dennis said.

"You're kidding!" Kelsi said, her eyes bulging.

Dennis laughed. "I am kidding," he said. "Is he related to you?"

"I don't know," Kelsi said. "I doubt it, but I would pretend he was. I'd take my lunch over there and eat it at his grave and talk to him."

"Did he ever answer?" Dennis asked, his voice teasing.

"No. I never saw or felt him like I do Gloria and some others," Kelsi said.

"You haven't visited since you came to live with me?" Dennis asked.

"No," she admitted.

"Let's go. Right now. Let's go visit Floyd," Dennis said.

"No, it's dumb. And I have friends who are alive now."

"I could use some of that peace and quiet you talked about," Dennis said. "Get my feet in the grass a little more today."

"Fine," Kelsi said, giving in to what she wanted to do, anyway.

The evening was wearing on and the shadows of the towering, cylindrical cedar trees and the taller of the grave markers stretched across the manicured lawn of the cemetery as Kelsi slowly drove along the narrow lane to the eastern edge. She parked as close as she could to the familiar grave, then got Dennis's chair out of the Buick's trunk as he pushed himself out of the passenger seat without help. Kelsi set up the chair to face the gravestone the same way she did the sycamore tree. When Dennis was safely in it and and pushed his loafers off to get his bare feet in the green grass, Kelsi sank into a cross-legged position beside him. She leaned back, bracing herself with her hands behind her.

"I can almost feel the charge from being on the ground," she said.

"I envy you being able to get down there and get back up," Dennis said. "So, this is Floyd Duncan?"

"Yep. Floyd, this is Dennis. He's the reason I haven't been around for a while," she said.

"Thank you for lending her to me," Dennis said, nodding toward the stone.

They sat in silence for a while and the darkness crept in around them. Cicadas chittered and nightbirds sang. Far off, there was the sound of traffic. With the night came a gentle breeze that ruffled Kelsi's hair and made the cedars sway as if slow dancing at a high school prom.

"I'm glad you came to live with me, Kelsi," Dennis said at last.

"I am, too."

"It was a lonely life before."

Kelsi smiled. "With all your friends?"

"They didn't come around much. The friends I have left aren't the kind who visit. We've talked about that. My best friends moved away or died." He paused, moved his feet in the grass, looked up at the stars. "I'll be following them soon."

"You're moving?" Kelsi asked. "Into a retirement home?" She knew that wasn't what he meant, but she wanted to derail the conversation train he seemed to want to drive.

"Since the accident, I've woke up twice outside my body," Dennis said. "Both times, Gloria has been there and told me it wasn't time." Now he looked down at Kelsi, who was looking back at him. "She promised it would be soon, though."

"Don't ..." Kelsi began, then stopped. "I understand," she said.

"She likes you a lot," Dennis said. "I do, too. When you took me downtown a while back and I sent you to have coffee, I was visiting with my lawyer. I made some changes to my will. I'm giving you my house. That's why Natalie came and took the last of her stuff."

"But ... Dennis ... You can't do that," Kelsi said, dumbfounded by the statement. "You have family ..."

"And I'm very fortunate that my family is doing just fine," he said. "The house isn't worth much. Maybe you've noticed nobody's building new businesses on Nokomis's east side. Natalie would sell the house and the money she'd get might pay for one of her elaborate vacations. It wouldn't mean much. I think ... I hope you've made friends and like it here and will make my home your home when I'm gone. Gloria loves watching you in her old kitchen."

Kelsi couldn't face him. Tears rolled down her cheeks and she could taste them on her lips. The lump in her throat prevented her from speaking for a while. Finally, she nodded and whispered, "Thank you, Dennis. So much. You ... you've always been so nice to me."

"There's some money, too," Dennis said. "Not a fortune, and I'm not leaving you all of it, but it will take care of any inheritance taxes and should pay off your college loans. You'll have to use that college degree and get a job when I'm gone."

Kelsi couldn't smother the crying any longer. She couldn't speak. She could barely see through the tears. She nodded her head and felt Dennis put a gentle hand on her shoulder. He squeezed once, then left the hand there. It was comforting being physically connected. He moved it away when Kelsi got herself under control enough to wipe at her eyes and cheeks.

"I love you, Dennis," she said at last. "You are the kindest person I've ever known. I want you to be with Gloria again, but I'm going to miss you so much."

"I'll be around," he promised. "And I'm not going yet. You may recall that we have a job to do."

Kelsi had to think for a minute before she remembered. "Gloria's ashes," she said.

"Yes. We should start getting some decent rain in September."

"We're really going to do it?"

"Gloria's orders," Dennis said, and grinned. "That's all I need."

Kelsi nodded. "We'll do it," she said.

Dennis sighed and looked away into the darkness. "And you'll do mine the same when the time comes, right?"

"Of course," Kelsi said quietly.

"Natalie will throw a fit, like I said. I'll try to tell her before it happens. I don't want to leave you to face her. William will stand with you. William Sheets. He's my attorney. You probably shouldn't tell them what you're doing with the ashes, though," Dennis said.

"Spreading dead people around a public park near a playground isn't cool here?" Kelsi tried to joke.

"Not so much," he said. "Natalie will want a memorial service. That's fine. It's for her. Let her do it. No body, no urn. I don't want to be there in any way."

They were quiet for a while, then Kelsi asked, "How long do you think?"

"I don't know," he answered.

Chapter Thirty-Nine

School started in late August and Kelsi immediately realized that, while she'd considered herself busy with Dennis's care and the upkeep of the house and meals and visiting friends, she soon decided she'd been living a life of leisure. She had two classes on campus three days each week and two more online classes. Fortunately, she had friends now and the time away from school spent studying and making notes was much more fun that it used to be. The women laughed and ate and talked about the professors and other students and drank enough wine to feel just a little lightheaded by the time the homework was done or the study session was over.

The bond of the study group was proven the night they found the bruises and burns on Cassie Phillips. Cassie was a petite woman, barely over five feet tall, with short brown hair streaked with black, like a pecan shell. She was always the quietest of the group of four to six women, but on a Thursday of the third week after classes resumed, she hardly spoke at all and barely touched her wine or tacos. Then Kinley bumped into her back reaching for a cord to plug in her computer. Cassie gasped and flinched away. The kitchen became very quiet and the other three women all looked at Cassie, who refused to meet the gaze of any of them.

"What's wrong?" Kelsi asked.

"Nothing," Cassie said.

"I barely touched you, Cass," Kinley said. "It shouldn't have hurt. What's going on?" Kinley moved her hand like she was going to touch Cassie's back again and the woman jerked away.

"That's a cigarette burn!" Joylynn Summers pointed to Cassie's upper arm.

"Stop," Cassie pleaded, trying to pull her short sleeve down to cover the mark.

Kinley gently took Cassie's hand and stopped her. She bent and looked closer. "It is a burn," she said. "The right size for a cigarette. And it's fresh."

They all knew. In the silence, they all considered their own pasts, their fears, and in that moment their individual rage became the anger of the group. Still, they needed confirmation, and it was Kelsi who asked for it.

"Did your boyfriend do that?" She had to think to get his name. "Did A.J. do that to you?"

Cassie swallowed hard and looked down. "It was my fault."

"Bullshit!" Joylynn's hand slapped down on the table, sounding like a gunshot. Cassie nearly jumped out of her seat. "How is that your fault?"

"We had an agreement," Cassie squeaked.

Trying to head off Joylynn's next outburst, Kelsi took Cassie's hand in hers. "What agreement?"

"He doesn't like me coming here," Cassie whispered. "He says evenings off work and out of school should be his time."

"What's the agreement?" Kelsi urged.

"Blowjob," Cassie said. "Before I go. Dinner took longer than I thought it would and I was running late and tried to get him to agree to after I got home."

"And he beat you for it?" Joylynn demanded.

"Shh," Kinley said, waving her away.

Cassie nodded. "I should have just done it. I was late, anyway."

"Honey, that's no reason," Kelsi said. "And you don't owe him anything. He doesn't own you. How bad is it?"

"The worst yet," Cassie said. "I didn't want to come after, but he said I'd earned it and made me come."

"He's done this before?" Kelsi asked. Cassie nodded. "Come to the bathroom and let me see."

Kelsi didn't wait for Cassie to agree or protest, but stood up and kept hold of the other woman's hand. Used to complying, Cassie stood and allowed Kelsi to lead her into the bathroom of Kinley's apartment. With Kelsi doing most of the work, they carefully removed Cassie's clothes. Kelsi was horrified by the bruises, burns, and scratches. There were welts that she knew were made by a leather belt. One breast was nearly all black and blue. Blood vessels were broken in her butt cheeks where he had apparently pinched her. Kelsi counted six burn marks from her thighs up to her shoulder. The whole time she examined her friend, Cassie simply stood with slumped shoulders.

"Did he rape you?" Kelsi asked softly.

Cassie nodded and a tear dislodged itself from her eye and slid down her cheek.

"Oh, baby, I'm sorry," Kelsi said, and she put her arms around the naked woman and pulled her close in a very careful embrace. Cassie hugged her back, gently at first, but as the silent tears turned into sobs, she clung to Kelsi, her voice rising to a wail of despair. Kelsi didn't say anything, but cried along with her friend. Until the knock came at the door.

"The police are here. They need to talk to Cassie," Joylynn said.

"No!" Cassie let go of Kelsi and stepped away, her eyes large and round like a trapped animal's.

Kelsi looked from the closed door to the naked woman. "It's the right thing to do," she said. "Even if you leave him, he'll move on and do this to someone else. You deserve better. Nobody deserves to be treated like this. But they shouldn't have called the police without asking you." She paused to think. "Get dressed. I'll go talk to them. Get in the bathtub and close the curtain so nobody sees."

Kelsi slipped out of the bathroom to find Kinley and Joylynn and two black-uniformed police officers, one an Hispanic man and the other a white woman. The guns on their hips looked huge and threatening. The man asked her, "Are you the victim?"

"No," Kelsi said. "She's getting dressed." She looked at her friends. "Who called the police? Cassie is scared to death now."

"It was either this or she was going over there with a baseball bat," Kinley said apologetically.

"It should be Cassie's decision," Kelsi argued.

"We're here now," the female cop said. "It will be her decision on whether or not anything is done to her boyfriend. Will she come out and talk to us?"

The bathroom door opened and Cassie stepped out. She had only put on her underwear and held her T-shirt over her breasts. A lot of the marks were visible. Kelsi heard the male cop suck in his breath at the sight.

The policewoman said, "Omar, will you step outside and call for a paramedic?" When he'd left, she turned back to Cassie. "Let me see, baby."

Cassie's hand dropped, pulling the T-shirt away. Everyone but Kelsi gasped. The police officer asked Cassie to turn around. Kinley began to cry. Joylynn swore. "If ya'll don't put him in jail I'm gonna kill him for this, the fucking bastard."

The cop seemed to ignore Joylynn's outburst. "Did he sexually assault you?" she asked. Cassie nodded. "How?"

Cassie's first attempt to answer failed. She cleared her throat and tried again. "He bent me over the table and ..." Her voice faltered.

"Vaginally?" the policewoman asked. Cassie shook her head. "Anally?" Cassie nodded. "Did he finish?" Another nod. "Was he wearing a condom?"

"No."

"We're going to get you some medical treatment," the officer said. "We can arrest him, but it's up to you to press charges. Will you do that?"

Cassie hesitated.

"Cassie, if you don't, I swear to God I'll go to prison for killing him," Joylynn said.

Kinley moved closer to Joylynn. "Me, too."

Cassie's eyes moved to her and Kelsi nodded. "Me, too. Cops or us. He's not getting away with this."

Kelsi looked around the small room and saw the anger and determination in the eyes of her friends. Her friends. They stood together, united in a cause, and it was something she had never experienced. She wanted to quote *The Three Musketeers* "One for all and all for one" but it wasn't the time. Still, her heart swelled with happiness to be part of this group.

Chapter Forty

Cassie had two major fears after her boyfriend was arrested. One was that the media would pick up the story and come after her for an interview. All that was reported, however, was a blip in the police blotter section of the local newspaper. The second was that he would get out on bond and kill her. It was Joylynn, who had taken to protecting and mothering Cassie, who sent a text message to the group the next day offering relief from that fear.

> The bastard has two previous assault and battery cases from fights in bars. There's a juvy record for sexual assault, but they probably can't use that. He's not getting bonded out. Held over for trial.

Kelsi, sitting in Dennis's favorite recliner with her legs dangling over the armrest, read the text and responded with a "Wooohoo!" She was happy her friend was safe, but her mind was elsewhere. It was after nine in the morning and Dennis was still in bed. That was very unlike him, and after what he'd shared with her in the cemetery, it worried her enough that she'd checked on him twice since she got up two hours ago. He'd been fine both times, snoring lightly, though Kelsi suspected the second time was fake. She went to her contacts page on her phone, thinking for an instant about how much longer that page had become over the past few weeks. She scrolled to the bottom until she found Peter Zook. She let her fingers dance over the keys before she could second-guess herself.

> I'm worried about Dennis. Could we meet so I can talk to you privately? He has therapy at 1 today.

> If you can come by the church we can talk for a while. 1:15?

> Thank you! See you then.

Shortly after, Kelsi finally heard the *shuffle-thump-shuffle* of Dennis coming down the hallway with his house slippers and cane. He went to the bathroom, where she heard him urinating, then flushing and washing. When he came into the living room, Kelsi gave up his recliner and propped herself on the couch so she could see him as he came over and settled into the chair. Gloria's urn of ashes and photograph were between them. Dennis grunted as he sat.

"I warmed it up for you," Kelsi said.

"I feel that," he answered with a mild grin. "I guess I only dreamed of bacon and scrambled eggs."

"I guess so," Kelsi said. "It's getting on to lunchtime, as you like to say." Dennis looked at the watch he only took off to shower, then grunted at her. "I'll make you some. Or, we can go out for breakfast. My treat. If you feel up to it."

"It was a rough night," Dennis said. "I didn't sleep well." He looked to the end table and took up the framed picture of his wife. He held it in his lap and stared at it. "I miss her," he said.

"Did you dream about her?"

"Yes."

"Did ... Was she there? Did she visit you?" Kelsi asked.

Dennis nodded. "Yes. I dreamed about her and woke up and she was there."

"Did she tell you anything?"

"Yes."

Kelsi waited, but there was nothing else coming. She prompted, "Do you want to tell me?"

Dennis shook his head. "No, I don't think so."

Kelsi popped up from the couch, making herself seem cheerier than she was. She bent and kissed Dennis on his bald head, then told him, "I'll make breakfast. You want toast, too?"

"Please," he said without looking away from the portrait.

She made the breakfast and put it on the table, then went to the kitchen doorway to call Dennis to come eat. He was still in the recliner, the framed picture hugged to his chest with one arm while he clutched the bronze urn against him with the other hand. Sunlight from the front window made the tears glisten on his face. Kelsi stepped away from the doorway, counted to ten, then called out, "Dennis, it's ready when you are," without looking back into the living room. It was a few minutes before she heard him making his way to the kitchen.

Kelsi sat with Dennis and did her best to keep up a cheerful banter about school and her friends and how the days seemed to be getting just a little bit cooler, but Dennis didn't participate much. He smiled weakly, nodded, and made a few listless comments here and there, but mostly just mechanically moved food from his plate to his mouth, chewed, and swallowed. When the food was gone, Kelsi gathered the dishes and put them in the dishwasher. Dennis was still in his chair when she turned back.

"We've got some time before your therapy appointment. How about we go outside and soak up some of that earth energy," she suggested. "I know some flowers that could use a morning drink."

"Don't you have some homework to do?" Dennis asked. "I thought I might go back to bed. I'd really like to skip rehab today."

"Dennis, you're not sick," Kelsi argued. "I think what you need is sunshine on your face, grass under your feet, and then to be around other people."

He sat quietly for a while and Kelsi was sure he was going to protest again, but then he simply said, "Okay."

She rubbed his back a moment with her open palm, then said, "Come on, lets get outside. Do you want to put on some shorts so we'll match?"

He managed a snort of laughter, then got up from his chair, putting his weight on the cane and the top of the table. "If I had your legs I'd do it," he said.

"Why, Dennis," Kelsi said in mock outrage. "Have you been ogling my legs?"

He laughed a little more, then gently swatted her bare foot with the rubber tip of his cane. "Get out, you scamp, before I run you and your indecent naked legs right over."

Both of them barefoot in the manicured green grass, Kelsi pulled a few weeds and then Dennis held the water hose and sprayed the last of the season's flowers until the bright petals and dark green leaves were dripping with water that glistened in the sunlight. The smell of the wet soil was loamy and comforting. A couple of bees buzzed around, avoiding the cascading water to dip and dive into the flowers.

An Asian child, older than a toddler but too young for school, appeared at the chain link fence next door. He was dressed only in dark blue shorts, his hair buzzed nearly to his scalp and his pudgy fingers clinging to the wire of the interlaced fence. He cackled and danced when Dennis moved the water in his direction, then stopped when it moved away. Kelsi watched this happen a few times.

"Will his mom get mad if you spray him?" she asked.

"I don't know," Dennis answered. "Should I try it and see?"

"I think he'd love it. Maybe don't soak him?" Kelsi suggested.

Dennis adjusted the nozzle of his sprayer so that it was a wider, gentler pattern, like soft rain, and increased the pressure so it would still reach, then slowly moved the arc of water over his flowers and toward the child, who again began to jump up and down and laugh. The boy's dark eyes widened when the water kept coming, moving out of the garden, over the grass beside it, and then Dennis flicked his wrist so that the water moved up and rained down on the child like a summer shower. The boy shrieked with delight. It was loud enough that a woman came out of the side door of the house to see what was going on. She looked at the boy with droplets of water on his skin, then at Dennis with the hose, and she laughed and waved at her neighbor. She said something in her native tongue while motioning at the boy, then she made motions like she was shooting him with water.

"I think that's permission," Kelsi said.

"I think you're right," Dennis agreed, and sprayed the boy with a little more water, earning more cackles from him. Kelsi saw Dennis finally break into a wide grin, too.

They played the game for a quarter of an hour. The boy's buzzed hair and his shorts were soaked and dripping. Kelsi said, "He's not going to get tired of this, you know?"

"I know," Dennis agreed.

"We need to get you ready for your therapy."

"You're a real party pooper, you know that?" Dennis said. He shot some water at her legs and Kelsi laughed at him.

"I'll be the bad guy," she said, and went to the house and turned off the water at the faucet. The last spray toward the little boy died in the air. The child looked at Dennis, then at Kelsi, then back at Dennis, who shrugged and made a sad face. The boy waved and turned away, disappearing around the corner of his house. "Come on, you overgrown little boy," Kelsi said, waving Dennis toward the house.

Her charge was in a better mood when Kelsi dropped Dennis off at the rehabilitation center. Since he'd moved up to just using the cane, she didn't go inside with him, but just dropped him off at the door of the circular drive. He waved as the door closed behind him and she tried not to hurry as she left, heading for the United Methodist Church and her appointment with the minister.

Chapter Forty-One

Peter's Zook's office was lined with dark-stained and full bookshelves, with a big, imposing desk that matched. It was a neat, spacious room, with everything in its place. On top of the desk was a blotter with a single file folder to one side. There was an inbox with a few envelopes that had been expertly opened with a sharp object. The office smelled of sage and Kelsi spotted a wooden incense tray on one of the shelves. The aroma reminded her of an occult store she had visited in Oklahoma City a couple of times and she found that to be odd.

The minister sat in his high-backed leather chair, his elbows on his desk and his intense but friendly eyes fixed on Kelsi, who sat in a wingback chair on the other side of the desk.

"Thanks for taking time to talk to me," Kelsi said. "I'm sorry the notice was so short, but I'm really glad I asked."

"I take it something's wrong," Peter said.

"I'm worried about Dennis," Kelsi said. "He says he's been waking up with his soul outside of his body and Gloria telling him he has to go back because it isn't his time yet."

The minister studied her for a moment before saying, "That's pretty extraordinary."

"I thought so," Kelsi agreed.

"Do you believe him?" he asked.

Kelsi hadn't even considered the possibility of *not* believing Dennis. "Yes, I believe him," she said. "I ... Well, I kind of see Gloria, myself, sometimes. Just, like, a shimmer in the air in the shape of a person, and sometimes a smell, like cinnamon and vanilla."

"I find that even more extraordinary," Peter said, his eyes unreadable. "But if you believe Dennis, what's the problem?"

"He's sad a lot of the time now," Kelsi said. "He wasn't when I first met him. Or, he never showed it." She told him about the morning, Dennis sleeping late, then weeping as he held his deceased wife's photo and ashes.

"Tell me something, Kelsi," Peter said. "Is this really about Dennis? Or about you?"

"What do you mean?" she asked.

"Dennis knows he's an old man and his time to leave us isn't far off," Peter said. "He misses Gloria and has since she passed. He's suffered a serious injury and with every step he's reminded that he's not the man he used to be. He's ready to go. You're not ready to let go."

"I ... " Kelsi sat with her mouth open, not knowing what to say. She clicked her teeth as she closed her mouth, then shook her head. "You're right," she whispered. Her eyes blurred with sudden, unexpected tears. She wiped at them, not caring that she was crying in front of this man. "My home life wasn't so good growing up," she said. "I never knew a grandparent. Mom tried for a while, but Dad was always in trouble and getting moved away, so I never stayed in one town or state very long, then he ... he did something bad and Mom moved us, but she became a drunk." She paused, sighed and looked away. Finally, she slapped her hands onto her bare thighs. "I'm just saying I never had anyone like Dennis in my life and I've only had him for a little while. I don't want to lose him."

With her vision blurred, she missed when Peter left his side of the barrier between them and came to the chair matching hers. He took her hands in his and squeezed them, ignoring the warm tears on her fingers. "He's quite a man, isn't he?" Peter asked. Kelsi could only nod her agreement. "He's helped a lot of people in this town. He's changed a lot of lives. You're his final gift to the town."

Confused, Kelsi asked, "What?"

"Dennis sees so much in you. So much potential," Peter said. "He says you are the kindest person he's met, other than Gloria. He's told me countless times how much you remind him of her. He hopes you'll stay here when he's gone and become involved with the people here."

"He said that?" Kelsi asked.

"He did."

"He's leaving me his house," she said.

"I know."

"I love him," Kelsi said. "Not like a boyfriend."

Peter chuckled. "I know. Have you told him that?"

"Once," Kelsi said. "I didn't know if it would be weird. He seemed okay with it"

"You would make his day if you told him often," Peter said.

Kelsi pulled her left hand away and swiped at her eyes and cheeks again. "He's not very religious, but he really likes you," she said.

Peter smiled and nodded. "Dennis is what we'd call spiritual but not religious. He's a good man. He follows his own spiritual path and sometimes it intersects with the more traditional path of the Methodists."

"Do you love him?" Kelsi asked.

"I do," Peter said.

"I guess you have to love everybody," she countered.

"I try to. Dennis makes it easy to love him." Peter paused and then squeezed her hand again. "We need to focus on you being ready for the day Dennis leaves us."

"God, I don't want to think about that," she said.

"It will come, whether you think about it or not," he promised.

"I know. His daughter hates me now. And his grandson," Kelsi said. "That's going to be awkward."

"Maybe," Peter said. "We'll deal with that later. Tell me, Kelsi, do you believe in an afterlife?"

"Yes," Kelsi said. "I know there's something. I've seen too many ghosts."

"So, you're confident Dennis will go on after he leaves this mortal plane?" Peter asked.

"Yes," Kelsi said.

"You know he won't be gone? Not really?"

"I do know it," Kelsi said. "But he won't be there where I can talk to him and he can talk to me. He can't tease me or sit and read with me or trick me into meeting people he thinks I need to be friends with."

"He's already done all of that," Peter said. "You'll miss him. That's normal. But you have wonderful memories, and there's time to make some more. Enjoy every moment you have with him. When his time comes, be happy for him. He wants to be with Gloria again so much."

"I know," Kelsi admitted quietly. "I have to give him back to her."

Peter chuckled again. "You can think of it that way if you want. He tells me she likes you a lot."

"Do *you* believe in ghosts?" Kelsi asked.

Peter grinned. "Officially, my response is not in the traditional sense, but personally, I believe in Dennis and I know that even though he loves a good prank, he wouldn't lie about this."

"You believe in burning sage in your office," Kelsi said. "To keep evil spirits away?"

"Maybe I just like the smell," Peter said.

"Thank you for talking to me. And seeing through my bullsh— My misunderstanding of the issue," she corrected, remembering where she was.

"It's what I'm here for," Peter said.

"I'm not even part of your flock," Kelsi said.

"You're welcome to join," he said.

Kelsi laughed softly. "I'm not ready for that kind of commitment. Plus, the witch with the tea shop has scones."

"We have bread and wine," he said.

Kelsi laughed again and squeezed both of his hands in hers. "Thank you again. I need to go pick him up."

"Did he get over the sadness you talked about this morning?" Peter asked.

"Yes," Kelsi said, and she related the story of the neighbor boy and how that had brought up the joy Dennis seemed to have buried inside himself.

Peter nodded. "He's always looking to make someone else happy." He released Kelsi's hands and stood up. She stood up with him. "Come see me any time, Kelsi. It's always a pleasure."

"Thank you," Kelsi said. They stood awkwardly for a moment, then laughed as they shook hands. She made her way through the silent sanctuary to the front door and her car beyond.

Chapter Forty-Two

Kelsi was doing her homework at the big kitchen table. It was dark outside, but she'd lost track of time. Two open textbooks and a spiral notebook full of her looping penmanship were spread on either side of the open laptop computer that cast a ghastly, death-like pallor on her face. In the living room, Dennis sat in his recliner watching the late news on the television. Kelsi was startled when he suddenly shouted her name.

"Kelsi! Come look at this!" he called, his voice full of excitement.

Kelsi nearly jumped out of her chair and hurried into the other room, her bare feet patting on the hardwood floor. "What?" she asked. "What is it?"

Dennis pointed to the television. "It's holding together. We're going to get it. A real autumn soaker."

On the screen, a nearly bald thin man in an expensive suit waved at a map of the state. Animation showed a field of green, interspersed with yellow and dots of red, creeping across Oklahoma until the whole state was covered. "It won't be a constant rain," the meteorologist said, "But it's going to be a very, very wet weekend, with parts of the state, especially up north around Sage Brush, Alva, Nokomis, and Ponca City getting up to three or four inches. We may have some flash flood warnings as the moisture actually gets here."

"That's a lot of rain," Kelsi said.

"It is," Dennis said. "It'll do."

"What do you ..." Kelsi stopped, her eyes moving to the urn on the table beside Dennis recliner. She nodded that she understood. "We'll take care of it," she promised.

The next day, Kelsi came home from her morning class to find Dennis sitting in his recliner, the footrest up and the back reclined. He snored gently, and snuggled against his side was the bronze urn of ashes. Kelsi didn't think much of it until later, when she called him to lunch and he brought the urn to the table with him. Evening came early because of the heavy cloud cover that had moved in late in the afternoon. A cool wind came with the clouds, so Kelsi suggested sitting on the porch for a while. She took a textbook. Dennis picked up a Western novel, and the urn, which he put on the table beside his old metal chair on the porch. Kelsi took the porch swing, tucked into one corner with her feet across the seat and under the other arm. She opened her book, but watched as Dennis read and occasionally reached over and stroked the cool bronze of the container beside him. The world got darker around them until neither of could read and they simply sat and listened to the wind blow through the leaves of the trees around them.

"We don't have to do it," Kelsi said.

Streetlight glinted off Dennis's reading glasses as he turned to look at her over the top of them. "We have to do it. I promised her, and I've waited too long."

"It comforts you having her in the house, though," Kelsi said. "She would understand."

"No, it's time," he argued.

"I could ... you know, do it with you, when that time comes. Together, you know?"

"I know." Dennis's voice was soft. "But this is something I want to do for her. I promised her I'd do it."

"Okay," Kelsi said, giving in. "You're a hell of a man, Dennis. I hope Gloria knew that. I think she did."

"I was nothing without her." His spectacles flashed again as he turned his eyes back toward the street.

"You can ask just about anybody in this city and they'll tell you that isn't true," Kelsi argued.

"Not many people left who knew me before we were married, let alone before we became a couple," Dennis replied.

"You're a hell of a man, but sometimes you are insufferably stubborn," Kelsi told him.

Dennis laughed a little. "I've heard that last part a few times."

They sat quietly for a while as the wind gusted around them. Kelsi could smell the coming rain and feel the energy of the storm in the air. She looked up and down the street, wondering if others felt it like she did. Then she smiled at an old memory. "When I was a kid and things were bad at home, I'd go for walks," she said. "I loved walking through neighborhoods as it got dark and looking at the windows with lights on inside the house. The best ones had a yellowish glow that I thought looked very warm and kind of welcoming. I would imagine the people inside living perfect, happy lives. Sometimes I'd wish the front door would open and the light would spill out and a father like on the television shows would come out and ask if I wanted to join his family."

"You're too young to be so full of sad stories," Dennis said.

"Maybe," Kelsi said. "But look at the windows up and down the street. Each one has people on the other side, living their lives in houses that have individual smells oozing from the walls, cracked ceilings, faucets you have to turn just right so they don't drip, and other quirks that all make the houses their homes."

"And you imagine the lives they're living, don't you?" Dennis asked.

"Sometimes, yeah," she admitted. She thought he might say something more about her silliness, but he didn't. She saw his hand go back to the urn. "Did she suffer very long?"

"She did," he whispered.

Kelsi waited a moment, considering, then asked, "Will you tell me about it?"

He looked at her again, then away, a double flash of streetlamps across his face. "Yes," he whispered. "I need to tell it."

Chapter Forty-Three

The withered, shrunken lady had skin as pale and creased as old paste smeared over a Halloween skull decades ago. Her breath rattled in her thin chest. Her hair was gone. There had been a few wisps that would float around her face when she wasn't wearing her wig, but she had insisted those be shaved off. The wig was on a stand on her dresser, long cornsilk waves like she'd had when she was a young woman. It had never looked right on her elderly head, but it had been what she wanted.

"If I'm going to wear fake hair, I'll damn well let everyone know it," she'd said about the color of the wig.

Her hand was tiny, thin, bony, and gnarled as a sparrow's talon. Her husband's large, work-hardened hand engulfed the human claw but did so in the gentlest way possible. Her other hand lay on the bed beside her, just as claw-like, the flesh just as papery thin.

She had been strong once. Invincible. A boulder in the river of time, with good and bad events battering against her, swirling, and rushing by without leaving any noticeable damage to the rock that had been the cornerstone of Dennis Aiken's world since childhood. She had directed committees, led rallies, raised a strong daughter, and had a hand in countless civic decisions through her husband. But now she was a dying old woman lying in a hospice bed in the living room of the house she had made a home for over fifty years. Her husband could have lifted what was left of her in one hand if he'd chosen to.

There were no tubes. No wires. Nothing to monitor her progress. This was the end. All of those things had been for an earlier time, a time when there had been hope that medicine, diet, and prayer would change her fate. Like poodle skirts, bell bottoms, and polyester pantsuits, those things were part of her past. She wore a thin hospital gown with a pattern of little blue flowers. It would be the last thing she wore in this world.

Dennis wept, even though she had told him not to. He promised he would stop before she woke up again. If she woke up again …

She would wake.

The hospice nurse said in the end there would be morphine every fifteen minutes, but they had a little while before that was necessary. Maybe a few hours. Maybe a day.

Dennis held his wife's hand and cried.

It had begun, like it did for so many women, with a lump in her breast. The left one. Mammogram. X-rays. An MRI. Biopsy. Diagnosis. Weeks of chemotherapy. Then the news got worse. Rather than shrinking, the cancer had spread throughout her body, almost like it was seeking revenge for the attempt to destroy it. A tall, gray-haired doctor saying Gloria should get her affairs in order and prepare those who love her.

"How long?" Dennis asked.

The doctor shook his head. "No more than a few months. I'm sorry."

That had been two months and three days ago. Gloria had aged years during the months of her treatment. She was nearly unrecognizable from photographs taken just a year ago. Only her humor and her will had remained unchanged as her body betrayed her.

On the bed, her eyes began to move under the tissue-like membranes of her eyelids. Dennis bent quickly and kissed her temple, then drew back and used his free hand to wipe the moisture from his face. Her head turned, her hand twitched in his, and her eyes opened. Her thin, colorless lips stretched in a weak smile.

"You haven't found a replacement for me yet?" she asked in a cracked whisper.

Dennis tried to laugh, but what came out was a barked sob that exploded from his mouth. Despite his promise, he broke down, and now it was her shrunken hand gripping his fingers, her voice too weak to offer words of comfort as she waited for the storm to pass. After a few minutes, Dennis got himself under control.

"When I go, you'll have widows swarming this house with their casseroles and pies and they'll be sizing you up," she whispered. "Pick one who'll take care of you. But not that Bessie Strombridge. I never liked her."

"You treat her like your best friend," Dennis said, surprised.

"Keep your friends close and your enemies closer," Gloria whispered, then smiled. "I know what she did to win that blue ribbon at the fair in 'Eighty-three. My pie was always better and she knew it. So did Ronald Bixby, but her apple pie wasn't the only pie he got from her that year."

"That was over forty years ago," Dennis said, grinning at the fire, however dim, that had come to his wife's eyes.

"A leopard doesn't change its spots," Gloria snapped back.

"Well, it doesn't matter," Dennis said. "I've never had anybody but you, and it'll stay that way. 'Til death do us part."

"Death will part us pretty soon," Gloria whispered. "You won't make it alone. Do you even know how to turn on the clothes dryer?"

"Natalie will help me," Dennis said.

"You'll spend your entire pension check on Werther's candies and wonder why you can't buy groceries," Gloria complained.

"No, you've taught me how to budget," he reminded.

Gloria sighed. "I worry about you."

"Hopefully I'll be with you soon," he said.

"Don't you dare talk like that, Dennis Jay Aiken," she warned, her voice almost more than the whisper. "You still have life to live. You're still needed around here. Time won't mean anything where I am. But you better squeeze every drop of living you can out of the time you have left. Promise me."

He fought back the tears this time but had to answer around a lump in his throat. "I promise."

The exertion of getting that promise out of him cost her. Gloria winced in pain, then drew her legs up as the agony made a crescendo through her body. That seemed to last forever, though it was only about ten minutes. Eventually, the fit passed, leaving the frail figure even weaker. She reached for her husband's hand and Dennis was there for her.

"Don't forget our tree," she whispered. "Don't forget Woody. I'll know."

Dennis worked hard to speak without choking on a sob. "I won't forget," he promised.

"Leave me there, like we talked about," she said, her voice little more than a breath.

"Yes," he promised.

There was a long pause and he thought she had fallen asleep or lost consciousness, but then she spoke for the last time. "Dennis? I hear singing." Her eyes closed, she smiled a little, then slept. Dennis strained his ears, but heard nothing except his wife's labored breathing and the ticking of a clock.

About two hours later, Gloria stopped breathing and there was only the clock ticking until Dennis's wails and sobs drowned it out. When the hospice nurse came to check on Gloria, she had to sedate Dennis and lead him to the bed he used to share with his wife. When he woke up hours later, the body was gone, the temporary hospital bed in the living room was gone, the nurse was gone. He was alone in the house. Gloria was gone.

Chapter Forty-Four

"Looking back, I know her spirit left her body when she said she heard singing," Dennis said to Kelsi, who sat across from him, wiping her cheeks. "It just took a while for her body to realize she'd left it."

"I'm sorry," Kelsi said, not knowing what else to say. "I wish I had known her."

"You would have loved her," Dennis said. "And she would have loved you. Even more than she does."

Kelsi laughed a little, but it was mixed with tears. "How did you get through it? I've never lost anyone to death, let alone anyone I've loved like that."

"It wasn't easy," Dennis said. "Natalie helped a lot. She's a great organizer, like her mom. We'd already arranged the cremation and paid all the expenses, but there was the funeral to plan and the death certificate and ... a lot of stuff. Natalie got me out of bed and back on my feet. I was numb through it all, and for a long time afterward, but she pushed me through it." He paused, reflecting, and his face seemed to droop a little. "Sometimes I think she pushed me through the stages of grief too quickly. But, here we are."

Kelsi blew her nose. She had gone inside for a box of tissue and a small trashcan less than halfway through the story. "You never thought about getting a dog or cat for company?"

"I did. But it just never happened. They're a lot of responsibility, and I had to learn to take care of myself," he said. He paused and cocked his head to one side like a puppy hearing a new sound. There was a faint rumble in the distance. "Thunder," he said, and looked down at the urn he held.

"Do you want to do it before the rain starts?" Kelsi asked. "Or go while it's raining?"

"Can we go at about midnight?" he asked. "It'll be raining by then. I think ... well, it's silly, I guess."

"No, what is it?" Kelsi asked.

Dennis gave a smile that was only on one side of his mouth as he looked at the urn. "Heaven's tears," he said. "And I just want to feel the rain on my face again, especially there in the park under our tree."

Kelsi didn't like the ominous sound of that, but of course she agreed. "I'll make us some tea and maybe we can watch a movie until it's time to go. I bought some really good tea downtown."

"From the town witch?" Dennis asked with a grin. "That sounds fine."

Kelsi went to the kitchen and made the tea and carried the two mugs back to the living room. Dennis hadn't moved, but sat in the chair holding the bronze container filled with his wife's remains. Kelsi set the mugs down and asked, "What was Gloria's favorite movie?"

"Oh, she had several. She loved *Forrest Gump* and *Gone with the Wind*. The last few years, she'd watch *Sweet Home Alabama* every time she saw it on TV even though we have it on tape and she could watch it any time," he said.

Kelsi smiled and nodded. "Okay. Let's watch that." She had cleaned and explored the house enough to know about the cabinet of VHS tapes at the bottom of one of the shelving units in the living room. The Aikens had never moved into the DVD world, let alone Blu-ray or streaming services. Kelsi took out the old tape and pushed it into the gray VCR. The machine clicked and whirred as she turned on the television. The credits came on with a line of distortion along the bottom, but that cleared up after a few seconds. She settled onto the sofa with her tea and they watched Reese Witherspoon fight against and then fall in love with Luke Perry and Kelsi tried not to notice Dennis weeping during most of the film.

The storm moved in as they watched. Lightning flashed outside the darkened window and thunder rumbled, then slammed against the house. The rain came softly at first, then in torrents, and then settled into a steady downpour that the meteorologists said would come and go, but that seemed to promise the world would end in water once again.

The movie ended and Kelsi put the tape away while Dennis discreetly wiped the tears from his face. She looked back at him where he sat in his recliner cradling the urn in the crook of one arm. "Are you sure this is what you want to do?" Kelsi asked.

He nodded. "I promised her I would."

"I understand that," Kelsi said. "But is it what *you* want to do?"

He looked at her as if he'd never considered the question, then nodded again. "It's the right thing. For her and for me. You'll do it for me? You promised. Let me be with her."

"Of course, Dennis," Kelsi said. "I'll do it. Your ashes will mingle and feed the tree you both love." She went to him and offered her hands. He put the urn back on the table long enough to accept her help up. As he came out of the recliner, Kelsi remembered the advice of Peter Zook and she put her arms around the elderly man and hugged him tight against her. "I love you, Dennis. You're the best parent and the best friend I've ever had."

Hesitantly, he arms rose and went around her middle, just above her waist and he returned a gentler hug. "I love you, too, Kelsi. I needed you in my life more than you'll ever know."

They let each other go, but looked at one another for a moment, smiling until it felt awkward, then Kelsi asked, "Do you have a raincoat?"

"In the closet by the door," he said. "Gloria's old one is in there, too. You should wear it."

In matching gray raincoats that came to their knees, they left the house and got into Kelsi's car, Dennis holding the urn tucked under his coat so no moisture would get inside despite the lid. They drove through puddles, sending arcs of water splashing up around the car as they maneuvered the deserted streets. Kelsi parked where she always parked, across the street at the side of the park. She killed the engine and they sat there for a few minutes, watching as the rain covered the windshield and distorted the world outside. There were no sounds other than the rain hitting the car.

"I don't think it's going to let up," Kelsi said.

"Doesn't sound like it," Dennis agreed.

"Are you ready?"

"Let's do it," he said.

Kelsi opened her door and swung her legs out of the car. She was wearing shorts and flip-flops under the raincoat and her bare legs were exposed to the cold rain as she got out of the car. She hurried around to help Dennis, who still struggled just a little getting out of the low car with his cane. He was having more trouble holding the cane in one hand and the urn in the other, but Kelsi got him out. He was wearing his usual khakis and loafers, which Kelsi knew were immediately soaked through by the puddle he stepped into at the curb. She opened the umbrella they'd brought from the house and together they crossed the street to the sidewalk that ran through the park. Overhead and in the distance, more thunder grumbled like an old man rolling over in bed.

Woody the sycamore stood tall and proud in the storm, his leafy branches offering some shelter from the falling rain, though the ground around his exposed, gnarled roots was wet and dark. The tree seemed to recognize the solemnity of the occasion and stood straighter than usual, Kelsi imagined. She felt Dennis gently pull his arm away from her, then he was pressing something into her hand.

"Hold these," he said. They were his eyeglasses. "The lenses are covered in water and fogging up so I can't see."

With his cane hooked on one forearm, Dennis pulled the urn from beneath his coat and gently removed the lid, which he handed over to Kelsi. He looked at her and smiled, then held the urn up as if making a toast. "For Gloria," he said.

"For Gloria," Kelsi echoed as he stepped forward.

Dennis put one hand on the trunk of the tree to steady himself, then began to sprinkle the ashes from the urn as if it was fertilizer on his flower garden. Kelsi wished desperately that she'd brought her camera, then considered the camera on her iPhone, but let it go. This wasn't a time for photographs. The gray ashes streamed out, staining the wet, black earth and knobby brown roots as Dennis, his hand still on the trunk, moved around the base of the tree, releasing his wife's ashes just as she'd wished.

Until his wet loafer slipped off a hump of root rising from the mud. He cried out as he fell sideways onto the ground, the urn slipping from his hand to clunk onto the base of the tree and roll a few inches away.

Kelsi gave a gasp of terror as soon as she saw Dennis toppling over. She dropped the umbrella, his glasses, and the urn lid as she ran to him, falling to her knees beside him on the ground. He'd rolled onto his back. His face was tight with pain. "How bad?" Kelsi asked. "Is it your hip?"

"It'll be okay," he said. "It'll be okay. Just give me a minute."

Kelsi tried to shield his exposed face from the falling rain, but he pulled her hands down and smiled wanly. "It feels so good. Like a baptism," he said. "Nice and cool."

"We need to get you home," Kelsi said.

"Help me sit up," he urged. Kelsi put her arms under him and helped him into a sitting position. He winced with the pain of the motion, but then waved her away. "You have to finish it," he told her, pointing at the urn and the tree. "Please, Kelsi. Do that for me."

She looked from him to the urn and nodded. She went to the tree and picked up the bronze container and reverently finished the circle around the tree's trunk, sprinkling the ashes all along the ground. As she came back to the starting point and let the last of the ash run from the mouth of the urn, she looked over at Dennis and sucked in her breath.

Beside him, outlined by the falling rain, was the clear shape of a woman. She squatted there, one hand on his shoulder, speaking into his ear while he smiled and looked into space.

Kelsi's hair stood up on her arms and neck. She had never seen a ghost so clearly before, other than that time on the beach when she had considered going into the water forever. She stood very still, unaware she was holding her breath, watching as the shape spoke words she could not hear.

Then Gloria turned and looked directly at Kelsi. She smiled, and then her shape dissolved in the rain and was gone.

"Oh my God," Kelsi whispered. Her voice seemed to bring Dennis back to the moment. He looked up at her.

"Help me up, please," he said.

With Dennis leaning too heavily on his cane, Kelsi gathered up the things she had dropped. They both gave a final look at the tree, particularly at the ground where the towering sycamore sprouted from the earth, at the gray ashes turning dark and soaking into the soil. Dennis nodded in satisfaction, and then they very slowly made their way back to the car.

"I should take you to the hospital to be looked at," Kelsi said once she had the Buick started.

"No, let's go home," he said. "I'll take some ibuprofen and go to bed. We'll see how it feels in the morning."

Kelsi wanted to argue, but he had walked on it and his voice didn't sound too strained, so she gave in and drove them home. Dennis struggled to get up the steps of the porch and insisted on pausing once they were there despite Kelsi having the front door open. He looked up and down the street, then shuffled over and looked down at his flowers.

"They needed this rain," he said. "We all did. But summer is over."

"Dennis, it's one o'clock in the morning," Kelsi said. "Come inside."

Once in the house, Kelsi shood him into his bedroom to put on dry pajamas while she made another cup of tea to help him sleep and take his pain medication. She brought them to his room, where he was already under the covers of his bed. She handed him the tea and the pills.

"Stay with me for a little bit, will you?" he asked. "I couldn't get to sleep yet. Not after all of that."

"Are you okay?" Kelsi asked.

He swallowed his pills with a sip of the tea. "I'll be fine. I want to talk, though."

Kelsi settled into the chair she had spent so much time in right after his accident and return home from the hospital. "What about?"

"Gloria, of course," he said.

"Okay," Kelsi said. She sipped at her own tea, a chamomile blend that reminded her of the smell of Dennis's flowers in full spring bloom. "But not a sad story. Tell me something happy. Tell me about a vacation you took together."

Dennis smiled. "We didn't get to take many. Money was always tight. Family vacations were always in-state or a state bordering Oklahoma. Kind of boring, I guess, but it was the best we could do. Except once. Natalie was sixteen or seventeen and old enough to be home alone with supervision from neighbors. The library sent me to Washington, D.C., for a conference on censorship and I got to take Gloria with me."

"That's a big trip," Kelsi said.

"Yes," Dennis agreed. His eyes were already back there, across half the country and several decades before he began telling the story.

Chapter Forty-Five

The flight from Oklahoma City to the District of Columbia had been an experience in itself. Neither Dennis nor Gloria had ever been on an airplane. They were traveling with Bernice Huffington, a librarian, and her sister, Angela, both of whom had flown once before to a similar conference in Miami, Florida. There had been turbulence over the Smoky Mountains. The airplane shook and Dennis just knew it was going to shred into a million pieces and drop bodies like seedlings all through the forest below them. Gloria's tight, pale face told him that she was thinking the same thing and all he could do was hold her hand and repeat over and over that it would be okay.

And it was. After a while, the flight returned to the smooth, if loud, journey it had been until the pilot brought them down. Still, Dennis was very happy when his feet made contact with the paved runway of the airport.

It was late afternoon and they took two taxis to their hotel, where they all checked in. Gloria was delighted with the room.

"The bed is so big!" she exclaimed, falling backward onto it as if falling into a swimming pool, her arms stretched out from her sides. Then she bounced off it and went to the window of their fifth-floor room and threw open the curtains. In the distance they could see the stark white obelisk of the Washington Monument. "Look at that view!" Then she was in the bathroom, popping out to show him the little soaps and bottles of shampoo before she emerged again modeling a thick white terry cloth bathrobe. "I want one of these for Christmas," she told him.

They met Bernice and Angela in the hotel restaurant for dinner, then went to the bar. The women ordered cocktails with patriotic names while Dennis drank bottles of Coca-Cola. Bernice recognized other library people and there was a fair amount of circulating and introductions as the night grew late. Finally, Dennis said he was going up to bed so he wouldn't doze off during the first day of the conference.

Despite the exoticness of the luxurious environment, the lovemaking with Gloria was no different than at home. She was a passionate, active lover in every setting in which they'd been able to experience one another. Dennis slept afterward, but knew that Gloria was still awake, thinking, evaluating, and planning. He knew by the time the first day of the conference ended, she would have a full agenda of things for them to do in the nation's capital.

There were a lot of bleary-eyed, hungover librarians sitting in the hotel conference room the next morning. Dennis was glad he had given up drinking. Bernice, who had stayed in the bar when he and Gloria left, wasn't in too bad of shape, but as the morning's presenter talked about rebuttals to the most challenged books, Dennis had to discreetly nudge her more than a couple of times. The hotel served them a lunch of sandwiches and potato chips.

"I might have had one or two too many Yankee Doodles last night," Bernice said to Dennis at the round table before they were joined by four other people.

"As a board member, I should probably motion to have you fired," Dennis teased. Bernice, a long-time friend, only laughed at him.

The afternoon was given over to another speaker who talked about pending or recently passed legislation in various states. His stomach full and the room warm, Dennis found himself struggling to stay awake. Finally, three o'clock came and the attendees were dismissed for the day. Dennis and Bernice rode the elevator up to the fifth floor, the conveyance nearly full as it took off from the ground floor. When they stepped off, Dennis said, "I'm sure Gloria has a full evening of activities for us. I hope she'll give me an hour for a nap."

She did allow him to lie down on the bed, and Dennis felt his eyelids grow heavy immediately, but then he sensed more than saw Gloria shimmying out of her green dress. He opened his eyes as she popped the snap on her bra, then she slithered onto the bed and pressed herself against his side. "I missed you," she whispered as her hand slid down his chest, over his belly, to cup what she found growing in his pants. His nap afterward was short, but he felt refreshed.

The four of them took a walking tour of the major sites in the city, trading cameras to snap pictures in front of the Lincoln Memorial and the far end of the Capitol Reflecting Pool with the towering Washington Monument in the background. They ate at a quaint little French restaurant, then Gloria dragged Dennis to a club where they could dance while Bernice begged off, saying she had to go to bed early to make up for the previous late night.

The next day was similar to the first, except the visitors were released at noon. Gloria had found a café for the four of them to patronize for lunch, then they all agreed to go off as separate couples to enjoy the rest of the day and reconvene in the hotel bar that evening. Dennis and Gloria remained in the café as Bernice and Angela made their way to the door and out to the sidewalk.

"I didn't even know Bernice had a sister," Dennis said. "They don't look anything alike."

Gloria pushed her cloth napkin to her mouth and gaped at Dennis with wide eyes while she smothered laughter. Her cheeks turned red as she fought to keep herself under control.

"What?" Dennis asked.

Gloria lowered her napkin. "Bernice may or may not have a sister, but Angela is most definitely *not* her sister."

"Then what ..." The truth dawned on him and Dennis felt his face flushing. "You mean ...?"

"Oh yeah," Gloria confirmed, grinning.

"How do you know?"

"Things happen in the women's restroom," Gloria said. "I might have walked in on a very unsisterly kiss last night. They begged me not to tell, but I know my husband won't hold their choices against them."

Dennis considered her words. Realization of what would happen if their little city in northern Oklahoma found out the head librarian was a lesbian crept over him like cold water. Was it his responsibility to tell the other board members? Was Bernice Huffington, who had been with the library for almost fifteen years, a dangerous degenerate? That was ridiculous. He shook his head slightly. "As far as I know, she has a sister named Angela."

Gloria smiled at him with satisfaction. "I knew you had a heart."

"Be that as it may, I'm so glad to finally be alone with you," he said.

Gloria fanned herself in mock modesty. "Mr. Aiken, what are your intentions?"

"To put our feet in the mighty Atlantic Ocean before the afternoon is over," Dennis said.

"It's over a hundred miles to the coast," Gloria protested.

"That's why we need to get to the bus stop right now," Dennis said.

It was a long, cramped, warm drive from downtown D.C. to Bethany Beach, Delaware. Dennis held Gloria's hand the whole time, including when they got off the bus, and pulled her into a taxi that would deposit them at the beach. The dry sand was warm under their bare feet, cooling as they moved over wet sand to the waves lapping toward them from deeper water.

"You should have worn shorts," Gloria teased as salt water crashed past her bare knees under her lemon-yellow mini dress.

"And scare the tourists away?" Dennis asked as he rolled up his khaki pants to just below his own knees and waded in after his wife. She turned as if to run, but he caught her and lifted her, kicking and laughing, out of the water. He twisted her around in his arms as he put her down. The wind had caught her hair and pulled it out of the scarf she had used to hold it back. Wisps of blonde tickled Dennis's cheek as he leaned in to kiss her. She put her arms around his shoulders and kissed him back, her mouth warm and moist, her tongue hard and mischievous as it probed and played with his. Dennis knew people would be watching them, but he didn't care.

"What's gotten into you?" Gloria asked over the sound of the surf when their kiss broke apart. "I like it!"

"It must be the salt air," Dennis answered, then kissed her again.

"I can't wait to get you back to the hotel room, mister," Gloria said when she was able to use her mouth to speak again.

They spent the next two hours walking along the beach or sitting to watch the waves roll in, whispering across the sand or sometimes crashing, the water spreading across the land, glistening in the afternoon sun. It was a clear day and the water was as brilliantly blue as the sky. The sun was beginning to sink behind them, sending their shadows stretching from the beach into the water, where they were washed clean.

Gloria leaned against Dennis's side and rested her cheek on his shoulder. "I'm having the best time of my life," she said quietly.

Dennis pressed his own cheek against the top of her head. "I'm the lucky one," he said. "I get to be here with you." He moved his sandy left foot over to tickle the bottom of her right with his big toe. He felt her smile against his shoulder.

"We have to go back, don't we?" Gloria asked.

"We do," he said. "The last bus leaves in just over an hour. We'll be late meeting Bernice and her loving sister in the bar."

"Then we should go," Gloria said, but didn't move.

It was up to Dennis to be the first to stand. He reached down with both hands and pulled his wife to her feet. They stood for a moment, holding hands, looking into each others' face. The evening sun made Gloria's face appear almost bronze and the light turned her brown eyes to drops of honey. She had never looked more beautiful to him than she did in that moment.

"Good God, I love you so much," he said, his voice a whisper because that's all he could muster through the emotion.

"I love you, too," Gloria answered, then pressed herself against him, wrapping her arms around him as he did the same to her. Most people had left the beach. The waves rustled and hissed while gulls dove for the human leftovers, but the couple didn't hear any of it.

"I wish I could marry you again, right here, every day until the world ends," Dennis said into Gloria's hair, which was now completely loose and wild in the coastal wind. "You make me feel like I matter."

Chapter Forty-Six

K elsi woke up with Dennis's story still on her mind. They had both cried as he told it and, although they'd both wiped their eyes before saying goodnight and her kissing the top of his bald head, she was sure they had both cried themselves to sleep. His face as he told the story had taken on that faraway look so that Kelsi knew he was reliving every moment, even the boring conference parts. He'd smiled and laughed as he told her about discovering that his head librarian was a secret lesbian. The longing in his voice as he spoke about the time on the beach with his wife had broken Kelsi's heart and left her wondering if she would ever find someone who would love her like that.

She didn't hear any movement, so guessed Dennis was still asleep after their late adventure. It was just after eight o'clock, early for Kelsi, but sometimes late for Dennis, who liked to read his actual real newspaper on the porch. But Kelsi could tell from the sound of passing cars that the front door of the house wasn't open. Rain still drummed on the roof. She threw the blanket off herself and went to the bathroom, where she showered quickly and threw her hair into a high ponytail, then made her way to the kitchen to cook biscuits and gravy with bacon and fried potatoes. It was a heavy, starchy meal, but it was Dennis's favorite and, between the fall and his story, he'd earned it. She sipped from a heavy ceramic mug of coffee as she flipped bacon and stirred gravy while potatoes popped and hissed in hot oil. The sound and smell was enough that the neighborhood had to know what she was doing, but Dennis never came shuffling and bumping down the hall with his cane.

Kelsi took the biscuits from the oven and put all the food on platters on the table, then laid out plates and poured Dennis's coffee and orange juice. If his hip was still hurting, she wanted to get him up and around so they could get in to see his doctor today. She went to his bedroom door and knocked.

There was no answer.

Everything was too quiet. With the food cooked and the oven off, all Kelsi could hear was the tick of the old clock in the living room and the rain falling outside. In her mind, she pictured a portable hospice bed and a withered woman lying silent on it while the clock continued to count off the march of time.

"Dennis!" Kelsi flung the door open and stepped into the room, sure she would catch him in the act of putting on his slippers.

He was dead. She knew it as soon as she saw his gray, still face on the pillow. He lay on his back, eyes closed, the slightest of smiles on his lips.

One hand still on the doorknob, Kelsi sank slowly to her knees as the tears came. They poured down her cheeks and fell onto her shirt and the floor. Her sobs were gentle but deep, shaking her chest. After several minutes, she wiped at her face and made herself stand up and step closer to the bed. Her eyes kept returning to his mouth.

"She came for you, didn't she?" Kelsi asked. She remembered the night before, the ghostly shape squatting beside him as he sat where he fell under the spreading branches of the tree they had planted so many decades before. "She told you it would be last night. She told you," Kelsi whispered. She felt like she should be upset that Dennis had known and not told her, but it was easy to guess why that was. She knew, as he had, that she would not have left his side if last night was to be his last on this side of the veil, as he called it.

Kelsi sat on the edge of the bed and continued to look at the face of the dead man. Now, with all animation and light gone out of him, she saw how skull-like his face was. Had he always looked so old? She didn't think so. He had been full of life until ... until he wasn't.

She knew she had to call someone, but she didn't know who. She got up and walked back to the kitchen where she'd left her phone. There were really only three options, and she chose Peter Zook. He answered quickly and she said, "Dennis died in his sleep last night. I don't know what to do."

"I'll be right there," he promised.

Kelsi opened the front door, then went back to Dennis's room and sat in her old chair beside the bed. She reached over and put a hand on Dennis's shoulder. The flesh beneath the thin cotton pajama shirt was cool and bony. Kelsi left her hand there.

"Thank you, Dennis," she said, her voice low. "You were the best friend anyone could ever ask for. I'm picturing you with Gloria right now, standing on a beach somewhere with the sun in your eyes as you hold each other. Together again. I won't forget my promise about your ashes."

A few moments later, she heard the front door open and footsteps in the living room. "Kelsi?" Peter Zook called.

She considered calling back to him, but thought raising her voice would be disrespectful. She got up and quickly went to the living room, where she found the minister standing with a closed umbrella and looking down at the empty urn and the photograph of Gloria on the end table between the sofa and recliner. He turned as she came in and Kelsi saw his eyes take her in and evaluate her condition.

"How are you?" he asked.

Kelsi shrugged. "Do you want to see him?"

"Yes."

Kelsi led him to the bedroom, where Peter checked for a pulse despite the obvious, then he stood straight and they looked at the corpse together.

"I already miss him," Kelsi said.

"He's smiling," Peter said as if it was an answer.

"Yes. I think Gloria came to take him away," Kelsi said. She felt the minister look at her, then back at the body.

"I know which funeral home he wanted," Peter said. "I'll call. They'll come to get him. They'll put him in a bag on a gurney, then in a van, and take him to the funeral home. Are you ready for that?"

"He wants to be cremated," Kelsi said.

"I know. He's left instructions with them," Peter told her.

"Okay," Kelsi said. "What about his daughter? Natalie?"

"Funeral home first, then I'll call her," Peter said. That's what he did. Kelsi overheard the calls. The funeral home phone was answered by a man who spoke in a cool, soothing voice, promising to have someone over within half an hour. Natalie was quiet for a moment, then thanked Peter for calling and said she would be in town that afternoon.

"Keep that gold-digging little tramp away from him," Natalie said. "I'll deal with her now that he's gone."

Peter looked at Kelsi and she could see that he was sorry she'd heard that. "If you mean Kelsi, she found him and she is very upset by his passing," Peter said. "She meant a lot to your father."

"That's exactly what she wanted," Natalie said.

"So, we'll see you this afternoon," Peter said. He hung up on her, and turned to Kelsi. "I'm sorry. She's going to be a problem. Dennis put you in his will, didn't he? Made it official?"

"That's what he said," Kelsi said.

The minister nodded.

The funeral director himself, a tall, tanned white-haired man named Aaron Murphy, came to collect Dennis. He had an assistant with him, a younger man introduced as Larry. "Dennis was a good man," Aaron said. "A cornerstone of this city." He moved around the bed, looking at Dennis. "This is how you found him? You didn't move anything?"

"Nothing," Kelsi said. "This is how he was."

"Did anything happen before bed? Bump on the head or anything?" Aaron asked.

"He fell last night," Kelsi said. "We were at the park and he tripped over a tree root. We got home and he took some ibuprofen and went to sleep."

"Did I hear right that he had a hip replacement recently?" the funeral director asked.

"Yes," Kelsi said.

The tall man straightened and rubbed at his bronzed chin. "Based on his look and what you've told me, I'm guessing a blood clot from the surgery. Falling knocked it loose and it reached his heart during the night. Heart attack."

Kelsi nodded, not knowing what else to say.

"We'll have to move him out of the bed," Aaron said. "Larry and I will get the gurney if you want to say good-bye or anything." The funeral director and his assistant left and Peter discreetly walked out with them.

Kelsi bent over the bed and whispered, "I love you," then kissed his temple one last time.

Chapter Forty-Seven

Peter Zook drove Kelsi to the funeral home that afternoon. The rain had stopped, but the sky was overcast and gray, threatening to let loose more buckets of rain at any moment. They were shown into the director's office, where they found Aaron Murphy in conversation with Natalie. The director sat on one side of a black desk and Natalie sat in a low-backed dark leather chair on the other side. Aaron turned a warm smile on Kelsi and Peter, but the look Natalie gave Kelsi told the younger woman that she was not wanted. Natalie punctuated that sentiment with her words.

"She has no business here," Dennis's daughter said in a tight, firm voice.

"Aaron," Peter said, addressing the funeral director, "Dennis made it known to me that he wants to be cremated and his remains turned over to Kelsi. It's in his will."

"Yes, I know," Aaron said, smiling. "That's what I was just telling Natalie. She ... wants to challenge that."

"You're challenging the will?" Peter asked the older woman.

"Of course I am," she snapped. "My father was not in his right mind. Not since Mom died. And then this hussy took advantage of his senility."

"He wasn't senile!" Kelsi shouted. She was going to say more, but Peter put a restraining hand on her arm. She looked at him and he gave a very brief shake of his head.

"Are arrangements for the cremation made?" Peter asked.

"Yes," Aaron answered. "There's no suspicion of foul play, so there won't be an inquest." He couldn't seem to help looking to Natalie as if for approval as he said these words, and Kelsi wondered if Natalie had suggested that she had killed Dennis.

"Natalie, will you be wanting the church for a memorial service?" Peter asked.

"I was going to ask about that," she answered coldly. "But you seem to be taken up with that girl."

"I'm interested in making sure Dennis's last wishes are fulfilled," Peter said. "And Kelsi has become a good friend. If that bothers you, I can help you make arrangements at one of the other churches."

"No. It's fine," she said. "But I am in charge of this. I will not be needing any assistance from *her*."

Kelsi remembered Dennis saying that Natalie would want to plan the memorial. She kept her mouth closed and didn't protest.

"Three days from now?" Peter asked.

"Yes. At one o'clock, if that's possible," she answered.

"We can do that," Peter agreed. "Is Aaron helping with the obituary?"

"We were going over that when you brought her in here," Natalie said.

"Then we will leave you to it," Peter said, adding his farewells before ushering Kelsi out of the office and then out of the building.

"I can't believe that bitch," Kelsi said in the car, then popped a hand over her mouth. "Sorry, Reverend."

Peter smiled quickly. "I can't believe it, either. We need to get to the lawyer's office before she does."

It was a short drive to the downtown law office where Kelsi had taken Dennis not so very long ago. Peter went inside with her and they met with a very old attorney named William Sheets, a tall bald man with brown age spots on his scalp and hands. They sat around his desk and Peter explained about Dennis's death.

"I'm very sorry to hear that," William said. "I enjoyed the company of Dennis and Gloria. They were good people."

"Yes," Peter said. "An issue has come up concerning Dennis's will, particularly the care of his remains. He told me he had made some recent changes to his will."

"That's true," William said. "He left everything to his caregiver." He nodded at Kelsi. "Including his mortal remains."

"Can that be challenged?" Peter asked.

William Sheets seemed to be sucking at his dentures while he considered the question. At last he said, "Anything can be challenged."

"If Dennis's daughter wanted to make a challenge, how long would that take?" Peter asked.

William shrugged with his shoulders and a flip of his hands. "Wouldn't happen today. My guess is that a petition could be filed today and heard tomorrow afternoon, at the earliest."

"But you have to read the will? Or she'd have to have a copy of it, right?" Peter asked.

"Yes," William answered.

"I don't suppose you'd take the rest of the day off, would you?" Peter asked.

"To slow her down?" William asked, grinning.

"Exactly," Peter said.

"Can he do that? Will that work?" Kelsi asked, finally getting in on the conversation.

"Yes," William said, nodding his bald head and grinning. "I've been hearing a big mouth bass calling me all morning."

"If I was Catholic, I'd put you up for sainthood, William. Thank you," Peter said, standing and shaking the attorney's hand. He turned to Kelsi. "We need to go so this man can catch his fish."

Back in the car, Peter pulled out his phone and began quickly texting.

"Who are you texting?" Kelsi asked.

"Aaron, the funeral director," Peter answered. "If there's no inquest, and Dennis paid ahead, maybe we can get the cremation to happen today and get the remains to you before Natalie can challenge the will."

"Why are you doing all of this for me?" Kelsi asked as Peter started the car.

"I'm really doing it for Dennis," he answered. "His wishes should be fulfilled." He backed his car out of the parking space in front of the attorney's office. "Not that you're bad company, of course." He shot her a quick smile.

"Where are we going now?"

"I'm taking you home," he told her. "If I know my flock, and I do, you'll be getting deliveries of food very soon."

"Really?" Kelsi asked, thinking of all the dishes they had returned earlier in the summer.

"Oh yeah. You won't have to cook for a long time," Peter assured her.

"I'll need help eating all that food," Kelsi said, keeping her eyes fixed firmly on the windshield and the houses passing by.

"I'll arrange for the city's homeless to line up on your porch," Peter teased.

Kelsi laughed, then said more casually, "You're welcome to come over anytime."

He looked at her quickly and nodded. "Thank you. I think I might enjoy that."

At home, Kelsi made sweet iced tea and the lemonade Dennis had loved so much and was ready when the first guests arrived. She spent the rest of the afternoon and early evening greeting people, either elderly friends of Dennis's, or younger relatives of friends. Evangeline came over when she got off work and helped Kelsi serve drinks and join the conversations. Kelsi was very grateful for the company.

"There'll be more tomorrow," Evangeline said when the stream of visitors had dissipated. "There are women all over the city cooking dishes tonight to deliver tomorrow."

"Where am I going to put it all?" Kelsi asked. "The refrigerator is already full. I can move some of it to the deep freeze, but ... how much?"

"You're a college girl," Evangeline reminded. "Invite your friends over. College students are always hungry."

"That's true," Kelsi agreed.

They sat on the porch, drinking the last of the lemonade and watching the evening darken. Around them, people washed cars, mowed lawns, barbecued, and went about their lives unaware that one of the neighborhoods oldest residents had died that morning. Had it really been this morning she'd found Dennis dead in his bed? Kelsi wondered. It had been such a long day.

"You got a text message while Mrs. White and her granddaughter were here," Evangeline said.

Kelsi picked up her phone and checked, then broke out in a grin.

"What is it?" Evangeline asked.

"I don't know if it's really good, but the funeral home worked Dennis in and he's ... well ... he's in the crematorium right now."

"Oh," Evangeline said. "Yeah, that's morbid, but necessary, I guess. How'd such a nice guy get such a bitch for a daughter?"

"That's the question of the year," Kelsi said. She thought back to earlier in the summer and how Natalie had been much nicer when Kelsi first took the job as Dennis's caregiver. "Breaking up with Tucker is what turned her against me. And she still thinks I'm the one who told his boss about him getting high at work."

"It really wasn't you?" Evangeline asked.

"Nope. I've never seen or spoken to his boss," Kelsi said.

Evangeline sighed and looked around the porch. "I guess this is all yours now."

"Oh," Kelsi said. "I guess so."

"Are you going to be okay here tonight?"

"Yeah. I'll be fine," Kelsi said.

Evangeline finished her drink, then held her glass loosely between her bare knees. She smoothed her navy blue skirt with her other hand. "Then I guess I'll leave you to your food."

"Thank you for coming over," Kelsi said. "It really means a lot to me."

"BFFs, girl," Evangeline said. They stood and embraced each other, then Kelsi took her friend's empty glass. "Call me if you need anything,"

"I will," Kelsi promised, then watched her friend drive away before going inside and locking up for the night.

Dennis's absence was palpable in the house. The dwelling felt as empty as if it had been abandoned decades ago. Silence lay heavily against the walls in small bricks separated by the ticking of the old black clock. Kelsi roamed through the house. In Dennis's room, she stripped the sheets off the bed to wash them. When she lifted the pillow, she was surprised to find a hardcover book with a dark red dustjacket. She picked it up and read the title, *Education of a Wandering Man* by Louis L'Amour, Dennis's favorite author. A tissue paper hung from the closed book. Kelsi opened it to what turned out to be the title page and was surprised to see her name in Dennis's firm script.

Kelsi,

I guess you'll find this once I'm gone. I hope you're not mourning for me. I'm with my Gloria now. I've done what I can to help you put down some roots. I hope you'll stay. Stay in my state, city, and house, and make it all your own. Louis had to educate himself and he became a great man. You're getting a different kind of education and have different plans, but I'm leaving you this book specifically as an inspiration. Whenever you think you can't do something, look in here and know that if Louis could live through all he did, you'll be fine. You're a beautiful, strong young woman and I look forward to meeting you again someday on the other side of the veil.

Love,

Dennis

Fighting back fresh tears, Kelsi took the sheets, pillowcases, and the blanket to the washing machine, then put some of the morning's bacon on a biscuit and ate it in Dennis's recliner, the book in her lap. She intended to open the book and read from it, but instead she took up Gloria's picture and held it in her lap.

"He's with you now," Kelsi said.

It had been a long day full of grief and trials. Soon, the framed photo sagged in her hands and came to rest against her chest as her head nodded forward. She slept the night there, but it was not a peaceful slumber. Behind her eyelids, a small boat was thrown around by giant waves as the girl in the boat looked desperately for solid ground.

Chapter Forty-Eight

ate the next day, Kelsi picked up Dennis's urn filled with his ashes and brought it home to rest on the table beside Gloria's empty urn. They made the little end table seem cluttered, so she moved them to the shelf that had the ever-ticking clock that had continued sounding when both the deceased stopped breathing. She put Gloria to the left and Dennis to the right and somehow it seemed like they belonged there.

For dinner, she heated up a plate of lasagna that someone had delivered, she couldn't remember who and was glad she'd made notes as the dishes arrived. She ate, then took the Louis L'Amour autobiography and settled into the corner of the sofa to read for a while. Her eyes kept straying to the urns, though.

"It's good to have you back in the house," she said to Dennis's container. Then she grinned, thinking of the look he would give her if he suspected she was considering reneging on her promise. "But I will do as I promised during the next rainstorm."

It had just gotten dark outside when her phone rang. She saw with dread that it was Natalie. Why couldn't her generation just send a text message? Kelsi answered the phone.

"How dare you claim my father's remains," the woman snarled into Kelsi's ear.

"It was his wish," Kelsi answered calmly.

"This isn't over," Natalie said, and then the line was dead.

The next day, Kelsi forced herself to go to class, then spend the rest of the day on the homework from the classes she'd missed since Dennis died. Her college friends arrived in the late afternoon and many of the delivered dishes were sampled with bottles of wine. A little more homework was done, notes were shared, and generous portions of food were sent home with the guests, then Kelsi crawled into her bed, but couldn't sleep for a long time. The memorial service was tomorrow, and she dreaded it.

That night, she once again clung to the sides of the small boat she had stolen and rode out killing ocean waves in her dream. She awoke more tired than she'd felt when she went to bed.

Dressed in a new black dress she'd bought for the occasion, Kelsi entered the church behind an elderly couple she didn't recognize, a man in a gray suit and a woman in a white dress with diffused orange roses printed on it. As they all stepped up to a podium to sign the guestbook, she was surprised to see Tucker standing there in a black suit and tie. She didn't know why she hadn't even thought of the fact her ex would be at his grandfather's memorial, but she hadn't, and she felt her heart hammering as the couple moved away and she was face to face with Tucker for the first time since leaving him in the restaurant.

His face was stony as he faced her and said, "Please sign the guestbook for my grandfather, ma'am."

Kelsi ignored him and signed her name, then walked past him to enter the sanctuary.

"Bitch," she heard him whisper at her back. It took a great effort on her part to pretend she hadn't even heard it and keep walking without so much as a faltered step.

The large sanctuary was almost full and Kelsi knew there were still people coming in from the parking lot of the church. She saw Peter Zook behind the pulpit on the stage, a few feet away from a large picture of Dennis that had been taken many years ago, when he still had sandy blond hair. Kelsi had seen such photos in the albums they had looked through together on some evenings, but it was still strange to see that large picture of him looking so young.

Natalie was moving from guest to guest in the aisle, directing people to empty spaces in the pews. Her eyes locked with Kelsi's for a moment and she actually paused and sneered. Kelsi immediately dreaded an encounter with Dennis's daughter, then she heard her name called off to her right. She turned and found Evangeline waving her to an empty space beside her. Excusing herself, Kelsi slipped past the people between her and her friend and fell into the pew beside Evangeline.

"That look she gave you would stop a clock," Evangeline said.

"Her son called me a bitch after I signed in," Kelsi told her.

"Hopefully they'll go back to Topeka or wherever they were right after this and leave you alone," Evangeline said.

Peter Zook stepped up to the podium — pulpit, Kelsi corrected herself — and looked out over the gathering with a benevolent smile. The murmur of conversation and the rustling of cloth quickly died away to silence, interrupted only occasionally by a brief, muffled cough. "Friends," he said, his voice carrying around the sanctuary through speakers mounted along the wall, amplified, but not overpowering. "We're here today to remember another friend. Dennis Jay Aiken lived to be eighty-two years old.

He touched the lives of so many of us, bringing smiles, advice, books, and in my case, difficult questions that often had me going back to my seminary textbooks." A ripple of soft laughter went through the crowd. "Dennis had a curious soul and a hungry mind. He didn't have any formal education, didn't even finish high school, but was a voracious reader and a staunch supporter of our public library and any idea that would put books in the hands of our city's youth."

Peter paused and looked around, as if gathering his thoughts. "What a man," he said quietly. "Ecclesiastes Chapter Three, versus four and five tell us there is, 'a time to weep and a time to laugh; A time to mourn and a time to dance.' This is a passage I know Dennis fully agreed with, and I know he would not want us to weep or mourn his death, but to laugh and dance in celebration of his life." Peter paused and looked around again. "We might be a little too crowded for dancing just right at the moment." There was general laughter, then a giant white screen descended from the ceiling and the lights dimmed. A slideshow of photographs flickered across the screen.

Kelsi watched through wet eyes as she saw Dennis as a little boy in black-and-white sitting on a spotted cow with a barn behind him. It was followed by digitized images of ancient school photos, the boy growing, his face round, then narrow, then almost pinched, his clothes never as fancy as the occasion might have called for. Then there were wedding photos of him and Gloria, both of them laughing and well dressed, holding champagne flutes and feeding each other cake. Photos from the late 1960s were in watery, blurred color, printed on square paper and featured Dennis with a huge, blooming red rose bush beside the house, something Kelsi knew was long gone now. There was a picture of him shirtless and mowing the lawn, and several of him holding Natalie as she grew. His hairline receded as the images came and went until eventually he was the elderly bald man she had come to know and love. The slideshow ended with what might have been the final picture of Dennis and Gloria together; she was obviously sick and the arm he had around her waist and the hand across his body to hold hers were loving gestures for a fragile figure.

Kelsi wiped at her eyes and nose with one of the many tissues she'd stuffed into her purse. All around the sanctuary there were sniffles and fumbling for tissues as Peter took his place in the pulpit again.

"It is better to go to a funeral than to a party, the author of Ecclesiastes tells us," Peter said. "He says, 'We all must die, and everyone living should think about this. Sorrow is better than laughter, and sadness has a good influence on you. A wise person thinks about death, but a fool thinks only about having a good time.' I would ask you, as we gather today to celebrate Dennis, to think about your own life, your own legacy, and compare it to his. Look around you. Do you want to fill a building with people you positively impacted? I can only hope to make such a difference that people will come together to remember me like this."

Heads nodded and there was a ripple of agreement. Kelsi wiped at her eyes some more.

"A time to weep and a time to laugh," Peter repeated. "At this time, I would invite you to stand up one at a time and share a story, memory, or thought about Dennis."

Several people rose, looked at each other, and laughed gently. Seeing it, others stood up, including Evangeline. Kelsi stood beside her. A woman who appeared to be in her mid-thirties with thick blonde hair and a black dress that seemed very businesslike made her way around the room with a microphone and people told short anecdotes about Dennis. Then she came to a very old man, short and stooped as he stood with arthritic hands clutching the pew in front of him. Tears ran down the man's face and he spoke in an aged, cracked voice.

"I led him wrong once," the man said. "I was young and stupid and gave him advice only a doctor should give. Him and Gloria fought when he accused her based on the bullsh... Based on what I'd told him. Pardon me, Reverend." The man lifted his hand and wiped at his nose with a twisted knuckle. "He almost lost her because of me. He became a drunk because of me." He waved the deformed hand. "He got her back and he kicked the bottle and ... and that man forgave me like I hadn't done anything worse than kick dirt on his shoe." The man broke down completely and Kelsi thought he was going to topple over into the pew ahead of him. He wasn't finished speaking. The woman with the microphone stepped away and he waved her back. "No! I have to say, Dennis wasn't real religious, but he was a good man. A good man with a pure spirit. The best man I ever knew. That's all."

"I'll never be able to do this," Kelsi said to her friend as fresh tears ran down her cheeks. Evangeline's hand found hers and gripped it tightly.

There were more stories. A man talked about Dennis being his T-ball coach when he was in second grade. A woman spoke about Dennis and Gloria visiting her when she lost her son in Vietnam. A retired principal remembered Dennis and Gloria providing paper and pencils for Adams Elementary School kids. Several younger former co-workers talked about pranks he'd pulled on them and advice he'd given when they desperately needed it. Then the microphone was in front of Evangeline.

"Dennis was just the best," she said. "He helped me get my job at the library and came in at least once a week to check on me and the rest of the staff even after his term on the library board ended. He found out I love sunflowers and he would ..." She paused, cleared her throat, and wiped at her eyes. "He'd randomly leave big, bright sunflowers on my desk. I never knew when to expect it and I could never catch him doing it, but I know it was him. That's Dennis. He was never rich, but he was always generous."

The microphone moved as Evangeline sat down but kept hold of Kelsi's hand. Kelsi stared at the black foam cover of the device, her mind racing. She swallowed hard and opened her mouth. "I was hired to care for Dennis after he broke his hip. I thought that's what I was doing, but really, he was caring for me. He taught me so much about life and community and love this summer. For the first time in my life, I felt like I belonged. Like I mattered. Because of Dennis." She fell into the pew and covered her face.

The rest of the service passed quickly. Kelsi was aware of Natalie standing up to speak at the end, telling some story from her childhood, but Kelsi couldn't focus. Her watery eyes were fixed on the lingering image of Dennis and Gloria on the screen, light and faded now that the sanctuary lights were on. Peter returned to the pulpit and said something that made most people laugh, then dismissed them. Evangeline pulled Kelsi out of the church and the sunshine brought her back to herself somewhat.

"Are you going to be okay to drive?" Evangeline asked.

Kelsi nodded. "Yeah, I'll be fine." She wiped at her eyes one more time and looked at the soaked, ragged tissue coming apart in her hand. She laughed a little. "So much for that time of laughing and dancing," she said.

Evangeline hugged her, then held her at arm's length. "I'm going back to work. I'm working on a proposal to name our Western section after Dennis."

"He'd roll his eyes over that," Kelsi said.

"That's why I waited until he couldn't protest," her friend said.

"Thank you for everything," Kelsi said. "I didn't sleep well. I'm going home to take a nap, then do homework."

Chapter Forty-Nine

K elsi was sitting at the dining table, deep into her homework with a piece of apple pie on a plate beside her when the doorbell rang. The sound slowly registered with her and she came out of her academic trance over textbook, notebook, and open laptop blinking and looking around. It was after six in the evening. The house was quiet except for the clock. The doorbell rang again and somehow it seemed urgent, or angry. Kelsi got up and walked barefoot through the living room to the door. What she saw in the peephole made her stomach drop.

Natalie stood on the front porch, glaring at the peephole. She had changed from her mourning clothes to jeans and an Oklahoma State University T-shirt.

Kelsi bowed her head and opened the door, but raised her eyes to face the other woman. "Hello, Natalie," she said.

"May I come in?" Natalie asked, but it was more a statement of intent than a question. Kelsi stepped aside and Natalie came into the house. She stopped a few paces in and looked around the room as if expecting that Kelsi would have already turned it into a Gen Z brothel. Her eyes fixed on the two urns flanking the ticking clock. Kelsi saw the slightest bob of her head, then she settled onto the sofa. Kelsi went to Dennis's recliner.

"I thought you would be on your way back to Kansas already," Kelsi said.

"In the morning," Natalie said curtly. "I have some business to settle first. Namely, this house." She ran her eyes over the living room again.

"What about it?" Kelsi asked cautiously.

"It should go to Tucker. Not you," she said. "Not some caretaker my father only knew for a few months. Let alone one who tried to get her ex-boyfriend fired from his job, embarrassing him and all his family in the process."

"Dennis left the house to me," Kelsi said, trying to sound firm and strong, but her voice sounded timid in her own ears.

"He obviously was not in his right mind," Natalie said. "His age and the surgery and pain medication ..." She shook her head. "He wasn't making rational decisions."

"You know that's not true," Kelsi protested.

"I have a lawyer who can make a judge believe it," Natalie said.

That was a lot. Kelsi wasn't sure what to say. She tried changing tactics. "You want to give this house to Tucker? He'll trash it. He'll sit here in this living room smoking weed and playing video games with his idiot friends and the girls he was cheating on me with."

"Better here than in my house," Natalie said in a voice that was almost a hiss. "Besides, this house has been in our family. It's ours. Not yours."

"Not according to Dennis's will," Kelsi said, her blood finally heating.

"My father left you this house and his money," Natalie said, her voice calm now. "The money came to just under fifty thousand dollars." She shook her head. "A pathetic amount considering his age, but he was never good at saving. Still, I suppose it's a lot of money to you. It would pay your college debt, which was his intention. If you vacate the house and sign it over to me, you can keep the money."

"But I legally have both," Kelsi said.

"If I have to take you to court, Kelsi, I will take the house and the money, you'll be labelled a gold-digging little harlot, and you'll have to pay all the court costs," Natalie promised. "Where will you get the money for that?"

"Not if I win," Kelsi said.

"The only money you have is what my father left you. A case like this would eat through that quickly. I will still have plenty of money to keep fighting. Think about that," Natalie challenged.

Kelsi couldn't hold the other woman's gaze and had to look away. She felt tears threatening to come to her eyes. "Did you ever like me? When me and Tucker were dating?"

"No. You were never good enough. Some girl from Montana or Wyoming or whatever with a past you wouldn't talk about," Natalie said. "But I found out enough. I thought Tucker would play with you for a while and toss you aside, but you had a hold on him."

"Get out!" Kelsi said, the words coming with a deep sob. "How can Dennis's daughter be such a stuck-up bitch? Just get out. Get the fuck out!"

Natalie seemed unmoved by Kelsi's outburst. "Not without an answer," she said. "Then I will leave my son's house."

"I don't have anywhere to go," Kelsi said, all the fire gone from her voice.

"I'm willing to give you thirty days to vacate the property," Natalie said.

"I'd like to talk to Dennis's lawyer first," Kelsi said.

Natalie laughed. "That old coot? He's senile himself. My attorneys will eat him alive on the stand. He can't help you."

"I'd still like to talk to him," Kelsi said.

"I need an answer now," Natalie insisted. "I have to leave."

"I can't," Kelsi said. "I can't answer you now."

"Then I'll go after everything. The house and the money." Natalie stood up and took a step toward the door.

"Wait," Kelsi said, defeated. She looked down at her bare feet. Her toenail polish was chipped. The hardwood of the floor beneath her feet needed to be polished, too. She knew she'd lost, and that Dennis would be disappointed in her. But all she could do was nod and say, "Okay."

"Okay, what?" Natalie demanded.

Kelsi chewed at her lower lip. "I'll keep the money and give you the house your father left to me," she said.

"I hoped you'd see the sensible thing," Natalie said, her voice dripping with smugness. She pulled a paper out of her purse and thrust it toward Kelsi. "Sign this."

In the barely understandable legal jargon, Kelsi saw she was giving up the house and that Natalie and her heirs would not come after her for anything else gifted to her by Dennis. She took the proffered pen from Natalie and put the contract on the end table beside Gloria's portrait to sign her name. She handed it all back and Natalie returned them to her purse.

"You have thirty days from today," Natalie said.

"Get out," Kelsi whispered.

Chapter Fifty

"What's this?" Kinley asked, holding up a Mason jar three-quarters filled with a gray substance. There was a small envelope taped to the glass canning jar.

Kelsi looked up from the box she was unpacking, then laughed. She stood up and went to her friend and took the jar from her hands. "This is Dennis," she said.

Kinley's eyes widened in shock and maybe disgust as she gaped at the jar. "*The* Dennis? Like ... that's *him*?"

"His ashes," Kelsi said.

"Ewww," Joylynn said, turning from her task of pulling books from a box. "Why do you have that?"

Kelsi took the jar and sat down in the recliner they had taken from Dennis's old house. "I made him a promise," Kelsi said. "And the contract with his bitch-ass daughter failed to say anything about the items inside the house. I could have taken the urns, just like we took this chair, but they don't really mean anything to me."

"Are you going to keep his ashes here?" Cassie asked. The bruises and burns were gone, leaving only some scars on her body. She was still timid and loud noises frightened her, but she was recovering. Joylynn was her near constant companion.

"Until the next good rainstorm," Kelsi said.

"What's in the envelope?" Kinley asked.

"Gloria," Kelsi said with a grin. "We spread her ashes, but it was raining and Dennis dropped her urn when he fell. A little water got in and stuck some ashes to the inside of the container. I scraped them out with his toothbrush since he won't ever need it again, and put her ashes in the envelope."

Kinley put her hands on her hips and stared at Kelsi. "Okay, but why?"

"Do you see the little jar in the box? Pull it out," Kelsi said.

Kinley reached into the box, rummaged through the packing paper, and pulled out a smaller jar that had once held a candle. Inside was a dull gold object about the size of a ping-pong ball. Kinley shook the jar so the thing bounced off the sides. "I know this is some kind of seed," she said.

"Yes," Kelsi said. "It's from Woody, the sycamore Dennis and Gloria planted when they were kids. I'm going to plant it and put what I still have of Gloria and just a pinch of Dennis in the soil. It'll be in a big pot, and someday, when I have my own house, I'll plant my own sycamore tree in the yard."

"Sounds like witchcraft to me," Joylynn said.

Kelsi only laughed. "Maybe it is."

"This is really where you lived before moving in with Dennis?" Cassie asked, looking around at the one-room garage apartment.

"Yes," Kelsi said, letting her own eyes travel from the living area with the twin bed to the kitchen with its appliances and little dining table, and the closed bathroom door beyond. "For a couple of years."

"You couldn't find any other place?" Kinley asked.

"I didn't look," Kelsi said. "I called my old landlord. He'd rented it, but after the police arrested the girl's boyfriend for beating her up the third time in the month she lived here, she went back to her mom, so he was glad to rent it back to me. And, it just felt fitting that I come back to where I started. At least for now. I don't plan to stay, but I'll finish college here."

At the mention of a boyfriend beating his girlfriend, Cassie had seemed to diminish until Joylynn moved over and put an arm around her. Kelsi couldn't help but think of the librarian Bernice Huffington and her sister Angela. She smiled, wondering.

"And what's this?" Kinley asked, pulling another, larger item from the box that had held the jars.

Kelsi grinned again. "That is the list of instructions Gloria gave to Dennis right after they planted the tree. See how they had a schedule for watering the tree? Isn't it just the cutest thing ever? After they got married, he didn't have money for an anniversary gift, so he framed that for her and it hung over their bed for years and years. Tucker sure as hell wouldn't have appreciated it. Or the boxes of recipes that are in there, too."

"I drove by that house on my way here," Kinley said sadly. "Tucker has thrown a lot of stuff out. It's just on the curb. Mostly books. There were little kids going through them when I drove by."

Kelsi shook her head. "He's an idiot. He could have sold those or donated them to the library. I hope the kids take them all. Dennis would love that."

Joylynn took another box from a stack and grunted at the surprised weight. "This one is heavy. And it's ticking," she said. "Is it a bomb?"

Kelsi laughed, put the jar of ashes on the floor beside the stolen recliner, and went to help her friend. "It's a clock," she said, taking the heavy box and carrying it to the table. "Dennis talked about how he heard it ticking when Gloria died, and it was all I could hear after I found him. Well, and the rain. Someday, it'll keep ticking when I'm gone."

"Damn, girl," Joylynn said. "That's some twisted shit. You were around old people way too much."

Kelsi rested her hand on top of the closed box. She could hear the muffled ticking within. "It gave me perspective," she said. "We're part of the earth, just like Dennis's ashes, and that's forever. But we're only alive for a little while. We have to do all we can to make life better for everyone around us during the short time we have. Before the real part of us passes through the veil, as he put it."

"Whoa, that's some deep shit for an empty stomach," Joylynn said. "On that note, how about you order the pizza while I go pick us up a couple bottles of wine. You three can have the rest of these boxes unpacked before I get back."

Kelsi, Kinley, and Cassie all laughed at her, and Kelsi agreed to order the food.

***

The October rain was cold and gusts of wind made it pelt Kelsi's face like tiny slaps from frigid little hands. Overhead, thunder grumbled across the night sky, but the lightning was far off in the distance. Holding the glass Mason chair tight against her belly, Kelsi jogged across the street and onto the grounds of the city park. It was nearly midnight and the playground equipment as well as the walking trail and empty space of the park were all deserted. She dashed along the trail to the relative safety of the sycamore, though its branches were now filled with only drying brown and gold leaves, many of which had already departed and were blowing across the ground in the brisk wind.

Kelsi put her hand against Woody's trunk, then pressed her face against the cool white wood, not caring about the water there or her hair catching on the bits of brown bark still mottling the trunk in some places. "I've missed you," she said to the tree. "I've brought Dennis to join Gloria. You'll have them both with you forever now."

She unscrewed the gold cap from the jar. She'd already shaken out the bit of ash she'd used to plant her sycamore seed in a pot on her apartment balcony. The rest would go here. "I'm keeping my promise, Dennis," she said, then bent low so the ash would hit the ground without the wind catching too much of it. Hunched over, she circled the base of the old tree, careful of the exposed roots, shaking gray ash onto the wet soil. When the jar was empty, she pounded the bottom of it and shook out the last bit of ash, then straightened.

She found herself facing the house across the street from the park. The run-down old house where Dennis had lived when the sycamore was planted. The house where he'd lived when his mother abandoned her two young sons to fend for themselves. The house where Dennis had hidden behind a curtain to watch young Gloria fulfill her part of the duty to take care of this tree for the first years after they'd planted it.

Looking around her, Kelsi sighed. She'd thought — maybe hoped — that she would see the spirits of Gloria and Dennis here when she left his ashes the way Gloria had appeared when she and Dennis and given her remains to the tree. But there was nothing. No translucent figures outlined by the falling rain. No cold spots or feelings of an other-worldly presence. A drop of cold rain hit her in the eye. Kelsi lowered her head to wipe at the eye. When she opened it, something glinted among the roots of the tree, reflecting the nearby streetlamp. She bent down and picked it up, rubbing off the bits of ash and mud that clung in some places.

Her eyes widened as she looked at the thing in the palm of her hand. It was a small gold heart, like one that might have been on an inexpensive charm bracelet purchased by a young boy. The story of Dennis giving such a bracelet to Gloria under this tree and the charm falling off and disappearing echoed in her mind. She fingered the small heart again, wondering.

Movement caught her eye and Kelsi turned. A dark figure stood about twenty-five feet from her, holding a black umbrella. It was a man, his face hidden in shadow. Kelsi let out a yelp and pressed her back against the tree. The man lowered the umbrella and stepped forward, one hand outstretched toward her.

"I'm sorry, Kelsi," Peter Zook said.

With the little heart clenched in a fist, she pressed it against her chest and gave a nervous smile while her own heart hammered. "You about scared me to death. How did you sneak up on me?"

"Well, I didn't mean to sneak," he said sheepishly. "I suspected you would be out here taking care of Dennis. I was walking up and about to call out to you when I saw you bend down to pick something up, and then you were staring at it and I wasn't sure if I should speak up." As he talked, he approached her and raised the umbrella again so that it covered them both. HIs presence was warm and comforting and Kelsi had to admit she liked the smell of his aftershave.

Opening her hand, Kelsi showed him the heart charm. "Do you know the story?" she asked.

"Story? No," Peter said.

Kelsi gave him the quick summary, then asked, "What are the chances this is it? The same one they lost?"

Peter's soft brown eyes studied her for a moment, then he smiled and shrugged. "A final gift from Dennis? I wouldn't put that past him at all."

"It could have been buried and as the tree grew, the roots pushed it back up to the surface," Kelsi said, trying to convince him with a logical explanation.

"Kelsi, Dennis was a mystic to some degree, and I know you are, too. I've seen it and he told me some things. You don't have to try to justify this," he said. "Is it the same charm?" He shrugged. "Maybe. Maybe some girl lost it here this afternoon. What's important is what you believe. Considering the timing and what you were doing ..." He shrugged again. "I can believe it really is a final gift from our friend."

Kelsi nodded slowly and closed her hand around the heart. "I believe it is," she said.

Lightning flashed and thunder rumbled over them like a hungry dragon. The wind was stronger and the rain was coming down harder.

"You're soaked through," Peter said. "You should get home before you catch a cold."

"I am cold," Kelsi admitted. "Thank you for coming out here. Were you checking on me, or did you want to help with the ashes?"

Peter shrugged and, though it was dark out, Kelsi thought she saw a blush come to his cheeks. "I guess I just wanted to witness the final act," he said.

"It won't compromise your reputation as a minister to be seen alone in the park with a woman after dark and in the rain?" Kelsi teased.

"A poor, lost lamb, possibly homeless," Peter said. "How could I have known from the street who it was over here?"

Laughing, and feeling suddenly mischievous with the charm in one hand and the empty jar in the other, Kelsi went up on her tiptoes and kissed Peter quickly on the cheek, then darted for her car. As she closed the door, she heard him laughing there under the tree where Dennis had first kissed Gloria.

***

Back in her garage apartment, Kelsi gloried in a hot shower, then dressed in one of the button-down work shirts Dennis had owned. It hung nearly to her knees. It didn't smell like the man, but the cloth did hold a faint aroma of the house and Kelsi loved it. She took up the Louis L'Amour autobiography, ignored the textbook she needed to read, and snuggled into her narrow bed beneath the framed instructions for caring for an American sycamore tree, and read until sleep overcame her.

Epilogue

The evening sun of spring cast eastward-reaching shadows as Kelsi used a sneakered foot to push the blade of her shovel into the soft earth. She lifted and turned, dumping the soil into a pile beside the hole she was digging. The yellow backside of the little three-bedroom house caught her eye and made her grin again. A year after graduating college, she was a homeowner. True, the house was on the city's poorer east side, but it was the side where Dennis and Gloria had lived and loved, and that was good enough for her.

She'd met her closest neighbors, making it a point to go and introduce herself, and she liked them.

Right out of college, she'd gotten a job with the state's Department of Human Services, working the regional office of Nokomis. It was a hard job full of sad cases, but she felt like she was making a small difference in the world and a big difference for the kids she helped and she loved what she did. Just today, she had taken a four-year-old boy out of a home while his parents, both high on methamphetamines they'd cooked in their kitchen, screamed they were good parents. The boy had been scared and he cried, but he was being checked out medically this evening and there was already a good foster family prepared to offer him a safe and stable home.

Kelsi turned more dirt until finally the hole was big enough. She dropped the shovel to the ground and plopped to her knees beside the two-gallon black plastic planter with the sycamore sapling growing from it. With a sharp pocket knife, she cut away the cheap planter and lifted the young tree and it's root ball to move them to their permanent home in her back yard. With the tree in place, she used her bare hands to scoop dirt back into the hole, patting it down to stabilize the tree and keep it upright.

Kelsi stood up, letting the fresh green grass of late April tickle the bottoms of her feet, enjoying her connection with the earth beneath her and the soil on her hands. She took up a watering can and poured a shower of water all around the base of the sapling, then put the the can down and surveyed her work.

"Alright, Woody Junior, you're home," she said. "I expect you to grow big and strong there."

Kelsi gathered her tools and put them away in a little metal shed in her back yard, then she went inside and cleaned up before putting a big pot of water on the stove to boil. Joylynn and Cassie and Evangeline would be over soon. Kinley had returned to Woodward after earning her degree. She was still in touch with her friends and they missed her. Kelsi sliced up a few chicken breasts, rolled them in a mix of egg and cornmeal, and put them in a skillet of hot oil, then added the pasta to the boiling water.

Her doorbell rang and she went to find Evangeline on her porch, a bottle of red wine in her hand as she threw her arms around Kelsi. "Congratulations to our new library board member, the youngest one ever," she gushed.

Kelsi hugged her back and thanked her. "I wouldn't have made it without your help," she said. "I hope it really isn't too much work."

"You'll be fine," Evangeline said as she came inside. "Look at this place! It's so cute. Is that us?" She went to a collage of framed photos on the wall to study a picture of the two of them posed beside a beautiful horse at last fall's county fair. Other pictures showed Kelsi with her college friends, eating pizza, or each peering over a stack of textbooks, or in their graduation robes. Many pictures were candid shots of her friends laughing or gesturing. A larger picture in a gold frame was of Dennis Aiken sitting in the recliner that was now in Kelsi's living room, holding a bronze urn of ashes, a distant look in his eyes and a portrait of his late wife on an end table beside him. Another larger picture showed a brown squirrel posed in the green leaves of a beloved sycamore tree.

"What's this one?" Evangeline asked, looking at another. She looked back at Kelsi and grinned. "I see the preacher man is still hanging around."

"Yeah," Kelsi admitted. It was a picture of her and Peter Zook having ice cream cones in a nearby Braum's. One of his parishioners had taken it and shared it to him, and him to her.

"You like him," Evangeline teased.

"I do," Kelsi admitted. "But the church could transfer him somewhere else at any time and he'd have to go. I've put down roots here. Literally, as of a few minutes ago."

"You planted the tree?" Evangeline asked, her voice excited.

"I did," Kelsi said. "In the back yard. I look forward to putting my lawn chairs in its shade someday. But now, I have to check on our chicken."

Cassie and Joylynn arrived minutes later, holding hands, and soon the four women were sitting around a dining table Kelsi bought used at a Salvation Army store, enjoying her pasta alfredo, Evangeline's wine, Cassie's homemade garlic bread, and Joylynn's store-bought cheesecake.

Evangeline raised her glass of deep red wine and said, "To Kelsi. May she help our library grow and prosper and nourish the minds of our community."

They drank, then Kelsi raised her own glass and looked around the table. "To friends, and to home. Thank you all."

Also By Steven E. Wedel

Visit the MoonHowler Press store for these titles and more

www.moonhowlerpress.net

The Werewolf Saga

Shara

Ulrik

Nadia's Children

First Born

The Werewolf Saga: Apocrypha

Call to the Hunt

Murdered by Human Wolves

Cody Treat Series

Afterlife

The Saga of Tarod the Nine-Fingered

Volume 1

The Travels of Jacob Wolf

The Broken Man

Apache Justice

Warhorse Trail

<u>**Standalone Novels/Novellas**</u>

A Light Beyond

Amara's Prayer

Inheritance

Little Graveyard on the Prairie

Love Curse

Mother

Orphan

Seven Days in Benevolence

Shim and Shay's Wish

Songbird

The Prometheus Syndrome

The Teacher

Yes or No

The Lost Pages Bookstore

With Carrie Jones

After Obsession

In the Woods

Sleeper (coming soon)

Short Story Collections

Darkscapes (third edition coming soon)

The God of Discord and Other Weird Tales

The Zombie Whisperer and Other Weird Tales

Unholy Womb and Other Halloween Tales

Non-Fiction

How to Fail as an Author

Now Not to Fail as an Author (companion workbook)

You Want to Do What? Things I've Learned as a Teacher

As Editor

Tales of the Pack

Milton Keynes UK
Ingram Content Group UK Ltd.
UKHW042006281024
450365UK00003B/215